NANCY
BUSH

"Nancy Bush is my go-to author. Always."

D0030987

THE
GOSSIP

DON'T MISS
THESE OTHER THRILLING NOVELS
BY NANCY BUSH!

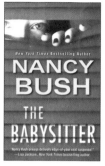

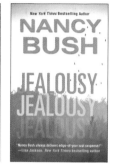

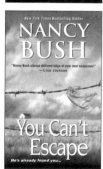

STALKING MACKENZIE

He followed after her as she headed back in the direction of her lover's place. How did she know what was in his mind? She was too attuned to him. Eerily so.

Was that why she'd been at the Waystation? Did she know? *Did she know?*

You approached her, not the other way around.

A cosmic connection, then?

He didn't know how to stop her. How to keep her from reaching the condo of her lover, the ex-cop. He had to stop her. He had to.

He needed to take her to the lair.

How? What did he have?

He had a pickup full of supplies. He could use something. What?

He had to stop her!

How?

And then he knew. It was mostly blocks of city between River Glen and Laurelton but there was that one stretch of county property with nothing built on it. They were almost there. She was rounding the corner. He pulled the truck up close to her SUV, hugging her bumper as she made that turn.

He punched the accelerator hard and the F-150 jumped forward.

Wham! He smashed his truck into her bumper. The RAV spun on the wet pavement and he hit her again, slamming into the SUV's side and pushing the vehicle off the road. . . .

Books by Nancy Bush

Published by Kensington Publishing Corp.

THE GOSSIP

NANCY BUSH

ZEBRA BOOKS
KENSINGTON PUBLISHING CORP.
www.kensingtonbooks.com

ZEBRA BOOKS are published by

Kensington Publishing Corp.
119 West 40th Street
New York, NY 10018

All Kensington titles, imprints, and distributed lines are available at special quantity discounts for bulk purchases for sales promotion, premiums, fund-raising, educational, or institutional use.

Special book excerpts or customized printings can also be created to fit specific needs. For details, write or phone the office of the Kensington Sales Manager: Attn.: Sales Department. Kensington Publishing Corp., 119 West 40th Street, New York, NY 10018. Phone: 1-800-221-2647.

Zebra and the Z logo Reg. U.S. Pat. & TM Off.

First Printing: July 2021
ISBN-13: 978-1-4201-5077-3
ISBN-10: 1-4201-5077-4

ISBN-13: 978-1-4201-5078-0 (eBook)
ISBN-10: 1-4201-5078-2 (eBook)

10 9 8 7 6 5 4 3 2 1

Printed in the United States of America

PROLOGUE

The cat placed her paws carefully into the dewy grass as she crossed the lawn to the glass doors of the building. She sat down on the WELCOME TO RIDGE POINTE mat and casually washed her face with one white-mittened paw. After several minutes passed and no one came to the door, she deigned to lift her paws against the glass panel. It took another minute before she started meowing. Finally, one of the assistants saw her and opened the door. She slipped inside and past him, then trotted down the hall. One of the residents, bent over her walker, looked up, saw the cat, and made kissing noises at her. The cat thought it over and decided to be amenable. She moved to the woman and rubbed against one leg.

"Oh, kitty, kitty," the woman crooned. She would have let go of the walker if she was able to bend down and pet the cat, but she wasn't steady enough.

A door opened at the end of the hall.

"I'll be back after breakfast," said the younger woman who stepped into the hallway, turning back toward the still open doorway. Her gaze was aimed downward, toward the ground. "Stay. I'll be right back."

She straightened, closed the door, and the cat heard muffled barking. The cat knew the dog inside that door. Once it had gotten out and chased after the cat, but the cat had slipped into a narrow alcove, too small for the dog, and hissed at it fiercely as people came and corralled the dog. This woman was one of them. She was fairly careful about letting the dog out. The cat disdained the dog, but she steered clear of it as much as possible.

The younger woman strode up the hallway. "Hi, Darla," she said to the lady bent over her walker.

"Eh?" said Darla.

"I SAID HI," the woman responded. "I'm Emma!"

"I know who you are."

"See you at breakfast," said Emma as she went on by.

The cat's nostrils quivered. The food was in the room that Emma had turned into. The cat could not go in there and had learned to wait outside. There was a short hallway where food was brought from one room to another. The cat could not go in that room either with its heat and noise and movement, even though good smells came from that direction, too. The cat had learned to wait patiently in the hallway, which she did now.

And then another smell drifted toward its nostrils; one that she recognized. A different kind of smell. The cat followed the scent and its eyes focused on the person who'd entered the room where the woman with the dog had gone. She stared unblinking at them, nose twitching with the odor. The cat would visit her later.

Emma Whelan glanced over at the black-and-white cat, sitting in the hallway, its black tail curled around its white toes. It had a tiny white stripe down the middle of its forehead, white whiskers, and the four white toes. Otherwise it was entirely black.

Emma wasn't sure what she thought of the cat. It was Ridge Pointe's resident mascot and it seemed nice enough, but Emma's dog, Duchess, did not approve of the cat and loudly complained about it.

"Ah . . . Twinkletoes."

Old Darla had finally worked her way into the breakfast room and she caught Emma's stare at the cat.

Twinkletoes was *not* the cat's name. Twinkletoes was a dumb name. Emma said succinctly, "The cat doesn't have a name."

"Just don't have her come to your room," Darla sing-songed, turning away.

Emma would have responded but Old Darla didn't hear well. Instead, Emma glanced one more time at the cat, who was meandering away. The cat sometimes sneaked into residents' rooms and curled into bed with them. Sometimes those residents died in their sleep.

Emma had seated herself at a table several over from where Old Darla was settling into a chair with a heavy sigh. She was the youngest member of Ridge Pointe by far and had become a resident the year before. Often Emma ate alone, which she didn't mind at all, but today Jewell Caldwell hurried in and plopped herself down across from her.

"Sara Throckmorton is a gossip, pure and simple," Jewell said in a lowered voice, looking over her shoulder as Mrs. Throckmorton walked in. Mrs. Throckmorton had steel-gray hair, a faint hunch on her back, and a slightly confused look on her face. Her brow cleared as she spied Old Darla and she lurched over to her table. "Don't tell Sara anything if you don't want it spread around everywhere,"

Jewell went on, waving her arm to include the whole room as Emma gazed around at the mostly empty tables. A lot of people preferred to eat in their rooms. Mrs. Throckmorton was leaning close to Old Darla and talking loudly about the menu.

"You gossip, too," said Emma.

Jewell looked affronted and shook her head. "I just relate the news! You know I do. Sara talks about one of the girls who used to work here all the time, but then that girl's a little hot pants, you know."

"Hot pants?" Emma cocked her head.

"Oh, your generation doesn't use that term." Her mouth pursed. "Let me put it this way. She doesn't discriminate with her bedmates. She *knows* a lot of men."

"You mean she's a whore."

Jewell barked out a little laugh. "Well . . . yes. You could say that. Rayne's had *lots* of boys. Never made any move to walk down the aisle with any of 'em, though Lord knows she can't apparently pick marriage material, even though I'm sure she lives with them." She turned a bright, birdlike eye on Emma. "Sara saw Rayne with her grandson—the one with the long hair?—outside, under the portico. They were kissing and there was no daylight between them, if you know what I mean. About gave her a heart attack. Right out in the portico, in front of God and everyone! But he must've gotten what he wanted because he hasn't been around much since."

"The boy with the long hair . . . is Mrs. Throckmorton's grandson?"

"Yes, ma'am."

"But Rayne's gone, too. She's been gone awhile."

"Well, obviously this was before she was told to leave," said Jewell with a sniff.

Emma had heard some of this from Jewell before, about the girl who'd left Ridge Pointe about the same time Emma moved in. When Jewell didn't have something to say, she seemed to go back to Rayne. Emma actually kind of liked boys with long hair, and she'd met Sara's grandson and she didn't remember he had long hair. It was a little confusing.

She opened her mouth to say as much, but Jewell ran right on. "Sara told me she doesn't know how many boys Rayne shacked up with, but somewhere along the way she and one of them got matching tattoos. Tattoos! I hear those are very painful to take off." She clucked her tongue. "Oh, I know you're young and think that's okay. Her going from one man to another and another . . . getting tattoos . . . In my day, there was a name for girls like that."

"Hot pants."

Jewell pressed her lips together and allowed, "Whore is closer. And Rayne . . . well, she's pretty enough, I suppose. But you don't give the milk away before buying the cow, you know." Jewell gave Emma a softer look. "Emma, I know you have trouble . . . understanding things like the rest of us. It's not your fault. But believe me, there are good people and bad people, and I'm afraid this girl falls into the bad category."

The waitress girl came by and told them the special was spaghetti and meatballs, then waited for their order. Emma liked pasta . . . well, she used to more than she did now, but she still really liked it so she picked the special. Jewell turned up her nose and said she would have the chicken salad.

As the waitress girl moved off, Emma decided she needed to set the record straight and so she said, "I know about good people and bad people." Her brain might not be the same as before she was hurt, but she knew things, too. She did know about good people and bad people. She understood she had "cognitive problems" and was more at peace with her own limitations these days. She didn't know Rayne, but she wasn't sure that Rayne was a bad person. She just sounded like she wanted to be with someone.

Jewell watched the waitress girl head over to Mrs. Throckmorton and Old Darla's table. As Mrs. Throckmorton switched her attention from Old Darla to the waitress girl, Jewell whispered again, "Sara Throckmorton's such a gossip."

Do not argue with Jewell, Emma reminded herself. It was hard advice to follow but Emma managed to keep her lip zipped as she recalled how Jewell had gossiped about her once after an argument about Emma's disability. You just couldn't trust Jewell.

The waitress girl brought Emma her spaghetti and Jewell her salad. Jewell made a face at the scoop of chicken atop the lettuce leaf. "They don't make anything good here," said Jewell.

"My lip is zipped," said Emma.

The cat strolled back to its station beside the dining room door and zeroed in again on the woman with the odor, ignoring the others who were drifting in and taking their seats. But then the cat heard the *pffft* sound that meant someone was getting her a treat. She whipped around toward the room with all the noise and saw the bowl of fluffy white coming her way.

"Your favorite, huh?" the man who smelled like skunk said as he set the bowl down. "I like whipped cream, too, and when no one's around, I give myself a hit. Squirt it right in my mouth from the can."

The cat ignored him as she delicately licked at the peaks of white.

"Who ya gonna hop in bed with next, huh?" he asked, leaning down toward her and speaking softly. "Let me know and I'll call the ambulance."

He patted her head a little hard and the cat shied away. When he left she got down to the business of eating.

CHAPTER ONE

Rayne Sealy stood in line at Miller's Market behind several mostly elderly women. One was definitely a Q-tip, her white hair glowing like a beacon beneath the grocery store's overhead lighting and she was really taking her time.

Rayne sighed and checked her phone again. Almost five. She was chasing daylight. It would be gone soon on this breezy March day if things didn't get moving and then all her plans would be over.

Hurry UP, lady!

Q-tip was pulling money out of a change purse, taking so long Rayne could have written a love poem to Chas—no, a full-on novel, thousands of pages long—in the time it took that woman to dig inside and drag out some carefully folded bills.

She hiked up the gray Hobo bag on her shoulder and checked her phone again. 4:55.

How long would Chas wait for her? They were supposed to be hiking along the trail that wound up to Percy's Peak, a small mountain that was really just a big hill, but it was a highlight around River Glen. Chas had said there was a lookout along the trail that was known for being where couples went to get engaged. OMG! Was Chas going to ask her to marry him today? Why not? So, theirs had been a whirlwind romance. So what? There was no limit on how fast two people could fall in love. Sometimes it happened in an instant. Across a crowded room, like Romeo and Juliet.

Rayne inhaled a calming breath. *Take it easy. Just a few more minutes.*

She'd teamed her red silk blouse with her black Athleta capris, the good ones that hugged her butt in a way that made her look skinnier, and her black sneakers just in case. Not exactly hiking gear, but who cared. This could be a monumental day and she wanted to look fantastic.

"Can I go in front of you?" Rayne blurted out to the woman with steel gray hair behind Q-tip who'd just loaded up the moving counter with groceries. "I'm really late."

"Honey, I've only got some produce," the woman threw over her shoulder. Didn't even bother looking her way.

Bitch.

Chas and her romance wasn't quite like Romeo and Juliet's, but it had been fast. Well . . . depending on how you looked at it. They'd known each other for years, but back in school she'd thought he was really nerdy and weird. The kind of guy who built radios or zapped bugs with electrified wires or something. She'd simply dismissed him. In high school she'd had her eye on Ryan Buck Ramsey, who'd played basketball and had unfairly thick lashes and an adorable, goofy smile. Every other girl in school felt the same way. But now, years later, it was sad to say, Buck had run to fat. He worked for his dad, who owned a business complex over in Laurelton, but he lived in an apartment and split custody of his daughter with his ex-wife, Anna, who'd been in Rayne's grade and was one of those girls who'd had it all.

Rayne smiled to herself. She was kind of glad Anna had gotten stuck with Buck.

But Chas . . .

He'd changed his name, changed his looks, changed everything about himself. She hadn't even recognized him at first. Whereas Buck had gone to seed, Chas had *developed*.

"Don't tell anyone about us," he'd whispered in her ear as he'd made excruciatingly slooowww love to her that first time.

"I won't," she'd gasped, holding back a scream of ecstasy, her fists clutched into the bedsheets.

"Our secret . . ."

She'd been too close to climax to suggest maybe she could tell her best friend, Bibi. There would be time for that later. As she'd floated down from ecstasy, he'd whispered, "I've always wanted you. I dreamed about you. We're made for each other."

She thrilled a little, every time she recalled his words, which she had countless times over the last few weeks. My God, he was wonderful and he wanted *her*.

Now Q-tip was moving off and Gray Hair was slipping into her place. Gray Hair was definitely more spunky, had her credit card in hand, thank God. And she had a helluva lot more than just produce going on there. Was that a bag of Chips Ahoy tucked in with the carrots, celery, and apples? *You're never gonna lose weight with those, honey.*

Rayne was really over old people. Her short-lived stint at Ridge Pointe had cured her of them.

Rayne still hadn't told Chas that she'd let Bibi in on their secret romance. He was death on anyone breaking into their perfect world. That's what he'd said, anyway, and she'd believed him. But it hadn't stopped her.

"No, what's he really like?" Bibi had demanded. "Where did you meet him? Why is he so secretive?"

"He's not secretive," Rayne had hotly denied. And then she'd gushed on about him. His looks. His intelligence. The way he made love. "He's what I've been waiting for my whole life," she'd told her friend, tears standing in her eyes. Bibi had given her that look that said, "I've heard this before," and Rayne had rushed to let her know that this time it was different. Really it was. It worried her that Bibi would somehow ruin this for her. Bibi had demanded more information, but Rayne was purposely lean on details. She couldn't tell her that she'd known Chas for years but under a different name. It would be a no-no in Chas's book, and, well, she was also kind of embarrassed about how much of a dweeb he'd been back then. He'd left around freshman year, maybe junior high, she thought. She hadn't even missed him.

Bibi had finally eased off with the questions. She was on the edge of divorce herself, so she was somewhat distracted. She'd also been drinking too much and trying to live her life through Rayne. Rayne had desperately wanted to tell her *absolutely everything*, but she had to be careful what she said about Chas. He'd been very serious about keeping their relationship under wraps and she wasn't going to blow it. No way. Uh-uh. Not until he was ready. She wanted a ring on her finger so she could wave her hand in front of her butthead older sister's face. And she wanted to get married, too, of course. She'd left her shitty apartment with rent due three days ago and had filled up her trunk with her belongings while she figured out what to do. Camping out at Mama's house was no answer, so she'd been living in her car and using the shower at Good Livin', even with Patti's glare knifing into her back whenever she entered. Her subscription to the club wasn't up for a few more weeks, but Patti sure as hell wanted to kick her butt out. All because of Seth. Well, fuck her . . . and him, for that matter. She had a much brighter future ahead than either of them. They could have each other.

She glanced down at her belly, protruding against the red silk of her blouse. She could admit she'd gained a couple of extra pounds since high school herself and well, she wasn't old by any means, but at thirty-two she kinda thought she'd better get on with it. The world could change in an instant.

If she and Chas had children . . . they would be smart like him, and cute like her. She was still cute. Even Bibi remarked on it. She just was a little pudgier than she'd been, although Chas had breathed in her ear as he'd squeezed her flesh, pinching her until it almost hurt, that all he wanted to do was be inside her, be enveloped by her.

"God, you make me hard," he'd whispered.

Thinking about him, Rayne felt desire zing right to her core. Man . . . Lord . . . was she about to orgasm just at the memory? Right here in the checkout line?

She fought a giggle and Gray Hair shot her a dark look. She wanted to stick her tongue out at the woman. She wanted to *tell* someone. Shout her love for Chas from the rooftops!

"Our secret . . ." he'd said.

Finally Gray Hair bagged up her groceries and left and it was Rayne's turn.

"ID," the checker said, giving Rayne a hard look as she scanned the bottle of wine.

Rayne already had slipped her small wallet from the back zippered pocket of her pants, a leather black-and-white-striped Kate Spade purchase that had cost her dearly. The wallet only had enough room for her driver's license, a few folded bills, and a credit card, if she should happen to possess one, which she didn't. She'd brought the Hobo bag for her purchases. Pulling out her license, she waited as the girl examined it closely. It might bug some people to be carded, but Rayne always liked it. Reminded her that she was still fairly young. Her whole life in front of her.

The girl gave her a long look, slowly handed the license back, and checked her through. Rayne paid, then hurried outside, tucking the bottle in the woven gray bag, holding it close to her body against the light drizzle of rain. No, no, no. The weather needed to hold so they could go to the lookout.

Rayne climbed in her Nissan with the bent fender that hadn't been her fault. That woman in the parking lot of the Olive Garden had just backed into her without looking. What a fight that had been. Luckily, Mama had helped out with Rayne's finances after a lot of bitching about her "inability to hold a job." Well, she'd been at the Coffee Club for a while, hadn't she? Ever since she'd left Good Livin' and she'd been there since Ridge Pointe. It wasn't like she didn't work!

But who knew . . . maybe she wouldn't have to work much longer anyway.

She drove like a madwoman to the parking lot at the base of the trail, the one in the strip mall that was right next to Ridge Pointe. Grabbing up her phone, she tucked it in her back pocket, then glanced inside the Hobo. Tucked in beside the bottle of wine were the two paper cups she'd taken from Starbucks and the wine opener from her mom's messy utility drawer. She slung the bag over her shoulder and headed across the blacktopped lot toward the trail that ran behind it. Luckily, the rain was holding off. She wasn't wearing a coat. She wanted Chas to see her blouse and how good she looked in it.

There were small sticks and leaves littered over the trail as its popularity had waned over the winter. Also, the construction of the three big houses built around twenty years earlier and situated about halfway to the outlook had gotten rid of a lot of the naturalists. Oh, man. The brouhaha that had taken place in River Glen over the sale of that land . . . the freaking out over the demolition of the massive house that had stood there as a landmark for years . . . the screaming nutjobs who couldn't handle any change . . . they'd all gone totally batshit crazy. Rayne's own father had howled about the injustice of it all. The neighbors had practically gotten out their pitchforks and chased down the builder, but then he'd moved on to that big development on the west side, Staffordshire Estates, and the whole thing had finally died down except for some of the oldies around town who still held a grudge. Q-tip and "only produce" Gray Hair were likely in that camp.

But, *Chas!*

It was crazy how she couldn't get enough of him. All she wanted to do was make love over and over again. Had she given herself to him too freely? Nobody cared about that anymore except . . . he'd made one comment about liking a challenge and she hadn't been sure if he meant her or not.

We're made for each other.

He'd said that, too. And they were. They really were! And if she could give up her job at the Coffee Club and live off his income—he'd told her he'd made a fortune in the stock market and been smart enough to know just when to get out and cash in—they could be happy forever.

She thought about telling her sister she was engaged. She could just imagine the look on her face. Elise had always treated Rayne like she was an idiot when *she* was the one who always screwed up. Elise was so easy to mess with. She grinned, but then she thought of what her mother would say when she found out and it kind of killed Rayne's joy.

"Three weeks? Not even?" Mama would say. "Rayne! Use your brain, girl. What are you thinking?"

"But I love him. And he loves me. HE LOVES ME."

She made a sound of frustration and picked up her pace. She passed the side path that led to the three houses above. A massive wrought-iron gate blocked access from the trail to the path that wound up the hill. Her eye followed it to a ridge above the trail before it disappeared through trees and brush. A line of Douglas firs had been planted into the hillside to screen the underlying structures of the houses from the hikers, trees that spread out at the base but were meticulously pruned higher up to keep from obscuring the views from windows that looked over the river.

Now Rayne was huffing and puffing as the trail grew steeper. The lookout was a helluva lot farther along than Chas had made it sound. It was apparently on the same upper height as the three houses but it was a good quarter of a mile along the trail past them. Jesus. Her chest burned and her thighs were killing her. She'd never been to the lookout. She hadn't been on this trail but once. She wasn't really into hiking.

Finally, up ahead, she saw Chas leaning against a tree. He straightened when he saw her and signaled her to hurry up. She did, though her heart was pounding. Maybe from seeing him. Maybe from the unaccustomed exercise.

"You brought a bottle of wine," he observed with a smile, though it didn't seem to quite reach his eyes. Her heart flipped painfully. Maybe he didn't think it was such a good idea.

She glanced down at her bag. The top of the wine bottle was visible. "I thought we could toast at the lookout," she said a bit anxiously.

"What are we toasting?" he asked.

"Us. Three weeks . . . almost."

"You haven't told anyone, have you?"

Rayne opened her mouth and tried to lie but couldn't say anything. Chas's face shuttered and she knew he'd recognized the tell. "Not really."

"What does that mean?"

"I've kept it secret, like you said."

"You told someone," he accused. "Your family?"

"No, of course not. I just . . . I just mentioned I was seeing someone to my friend, Bibi. I didn't tell anyone else. Promise."

"What did you say?" he demanded tersely.

"Nothing! Really. I just said that I was . . . falling in love with you."

"Did you tell her my name?"

"No . . ."

"Rayne."

"Just your first name," she admitted. "I'm sorry. Is it really that much of a secret?"

His whole body was tense. He tore his eyes from hers and stared out toward the overlook, which jutted above the river about ten yards from the trail. Rayne also gazed at the small spur of land that ended in a railed arc above the river.

Chas drew a deep breath, exhaled, and shook his head. "It's fine. Let's open that bottle, huh?" He smiled with an effort and reached a palm toward her. She handed him the bottle with the Starbucks cups upside down on its top, worried, needing him to say everything was all right. She shouldn't have said anything about Bibi. She should have kept it secret, secret, secret until he was ready to let the world know. God, could he have a wife somewhere? Was there some reason that had real consequences attached to it? She wanted to ask him, but bit her tongue. Now was not the time.

They walked toward the edge of the overlook and stood at the semicircle of the wrought-iron rail, both gazing across the chasm to more Douglas firs and a line of native white dogwoods that dotted the opposite bank. The East Glen River wound slowly along far below, its surface ruffled by a light wind that didn't reach upward where they stood. Chas kicked a small pebble off the edge and it rattled down the side of the cliff toward the river.

Rayne pulled the wine cork and her phone from her pocket, handing him the former. She set her phone on the ground as he gave her back the Starbucks cups, then expertly opened the wine, peeling back the foil and loosening the cork. It was a pinot noir that she'd paid dearly for, money she'd actually stolen out of her sister's purse because it was open and *just there*.

She held out the cups and he poured several inches in the bottom of each one.

"To us," he said.

"To us." She glanced down at her phone, her heart pounding hard. How she wanted to take a picture and share it on social media. Man, she would love to be an influencer, someone everyone else followed. But she felt kind of uncertain with Chas. Things were a little odd.

"You want a picture," Chas said, reading her mind as he took a sip.

"I know you don't want them. It's okay."

"This is our secret. You know that."

"I do."

She just didn't know why it had to be soooo secret. The thought that he could be married again made her heart jerk painfully. But even if that was true, she wasn't giving him up. She couldn't. She gulped her wine.

He bent down and picked up her phone. Immediately she wanted to snatch it from his hands, afraid. She realized she'd never seen him use his phone, though its outline was in his back pocket.

"Okay. Just one," he said.

"Really?"

"Hold up your glass . . . no, wait . . . stand back here." He pointed to the railing as she'd automatically moved several steps forward. She resumed her position against the rail as he set down his cup, moved back, and aimed the phone at her.

"I want one with the two of us," she protested.

He made a face. "Let me get one of you first."

She was ecstatic. He'd never allowed a picture before, which was silly, because he was in her junior high yearbook, maybe even her high school one from freshman year, for God's sakes. He hadn't been as averse to photos then.

Maybe he's on the run.

Bullshit.

"Okay, stay there." He touched her arm, lightly grabbing her wrist. "Yeah. Good." He held up the phone again.

"You're too close," she said. He was right in front of her.

"Am I?"

"Yeah . . ."

He peeked over the top of the phone mischievously, then leaned in for a deep kiss. She wrapped her arms around him and he pressed himself against her. She could feel his hard-on and said, "Mmmmmm," against his lips.

He pulled back and laughed.

"Now, take the picture so I can get one of you," she said.

He gave her an "Oh, you . . ." look accompanied by a small smile.

He lifted the phone, then slowly lowered it again.

"Chas!" she complained on a laugh.

"I just can't leave you alone."

He suddenly tossed the phone behind himself and it hit the ground hard.

"Be careful!" she said, shocked.

His smile froze. "What did you say?"

"I just didn't want you to throw my phone like that. I just . . . don't want it to break."

"Don't you mean, be careful, Mr. Toad?"

"What?"

"Isn't that what you said?"

She blinked. "I don't know—"

"I hate people who talk about me," he said with heavy disappointment.

"I'm . . . I'm sorry. I didn't really say anything. I'll tell Bibi we broke up. She doesn't even hardly care. She just—"

He moved so swiftly she didn't have time to catch her breath. Bending down, he grabbed her by her knees. Hoisted her up. Flung her over the rail. She inhaled, barely had enough air to shriek, "Chas!" as her foot caught in the rail. Her arms flailed. Her cup flew out of her hand. Then her head smacked hard into the cliff side and she saw stars.

Through a haze of pain, she felt him grab her snagged foot. She moaned and vaguely swatted around to grip the rail.

"Chas . . ." she murmured brokenly.

"Goodbye," he said with a sigh of regret. He shoved her foot through the rail. Rayne's fingers scrabbled wildly, touched the metal rail, never gaining purchase. She hurtled headfirst over the cliff's edge, hitting the edge of the headland once, then again, bouncing against hard dirt and rock, spinning and tumbling the long way down into the slow-moving river far below.

CHAPTER TWO

When are you going to learn not to take on something you don't want? Why did you listen to Bibi? You know she's teetering on the edge of crazy. C'mon, Mac. Be smart.

Mackenzie Laughlin looked at her reflection in the mirror behind the Waystation's bar. She lifted her glass of neat vodka to her mouth and wetted her lips. She wanted to appear like she was drinking, but she couldn't afford to get inebriated. She'd told Bibi she would look into Rayne Sealy's disappearance and so here she was, day drinking at the Waystation while keeping an eye on the couple at the table in the corner, Rayne's ex and his latest girl.

"Hey, Mac!"

The unwelcome shout from down the bar caused her to stiffen. Someone had recognized her? Just what she needed.

Mackenzie cautiously slid a look out of the corner of her eye. The guy just strolling into the bar was tricked out in cowboy gear complete with Stetson, which he pushed higher onto his head with one finger as he caught her gaze and winked. She inwardly groaned. Donnie Gillis. She'd picked him up for DUI twice while she was still with the force and now he'd caught her in the middle of her surveillance. Well, shit. Pulling her gaze away, she picked up her drink again, refocusing on the mirror behind the bar, noting her own sour expression.

"You on duty, copper?" Gillis asked gleefully, sliding onto an empty stool next to her. He was tall and thin and wasn't terrible looking, but his weak chin was right on full display as he leaned toward her.

She had to force herself not to move a stool over. "That's when I drink the most."

"Hah. Funny. You're funny."

He'd asked her out both times she'd taken him into the station. She'd told him she was in a relationship, which was a lie, but Donnie Gillis, known as Dobie to his friends, from the title character in an ancient television show, which was sometimes changed to Doobie because of one of his favorite choices of recreational drugs, was no slouch when it came to persistence.

"I'm no longer a cop," she informed him.

"Really?" He looked surprised.

"Really."

He was now blocking what had been a clean view of Rayne's ex, Seth Keppler, and his girlfriend/roommate Patti Warner, who were seated at a table by the door. They'd been arguing, but now appeared to be lost in a silent, furious, standoff.

"Let me buy you another," Gillis said. "To celebrate."

"Not interested."

"Oh, come on."

"Thanks, but no thanks, Gillis. Need to stop you before you get started. Save us both some time."

He spread his hands. "Time, I got."

Mackenzie leaned back again to catch a quick look at her quarry, worried they'd heard him call her "copper" . . . but they didn't seem to care.

He lifted his chin at the bartender, getting the man's attention. "Bring me a Bud."

Then he glanced at her drink. "What're you having?"

"Vodka."

"Hey, man. Changed my mind. I'll take the same as her."

Mackenzie felt a stab of impatience. She'd agreed to this "job" more as a lark than a means of making income because Bibi Engstrom was in the midst of an ugly divorce and barely making ends meet. Bibi had contacted Mackenzie because she'd thought Mac was still with the River Glen Police Department. Her friend Rayne had gone missing and no one seemed to be looking for her. Rayne's family had told Bibi she'd likely taken off for parts unknown, possibly with a new romantic interest as Rayne tended to flit from one affair to another, but Bibi didn't think so.

"Rayne doesn't just take off," Bibi had said, flipping back a dry end of over-dyed red hair. Bibi's roots were showing and there was a weariness around her eyes. She and Mackenzie had shared some classes at Portland State but they'd never been exactly friends. They'd remet in River Glen when Bibi had called the police on her husband. She'd thrown his clothes onto the front yard and locked him out. His answer was to break a back window and climb back inside and then they'd screamed at each other for a long while. A skirmish of some kind occurred, in which Bibi's arm was hurt. But Bibi had refused to charge him with battery, when all was said and done. The red handprint on Hank Engstrom's cheek hadn't helped her case. They'd reconciled, and apparently the clothes had been put back in the closet, but Bibi had recently confided in Mac that she and her husband had hit the end of the road. There was the intimation that Hank was seeing someone else. Neither of them seemed to be willing to give up the rental, so they were at a stalemate.

"Well, I mean, okay, Rayne does leave sometimes," Bibi had corrected herself. "But not this time. She has a new boyfriend and she wouldn't tell me about him. Honestly, she was . . . I don't know, kinda weird about it. I thought maybe he wasn't real? Like maybe she was still seeing one of her exes? I get the feeling it might be Seth and she just didn't want to tell me? But she's been gone for over a week. Not answering her phone? And she always picks up. Would you check it out?"

That's when Mackenzie had explained that she'd left River Glen PD, but that fact had scarcely slowed Bibi down. When Mac told her to report Rayne missing to the department, Bibi said that's what she'd thought she was doing when she ran into Mackenzie at the local coffee hangout, the Coffee Club, Rayne's last place of employment.

"Talk to Gary," Bibi had pleaded, waving an arm toward the middle-aged man with the hangdog face who cruised in and out of the Coffee Club's back room to check on the girls working the counter. "Rayne hasn't shown up for work for over a week. She's not at her apartment. Okay, she ran out on the rent, but she would be here if she could. Hey, Gary!"

Mac vaguely recalled Rayne as the chubby, dark-haired woman with the beaming smile mostly reserved for the male customers as Bibi told Gary that her friend Mackenzie would be looking to find out what happened to her, why she wasn't coming to work. Gary shrugged and said Rayne was unreliable. It's just how she was. It wasn't the first time she'd run out on him and maybe he'd take her back when she showed up, or maybe he wouldn't. He had a business to run.

"If you find her, tell her it's the last time," he tossed over his shoulder as he resumed his place behind the counter.

Bibi had gone on to explain that she'd approached Rayne's equally blasé mother, Sharon Sealy, and sister, Elise. Neither of them was apparently getting too worked up about Rayne's sudden disappearance, either. "Would you just please find out where she is? She also owes me some money," Bibi had admitted. "I'd like it back, but I also want to know what happened to her. She's a flake, okay? But like this? I don't think so. I have half a mind to go up to Seth myself and call him out, but he's got guns. Even my husband, the asshole, thinks Seth's trigger happy. So be careful, okay? I wish you were still with the police."

Mackenzie, with no clear career path currently in sight, had grudgingly promised to look into the issue. A fool's errand, most likely. Maybe a dangerous fool's errand. But at some level it beat hanging around her mother's house, her current place of residence while Mom recovered from surgery from breast cancer.

Mom . . . For a moment Mackenzie tuned out Doobie's rambling. She'd been living with her mother at the insistence of her stepsister, Stephanie, daughter of the odious Dan "The Man" Gerber. Her mother was doing okay enough that Mackenzie could probably move out of the house now, but she'd let her apartment go when she'd moved in, so there was that. And then she'd quit her job, so there was that, too.

Mom had asked why Mackenzie had quit the force but Mac hadn't felt like going into it all. Her emotions were still whipsawing back and forth over what she maybe could've done, should've done, but hadn't. The sexual harassment had been mostly implicit. Nothing concrete enough to be definitive. A move in front of a door to make it hard to leave the room. A casual brush by. The evidence of his erection inside his trousers, something he wanted her to see.

The fact that he was the River Glen chief of police was what determined it for Mac. He wanted to promote her, but . . . there were steps she needed to take to earn that promotion. Those steps had never been outlined, but Mackenzie had understood they weren't the kind of steps described in the department manual.

As if he could read her mind, Gillis asked now, "Why'd ya quit?" as the bartender slid his drink to him.

"Dissatisfaction with the job."

"Didn't get the promotion you asked for?"

Well, yeah, Doobie. The truth was she had half hoped she'd be promoted to detective when one of the River Glen PD's detectives, Howard Eversgard, went on administrative leave. Eversgard had gone on to take early retirement after a dangerous domestic violence incident that left him no choice but to shoot the belligerent, angry husband aiming at him with his own handgun. An investigation had followed with Eversgard put on administrative leave, and though he was eventually cleared of wrongdoing, the man's unfortunate death had gotten to him. He'd surprised everyone by giving up his job and starting a new life. Mac had secretly hoped for a promotion then, but Chief Bennihof had quashed that wish in a way that had left Mac no choice, she'd felt, but to quit herself.

And then Bibi had run into her at the Coffee Club.

"Look into Seth. There's something there, I just know it," she'd insisted as they were leaving, latching onto Mac as if they were long lost friends.

"An investigation takes time," Mac had reminded.

"But you'll do it?"

"Yesss . . . okay. No promises, but I'll check it out."

"Good. You know Seth?"

"No."

"He might be a . . . dealer . . . drug dealer, kind of. Small-time. But his day job's as a trainer at Good Livin'. I guess his latest girlfriend is a receptionist there."

So, now Mac was following Seth and Patti. Seth was nice enough looking in a sneery sort of way with hipster hair and clothes, and Patti was short and tough looking with dyed black hair scraped into a ponytail. Good Livin' was situated near River Glen General Hospital, Glen Gen to the locals, and it tried to trade on its proximity to the hospital as part of the club's overall health experience, which had earned them several reprimands and fines from the hospital itself. As far as Mackenzie knew, those charges hadn't slowed Good Livin' down one bit.

Her drinking today was to give legitimacy to her afternoon trip to the Waystation should Seth and Patti recognize she had more than a passing interest in them. She'd been following Seth for about a week back and forth to the club and his house and back again and so far had learned nothing. If he was a dealer he must be doing it at the club because no one was showing up at his house and he and Patti weren't going anywhere but the club. Until today, that is, when they had suddenly taken a detour to the Waystation in the middle of the afternoon. So far, neither of them had paid her any attention. They were too involved in themselves and their own quiet fury at each other. Mac was kind of curious about whatever that was about, but hadn't moved close enough to listen. And now Gillis was trying to ruin her game as he edged nearer again and she got a whiff of his sour breath. He might dress like he was headed for a rodeo, but he smelled like what might be found on the bottom of a cowboy boot.

"We're not on a date," Mac said, sliding over another barstool.

Gillis seemed about to follow, then shrugged and stayed where he was. "You're really hard to get to know."

"So I've been told."

"I thought you'd get those doo-ees taken care of for me."

"You deserved those DUIs."

"For somebody so cute, you sure are a tough bitch, aren't ya?" he said.

"That's a compliment, right?"

"You bet your sweet ass." He leaned back to catch a glimpse of her derriere.

If he touches me, I'll smack him, she thought mildly, aware the vodka she'd been so carefully sipping might be moving through her system anyway. She'd made a show of tipping back the glass a time or two. Now she had a second one in front of her, which she had no intention of drinking. When Seth and Patti decided to leave, she needed to be sober and ready to follow.

"So, they fire you, or what?" asked Gillis.

"Or what."

He snorted. "They *didn't* fire you?"

She allowed herself a heavy sigh. She didn't want to talk to him. But she also didn't want to make a scene. "I quit."

"Why?"

"It was time."

"Yeah, well, there's always a reason."

You wanna know the reason, Doobie? The chief made a pass at me, then acted like it never happened. And after that, though I thought things were maybe cool, they weren't. Same old story. My career, such as it was, wasn't going anywhere. He wasn't going to get over the rejection. . . .

"Sometimes you know when time's up," she said.

"You were a pretty good cop," he said grudgingly. High praise indeed from someone she'd arrested twice and who complained long and loudly about River Glen's finest on a good day.

Suddenly Seth and Patti got up from the table. Patti walked out of the bar, stiff-backed, head high, totally pissed. Seth threw some money down and followed after her, swearing furiously beneath his breath. Mac caught a few pungent words. The "F" word chief among them. *Trouble in paradise.*

"They're pretty mad at each other," Gillis observed.

"What was your first clue?" Mac asked.

Gillis guffawed as the bartender, a guy in his thirties with a bald head and full beard, leaned in and observed, "They're always like that."

"They in here a lot?" Mac asked him, getting to her feet.

He shrugged. "Seen 'em in here a time or two."

"Bet they jump on each other as soon as they're in the car," said Gillis. "Makes me horny."

"Gotta go." Mackenzie dropped a twenty on the bar. The Waystation was a dive bar with moderate to cheap prices, its most appealing feature. Maybe it was the reason people like Seth and Patti came here because it sure wasn't for the ambiance or the food.

"I got this," Gillis said magnanimously.

"Appreciate it, but no thanks." Mac left her twenty where it sat and pretended to mosey out the door but inside she was hurrying. She knew where Seth and Patti lived, but maybe they had other plans. Maybe this was where they broke routine. Maybe there was a dinner scheduled. At some Portland restaurant? Or another bar? There were hours of daylight left.

She hurried to her SUV, a dark blue RAV4, and eased in behind the wheel, pulling out after Seth and Patti, but staying back several blocks. Maybe they were going somewhere else, but they seemed to be heading in the direction of their rented town house on the west side, the newest side of town. She always felt nervous when she was following someone. What could she say if she were caught? With that in mind, she let herself fall back even farther, but when Seth and Patti started up Stillwell Hill Mac let out a pent-up breath. They were likely going home. She made a face. Well, whatever. She could follow them back or head to her mother's. But Dan the Man would be home from his job in insurance sales soon and there would be a lot of hours trying to figure out what to say to him. He spent a little too much time sliding his gaze over Mackenzie's body when he thought no one was looking. She'd thought about complaining to Stephanie, but Stephanie was his daughter and . . . she'd probably get told she was imagining it. She wondered if it was a function of being single, this unwanted male attention.

"Maybe you need a relationship," she said aloud.

You would have to try. Have to be nice. Have to SMILE, and you know that's never going to happen.

She made a face. It had been a while since her last relationship. Maybe it was just the males she was around.

Maybe it's you . . .

She followed Seth's white Ford F-150 from a discreet distance and when they turned into their small cul-de-sac on the edge of the Staffordshire Estates development, she cruised on by, driving through the part of the development where most of the two hundred plus homes were completed. The overall construction had slowed a bit from its earlier furious pace, but the houses, which had seemed to languish partway through construction, were now finished and they were breaking ground on new ones. The completed homes were all large and modern; every Realtor's dream. A new phase of development was starting soon, according to the billboard with the grinning man in a hard hat holding a rolled-up set of plans in one hand. Andrew Best, owner of Best Homes. Her stepsister's husband, Nolan, had quit working for Best Homes after suffering a falling-out with Best, who was an unbelievable tyrant, according to Nolan, who now worked as a foreman for Laidlaw Construction, which had purchased a number of lots from Best and was also building homes in the development. Nolan and her stepsister had been planning to have a baby, but Stephanie and Nolan had put those plans on hold after Nolan lost his job. Mac wasn't sure what the status on baby making was now that Nolan had been with Laidlaw nearly a year.

She circled back and drove past the opening to the cul-de-sac, pulling into an open spot a block ahead, watching through her side mirror as Seth and Patti climbed from the truck and walked toward the town house's front door. They let themselves in and Mac saw lights flicker on in first the bottom floor, and then the top. It looked like they were in for the night. Though Bibi was convinced Seth had something to do with Rayne's disappearance, Mac suspected she was on a wild goose chase. She would be better served looking for another job. A real job. She just wasn't sure what that job could be. She could try for a spot with either Portland or Laurelton PD, but any job she would be offered would mean starting at the bottom again and honestly, she wasn't sure that's what she wanted. She had a bit of a problem with authority . . . maybe more than a bit . . . and though she might be wasting her time chasing after Seth Keppler, she loved the freedom of doing what she wanted and not being under someone else's control.

Her inner eye woke and rewatched the events that had brought her to this place. The chief locking his office door while she'd swiveled slowly around in the chair in front of his desk, refusing to believe what she was seeing. The curtains to the office were already closed. After hours. No one around. No officers, no detectives. No one. She'd risen from her chair, trying to tamp down her alarm. "Hey," she'd said, while he'd leaned back against the door and eyed her in a way that could only be described as lascivious. Her pulse had skyrocketed, and not in a good way. She'd understood, from what others had said, that the chief wasn't much of a leader, but no one had totally condemned him nor accused him of sexual harassment.

"Hey," he'd responded quietly, moving from his position at the door toward her.

Holy . . . hell.

To this day she couldn't remember exactly what she'd said to get herself out of there. He hadn't chased her around the desk. He hadn't completely blocked her escape. He hadn't *touched* her. But she'd had to do some fast talking to get him to unlock that door and allow her to escape.

After that, she hadn't looked at her job quite the same way, and neither had he, apparently. He found little ways to criticize her work. Nothing huge, just enough to sow the seeds of doubt in her coworkers' minds, though they swore they knew she was hardworking and uncomplaining. It wore her down though. She quit without a real plan. Being a cop had lost its luster. She'd never really fit in and so she left.

And here she was, playing private detective. She didn't have the credentials. Wasn't sure that was the route she was going to take. She'd just listened to Bibi and—

Her passenger door suddenly flew open. Mac gasped and immediately bent over, searching for the gun under the front seat before remembering she didn't keep it there since she quit the force.

"Just me, Officer Mac," a familiar male voice said, catching her arm before she could grab for it.

"Taft!" she exclaimed, getting a good look at him.

"What are you doing here?" he demanded. "Staking out the place? Who're you looking for? I thought you quit the PD. This your car?"

She snapped her arm free and pushed his shoulder hard. "Jesus Christ, you scared the crap out of me."

"You following Seth?"

He was so good-looking, and such a pain in the butt. Here, then, was a real PI. She'd run into him several times during the course of her two years on the job. He was the bane of the department, although Cooper Haynes, one of River Glen's two remaining detectives, had admitted that

Taft had done some good investigative work on more than one occasion. Elena Verbena, the other detective, didn't think so, but Elena was a hard-ass and determined not to like him in that way that really said she might be attracted to him.

And for good reason. Sporting a three day's growth of dark beard, dimples hidden in the fur, blue eyes regarding her with faint humor, Jesse James Taft was too attractive to be any good, Mac had thought. She'd learned differently, but the man was unorthodox and if she thought she had a problem with authority, Taft took the cake. Rumor had it he'd been fired from not one, but two, separate police departments, and then had gone on his own. He was a fixer for the wealthy around River Glen and Laurelton and the Greater Portland area. He was also a guy who worked for free sometimes, if he felt his clients deserved a break and the police weren't doing the job. Mackenzie's dealings with him had been fairly benign, although she'd been warned his bonhomie was an act, something he could switch on and off at will. He was charming and dangerous and exactly what she did not need right now.

He said, with a smile that she didn't trust, "I'm on a job and you're ruining my mojo."

"I'm on a job, too."

"What kind of job?"

"I don't think I want to tell you," she said.

"What kind of job?" he repeated.

"An errand for a friend."

"What kind of errand?"

"I don't have to talk to you. Get out of my car. Where's yours?" She glanced around. There weren't many vehicles parked on this stretch of road.

"I'm around the corner." He inclined his head. "What kind of errand? I need to know why you're in the way."

"Yeah? Well, I don't have to tell you. And this conversation has just hit a junior-high low, so go away." She motioned him to get out of her car.

"You're watching Seth Keppler." She tried not to let him see he'd hit pay dirt, but he was too good at reading people. "Why?" he asked.

"Like I said, an errand for a friend."

"What friend?"

"Stop with the questions. You can't grill me."

"Why'd you quit the force?"

"I just told you—"

"Was it Bennihof? He come on to you?"

She opened her mouth but couldn't answer. She could lie with the best of them at times, but Taft's bombastic style made it near impossible. "That's none of your business," she finally sputtered. "Get out!"

His face shuttered. He'd heard the right answer even if she hadn't given it. After a moment, he said, "Probably good that you left. Whatever you're doing now, let it go. Seth and Patti are in for a while, maybe for the night. It's their routine."

"Why are *you* watching them?"

"An errand for a friend," he tossed back at her, sliding out of her car. He motioned her to take off as he closed the door and then headed around the hedge she now realized he'd been hiding behind.

She felt like staying where she was, just to be obstinate, but that wouldn't get her anywhere. Taft was surveilling Seth and Patti for some other reason. It might serve her better to work with him than against him.

She drove around the corner and found his black Jeep Rubicon with him just climbing into it. She pulled up next to the Jeep, rolled down her passenger window, and called out, "Give me your cell number."

He was only halfway into the driver's seat and stopped for a moment. "You looking for a date? After Bennihof, I thought—"

"Just tell me."

"Hand me your phone, and I'll do you one better." He shut the Rubicon's door and walked around to the driver's side of her car.

Reluctantly, she rolled down her window, pulled her phone from its iOttie holder, unlocked it, and passed it to him. He quickly entered his information into her phone, then sent himself a text with hers.

"We good?" she asked, letting her annoyance show.

She saw the dimples beneath his beard momentarily deepen. "Yep."

"I don't like you very much," she said.

He laughed. "That's a lie."

"I want to know more about Seth Keppler."

He patted her car and moved away.

"C'mon, Taft. Be a pal," she called. He shook his head as he walked back to his Jeep. Her passenger window was still down, so she added loudly, "I just want to know what his deal is. Is he a big bad criminal, or just another loser that I'm wasting my time on?"

"Both." He climbed into his vehicle and rolled his window down so he could still hear her.

She stared across at him. "My friend thinks he's responsible for her friend's disappearance."

"Who's your friend?"

"Who're you working for?"

Taft screwed up his face in thought, then said, "Text me. We'll get something to eat sometime and exchange information."

She was jubilant. She hadn't really expected him to comply. She didn't have much information to bargain with, but he didn't need to know that. "I will," she said, putting the RAV in gear.

"Goodbye for now, Officer Mac."

"Ex-officer Mac."

He saluted her as she hit the gas and drove away and she felt his gaze on the back of her neck long after she was out of sight.

CHAPTER THREE

Mackenzie parked in the driveway of her mother's house and started a text to Taft. No reason to let grass grow beneath her feet. Strike while the iron's hot and all that. But then she hesitated over the phraseology. She wanted him to open up to her, but she didn't know him well enough nor possess the key that would unlock his reticence. He was brash and forthright, but she sensed his lips were tightly sealed. She'd heard a lot of adjectives used about him, but blabbermouth was not one of them.

Finally, she just texted: Tonight. 7:00. Deno's or Pizza Joe's. Your choice.

She waited for five minutes, her teeth on edge. If he didn't get back to her, she was going to have to push. She needed him a whole lot more than he needed her.

The front door opened and Dan the Man squinted out at her car. She'd been sitting inside it for too long and he was wondering what she was up to. He was very fussy about her loose hours, and to be fair, her mother was equally concerned. Mackenzie sometimes felt like she was back in high school and that was a no-go. Since Mom was loads better, maybe it was time to leave. But where to go? She had some savings but she wasn't exactly rolling in the dough right now, either.

When her cell remained silent, she finally got out of the car, thinking about what her next text should be. She didn't know where Taft lived, or where he worked, if he even had an office. She knew only the gossip about him, and what she'd seen, which was very little. She'd run into him a time or two during the course of police work. Her ex-partner, Bryan "Ricky" Richards, had had a beef with him over Taft's "interference" of the arrest of a wealthy "captain of industry," Mitchell Mangella. Mangella, who'd grown up in River Glen, moved to New York and became a hedge fund guy, apparently made scads of money and bought homes and businesses around the world, had then sold most of his assets and moved back to River Glen. He'd been accused of stealing his own wife's jewelry, by his wife, and the wife had lodged a complaint with the River Glen PD, which hadn't taken the accusation too seriously since Mangella had bought the jewelry, a necklace and bracelet, for the woman in the first place and the two of them were still living together. Still, an investigation had been opened. Mackenzie had reserved judgment on the whole debacle, but Ricky had landed firmly on the beautiful Prudence Mangella's side. Taft had beat River Glen's finest to the punch when he uncovered said stolen pieces at a pawn shop in Northeast Portland, which, naturally, had cameras, and showed that a woman had dropped the jewelry there. The woman turned out to be a friend of Prudence's, not Mitchell's, and the two women had been working together to get either Mitchell, or an insurance company, to pay for the stolen pieces. Prudence had zeroed in on Ricky's allegiance to her during the course of the investigation and had stoked his adulation, promising . . .

what . . . Mackenzie still didn't know. But then it had all come crashing down and accusations were hurled right and left. Mangella roared at Prudence, and Prudence roared right back, and the River Glen PD gently tiptoed backward out of the whole affair. As far as Mac knew, Mangella and Prudence were still battling it out, though still living together. Marriages . . . there was no telling what made them work.

But Ricky had fallen for the lady hook, line, and sinker, even though her partner had been merely a pawn in the Mangellas' ongoing war. Mac had told him to get over it, which had only served to piss him off at her. And the department had been made to look bad at being beaten to the punch by Taft, so nobody was happy, especially after Taft, having been called into the department by Chief Bennihof, had essentially breezed through and made it clear the department shouldn't blame him for doing *their* job. He'd cruised out about the same time Mac was leaving for the day and they'd struck up an acquaintanceship, one that consisted until today of a few witty remarks and some unspoken mutual awareness but not much more. Of course the department considered him a turncoat to law enforcement, and Ricky seemed to somehow blame him for ending Prudence's interest in him. Ricky still had trouble seeing that Prudence had used him for her own ends and that when those ends failed to materialize, she had no further use for him.

The male ego . . .

Mac ignored Dan the Man and hit the remote for the garage door. She locked up her car, walked through the garage, and let herself into the house through the kitchen door as much to avoid her stepfather as to see if her mother might be at the table doing a jigsaw puzzle, her favorite pastime throughout her chemotherapy, surgery, and recovery, one she hadn't as yet given up.

"Hey, Mom," Mac said, finding her just where she'd expected her to be.

"Hi there." She barely glanced up from the thousand-piece puzzle of various African animals.

"A lot of grass," Mac observed.

"A lot of grass," her mother agreed. "A lot of stripes, too."

Mac looked at the picture of what the puzzle should look like when finished on the front of the box. Zebras and okapis. Yep. A lot of stripes.

Dan the Man entered the room from the living room. He smiled at Mac and said, "You sure spend a lot of time in your car."

"I sure do."

"What takes so long?"

"My RAV is kind of my office these days, Dan."

Her mother looked up. "You can stay here as long as you like," she said, jumping ahead to the unspoken question hanging between them. "It's really helped having you around after the surgery and I like having you here."

Mac pulled her attention back to her mother. Beverly Gerber's pallor, though still pale, was showing a faint pinkness underneath, a slow return to health that filled Mac with relief. Mom's illness the last year and a half had taken over all their lives and scared Mac to her core. Mac and her mother had never been what you could call close, and there had definitely been a rift when Mom had married Dan, but recognizing she could lose her had chilled Mackenzie to the bone. She'd moved in to help care for her and in the process they'd found each other again. If Dan weren't around, Mac felt she and Mom might even find their way to a kind of friendship they'd never had before. But Dan the Man was entrenched.

As if to prove that point, Dan said, "I was just talking to your mother about ordering from the River Glen Grill. She loves that chicken salad. Think you could pick up for us?"

Mac immediately felt herself resist. He always volunteered her without asking. Not that she minded helping out her mother. That's why she'd moved in in the first place. But Dan was that guy who always seemed to be asking for something. "Sure," she clipped out.

"You're part of dinner, too," said Mom.

"Well, there is our budget—" Dan started.

"Thanks, I've got other plans," Mac said at the same time.

Mom looked like she was going to argue, but Dan clapped his hands together and said, "What else would you like, honey? Feeling up for a glass of white? I'm sure Mackenzie would pick up a bottle of chardonnay?" He turned and smiled at Mac.

Mackenzie slid a glance at her mother, whose brows had knit into mild consternation. Mac said to her, "I could get you a rosé," knowing her mother's favorite.

"Oh . . . no, thanks." She met Mac's gaze and they shared a moment of silent understanding. Mackenzie had a memory of her mom smiling at her that same way from a seat in the audience, silently encouraging her as she emoted her way through whatever small part she'd been assigned, drama being Mac's favorite subject in school. She recalled the animation in Mom's face. The fun they'd had. Before the disappointment when, following her father's death, Mac had given up any dreams she might have had in the arts and had determined to go into law enforcement, just like her father. Though she'd never outwardly voiced it, Mac knew her mother had been sorely disappointed, even though she'd agreed with Mac's declaration that she needed a paying job.

"Still not feeling like a drink?" Dan asked Mom, his voice oozing with empathy.

She smiled faintly and nodded, turning back to her puzzle.

Mackenzie pivoted and walked back out the kitchen door. Dan was never going to listen hard enough to recall that Mom didn't really like chardonnay. He had it in his mind that chardonnay was the white wine all women drank and no matter how many times he was told differently, he reverted to his own rock bottom notions.

She glanced at her phone as she placed it back in its car holder. Still silent. Her other plans might not be materializing but she wasn't giving up yet. In the meantime, she would head to the River Glen Grill. A couple hundred rungs higher up on the sophistication scale than the Waystation, it was probably the nicest place in River Glen and nearby Laurelton combined. An expensive meal for Dan to be ordering; he was notoriously cheap. But then she hadn't gotten Dan to cough up the money for whatever he'd ordered for Mom and himself, so maybe he hoped Mackenzie would also foot the bill, even though he had to know her current financial situation wasn't the best. She would need to demand payment from him. One thing Mac had learned over her months of living with him: You needed to nag him until he caved. Though as a rule nagging didn't come naturally to Mac, she almost lived for it with Dan.

* * *

After watching Mackenzie Laughlin drive off from Seth Keppler's, Taft drove past the town house once more, just to be sure the lowlife was staying home. His F-150 was still in the drive and the house lights were blazing against the damp March evening. A sporadic wind had kicked up and was currently sending an escapee plastic bag jigging and jagging across the property to cross the road and land in the laurel hedge he'd been standing behind while he'd been surveilling Seth and Patti's home earlier.

Patti came into view in the living room window as Taft slowly cruised by. She was carrying two drinks and looking down at someone seated on the couch below his line of sight. Behind her the wall-mounted television was set to some speed-racing event that probably was prerecorded. In his research Taft had determined Keppler loved anything that had to do with vehicles in general, racing in particular. The fact that his truck was over a decade old was either because Seth didn't have the funds to buy a new one, something Taft was pretty sure was untrue based on the man's illegal side ventures, or it was indicative of his desire to stay deep, deep under the radar with a vehicle that wouldn't deserve a second look in an area rife with trucks. If River Glen's finest was onto Seth's side deals, they sure weren't acting like it. Maybe it was some overall quiet, clandestine investigation by them that would result in a sting, but Taft would bet his last George Washington that just wasn't so. He knew enough about River Glen PD's operation to have little respect for some of them. The detectives on the force were the only ones worth their salt, and one of them had quit. That left only Haynes and Verbena to uphold "protect and serve" along with a group of other street cops and departmental police who were varying degrees of incompetent, too gung-ho or just putting in their time . . . in Taft's biased opinion.

He'd never been part of the River Glen PD, as he had several other police departments, mistakes he'd made in his youth, mistakes he wasn't going to make again. His questioning of authority had rubbed the old guard the wrong way, which he'd ignored, and he'd naturally bucked the bad aspects of the cop culture he'd experienced, naively expecting it would change. The expectation was that he should be the one to change, not them, which had forced him to say adios *twice* before he'd really understood that being a cop just wasn't going to work for him.

His sister had often told him he had a thick skull. He smiled faintly now and sketched the sign of the cross even though he wasn't Catholic or even particularly religious. It was just what he did when he thought of Helene. She'd been a decade older than he was, and she'd been gone about a decade as well. She'd warned him about being too cocky, too sure, too rash. He'd ignored those warnings throughout his years with the police. He was a little more seasoned now, but his reputation had been formed. The result: The cops didn't like him much.

He mentally shrugged. He worked for law and order in his own way. Too bad if it sometimes stepped on others' toes.

With Seth and Patti apparently in for the evening, he turned the Rubicon west toward Laurelton and his own condo. Helene had told him to save up and buy real estate, and he'd listened to her advice. She'd left him a small amount, which he'd saved and then had added to that amount, exercising the lease option to buy his condo at the end of the contract. Now, seven years later, he lived in the two-bedroom end unit of a onetime motel that had been renovated and converted, and he sometimes took care of neighborly duties for some of the others in the rambling, one-story, sixteen-unit complex. It wasn't a whole lot of space but it worked for him. He'd resisted the requests to "move in together" from his list of sometime girlfriends, which had resulted in more than one screaming breakup when he hadn't even realized he and said girlfriend were supposedly exclusive. He'd had a dog once, Helene's golden retriever, but John-Boy had been aged even then, and he hadn't lasted a year and a half after his mistress's death. Nowadays he took care of Tommy Carnoff's two pugs whenever the older gent in the unit next door decided on a trip somewhere with his latest lady friend. Taft might have had a few women in his life, but Casanova Carnoff beat him hands down at playing the field.

Today, Taft parked his car beneath the carport in his allotted slot, remote locked the Rubicon, and entered the condo, tossing his keys on the small console table near the front door. He walked through the living room and past the small galley kitchen to the bathroom that sat between the two bedrooms. One bedroom had his bed and dresser; the other was filled with boxes of stuff. Junk, Helene would say, if she could see it. The same junk he'd transferred from his apartment when he'd moved in. An acoustic guitar gathered dust next to his desk. The desk, chair, and lamp were the only pieces in the junk room that were used, unless you counted his laptop and portable printer, both of which he often kept in his vehicle. This was the extent of his office. Oh, and the safe he'd installed in the wall, which housed his Glock and some cold hard cash. Welcome to Taft Investigations.

He stripped down and took a quick shower. There was work to be done tonight and he wanted to both clean up and wake up before he met with Mangella. The man was wealthy and eccentric and his wife was even worse. Nothing about Prudence Mangella was prudent. She was excessive, loud, and indiscreet. A perfect complement to her husband, who was exactly the same. Strangely, they both liked and trusted him, even when they were viciously fighting with each other, which was most of the time. He thought over her last dido, expecting that Prudence would resent him finding her "stolen" jewels, but no. All was well again in Mangella-land. Taft worked for Mitch and Mitch's business and therefore he was part of the team. Prudence had her eye on the money, always, and if she tried to sneak a little extra off the top from time to time, well, apparently that was—after much Sturm und Drang—a forgivable offense. The Mangellas lived a strange partnership that somehow seemed to work for them both.

Taft dressed in jeans, a black T-shirt, and a black jacket. As he was heading out he saw the text from Mackenzie on his phone: Tonight. 7:00. Deno's or Pizza Joe's. Your choice.

Mackenzie Laughlin.

He thought about it, caught sight of himself in the mirror by the front door, recognized the faint, interested smile on his lips, and purposely wiped it off. Not a woman to mess with. A cop, *ex-cop*, he reminded himself. Maybe not seasoned, not hardened . . . maybe not even any good. Hard to know, at this juncture. Ex-cop or no, she had recently been a police officer, and Taft had learned long ago to keep those kind of women at arm's length romantically.

Those kind of women? his mind taunted him as he headed outside, locked up, and strode into the carport.

Was it sexist that he found policewomen too . . . rigid?

You want every woman to be like me, Helene's ghost reminded him, like she always did. He could almost see her standing by the Rubicon, her eyebrows lifted and gazing at him in that way that let him know that *Yes, you are a full-of-shit male and I only love you because you're my brother.*

The image darkened and faded and he climbed in the vehicle, his mood sobering. His sister haunted him less and less, but she was still there. One of these days he might even forgive her for leaving him.

Mackenzie waited by the maitre d's station at the River Glen Grill, an ivy-covered brick building that had once been a hotel and now was the restaurant on the first floor with very nice apartments above that, each spanning the entire floor of the twelve-story building. At one time Dan the Man had said that he and Mac's mother might move there, but that, like so many other of Dan's plans, never materialized. Stephanie had said of her father, "Yeah, you can't believe him. My mother finally figured that out and left him. He's never forgiven her and she's never looked back." According to Stephanie, her own mother had married a man from Scottsdale and moved there while the ink was still drying on the divorce papers. Left high and dry by his ex, Dan had then entered Mom's circle of friends, introduced by one of them who'd apparently had designs on Dan herself. Unfortunately, Dan had zeroed in on Mom, recently widowed, who owned her own home and had only one child, who was about to graduate high school.

Mac made a face. The only good thing about Dan was that he'd brought Stephanie, also an only child, into Mackenzie's life, and the two stepsisters had become close friends. That almost made up for the man's other transgressions. Almost.

"Order for Dan Gerber," Mackenzie said to the girl behind the maitre d's podium when she finally looked up.

"Okay."

The girl checked with another member of the waitstaff, who turned on his heel and headed out to collect Mac's order. Mackenzie looked past the podium and into the dining area. The room was full of semicircular blood-red leather booths. There were no white tablecloths, but the amount of glassware glistening under the muted lights and the deferential attitude of the waiters suggested a place out of the fifties where Frank Sinatra or his like would order a black telephone brought to the table and lean back, puffing on cigars. There was something wasteful about the whole shebang that bugged Mac in a way she couldn't quite define. The food was good at the Grill; there was no denying that. But the dollar signs on the restaurant Internet's ratings denoting price were many.

The maitre d', a forty-something man with a straight back and prematurely gray hair, came up to the podium as the girl rang up the order. The younger man returned at that moment with the order and he set the white plastic bag on the counter as the girl handed Mac the bill. The total wasn't as bad as it could have been, but it did make her grimace. She talked with Art, the maitre d', whom she knew from other trips to the River Glen Grill, to make certain she wasn't on the hook for the bill. He assured her it was taken care of and hefted up the order for her to grasp. Mac slipped her fingers into the handholds in the white plastic bag. "Thanks, Art," she said before carrying the bag of food to her car.

She drove the meal home and dropped it off, sketching a goodbye to her mother when Dan's back was turned as he busied himself with digging into the bags. "You didn't pay for this, did you?" Mom asked, as Mackenzie turned to leave.

"Heck, no. Gave them Dan's credit card."

"What?" Dan asked, looking up in surprise.

"Just kidding," Mackenzie said. "They have your number on file. Remember?"

"Oh, do they . . . ?" He looked discomfited, even though he knew full well they did. Art had called Dan and gotten the information from him the last time Mackenzie had been tasked to bring home the takeout and had asked Dan if he could keep the number on file. Dan had agreed but either had forgotten, or more likely, hoped Mac had. Like that was gonna happen. You had to stay one step ahead of a guy like Dan or you found yourself left holding the bag.

From her time on the force, Mackenzie had gotten to know a number of people around River Glen who were stationed in various jobs and who willingly helped her if she asked. It was one of the best things that had come from the job.

"See ya later." Mackenzie walked out into a brisk night. The air felt thick with moisture, but for the moment the clouds were holding on tight. It was full dark now. Taft hadn't gotten back to her, so she was in a quandary. "Screw it," she muttered, yanking out her phone and typing in: *Heading to Pizza Joe's. Hope to see you there.*

She drove to the pizza parlor and parked in the back lot. Pizza Joe's was in the middle of a center with a Safeway, a nail salon, a small deli, a Great Clips, and one of the Good Livin' fitness centers. Mac strode through the front door, which had an annoyingly cheery little bell. Immediately she wished she'd chosen Deno's. She'd forgotten how chipper Pizza Joe's was with Pizza Joe's smiling, mustachioed face painted on one wall, a near-perfect replica of Nintendo's Mario or Luigi, surrounded by a kabillion miniature red, white, and green Italian flags, which were spread just as cheerily all over the place. As Mackenzie sat herself at a two-person table with a good view of the front door, she eyed the little bouquet of flags sprouting from the top of her napkin dispenser. Pizza Joe seemed to have forgotten the warning: too much of a good thing.

She was debating whether to order a personal pepperoni pizza or to attempt something more exotic, like Canadian bacon and pineapple. That's about as far as she liked to venture when it came to the pizza menu, and even then she was generally sorry she'd left her comfort zone, which was pretty much pepperoni.

The bell above the door jangled and she looked up and there was Taft. He spied her at the same moment and she felt a small jolt of awareness. She clocked it as a normal reaction to a good-looking male.

"Hey," he said, swinging the other chair at her table around and half sitting, half slouching in it, his arms over the back of it.

"Are you preparing to jump up and leave, or are you staying for a while?" she asked.

"I'm staying."

"Are you?"

He looked amused, but he turned the chair back around,

sat down on it, and scooted up to the table, folding his hands on the tabletop and regarding her expectantly.

"What?" she asked.

"You wanted to share information. I had an appointment that I rearranged to come here, so give me what you've got and I'll see where we are."

"I get a choice in this, you know. This is a two-way street."

His answer was a faint twitch of his lips.

"You're going to give me information, too," she said, in case he had some other idea bubbling around in his brain.

"You're making up the rules here?"

"Let's just talk like adults, okay? I want to know why you were surveilling"—he shot her a look of warning and she lowered her voice—"our mutual *friend*. You want to know what I was doing, and I want to know what you're looking at. Let's get to it."

"You gonna order?" He inclined his head toward the menu, still in her hand.

Mackenzie bit back a sharp remark. "I was thinking about pepperoni."

"With mushrooms?"

"No."

"Pepperoncinis and some onions, maybe tomatoes."

"Taft . . ."

He lifted his palms. "You like it plain. I get it. Just pepperoni." He nodded, as if that made sense, and it pissed Mackenzie off anew for reasons she couldn't immediately place.

"No, I don't care. You order."

"You buying?"

She was about to object but saw he was baiting her. "Yeah, I'm buying."

He laughed. "I've got it."

"Jesus, Taft. Don't make everything so difficult."

"Okay, I'll place the order."

He got up and walked to the line at the counter, his gaze scouring the menu posted on the wall behind. Mackenzie watched the pretty gal taking his order smile and flirt a little and almost sighed. Taft was a wild card, his aims hewing closer to his client's rather than the letter of the law. It was why he'd washed out as a cop. Too much leeway. Though he'd never been on the River Glen force, everyone in the department was well aware of him and there were those who felt he'd gone over to the dark side. Mac didn't necessarily believe that, but she certainly knew she needed to be on her toes around him.

But then the River Glen PD had no reason to be on their high and mighty, either. They were in the midst of challenges in the department. A rogue cop, one of their own, had accidentally shot and killed another officer during a robbery at a convenience store. It was an ugly and sad affair and the cop, Keith Silva, had left on bad terms. Though Mac had her problems with Bennihof, she had to admit the chief had stuck to his guns, fought with the union, and fired Silva, who'd been universally disliked in the department anyway. She just hadn't figured she'd be the next to go, for totally different reasons.

Taft headed back to their table, bringing them each a beer on his return.

"I don't drink beer," Mac said.

"A lie. You occasionally drink light beer." He pointed at the mug he'd set in front of her. "That's a Coors Light."

"Very occasionally."

He shrugged. "Your choice." Picking up his beer, he took a long swallow.

She wasn't sure what she thought about how much he knew about her, but then hadn't she just been thinking about what she knew about him? Dragging her eyes from the sight of his strong throat as he swallowed, she asked, "What did you order?"

"Pepperoni straight up."

"You could've added some other stuff."

"It'll be good anyway."

Was this flirting? It felt like flirting. There was a spark of humor lurking in his eyes that put her a little on edge. "So, why're you following Seth?"

"He's a low-level drug dealer."

She blinked at this admission. "What's your interest? You trying to go up the chain?"

"Something like that. What's *your* interest?"

"Why do I feel I just got fobbed off?"

"I can't go into it further right now. Maybe later. We're doing a little tit for tat here. I got something, you got something . . . Tell me the name of your client?"

"'Client' might be too strong a word. A friend . . . more like an acquaintance who thought I was still with the department. Bibi Engstrom. She wants me to find a friend of hers who just disappeared. Rayne Sealy. Rayne's apparently a bit of a flake. I talked to her boss at the Coffee Club and he just acted like she'd done this before, and said he wasn't interested in hiring her back this time, if and when she returns."

"What do you think?"

"I think . . . the boss probably knows her character, but I said I'd look into it and I'm not real busy at the moment, so fine. I'll see what I can come up with."

"What are your future employment plans?" he asked.

"I don't know yet. Who're you working for on this?"

"I really can't say."

"Bullshit."

Another smile crossed his lips, one that she suspected had worked its magic throughout his life. She kept her expression neutral, a trick she'd learned on the job. *Don't give anything away.*

Into the silence that followed, Taft admitted, "Mostly I'm working for myself."

"More bullshit."

"No, it's true. There are . . . reasons to keep Seth under tight scrutiny. Call it more of a hunch than anything else. Yeah, he's low level, but he's on the way to something more."

"Like what?"

"You're a cop. Ever just known when you were onto something?"

"Was a cop," she corrected.

"Something that doesn't feel right. Maybe on the surface it looks one way, but underneath you just know that there's more. And I don't mean bigger and badder drug czars up the ladder to the kingpin. Leave that to the DEA. It's personalities that make up these crime . . ."

"Syndicates?" Mac finished for him when he trailed off.

"Smaller than that. More like crime groups. Small-time, but deadly. It's amazing what you can get killed for if you try to carve out your own niche within the family hierarchy. You half expect it in the big families, but it can be as vicious at a lower level. And sometimes it gets quirky."

"Quirky," Mac repeated.

"I knew this guy over in Laurelton who raised llamas. Look sweet, but terrible beasts. They spit at you."

"Maybe they spit at *you*," said Mac dryly.

He inclined his head to her on making a good point. "There was one llama in particular who was the spitter. Apparently, he's the angry one. He got me twice before I knew to stay out of range. The rest of the herd was apparently benign, but if you're ever around 'em, I advise to stay back. Just a warning."

"Got it."

"So, there was this member of the family that owned the herd. A younger brother, who was . . ."

"Quirky?"

"And then some. Stole some of the prize stud's semen to start his own herd. Got caught, asked forgiveness, then did it again about six months later."

"Llama semen?"

He nodded.

"How did he get this semen?" she asked tentatively.

Taft spread his hands. "There are ways, apparently. This particular sample was in a vial in a refrigerator. Used for artificial insemination from the prize llama stud."

"Ah. So, the brother got caught a second time?"

"Started a melee. A huge fight, which resulted in the vial breaking and the prize stud's semen leaking onto the floor, which then further resulted in the younger brother being pummeled hard enough by the 'family' to send him to the hospital. He survived, but it was touch and go. Like I said, small-time but vicious."

"But Seth and Patti aren't into llama breeding."

"No."

"You think they're a small-time drug . . . family?"

"Along those lines . . ." His voice trailed off thoughtfully. She sensed he was thinking something over and waited for him to come to a conclusion. About her? About Seth and Patti? She wasn't sure, so she just waited.

His name was called and he got up and retrieved the pepperoni pizza and some paper plates. He brought everything to the table and they spent a few minutes sliding hot and gooey pieces onto their plates and doctoring them with Parmesan (Mac) and hot chili flakes (Taft).

After a few bites, Taft gave Mac a speculative look. She noticed the dark lashes that framed the icy blue depths of his eyes. In her limited experience good-looking men were wrapped up in layers of ego. The jury was still out on Taft, but she couldn't think of one good reason he would be any different from Pete Fetzler, the last guy she'd been with, who was all front and no rear. Pete could sure put out the advertisement, but there was never any follow-through. The worst part was, she'd suspected it from the start and had dated him anyway. She liked to think of herself as above being swayed by good looks, but she'd really fallen off her high horse on that one.

"Want to work together?" Taft asked, wiping his mouth with a napkin. The movement brought attention to his mouth. The shape of his lips seemed embedded on her retina.

"On this case?"

"I could use someone."

"What do I get out of it?"

He barked out a laugh. "My expertise?"

She sensed she was being led down the primrose path. Still . . . "What would I have to do?"

"Sometimes I have to be two places at the same time. Since you're already watching Seth, it could free me up to do something else. I have other . . . jobs."

"Clients?"

"I work for different people at different times."

"I have a feeling your expertise isn't going to be enough for me."

"I'll pay you," he said.

"How much?"

"What do you think you're worth?"

Mackenzie said slowly, "I'll have to get back to you on that."

They stared each other down. After several long moments, Mac said, "You make me feel like I'm about to dance with the devil."

"That sounds vaguely like a yes. Is it a yes?"

"Yes."

He reached for another piece of pizza and pushed the rest her way, even though she'd barely touched her first slice. "Want another beer while we get down to it?"

"Yes," she said again. What the hell. She was already on the path.

Chapter Four

"How did you know I occasionally drink light beer?" asked Mac as she sat back in her chair. She'd made it through one piece of pizza. Normally she would eat two and eye a third, but Taft had put her on edge.

"I know people."

Ah. Okay. "Ricky. Bryan 'Ricky' Richards. My ex-partner," she guessed.

"Ricky . . ." He cocked his head and thought that over.

"He became one of Prudence Mangella's surrogates during the 'stolen' jewelry that was in the pawn shops. She relied on Ricky and he let her."

"That guy's your partner?" Taft's brows lifted. "The one Pru flattered and pretended interest in."

"Ex-partner," she reminded. "And yes."

He shook his head. "I know other people."

"Someone at the department." She didn't wait for his answer, just listed everyone she could think of at the River Glen PD, but Taft didn't react to any of the names.

"I'm an investigator," he said, shrugging it off.

Mackenzie formed the words to point out that she'd hardly ever talked to him before today. That she didn't see how he could know so much about her without a deep dive into who she was. But she decided to let the questions wither on her tongue. The truth was, she was kind of flattered that he'd taken the time to note that small detail about herself.

After a long silence, Taft spread his hands and said, "Okay, I saw you pouring Tecate Light into a glass at Mexicali Rose. You were with a woman with hair pulled up into a bun who's about your same age and a man, likely her husband, based on the wedding bands, with a trimmed beard, no mustache, left-handed, wearing a Best Homes jacket."

"That had to be two years ago," Mackenzie said, not quite able to hide her surprise. "My stepsister and her husband. I didn't see you."

"I was in the restaurant," he said offhandedly.

Mackenzie took a swallow of her now warm beer, needing a moment to think. He'd impressed her. She had a lot of half-formed ideas about him, some not so great, but he'd definitely risen in her opinion with that one. "Nolan doesn't work for Best Homes anymore. He's with Laidlaw Construction."

"Didn't get along with Best?"

"Didn't get along with Best," she agreed.

"What happened with Bennihof?"

She should have figured they'd get back to that again. She shook her head. "I'm not going there."

"Hmm."

But she couldn't help herself from asking, "How'd you know about him?"

"Open secret."

"Open secret, my ass," she said. "Someone would've told me."

"There was a woman in dispatch I knew who found herself alone with him in his office after hours."

Mackenzie blinked several times. "After hours . . . ?"

He eyed her shrewdly. "I'm guessing you had a similar experience."

The woman who was currently in dispatch, Barbara Erdlich, was built like a fifty-gallon drum and tough as nails. She was affectionately known as the Battle-axe and enjoyed the moniker, apparently, as she even addressed herself with the same pejorative and glared down anyone who tried to suggest it was improper. The woman before her, however, had been young and exceptionally pretty. She'd only worked a week or two while Mackenzie was on the job, then she was gone and the Battle-axe took over. Now Mac wondered if the Battle-axe had been purposely hired. Maybe more people knew about Bennihof than she thought. "What was her name?" asked Mac.

"Katy."

"That's right. I didn't know she left because of Bennihof."

"She'll only tell you that if she's drunk enough."

"Oh." Mackenzie tried not to roll her eyes.

"It wasn't like that. I interviewed her, several times. That's all."

"Sure."

"I told her she should Me-Too him. Exposing him's the only way he'll leave. She didn't want to."

"If that look is because you think I should've been the one to do that, put it to rest. He didn't touch me. He didn't get that far," said Mac.

"I'm not giving you a look."

"Yeah." She snorted.

"You quit the job."

"Because it wasn't working for me." She hesitated. "And it wasn't going to work for me in the future, either."

He lifted his palms.

"Why do you want Bennihof out so badly?" she asked.

"He's bad for the department as a whole, bad for morale, bad for any woman he sets his sights on. I don't like guys like that."

He'd left two different police departments on bad terms and might have his own axe to grind. "Bad for the department?" she questioned.

He didn't rise to the bait, said instead, "I've seen my share of those guys, in one form or another, in one job or another. Political appointments, mainly, though a lot of them don't make it to chief. I don't have a lot of success with them, and I don't have any respect."

"Okay."

"A lot of good cops out there. I wouldn't call Bennihof a cop. I left the job . . . or it was suggested I leave the job . . ." His smile was ironic. "But I didn't leave the work. I'm still investigating, which is why we're here."

He'd unfolded himself from the chair and his height made her feel small, so she scrambled to her feet as well. He stuck out his hand and she cautiously did as well. They shook hands.

"So, am I on for surveilling Seth and Patti, starting tomorrow . . . morning?" she asked.

"As much as you can keep tabs on them. He's dealing the stuff. Maybe she is, too. They're going to make some move soon. It's like they know they're being tailed, so maybe they caught me at it." He said it like there was no way for that to be true. "Whatever the case, something will break. I'm counting on you to take this seriously."

"Absolutely."

"Okay. Keep in contact. If something happens, let me know. Otherwise we'll circle back in about a week?"

"Sounds good."

He nodded and held the door. She walked out ahead of him, inhaling deeply as she passed, far too aware that she liked the clean, male scent of him.

As soon as she was in her SUV she headed toward Seth and Patti's place, needing to assure herself that they were still in their current rut of work, home, and the Waystation. The lights were dimmed but she could see the flickering of the television and more importantly, Seth's truck in the driveway.

Satisfied, Mac drove back to Mom's house. She would make keeping eyes on Seth and Patti a priority for Taft, but she hadn't forgotten Bibi's request to find out what had happened to Rayne Sealy. Though Bibi had pointed to Seth, the ex-boyfriend, as a likely place to start, there were other avenues of investigation as well. Mac had planned to try to interview Seth and see what he knew about Rayne, but she was going to put that off for a bit now. Other people knew Rayne. Other people who worked for the Coffee Club and there was Rayne's mother and her sister, who Bibi had said still lived together in River Glen. Mac had the address. It was possible that they had information on the mysterious boyfriend among other things. She hoped to interview them soon, although they were playing a little fast and loose about getting together. Nobody appeared to be all that concerned about what had happened to Rayne. Mackenzie had gone to Rayne's apartment and learned that she'd told the manager she was leaving, given

her thirty-day notice, only to take off both early and shy
of a few days' rent. Maybe it was true that she'd just disappeared with her latest Mr. Right. It definitely seemed to
be within her modus operandi.

Monday morning Emma stood behind the counter at
Theo's Thrift Shop, her place of work. Theo had arranged
the donated clothing on metal rounders and there were
stacks of items on tables, folded shirts, pants, shorts, toys,
and household goods. Bigger items were in the back or
along the wall. There was one bike that Emma liked. She
didn't have anywhere to ride it, but she thought maybe she
should use one. She could see herself riding along with
Duchess trotting beside her.

As if discerning her mistress's thoughts, Duchess
looked up at her from where she was lying next to the
counter and gave Emma the eye before turning her attention toward the front door. She liked to watch. At first Theo
had resisted Emma bringing Duchess to work, but Emma
couldn't leave her at Ridge Pointe every day and make
someone else take care of her. Realizing the issue, Theo
had allowed Emma to bring Duchess as long as the dog
behaved herself. Duchess got along with Dummy . . . well,
Bartholomew, Theo's little dog, so it worked out okay, and
luckily, Duchess seemed to get it. She was well behaved
at work, and well behaved at Ridge Pointe, except when it
came to the cat.

"Twinkletoes," Emma muttered in disgust. No, that was
not the cat's name.

The door opened and a mom with two young blond-
haired daughters entered. Emma recognized her. She came
in once in a while by herself, once in a while with her kids.

"Is Theo here?" the woman asked, craning her neck to look around.

Emma hesitated. Theo was out picking up lunch, but she didn't like people thinking Emma was alone. That's why she kept the television on low in the back room to one of those stations where people yakked, yakked, yakked about politics. Emma didn't think much of politics. She preferred food shows and was still glum over the fact that all her favorite episodes had been erased when her sister upgraded their cable subscription and got new DVR boxes. But now, at her own place at Ridge Pointe, she'd found a few new shows that were pretty good and she was filling up her own DVR. She was proud of the fact she was a good programmer. A lot of people at Ridge Pointe weren't.

"I'm Kendra. I don't know if you know me?" the woman asked, looking at Emma anxiously. There were deep lines in her forehead.

Emma shook her head.

"I keep hoping you'll have children's bikes. They've outgrown the ones they have. You'd think the girls were twins, but they're not. They're just the same size. It's a problem."

"We have one bike," Emma said. It was hard to get the words out. She didn't want the bike to leave. But it wasn't her bike. It was the thrift shop's.

"Oh, I know. That one's too big. Theo said if one came in in a children's size that she would let me know."

"None came in," said Emma.

Kendra tilted her head a bit, as if to really check Emma out. This happened a lot. When people looked at her strangely Emma knew she'd said something wrong some-how. Jamie had told her that it was her deadpan delivery.

"It sometimes stops people. They're not sure if you're serious or you're putting them on," her sister had explained.

"I'm always serious," Emma had responded, affronted.

"I know that, Emma. But they don't know that."

"I'll tell them I have a problem," Emma had assured her.

Jamie had screwed up her face and said, "I don't think you need to say that. Just, if they look unsure? Like they want to ask a question, but don't know quite how? Tell them you mean what you say."

"That I'm serious."

"Exactly. You don't have to give them your life story. Just make them feel comfortable."

Now Kendra looked longingly over at the bike. One of the girls was reaching toward a pile of toys and just as Kendra turned toward her, she picked up a big bag of blocks that she couldn't handle.

"Paige! Stop!" Kendra yelled, as all the colored blocks crashed out of the bag and onto the wood floor, making a huge clatter.

Duchess barked and Emma put her hands over her ears before she could stop herself.

"Sorry, sorry!" the little girl cried as Emma dropped her hands and shushed Duchess, who'd jumped to her feet.

Kendra rushed over to the girl. "Oh, Paige," she sighed. She looked at Duchess and Emma. "I'm sorry. I'm just so . . . I'm sorry."

"It's okay," said Emma as Duchess lay back down, her chin on her paws, watching.

The other little girl rushed over. Paige broke into sniffles and cried, "I didn't mean to! I didn't mean to!"

"Mom told us not to touch anything," the second girl tattled.

"I can handle this, Brianne," Kendra said, exasperated.

Emma went over to help pick up. She looked down at the yellow, blue, red, and green blocks that Kendra was feverishly grabbing up and trying to put in the bag. There was, however, a big hole in the bag's netting and the blocks kept tumbling out. "That isn't going to work," said Emma.

"I'm really sorry." Kendra kept putting blocks in the bag, oblivious to the fact that as soon as there were enough of them, they would squeeze out through the hole.

"I'm serious," said Emma.

"I promise I'll take care of it," Kendra said shortly. She gave Paige and Brianne a mean look.

"I didn't do anything!" Brianne shrieked as Paige started to cry again.

"There's a hole in the bag," said Emma.

Kendra shot her a dark look. "What?"

"There's a hole in the bag. Just leave the blocks on the floor. We need a new bag."

"Oh . . ." Kendra looked flustered for a moment, saw what Emma meant, and straightened to full height. "Okay, well, then I guess we'll just go. I . . . tell Theo I was here. I'll come back tomorrow. I just really need . . . Wait. Let me leave my number."

Emma went to the counter and ripped off a sticky note from its pad. Kendra scratched down her number and then she hustled the two girls out the door as if she couldn't bear to stay another minute.

When Theo returned about ten minutes later Emma was just finishing picking up the blocks and putting them in a paper bag instead of the navy netting. Theo was holding Dummy . . . Bartholomew . . . under one arm and a paper plate with a sandwich covered in plastic wrap in her other hand. She set the paper plate on the counter for Emma.

"What happened?" Theo asked. Theo had gray hair and

was small and wiry. Dummy was the same and he was trying to scramble out of Theo's arms to Emma. Emma took the dog, who tried to wash her face with his tongue. He was one of the main reasons Emma had gotten Duchess. Jamie had seen that Emma wanted a dog and so Emma, Jamie, and Jamie's daughter, Harley, had trooped to the dog place that Jamie's friend had recommended and *voilà!*, there was Duchess.

"*Voilà,*" Emma said as Duchess lifted her head and stared hard at the wriggling dog Emma placed on the ground. Dummy raced over to Duchess, tail snapping back and forth. Duchess rolled her eyes up at Emma. Emma knew sometimes that Duchess felt Dummy was a little too much. That's what Mom used to say before she died. "Emma, that's just a little too much."

Emma picked up the plate with the sandwich and told Theo about Kendra and the little girls and Theo shook her head as if she didn't want to hear it.

"I wish I could get her what she wants, but it's not like I can magically make someone donate a couple of kids' bikes the right size. You just have to come and see what we've got."

"She saw nothing."

Theo nodded. "If you want to knock off early, go right ahead. Your bus'll be here in about twenty minutes. Oh, right. Jamie dropped you off with Duchess."

"I'll stay the whole day. Jamie will pick me up."

"Okay, then would you mind bringing down the Easter supplies after lunch?"

"Yes, I will."

As Theo took over the counter Emma went into the back room kitchenette. She set the plate on the counter, then washed her hands. After drying them, she removed the plastic wrap from the sandwich and then picked up one of the cut halves. She really liked her sandwiches in four pieces, but she wasn't supposed to use knives. She thought maybe she could use a knife and it would be okay, but sometimes when she looked at the sharp blade she would shy away because she would think of how you could be hurt by a knife, just like you could be hurt by banging your head on a fireplace or something else. Emma knew by experience. She tore both halves of the sandwich in half, then ate the four pieces one by one. Every day she worked at the Thrift Store Theo would bring her a tuna sandwich. Occasionally Emma worked when Theo wasn't there, but Emma didn't like it as much. Theo would have one or the other people work with her and Emma didn't feel as comfortable with them.

Finished, she recycled the paper bag and threw the plastic in the trash, then she collected a bottle of water from the refrigerator and drank about half of it down, before putting it back in the refrigerator. She would drink the rest in the afternoon.

Before she left the kitchenette she grabbed the sponge and disinfectant cleaner and wiped down the table. She then lined up the sponge next to the faucet on the sink, straightened the salt and pepper shakers, and headed toward the narrow flight of stairs at the back of the kitchenette that led to the attic storeroom. There wasn't a lot of headroom on the top floor so she had to duck as she started looking through the holiday supplies. She found Easter and started pulling them out. She preferred organization to working the front of the shop. She was good at putting things away and making sure they were in the right spots.

St. Paddy's Day was over and she needed to also pack leftover items into boxes for next year.

Several hours later she was back on the main floor when she heard her sister's and niece's voices outside. They came in and Emma was glad Harley had come to pick her up as well. She loved Jamie and Harley. They were her family. And Duchess, of course.

"Hey," Harley greeted her with a high five. Emma didn't mind high fives, but she didn't like hugs very much. Harley was a junior at River Glen High. She'd been a sophomore last year when she and Jamie had moved back to River Glen from Los Angeles. Harley had fallen in love with a boy from school, but he'd graduated and had left town. Harley said they kept in touch, but she didn't talk about him much anymore. Emma thought maybe it was over. That's what happened with relationships sometimes. They were over.

Harley had dark hair and it was long now and pulled into a ponytail. She'd started wearing more makeup and Jamie had told her it was "over the top," which had made Harley mad but she'd stopped putting on the smoky eyeshadow some. Jamie's hair was light brown, like Emma's. Now Jamie smiled at Emma and asked, "So, how'd it go today?"

"Fine." This was the question Jamie always asked her. It was okay, though. It was just her sister's way. Jamie was in love with Cooper Haynes, who'd been a friend and classmate of Emma's in high school. If Emma had to leave Duchess at Ridge Pointe, either Harley or Emma or even Cooper usually came to take her outside during the day. But sometimes Emma had to ask that waiter-guy, Ian, the one who smoked marijuana cigarettes outside the building after hours. Emma and Duchess had caught him when they were outside on a walk to let Duchess do her business. "Want a hit?" he'd asked in a squeaky voice, holding the smoke in his lungs.

"I don't do drugs," Emma had told him.

"Neither do I," he said, exhaling a cloud of smelly smoke. "Just toke a little."

Emma wasn't sure whether she liked Ian or not. He was good with Duchess, but he also liked the cat and Duchess didn't like the cat. There had been several hissy fits from the cat when Duchess barked at her.

Emma said to Jamie, "Paige knocked over the blocks and they fell out of their net bag. I had to put them in a paper bag." She picked up the net bag with the hole in it from the counter and showed them.

"Excitement at the Thrift Shop, huh?" said Harley. "Who's Paige?"

"One of our customers' little girls," explained Theo.

Duchess was on her feet and staring up at Harley expectantly.

"No treats," Emma warned her niece.

"What did I do?" asked Harley.

"You have treats in your pocket," said Emma. She was pretty sure Harley knew that already.

Harley made a sad face at Duchess, who got to her feet and nearly rushed Harley for a pet. "I know. It sucks," Harley murmured. "You're on doggy Weight Watchers."

"But she's in good shape now," Jamie reminded.

Duchess had been eating too much after Emma went to Ridge Pointe. It had been hard for both of them to make the change, even though it was a good thing to do. Emma hadn't been careful enough with Duchess, but like

Jamie said, the dog was in good shape now. They were both happier.

"Well, let's get going," said Jamie. "We've got dinner in our future and I'm substituting tomorrow." Harley gave her a sharp look, and Jamie made a sound in her throat. "Freshman class. Not you," she said on a huge sigh.

"It doesn't matter," said Harley with a shrug.

Emma kinda thought it did. Harley never liked her mom substituting for any of her classes, though Harley had admitted it didn't bug her as much as when she was an underclassman. But it still bugged her.

They drove directly to Jamie's house, the house that was their mom's before she died, the one they grew up in. Jamie was thinking of selling it but Harley had put her foot down. She didn't want to move again, even across town. Also, Cooper was over a lot and Harley argued that they needed the space.

"He practically lives with us," Harley had told Emma. "Which is fine, but why do we have to move? I'd be okay if Marissa wanted to move in and take over your old room."

Marissa was Cooper's daughter and Harley's best friend. Emma had almost stayed at the house, too, because she loved her family, but she'd always wanted to go to Ridge Pointe. Mom had wanted that for her, too, when she was alive, so Emma had moved out. It made her feel a little funny, though, thinking about Marissa taking over her old room.

"Marissa lives with her mother," Emma had said, starting to feel anxious.

"Well, yeah, but sometimes she could be with us. Right?" Harley had looked at Emma for assurance.

"I'm welcome back anytime," Emma had pointed out.

"Absolutely. I was just saying sometimes Marissa could live with us. It would be cool."

"She's your BFF."

"Hell, yeah. And no swearing. I know."

Emma hadn't been about to chastise her, but it was the rule that they were all supposed to follow. It was good that Harley knew that, but it didn't stop her much.

"What are you making for dinner?" Emma asked Jamie now, as they all trooped into the house through the back door.

"Lasagna," said Harley as she raced up the stairs to the second floor. Duchess didn't hesitate, just chased after her as she did whenever they were at Jamie and Harley's.

"Close. Rigatoni," Jamie said to Emma as they heard Harley's bedroom door shut behind her and Duchess. She glanced at the kitchen clock. "Cooper should be here in about an hour."

Whenever Jamie picked up Emma from work they all had dinner all together.

"I don't have to have pasta," said Emma. "I like sushi, too, now."

"And tuna sandwiches. I know. But I was in the mood to make some. Tell me what's been going on at Ridge Pointe while I get things ready."

Emma sat down at the table and clasped her hands on the tabletop. Sometimes she helped Jamie cook, but she had to be asked. Sometimes she made some mistakes while cooking. "Jewell says Rayne's a hot pants," she informed Jamie.

Her sister gave her a quick look. "Older Jewell with the white hair?"

"It's Old Darla. Not older Jewell. Jewell's hair is gray."

"Who's Rayne?"

"That girl that worked in the kitchen for a while. She had a boyfriend with long hair that she was kissing under the portico. Mrs. Throckmorton saw her. She said it was her grandson. . . ." Emma frowned. Her head hurt a little as she bore down on her thoughts. Very hard to put things together sometimes. "Jewell said Rayne had lots of boyfriends and that Mrs. Throckmorton's a gossip."

"Sounds like Jewell might be the gossip."

Emma looked at her sister in wonder. "That's what I said!"

"So, it's news that one of the younger people who works there has or had several boyfriends?" Jamie asked dryly.

"She doesn't work at Ridge Pointe anymore. Jewell said she has tattoos."

"A lot of people have tattoos. Harley wants a tattoo."

Emma heard something in her voice. "You don't want her to have one?"

Jamie ripped open a box of rigatoni with a little more force than necessary. "I don't mind tattoos. I just remember when Harley was a baby and her beautiful, soft skin. I can't get that image out of my head. This unblemished skin, just so . . . perfect." She shrugged. "I told her when she's eighteen, to have at it. She'll be an adult and can make her own choices. I don't really care, I just . . ." She shook her head and poured water into a pot, then put the pot on the range top. "It's just confusing. I don't know. Parenting's different and it doesn't really end at eighteen, either. I mean, they might be adults, but there're still a lot of years ahead, and I still want some influence, too, you know? I've never been a helicopter parent. Harley would never allow that, even when she was little. But I hate to be completely irrelevant and that's where it feels like I'm heading."

She looked at Emma and Emma felt a certain pressure to answer her, but Jamie held up her hand. "Don't look so worried. I'm just working through stuff. Other parents with teenagers are struggling with these issues, too."

"It's confusing."

"Yes. Confusing. Uncertain. I wish I had more answers than questions. All of the above. Parents of my students sometimes ask me for advice, and they want answers and it feels like all I can give them are platitudes that they've heard before."

"You don't have to give them your life story," said Emma.

Jamie stopped short, then laughed. "No. You're right. I don't."

"You said those words," reminded Emma.

"I know."

Emma shrank back when her sister headed her way. She could tell Jamie intended to hug her and she didn't like to be hugged. But her sister just came over and held up her palm for a high five. "Thanks for listening to me," said Jamie as Emma slapped her hand.

Bibi Engstrom drove home carefully from the bar, on the lookout for cop cars tucked into hidey-holes alongside the road. She'd had more to drink at the River Glen Grill than she'd intended. It was a Monday night. She'd sat at the bar during Happy Hour and forced herself not to have more than two drinks . . . which had turned into three, maybe four, when that guy had started flirting with her. He'd bought her a drink, maybe two. It was a little hazy.

She should've taken Uber or Lyft, but she only lived a few miles from the restaurant. She hadn't even meant to stop. She'd just . . . been tired. Her asshole of a husband, Hank, had packed up and moved in with his bitch of a girlfriend. He'd left . . . really left . . . and he wasn't planning on paying the rent next month and she had nowhere to go and there was hardly any savings and she was going to be broke.

Tears filled her eyes. She didn't want Hank anymore but she didn't want him to want someone else, either. And the rent . . . and utilities . . . what was she going to do?

Rayne owes you money. . . .

She exhaled as she turned onto her street. Like she was going to get that back anytime soon. She'd loaned the money, knowing full well it was probably a gift where Rayne was concerned. It hadn't been a lot of money anyway, but now she needed it.

She pulled into the driveway and parked in front of the garage. The garage was full of Hank's stuff.

As she climbed out of the car she heard a knocking under the hood. The car was probably going to conk out on her. And she didn't have any way to fix it when it did. She didn't have a job. She'd once thought about being a hairdresser, but never gone through the training. She'd worked as a waitress for a New York minute, but then she'd married Hank and she'd quit. That was four years ago now. A lifetime . . .

Swiping at her tears, she aimed for the front door, stumbling a little. A car drove by slowly and she looked around, a shiver sliding down her spine. She couldn't make it out in the dark because . . . well . . . she was a little buzzed, but it felt . . . bad, like someone was watching her.

The keys fell out of her hand as she tried to thread one in the lock. She bent down to pick them up and nearly toppled over. Her head was whirling. She grabbed on to one of the porch posts, wishing she'd left a light on for herself.

You did, didn't you?

She blinked in the dark. Yes. She'd definitely left the light on, but it wasn't on now.

Had Hank come back?

Or was it something else?

She finally managed to get the key in the lock and she threw her shoulder into the door as it always stuck. It gave way and she was in her living room. She switched on a table lamp and the room flooded with light . . . only to reveal that half the furniture was gone. Hank had cleared out what he felt was his. And he'd turned out the light.

Well, shit.

Now that the split was really upon her, Bibi was sad, really, really sad. She'd liked being married. Liked to say that she was married. Liked having just one man.

She worked her way to the kitchen. She hadn't eaten enough at the restaurant, just some peanuts and one order of french fries. Too expensive. Now she dug through the refrigerator and pulled out some celery that was an anemic white-green. She ate without tasting, wondering if there was a bottle of wine left in the garage mini fridge. Unlikely. Hank had made sure there was no extra booze around weeks ago.

She decided to look anyway and walked carefully toward the door to the garage. Her equilibrium wasn't so hot. Turning the handle, she yanked the door open and flipped the switch.

Nancy Bush

She stared in open-mouthed horror at the cleaned out, empty space.

"Hank!" she cried aloud.

He'd come in and emptied the place! She'd nagged him throughout their marriage to clean up his shit, and he'd done it in one day, the few hours she was at the bar.

"Asshole!" she shouted, then burst into tears, sank to the step that led from the kitchen into the garage, and bawled her eyes out.

She was too distraught to look out a window and see the vehicle that had turned around at the end of her street and was driving slowly, slowly past again.

CHAPTER FIVE

Following Seth and Patti was all well and good, but it wasn't moving Mackenzie forward in any measurable way. Nothing was happening. After about a week of keeping them in her sights, while they went to their respective jobs at Good Livin', she grew bored and played games on her phone to idly pass the time as she sat in her SUV. Calling in to Taft with updates had begun to feel almost silly as there was no change. When he said to stop by his place and he would pay her for her hours, she was oddly torn. Yes, she could use the funds, but had she really done anything to deserve them? She'd definitely put in the hours, but apart from Seth taking several trips to Best Homes—was he planning a job switch, or was this something else?—there was nothing to report. When she wasn't watching Seth and Patti, she'd tried to connect again with Sharon Sealy and her daughter, Elise, hoping for an interview. Both women were singularly disinterested. It felt as if they were deliberately putting her off, but maybe that was just her own frustration at making little to no progress.

Still, Bibi wasn't paying for her to follow up on Rayne, whereas Taft was for keeping tabs on Seth and Patti, so there was no question about where her allegiance should lie. If she really wanted information from Sharon or Elise, she was going to have to just show up on their doorstep one day and stick her foot in the door.

It was Friday afternoon and she was waiting in her car, her angle of sight allowing her a clear view of Seth's truck, currently in the parking lot outside the Best Homes two-story office building with BEST HOMES in enormous, painted red letters reaching diagonally up the short end of the concrete building. A blue ribbon was painted at the end, with a white #1 in the ribbon's center. A wide, painted red strip ran up the front concrete steps, a "red carpet" leading into the building's foyer. Whether they truly were the best home builder in the area was debatable, but they certainly felt that way.

Seth had entered about fifteen minutes earlier. This departure for him was the third this week, a new addition to his daily routine. The first time he'd made the trip to Best Homes Mac had sat up straight with interest. Something, anything, to break the routine was certainly worth taking note of.

Patti was still at Good Livin' but since she and Seth carpooled and the workday wasn't over, it was a safe bet she would wait for him to return, as he had both other times. Was this something to do with his "side business"? Mackenzie had texted Taft with the information and all he'd done was text back: Good. Stay on them.

She'd briefly thought about following Seth inside and making up some excuse to be there, see what he was like at work, his clients, who he talked to. But . . . she needed to talk to Taft before she went off script, and she hadn't forgotten what Bibi had said about Seth having guns. She was supposed to see Taft tonight at his place, as he didn't have an outside office. She was both anticipating and dreading that meeting.

She sank down in the seat and leaned her head back, momentarily closing her eyes. Forcing herself awake again, she scrolled through her phone to Facebook and looked again at as much of Rayne's account as she could. Same pictures. She then went to Instagram. Same pictures. She tried a couple of other platforms, but nothing had changed. It was always Rayne and a bunch of friends, drinking, partying, and generally hanging out.

I could fall asleep, she thought. Her lids were heavy as bricks. It was warm in the car. March had come in like a lion, but appeared to be leaving like a lamb. The sky was a grayish blue, visible between scudding white clouds. It was a really nice spring day.

She tried to shake herself out of it by reminding herself how it bugged her that Sharon Sealy and Elise had put her off. She'd phoned Sharon and asked to speak to her about Rayne, and Sharon had snapped back that Rayne was always taking off and not to worry about it. Rayne's sister, Elise, had echoed the sentiment when Mac had finally gotten through to her. Neither Rayne's mother nor sister wanted to talk to Mac and had basically hung up on her. Their rudeness had kind of pissed Mackenzie off, even while she wondered why she cared to keep on investigating. Bibi had thrown Rayne's disappearance at Mac because she'd thought Mac was still with the police. Mac didn't owe her anything, yet she felt indebted somehow. She should just give it all up.

Still . . . Rayne's disappearance bothered her in a way she still hadn't quite defined. Mac searched her feelings and decided it was because everyone's lack of real interest got under her skin. No one seemed to care. It felt like Rayne needed a better shake than that.

She determined she would go to Sharon Sealy's house before meeting with Taft. Bibi had given her the directions so after she followed Seth back to his place, and it looked like he was tucked in for the night, she would head over to the Sealy home and knock on the door, see if she could talk her way inside. If they weren't there, she could camp out until they were.

She'd just decided as much when Seth strolled out of the building with another guy with longish, dirty-blond hair and a darker three days' growth of beard that could either be a fashion statement or idle neglect. He wore a gray work shirt, dusty jeans, and worn, leather work boots, the kind that looked as if he could break your rib if he kicked it just right. Mac twisted her key in the ignition to engage the battery, pressed her finger on the button to depress her window, and heard Seth, talking fast and urgently, call him "Troy." She grabbed her phone from its holder and quickly brought up the Best Homes company website, all the while keeping her eyes mainly on Seth, who stood with Troy by his truck. Scrolling through the personnel, she saw Andrew Best's smiling face again. A snake-oil salesman's smile, she decided. A little untrustworthy somehow. Or maybe she'd just been infected by Nolan's assessment of the man.

Troi Bevins was employed with the company. There didn't appear to be any other information.

Okay. Troi with an *i*. Had he taken Nolan's old job? When she thought of her brother-in-law she recalled his strong, clean-shaven jaw and trimmed dark hair. Kind of a sea change there in terms of employees, but maybe Troi's appearance belied a terrific work ethic . . . ? Fat chance. Probably someone else had taken that position.

Mac carefully took a picture of the two men with her phone. Seth's arm was stretched lovingly across the bed of his F-150. Something possessive and maybe a little show-offy about it. He seemed to be trying to impress Troi. If so, Mac couldn't tell if Troi was buying it. His back was to her and he had most of his weight thrown on one hip. Maybe Seth was applying for a job?

After a few minutes the two men said goodbye with a kind of lift of their chins, and her gaze followed Troi as he climbed into a fairly new-looking silver Audi. She automatically calculated the cost in her head, as his ride looked a lot more expensive than Seth's older truck.

Seth pulled out of the lot and after a moment or two, Mac fired up the RAV's engine and slid into traffic behind him. As ever she was careful to stay back from the white truck. She expected him to head to Good Livin' for Patti, which he did, but then, with her mind wandering some, she almost missed his turnoff toward what turned out to be the Waystation again. As far as she knew, he and Patti hadn't been back to the bar since she'd seen him there nearly two weeks earlier.

After Patti and Seth entered, she sat in her car for a while, thinking. Should she go in again? What if they remembered her? They hadn't appeared to notice her last time, but what if they twigged to it if she walked right by them?

She twisted in her seat and searched the interior of the RAV. Her eye fell on a Mariner's baseball cap. She honestly couldn't remember where it came from as she wasn't much of a sports fan, but she swooped it up and crammed it on her head. Nolan, she decided. Steph's husband was a fan and she could almost recall her stepsister wearing it one day when they'd gone jogging together.

She strolled into the bar and slid a look out of the side of her eyes. Seth and Patti were at the same table they'd inhabited last time. Maybe it was their spot. Someone had cranked up the country music and Mackenzie could feel it throbbing in her chest. She started to head to the bar and then nearly stumbled as she put it in reverse. Doobie Gillis was plopped in his same seat. At least it was the same one he'd occupied the last time she'd been here.

She glanced around for another place to sit. There were several empty booths circling the pool table. Beneath the overhead, low-hanging, faux stained-glass lamp, one lone man was playing a game of pool by himself, squaring up his shot on the eight ball.

Before she could move, Doobie twisted around to see who'd come in and grinned when he saw her. "Hey, copper," he greeted her.

Ugh. She didn't look, but felt that this time she was almost certain Seth or Patti swiveled a head her way; she could sense the motion in her periphery vision. Rather than draw further attention to herself, she headed toward the bar and seated herself next to Gillis, shielding herself from Seth and Patti's sight line. "I'm not a cop," she reminded him.

He seemed to take her joining him as a good sign. "What can I do you for?" He waved an arm expansively toward the array of bottles against the mirror behind the bar. Several of them looked to have a light fur of dust.

The bartender, a woman this time, glanced over at Mackenzie. She looked to be in her mid-forties with thin, ropy arms, eyes heavy with mascara, and a tattoo of a ring around the third finger of her left hand.

"Wedding band?" Mac asked curiously.

"I married myself after I caught my last boyfriend doing my best friend. Haven't seen either of them in a decade and that's fine by me. You want something?"

"Vodka and lime."

Mackenzie had to force herself not to peek over Gillis's shoulders toward Seth and Patti. She could just see around him to the door and therefore could catch any movement with her eye should Seth and Patti decide to leave, which was great as she doubted she'd hear anything above the thumping music.

"Whatcha been doin' since we last met?" Gillis asked loudly, tipping his cowboy hat back to get a better look at her.

"Not much."

"You becomin' a regular here?"

"You mean like you?"

"Who says I'm a regular."

"I don't know. When was the last time you were here?"

"Before today, you mean?"

She nodded.

"Yesterday."

She smiled and he chuckled deeply.

"I like you," he said.

The door opened and another couple came in, taking a table near Seth and Patti. Mackenzie lifted up a bit to see past Gillis and noticed that Seth was looking the other couple over, his gaze lingering on the woman's shapely legs. Patti twisted around to see where his gaze had landed and her expression darkened.

Mac's drink came and she picked it up and took a sip. Damn near straight alcohol. She pulled her phone from her back pocket and checked the time. She might have to forgo that trip to Sharon Sealy's if Seth and Patti decided to stay awhile.

Another man came into the bar, sporting a cowboy hat like Gillis. His jeans were tight, and the collarless tee showed off a pair of arms that had seen a lot of hours at the gym. Or maybe he actually worked outdoors. Hard to say. He caught her eye and his look said he knew she'd been admiring him. She dragged her gaze back to Gillis. Like Taft, the newcomer knew he was good-looking.

Seth's gaze had swept from the girl to the single guy who'd just entered. He squinted at the man, then seemed to remember he was there with Patti and gave her his full attention. She glared at him.

The newcomer engaged with the man at the pool table and they started up a game together. The first man whistled at the bartender and yelled, "Can ya turn that shit down?"

The bartender gave him a cold look, but went into the back for a quick moment and shaved a few decibels off the music before she returned.

Mackenzie relaxed back onto her stool. Didn't want to appear to be gawking too much.

Gillis said, "Feel like dancin'? I feel like dancin'. There's kind of a honky-tonk place over in Laurelton that—"

"No."

"—is a helluva lot of fun. Oh, c'mon. Gets going around nine o'clock. Used to be later but they kept running up against the fucking noise ordinance. I say—"

"No. Don't dance."

"—we mosey on over and give a little two-step." He wriggled on his stool and gave her a wink. "C'mon, Mac.

You can't be as uptight as you seem or you wouldn't be here at all. We could smoke a little weed. There's a dispensary right there, but I happen to have some on me. . . ." He waggled his eyebrows beneath his hat.

"Don't do weed. Don't dance. Don't have time. Don't want to."

"You don't do weed?" He looked aghast.

"Thanks for the drink, Doobie. But no. Alcohol's the boring limit to my boring existence." Maybe it would be better to just wait outside before anyone else in the bar took more interest in her.

The first man at the pool table was in a nine-ball battle with the newcomer, but something was going down because though they were standing pretty close to each other neither man was lifting a cue stick. Mackenzie sensed a fight brewing, but then the first man folded like a fan, picked up his beer from the elbow-height shelf that ran on one side of the table, drank it fast, crushed the can, and left.

The new guy watched him leave, a slight smile on his lips. He felt Mac's gaze and looked her over, lifting his brows in invitation.

Not exactly a stealth kind of surveillance she had going here.

She declined his invitation with a regretful smile as she put some bills on the bar and slid off the stool.

"You gotta finish your drink," Gillis protested.

She hesitated, took a hefty sip, more for him than her, then set the glass down and headed for the door. If Seth or Patti noticed her leave, she didn't see because she pretended to be looking at her phone as she pushed outside.

As the door shut behind her, she raced to her car and drove the RAV out of the lot and around the block, slipping into a spot between two cars that looked like they'd been parked in those same spots for a millennium by the dust, dirt and bird poop on their hoods, fenders, and roofs. She swept off the Mariner's cap and squinched down in the seat till only the top of her head and eyes were visible. She couldn't see Seth's car or the door to the bar, but she had a view of the street. If he drove out of the lot and headed west, toward his home, she would likely be able to see him for half a block, or if he headed east he would drive right past her, which could be a problem if they took much longer. Right now she could pretend to be yakking on her phone to explain what she was still doing in the area, if Seth and Patti even noticed, though they hadn't shown that they knew she'd been following them for the better part of ten days.

To her consternation, the good-looking dude was the first car to leave. He drove an F-150 Ford truck like Seth's but it was much newer, its gunmetal gray color gleaming in the late afternoon sun. He pulled up next to her car, his engine throbbing. Mac had been trying the phone-yakking ploy, but he just stopped the truck beside her and waited.

"I'll call you back," Mac said, and pretended to click off as she lowered her window.

"That guy at the bar your boyfriend?" he asked, jerking his head in the direction of the bar.

"More like an acquaintance."

"You hooked up with anybody?"

"Does it look like it?"

His smile was quick. "Anybody at home expecting you?"

"My mother and stepfather."

"I mean . . ." He gave her a searing look that was meant to be sexy but didn't quite do the trick.

"My mother and stepfather," she repeated. She wasn't in the habit of flirting with strangers, and there was something about this guy she found somewhat intriguing and repellant at the same time. Like if she actually thought about taking things a step further, it wouldn't be good . . . but it might not be all bad, either. It had been a long while since Pete. It was a shame she was attracted to good-looking men who seemed too aware of their own charms.

"We could go to—"

"I'm not your type, believe me. Goodbye . . . ? It was nice meeting you?" She smiled to take the sting out of it.

"You sure?"

"I'm sure."

."Next time, then," he said, putting the idling truck in gear. His smile seemed to have grown icier.

Mackenzie watched him depart in her rearview, feeling slightly disappointed. Maybe she should've gone for him. Maybe it would have scratched that itch for a romantic encounter that seemed to have infected her.

"Nah," she said aloud, then settled back to wait for Seth and Patti.

Chapter Six

The kayakers were friends from grade school. They challenged each other at every opportunity and had spent last summer windsurfing outside of Hood River, the best place in Oregon to windsurf, or so they'd heard, and they had no reason to doubt it. This March had been a tough time for outdoor sports. Rain and wind and cold. Coulda been the middle of winter. Only toward the end of the month had the weather grown favorable, and the two friends had been on several weekend biking trips, tuning up for their next adventure. This afternoon they'd headed down the East Glen River, which wasn't much of a challenge overall, but it did have a few rapids that required some serious skill.

Coming out of one of those breathtaking, white-water spots, the first boy, Ryan, had caught an oar and capsized, turning a three-sixty and popping up again. The second boy, his friend Kurt, was still razzing him as they turned the corner along a brushy expanse, which held a far slower current. This section of the river was practically a canyon, with steep slopes on either side rising up toward a darkening sky.

"What the fuck's that?" Ryan asked, pointing. He really wanted his friend to get off his ass.

Kurt looked over and saw some red material caught in a thicket of blackberry vines that had overrun the bank. "Somebody lost their trunks," he said, uncaring.

"It's not trunks. It's . . . a sleeve."

"Well, excuse me. Somebody lost their *shirt*," Kurt corrected.

They cruised closer and both stared and stared. There was an arm sticking out of the red sleeve . . . and there was a hand at the end of it with matching red fingernails, frozen in a clawlike grab.

"Fuck me," whispered Ryan.

"You think that's real?" asked Kurt.

The wind switched direction, blowing in their faces. The dank, rank, rotten smell answered the question.

Ryan heard a moaning sound and realized it was coming from Kurt. His own heart was pounding triple time. He reached inside his waterproof pack, pulled out the cell phone from its interior clear-plastic sack, and stopped. "Who should I call?" he asked, his voice tight.

Kurt's eyes were wide, glued on the grasping hand. He blinked, then croaked out, "Nine-one-one." Any other time, he would have likely responded, "Nine-one-one, moron," but today he didn't even think of it.

Detective Cooper Haynes was having dinner with Jamie, Harley, and Emma when the call came through. He didn't immediately take it because he had a mouthful of arrabbiata sauce, loosely translated as "angry" sauce, and the hot red chilis were bringing tears to his eyes.

"I made the sauce," said Emma proudly.

Duchess slapped her tail against the floor in approval at the sound of her mistress's voice.

Cooper had known Emma for years, before and after the tragedy that had mentally debilitated her when she was a teenager. Still struggling to talk, he looked from Emma to Jamie, Emma's sister and the woman he'd fallen in love with. Jamie was regarding him with a guilty "oops" face. "You okay?" she asked.

"Spicy, huh," said Harley, Jamie's daughter. She had nibbled at a bite, but most of the red-coated linguine remained on her fork, uneaten.

Emma frowned and took a bite herself, chewing hard. Moments later she dropped her fork with a clatter and grabbed for her water glass. Cooper had already done the same.

Jamie hadn't tasted her food yet. She'd loaded up her plate mostly with salad and had taken her time. Now she set down her fork and picked up her napkin, covering her mouth while the rest of them swilled water, but Cooper could see that she was fighting laughter.

Emma set down her glass and drew a breath, her eyes watering. "I can't eat it."

"Maybe it's a tad hot," Jamie said from behind her napkin, trying to be conciliatory, but Emma gave her a sharp look.

"It's uneatable," Emma said gravely.

"We might be able to save it," Jamie said, putting down the napkin, her face mostly under control though she had her lips pressed together as if she were afraid they would betray her.

"It's DOA, Mom," Harley disagreed. "Sorry, Emma.

Good try." She got up from her seat and went to the sink to clean off her plate.

"Too many chilies," said Emma.

"Maybe a few too many," said Jamie generously.

Emma considered. "You do better than I do. You didn't ruin the garlic shrimp last week."

"Well . . . that was a different dish."

"We should order pizza," said Emma.

"Good idea." Harley swept her cell phone from her back pocket. "Deno's."

Cooper's cell phone had fallen silent after its *ding* to let him know he had a voice mail. It was on the edge of the counter where he'd plugged it in upon returning "home" from the station. He didn't actually live with Jamie; he had his own house. But he spent most of his free time here and a whole lot of meals, so, yeah. It was home. "It's the station," he said, getting up from the table.

While Jamie tried to convince Emma to let her try to take out the heat with more marinara sauce, Harley ignored them both and ordered pizzas, and Cooper moved away to listen to the message from dispatch. A recovery was underway on the East Glen River, below the trail that led to Percy's Peak. A young woman's body had been found.

"I gotta go out for a while," he said, clicking off.

"What?" Jamie looked over at him, her voice serious. She knew his routine well enough to recognize this was something unusual. River Glen was a bedroom community to Portland and it had its share of smaller crimes, but Cooper was a detective and his involvement meant there was something more to the story.

Harley had frozen and was waiting for his answer.

Even Emma sensed his casualness might be somewhat manufactured and frowned at him in that way that meant she was in deep thought.

"Looks like an accident along the East Glen River." He didn't want to get into too many details before he knew what was going on himself.

"By Ridge Pointe?" asked Emma.

"Down the river a ways from there."

"By the overlook?" Again, Emma. She struggled with commonplace things, sometimes, but when her interest was piqued, she could be a terrier. It was amazing what she knew. And she seemed to always sense when you weren't being completely truthful with her.

"Down that way," Cooper agreed.

"What kind of accident?" asked Harley.

"That's what I'm going to find out."

"Somebody's dead," said Emma.

"Emma," Jamie warned.

Cooper walked over to Jamie and kissed her goodbye, but when he turned to leave she followed him to the back door. "Is Emma right?" she asked.

Cooper glanced over her head toward the kitchen where Harley and Emma were watching them. He pulled Jamie out the back door and onto the porch into the cool night. "A young woman's body has been found," he admitted. "I'll know more later."

"In the river?"

"Along the bank, I think." He gave her another quick kiss, then headed out to his truck.

* * *

Twenty minutes later Cooper stood on the south bank of the East Glen River. Across from him the rescue workers were untangling the body from the blackberry vines that covered the opposite bank. They loaded the woman's body into a flat-bottomed police boat they'd launched from the boat ramp about a mile downriver near Ridge Pointe, Emma's place of residence. He'd thought about waiting at the marina, if you could call it that, as it was a shed, ramp, and short pier with a couple of tired houseboats listing nearby, their right to be on that stretch of riverfront still in litigation. But he hadn't been able to wait and when he'd learned the body was opposite some undeveloped acreage owned by a wealthy local family, he made a couple of phone calls and got permission to hike down a dusty track that led to the water through a wall of brush. He'd been slapped by limbs and leaves, but was finally dumped out almost directly across from the body.

His eye traveled upward. The wrought-iron arc of the overlook jutting out from the trail that led to Percy's Peak was just to the left of where the body had landed and about five stories up. Had she fallen from the overlook?

He glanced back at the body, now aboard the boat. They'd put her on her back on a gurney and her lank, wet hair hung down from her temples. Her mouth was open. She wore red lipstick that matched her red shirt.

His stomach churned. He could tell she was fairly young. His mind naturally went to Emma and the tragedy that had befallen her. Twenty years later, Emma had been changed forever and it still felt like he should've been able to do something about it, even though he knew that wasn't the case. For years, whoever had attacked her had remained a mystery. Only recently had the truth come to light.

He heard some crashing through the brush behind him and turned just as another cop, Bryan "Ricky" Richards, broke through, rubbing at his arms and swearing under his breath. Upon spying Cooper he cut himself off, finishing with, "It's a bitch to get here."

"You coulda waited at the marina."

"Marina." He snorted. "When I heard you came here, I decided to join you."

As the closest officer on scene when the information from the 911 call station had come in, Ricky had told Cooper he was heading to the marina while the patrol boat was ordered. The boat was just leaving as he got there, but he'd let it go without him when he'd learned Cooper was on his way and planning to approach from the water's edge on the opposite bank. Ricky was bucking to move up to detective and had become Cooper's unasked-for shadow. Cooper also thought maybe Ricky hadn't been quite as eager to be up close to the body as he pretended.

Ricky glanced skyward and his gaze caught on the overlook. "Think she fell from there?"

"It's a good bet."

"Taking a selfie?"

Cooper grunted. The scenario of the girl stepping onto or over the fence for the perfect picture had crossed his mind, but he hated the thought of a life cut short by such a reckless decision.

"Looked pretty young," Ricky said somewhat mournfully as the boat pulled away. Cooper turned to fight his way back through the brush along the track. He could have pointed out to Ricky that accidental death was a tragedy at any age, but knew before speaking that it would probably be a waste of breath. Ricky's attitude was a product of his own youth, and Cooper had made enough mistakes when he was young to let others blunder their way into adulthood without a lecture every time they said or did something thoughtless and callow.

Evening descended in full before Seth and Patti left the Waystation, and Mackenzie had to put on her lights to follow them back to their town house, which was exactly where they went after another basically uneventful evening. She was chafing inside at the waste of time when she got the text from Taft, pushing their meeting till eight p.m. She texted back that she would be there, then let out a long breath. Surveillance was like that. Sometimes hours upon hours. There was still time to stop by the Sealys.

But first, she was hungry. And she had to pee.

She waited around till she saw Seth and Patti's TV go on, then headed back toward her mom's house, changing her mind at the last minute and dropping into the McDonald's on the border of Laurelton and River Glen for a Quarter Pounder with Cheese and a trip to the loo. She ate the burger back in her car, then aimed her vehicle toward Sharon Sealy's house. Friday night drop-in. What were the chances either of them would be home?

It was after seven when she pulled up in front of the slightly shabby-looking house. The outdoor lights were on and it was clear Sharon could really use some Moss Out! on the roof. The paint was peeling on the edges of the posts that held up the front porch, the shingles graying and warping in the bright, white illumination of an LED light.

Mac walked up the front walkway through a faintly misting rain. It had been nice up till now, but the weather was growing wilder again. She'd snapped her hair back into a ponytail after she'd parked, which made her look about ten years younger. This wasn't necessarily a calculated move on her part, more a way to keep her hair from being plastered to her head by the rain, but she thought it might make her feel less threatening should anybody be home. There wasn't a car in the driveway but there could be one in the garage, and there were a number of vehicles parked along the residential street that could be either Sharon's or Elise's.

Interior lights glowed from somewhere down the front hall. Maybe the kitchen?

Mackenzie lifted her hand to knock, then hesitated. She was definitely pushing things if she wanted to be at Taft's place in Laurelton by eight. She was second-guessing herself. Should she put this off? Now that she was here, it seemed almost intrusive. She had no authority. None at all. In fact, it was downright snoopy.

Fortune favors the bold.

Well, hell. She banged on the door with more force than necessary. When no one immediately answered, she banged on it again.

Through one of three diamond-shaped panes in the front door panel, she saw a figure pause, and then head her way. Someone *was* home. Okay. Good. Maybe now she'd learn something.

It was Sharon Sealy who opened the door, Mackenzie presumed, based on her age. She was somewhere in her fifties with a straight, light brown bob and a bit of middle-aged spread at the hips. She spied Mackenzie through the little window and after a moment, unlocked the door, edging it open with a *creaaaakkk* that was ear-splitting but mercifully short in duration.

"Yes?" she said tersely.

"I'm Mackenzie Laughlin. I called and wanted to meet with you about your daughter Rayne?"

She recoiled as if she'd smelled something bad. "I don't know what you're doing."

"Her friend Bibi Engstrom is worried about her," Mac quickly reminded. "I just said I'd talk to family and friends and see if they knew anything."

"You're getting rained on out there."

It was more like mist coalescing on her hair and forehead, but Mackenzie took this as a possible invitation and simply nodded, wondering if she should grimace and look pathetic or if that would be overplaying it.

The door opened wider, still creaking but with less volume. Mac stepped inside before Sharon could change her mind.

"Elise is in her room. My other daughter," she said grudgingly, hitching a chin in the direction of the dark hallway. Mac could see a line of light beneath one door. Both of them at home. Bonanza.

Sharon led her into a small family room next to a kitchen. The smell of burned toast filled the air and Mac got a quick glance of the makings of a BLT spread across the counter.

"I didn't mean to interrupt your dinner," she said.

"We're just eating sandwiches. I think Elise has plans. I don't know."

It didn't sound like she cared much, either.

Sharon glanced at the food and shrugged before sinking

onto a sofa whose worn cushion nearly swallowed her up. "So, you're a friend of Rayne's?"

"Actually, I frequent the Coffee Club," said Mac, tiptoeing around her relationship with Rayne. "If you'd like your sandwich I could—"

"Rayne knows a lot of people from work, I suppose," Sharon cut her off. "Take a seat." She waved an arm toward an overstuffed chair that matched the couch.

Mac gingerly sat down and also sank into the cushion. "I haven't seen her in a while. Both Bibi and I are worried."

"Bibi . . ." She frowned.

Mac had thought throwing out Bibi's name would help, but maybe not.

A door opened from down the hallway, also creaking, but not as intense as the front one. Footsteps sounded on the thin carpet and then Elise appeared in the doorway. She was slightly pudgy and her dark brown hair had a bleached white-blond streak that framed a face of big blue eyes, pouty lips, and a pugnacious chin. She wore a pair of purposely tattered black jeans, black boots, and a white blouse that was cut low enough to expose a lot of flesh over the hills of her breasts.

"Who are you?" she demanded, frowning, and Mackenzie introduced herself again as a friend of Rayne's.

"She brought up Bibi," Sharon said, surprising Mac.

Mac's attention snapped back to her. "You do know her."

Elise snorted and searched inside a black leather purse for what Mackenzie expected to be a pack of cigarettes but turned out to be a tin of Altoids. "Oh, yeah, Bibi. She's a piece of work."

"Elise . . ." Sharon admonished.

"If you're Bibi's friend, you already know it, right?"

Elise flipped her hair over her shoulder. "What a pain in the ass she is? So dramatic." She rolled her eyes.

"She's worried about Rayne. So am I," Mac said.

"Oh, don't." Elise held a hand up to her mother, who was about to protest. "Rayne can't get her life in order. She can't keep a job. She basically slept her way through high school and as soon as she was done, moved in with her boyfriend and lived off him. She's tried to live off Mama, too, but I won't let her." As if realizing she was currently living with her mother and what impression that might deliver, she added quickly, "I got my associate's degree and I'm planning on becoming a nurse."

"Someday," Sharon put in, ironically.

"Anyway . . ." Elise gave her mother a speaking look. "Rayne will show up when her latest relationship ends. That's what happens. He'll dump her and she'll come crying home with no money and no job."

Mac decided to try to direct the conversation. "Bibi mentioned a new boyfriend, but she didn't know who he was."

Elise made a face. "Have you checked her Instagram account? There's no new guy on there and Rayne always takes pictures of her latest sucker. *Always.* So, no, there's no new guy."

"There was someone she was seeing," Sharon said.

"The last pictures were Seth. And Troy, I guess," snapped Elise.

"Troy?" Mackenzie came to sharp attention.

"He's the reason she lost that job at the old people's place. Got told to leave," Elise said in a mocking tone. "But then he dumped her and she moved on to his friend, Seth. That's how she operates."

"Is that the Troi that works for Best Homes?" asked Mackenzie.

"That's the one." She bit off the words. "So, you know about him." Elise's lips were tight.

"Not really. I think I've seen Seth and Troi together."

"Well, that would be a trick, as they hate each other. Rayne ruined that friendship like she's ruined everything else."

"That's not fair, Elise." Sharon pressed her lips together, as if holding in a lot more she wanted to say.

"She stole money out of my purse, Mama. You know she did. She's done it to you."

Sharon crossed her arms over her chest. "Rayne's just flighty."

Elise turned to Mackenzie as if she were pleading a case. "She tried to get a job at Best, but it didn't happen. She'd be going after Andrew Best, if she could."

Sharon said distinctly, "Rayne's just outgoing. She was really popular in school. Lots of girlfriends. And lots of boyfriends." Elise opened her mouth to speak up again, but her mother rushed in with, "Everyone loves her. If that's a fault, then let God hit me with it."

Elise shut her mouth and subsided into injured silence.

"Can you remember the last time you saw her?" Mac asked them both.

They slowly looked at each other, neither wanting to give up their resentment. After a few moments, Sharon suggested, "A week ago?"

"More like two weeks . . . or so . . ." Elise finally muttered.

"That's not unusual," Sharon said quickly.

"It's not unusual when she's with a guy," Elise qualified. "But she's not with a guy. That's what I just said!"

"Could it be a secret romance?" asked Mackenzie.

"With Rayne?" Elise laughed harshly. "The girl who let a guy feel her up in the dentist's office?"

"Elise!"

"It's true, Mama! It's true." Elise turned back to Mackenzie. "She's there and waiting to have her teeth cleaned and some random guy who knew her from work, I guess, or somewhere, sees her through the glass door and comes in and before you know it they're making out and he's got his hand up her shirt. The receptionist, Giselle— I know her from cycle class—had to pretend she didn't *see*! It was crazy! And then Rayne didn't act like it was any big deal."

"He worked with Rayne at the care center," said Sharon.

"No, he didn't," Elise said, annoyed. "Rayne dated a lot, and that's putting it mildly."

They both seemed to shut down at the same moment. Bibi had told Mac that Rayne's latest crush had been death on anyone knowing about their relationship, so she tried pushing that further. "Maybe she rekindled something with one of her old boyfriends."

"Fat chance. Once they were done with her, they were done with her," said Elise.

"Stop it." Sharon's face was red. "Those boys liked her."

"They liked the fact that she would fuck any of them."

"Elise!"

Her daughter lifted a hand and stormed out of the room, back down the hall to her bedroom apparently. The door slammed hard enough to shake the house.

"She's leaving to go out to a bar and do exactly what

she accuses her sister of," Sharon said tightly. "But if Rayne does it, she's a whore." She gazed angrily in the direction Elise had stormed. "Elise will never forgive her."

"Forgive her?"

Sharon's lips parted. She looked like she was sorry she'd revealed that. Mackenzie waited, and Rayne's mother finally admitted, "Rayne stole a boy from Elise."

Ah.

"It was . . . a challenge to Rayne and Elise was hurt and the two of them can't get over it." There was a long moment, and then she added, "Rayne's impulsive. I've tried to . . . well . . . it's just been hard to get her to stay on track."

There was a finality to her words that sounded like a dismissal. Mackenzie tried to think of what she could say to extend the interview, but she wasn't certain there was any further information to mine. Also, after this last admission, Sharon Sealy had shut down. Mackenzie expected Elise to reappear and head out to wherever she was going, but there was no sound from the bedroom down the hall.

It appeared that Seth was only one in a long line of Rayne's lovers and that was a tidbit of information Bibi had neglected to tell her.

Time to check in with Bibi again and see what was what. She struggled out of the chair and said goodbye to Sharon, hesitating a moment, but Sharon didn't get up from the couch to show her out, so she walked out on her own, wincing a bit at the door's screaming as she shut it behind her. In her RAV, she placed a call to Bibi.

She was waiting for it to go through when she saw the police car pull up on the opposite side of the street and her ex-partner, Ricky Richards, along with Detective Haynes, slam out and walk toward Sharon Sealy's front door.

Mackenzie clicked off and dropped her phone to her lap, staring through her windshield at the two officers.

Uh . . . oh . . .

Her heart started a hard beat. She was guessing by the appearance of the two officers that Rayne had been found and, based upon what she knew about police procedure, the circumstances did not look good.

CHAPTER SEVEN

Mackenzie couldn't decide whether to make her whereabouts known, wait for the officers to come back out, or drive away. If this was about Rayne the questions she would be asked would never end. Her ex-partner was a hard-ass. If Ricky had a new partner, she hadn't heard who it was, but she knew his aspirations were to be a detective. How he'd hooked up with Haynes she didn't know. She was pretty sure Ricky hadn't been promoted to detective. Anyway, though Detective Haynes was known for being fair-minded, he would want to know about her involvement, too.

She hesitated, her hands on the wheel.

"Hello?" Bibi answered, her voice tinny.

Mac glanced down at the phone she'd tossed onto the passenger seat. She hadn't managed to switch it off, apparently. Now she swept it up and pressed it to her ear. "Bibi. It's Mackenzie. I was going to ask you about . . ."

Bibi waited, then snapped, "About?"

"Uh . . . Rayne. But I can't talk now. I'll have to call you back."

"What—"

Mac clicked off, checked to make sure the phone was

really dead this time, then pressed it into her iOttie holder. She needed to wait till the officers returned. She knew better than to intrude. Ricky and Haynes were there to deliver bad news, the worst news, she was pretty sure. The two of them wouldn't be together if it was for anything else, as far as she could see.

What had happened to Rayne?

She switched on the engine and put the RAV in gear, driving to the end of the block. She turned the SUV around, thinking she would try to catch them on the way out. She and Ricky had been partners, and though they'd never quite gelled, that didn't mean they hadn't managed to work together. Maybe he would understand that she'd been looking into Rayne's disappearance and it was merely a coincidence that she'd ended up at the Sealy home just when he and Haynes arrived.

But she hesitated. If the situation were reversed, how would she feel about it? She suspected she wouldn't be all that welcoming to Ricky if he suddenly turned up asking questions.

She exhaled heavily. Time to call Taft and explain why she was going to be late. She picked up her phone and punched in his number.

"You on your way?" he answered before she could even utter a syllable.

"Not yet. Something came up. I'm outside Sharon Sealy's house. Rayne's mother and sister, Elise, live there together and I wanted to talk to them."

"Ah. You're going in now?"

"Actually, I'm just leaving. I should be at your place . . . in a while." She still had time.

"Okay. Have you eaten?"

"Umm . . . yes. Earlier. Taft, Ricky Richards, and

Cooper Haynes just went in the door. Bryan Ricky Richards," she clarified.

"I know Richards," he said slowly, waiting for her to continue.

"Yeah, well, he's not usually with Haynes and they just went into the Sealy house together."

"You think they're there to tell Sharon her daughter's dead."

Taft had a way of jumping ahead of the conversation that sometimes threw her off her game. "Yes. To tell both of them, Sharon and Elise. They're both there."

"You spoke to them?"

"I did. I came here after I put Seth and Patti to bed. I figured I had enough time to interview them before I came to your place, but I ran over."

"Richards and Haynes are going to learn you were there."

"I know that," she said patiently. "I thought maybe I'd talk to them—"

"No. Get out of there."

"—and share information. What are you talking about? I can talk to them."

"You're on the wrong side of the law now, Laughlin. Get out. Now. Call me back when you're miles away." And he hung up.

Well.

She took a moment, half-inclined to ignore his advice just for the need to reassert some independence and control. Reluctantly, she put the car in gear and drove toward the main road that led away from the Sealys'. She stopped at the intersection. Taft's insistence prickled. She'd worked with these people. Not so long ago. He was the one who'd gone to the dark side. All she'd done was quit the department.

But . . . he'd also infected her with an urgency to run that seemed out of sync with the circumstances. She didn't want to race to his place like she was scared and it was some kind of haven.

She split the difference, giving herself time to think, texting him that she would be delayed. Then she headed to her mom's house. She let herself through the back door and luckily didn't run into Dan the Man as she turned down the hallway toward her bedroom, the spare bedroom. She could hear the television tuned to some game show as she sneaked into the room. As soon as she shut the door behind her, she determined she had to move out and soon. There was no need for her to be here any longer.

Her belongings were in storage. A couch, two chairs, a bed, and bins of household and personal items. She decided she was going to move to Laurelton; it was where she'd been living before and there were a lot more apartments available within its city limits. River Glen was an older city and had been laid out in treelined blocks, although the newer housing developments and infill had added a few multi-family housing units.

She changed her clothes and combed her hair, checked her makeup. She surfaced as if from a dream and snorted at herself. What did she think, this was a date? She was dawdling and primping as if it mattered. Berating herself, she tiptoed out of the house and drove away. Passing beneath streetlights, she caught a glimpse of her image in the rearview. Too much lipstick. She grabbed a tissue from her console and rubbed at her lips.

She'd almost reached the address Taft had given her

when she pulled over to the side of the road, fingers clenched around the wheel. It had been about forty minutes since she'd seen Ricky and Haynes enter the Sealy house. Were they still there?

Setting her jaw, she turned the RAV around and headed back toward the Sealy house. She arrived in time to see that the two men were now standing outside their respective vehicles, Haynes on the phone, Ricky hovering nearby. Immediately she realized Taft had been right. She was the interloper here and her intervention wouldn't be appreciated.

Too late. Ricky saw her and practically jumped in front of her RAV, causing her to slam on the brakes. Her temper fizzed. She'd had her problems with him while they'd been partners but she'd swallowed all objections as he was her senior officer. That might have been a mistake.

"What the hell, Laughlin?" he demanded as she rolled down her window. "They said you were here asking questions. What are you doing? In case you forgot, you're no longer with the department."

She was stopped in the middle of the street, her engine idling. "I'm helping someone who said Rayne Sealy was missing."

"Who?"

"Is she dead?"

"You can't ask me that!" he practically exploded.

"Hey." Cooper had ended his call and now frowned at Ricky.

"I was just explaining things to *Ms*. Laughlin," Ricky said coolly.

Mackenzie watched as Cooper walked closer to her window. He flicked Mac a look that she couldn't read. She repeated her question to him. "Is she dead?"

Ricky started to object again, but Cooper said, "Yes," and explained about finding the body along the East Glen River below the overlook to Percy's Peak. The police had then discovered Rayne's car in the parking lot next to the trail. He turned to Ricky, who was clearly disturbed that he was giving out so much information, and pointed out, "It'll be on the news."

Ricky's mouth was a thin line of obstinance, but he gave Haynes a curt nod. His anger was directed entirely at Mackenzie.

Mac asked, "So, it's definitely her?"

"She had a small wallet in her back pocket with her driver's license," Haynes added as Ricky sucked in his breath.

Mackenzie hardly knew how to feel. She was definitely discombobulated. She'd half believed all the talk of Rayne running off with a boyfriend. Seth had been an unlikely candidate, given his tight schedule with Patti, but she'd taken the job of watching them from Taft so she hadn't really ventured any further. Now the police would take over, which made her feel like she'd let both Bibi and Rayne down.

"How well did you know Rayne?" Ricky demanded.

"Not at all. I was hoping to learn more about her from her mother and sister."

A car turned onto the Sealys' street, so Ricky and Haynes moved away from Mackenzie's vehicle allowing her to pull forward and park, which she did as the misting rain began to turn into serious precipitation. Haynes bent his head against the wet deluge as Ricky ran for the prowler that he'd apparently arrived in. Haynes was in his favorite city ride, a navy blue Trailblazer with a tow hitch that had come in handy for him more than once. It had been well-known around the squad room and everyone mostly left it for him if they could.

Mackenzie's window was still rolled down and she called to Haynes, "If you want me to come in and talk about it, I'd be happy to."

He moved her way again, letting the rain wash over him. "That might work. I'll let you know. Who asked you to look into Rayne's disappearance?"

"Bibi Engstrom. A friend of Rayne's."

He nodded. Mac was pretty sure he'd gotten that much from Sharon and/or Elise already and was just verifying. "How long have you been on the case?" he asked.

"A week, almost two and no, I haven't really learned anything. That's why I wanted to talk to her mother and sister."

Ricky yelled from the prowler's open driver's window. "You a PI now?"

"Something like that," she answered coolly.

It might not be true, but she was pretty sick of her ex-partner. He'd made a fool of himself over Prudence Mangella, and she didn't think he was scoring any points with Cooper Haynes, though it sure as hell looked like he wanted to.

A few minutes later, Haynes returned to his SUV and Mackenzie made another U-turn back to the highway toward Jesse Taft's.

It took her a lot longer than she'd expected through Friday night traffic and by the time she arrived she was abysmally late. She found the one-story condominium complex fairly easily, then had to circle around a few times before she discovered a parking spot three blocks away.

She hurried back to his end unit, spying his black Rubicon parked in the carport. As she drew near, she rubbed at her lips again, making sure she wouldn't blast him with neon pink. Pink Promise. Jesus. She hadn't been sure what kind of impression she wanted to make and had gone for the girly stuff because well, Taft was attractive. But after the way Ricky had sneered, "You a PI now?" she now wanted to make sure Taft took her seriously because maybe she *did* want to be one. Something she'd hardly thought of until she'd taken on Bibi's request. Whatever the case, she was walking into a business meeting, nothing more, nothing less, and she had an image to project that did not include Pink Promise.

After Taft hung up from Mackenzie he'd turned back to the hamburger patty he'd been about to fry on the stove. He'd learned she'd already eaten so he went about fixing his own dinner. He piled a tomato, lettuce, onion, pickles, mayo, mustard, and ketchup on the bun, and a few slices of avocado for good measure, then cooked up the patty and sat down at his kitchen bar to eat the burger. He'd barely taken a bite when there was a knock on his door. He hadn't expected her to get here that fast. Swallowing, he went to answer and found there was no one there. Senses on high alert, he looked around the carport.

Hmmm.

Taft thought about it a minute, then noticed that Tommy Carnoff's door was slightly ajar. He stepped over to the next unit and pushed the door in a bit farther with one finger. Tommy was bustling around in the kitchen and the pugs were snorting and milling around his feet. The black one looked over at him and started yapping. The fawn one recognized Taft and came running over, his clown-like face pulled back in a pug smile.

Tommy turned around. "Oh. Taft. Yeah, I knocked. Sorry. Had to get these guys fed. I wonder if you can take care of them for a few days? Got a late weekend trip to Palm Desert."

"Sure."

"Good. Good. Can I get you a drink?"

"No, I'm having a burger and expecting company."

Tommy looked interested, his blue eyes twinkling beneath white brows. "Anyone I've met before."

"Nope. Not like that. This one's a . . . coworker."

"You hesitated on that, man."

"I was going to say protégée, but she's an ex-cop, too."

"Interesting." Tommy looked like he wanted to say more, but Taft sketched him a goodbye and returned to his condo. He ate the rest of his burger and thought about Tommy, who was more than likely taking a female guest along for the trip.

His phone bleeped out a text. He looked at it and saw that Mackenzie was going to be later still. He hoped to hell she hadn't tried to get information out of Richards and Haynes. Richards would play games with her for the information and never come through anyway. Haynes was a straight shooter, but he would be tight-lipped as well.

Finishing the last bite, he cleaned up, reflecting on that last troublesome call with Mitch Mangella. Taft had worked for the man off and on since leaving Portland PD and had found himself navigating the line between permissible and illegal. Mangella wasn't a full-on crook, but he was "fluid" with the law. While Taft felt the letter of the law was sometimes too restrictive—one of the many reasons he didn't fit into the quasi-military structure of the police department—he had nevertheless worked hard to keep Mangella from outright criminal choices.

But . . . they'd maybe reached a bridge too far.

There was a case with the River Glen PD that involved Keith Silva, a River Glen cop whose disregard for the rule of law was legendary. Silva had shot and killed a fellow officer while attempting to chase down a robber. The suspect got away during the melee, but was captured later trying to hit up another convenience store. Silva had been asked to leave the department, according to those who were in the know. He'd initially resisted and appealed to the union, but had eventually given in and had managed to walk away with his pension. Just recently it had come to Taft's attention that the cop's widow, who'd purportedly raked in a multimillion-dollar government settlement, was a friend of Mitch and Prudence Mangella. But it was that the Mangellas had an acquaintanceship with Silva that had really spoken to Taft. How did the Mangellas balance their relationship with both the widow and Silva?

The suspect in the robbery had contacted Taft and told him the widow was in on it and had used Silva to get rid of her pesky husband. Taft would've gone straight to the River Glen PD except for the fact the guy was a lying scumbag looking for a get-out-of-jail-free card. Taft had taken the information with a grain of salt and had been quietly looking into it. It was possible that River Glen's Chief Bennihof had made Silva's case go away rather than have the stain of a premeditated cop murderer within his ranks on his record. Nothing was certain yet.

But it all sat hard on Taft's conscience because if the robber was telling the truth and Mangella had lied to him and/or worked with Silva to cover up a murder . . .

He shook his head at the thought. Recently he'd made a point of looking up Silva, asking about his relationship with Mangella. Silva had smiled with his teeth and said,

"Checking on your buddy Mitch? He's a very, very smart guy, you know. Like you're smart, right? You know when to ask questions and when not to, right?"

"I agree that Mitch is a smart guy," Taft had answered, not wanting to derail the man if he was offering up unsolicited information. He'd refrained from pointing out that Mangella wasn't really his "buddy."

"Smart enough to see the future. Are you smart enough for that?" Silva had laughed then and shrugged. He was finished saying anything further about Mangella. The meeting had increased Taft's unease, leaving him with a gnawing worry. He liked Mangella; Mangella was likeable. But thoroughly trusting the man was a mistake. He'd blown off a meeting with him the week before to meet Mackenzie, and though Mitch had said it was no big deal, when he'd asked Taft later about where he'd been, and Taft had explained about having pizza with a female ex-cop—he'd purposely left out that it was more business than pleasure—Mangella had wanted to know every detail.

In fact, he'd really poured on the pressure.

"It was just a date," Taft had answered.

"Was it? With an ex-cop?"

"Since when are you interested in my life?" he'd rejoined. The more Mangella pushed, the less he wanted to say.

Mangella spread his hands. "I'm always interested in your life. Like you're interested in mine. And yes, I know Keith Silva."

Taft had expected Silva to talk to Mangella, but it did put a cold hand around his heart. There was just the tinge of Mafia Don about the man. So welcoming, so much bonhomie . . . but so much power. Taft was leery of power even though he worked with and for powerful men.

"The next time you take out your ex-cop lady friend, you let me know." Mangella smiled.

That's when the decision to keep Mackenzie Laughlin far, far away from Mitch Mangella had solidified into a hard stone of determination. As long as Mangella's needs were legitimate, Taft could work for the man, but that's as far as it went. Mangella might be River Glen's most successful native son and generous philanthropist, but he was a cagey and powerful man who didn't allow others to get in his way . . . and that included Jesse James Taft.

He heard a car pull up and came out of his thoughts on Mangella. It parked outside the carport, so he figured it was Mackenzie. He next listened as her quick footsteps came to his door. He waited, somewhat amused at her hesitation as there were several long seconds before she actually rapped lightly on the panels. He opened the door and looked into her eyes. Her hair was down and brushed the shoulders of a light blue shirt that she wore with jeans and black sneakers. He noticed a bit more makeup.

He smiled and greeted her with, "You clean up good."

"I'm just in jeans," she was quick to respond.

He spread his hands. If she didn't want to be complimented, he could go with that.

She crossed the threshold and looked around his living room.

"I'll get us something to drink. No Tecate, but I do have some wine."

"I'm not drinking, thanks. I'm just here to work."

"Okay. Come on in then."

He headed back to the U-shaped kitchen and she followed slowly after him. He pointed to the two stools at the end of the section of counter that jutted out to form a bar. She perched on one as Taft pulled out a bottle of red, a medium-priced blend that he liked. He drew the cork and opened a cupboard to grab two stemmed glasses, then poured one for himself, leaving the other as an open invitation should she change her mind.

"I had vodka earlier," she said.

"You don't have to have wine. I could—"

"Actually, I've changed my mind. I'd like a glass, thank you."

Taft inclined his head in agreement, recognizing how edgy she was. He poured her glass, then slid it across the counter to her. He leaned back against the counter perpendicular to the bar, waiting for her to make the next move. She was prickly in a way he hadn't seen before.

It didn't take long. She gulped half her drink, then set the glass down with a little more force than necessary. Exhaling on a deep breath, she stated, "Rayne Sealy's dead. They found her body on a bank of the East Glen River. I talked to Detective Haynes. He said there was a small wallet in her back pocket with her ID. They think she fell from the overlook on the way to Percy's Peak."

She clearly hadn't taken his advice to leave well enough alone, though it sounded like Haynes had been amenable. "She was on the trail above?"

"That's what they think. They're investigating."

"An accident?" asked Taft.

"Maybe she crossed the fence to take a selfie." She took another hefty swallow. "I know you told me to get out, but I wanted to know. I told Bibi I'd try to find Rayne and I just wanted to know."

"Richards was there, too, you said."

"Yeah, well . . ." She shot him a glance he couldn't read. After a few moments, she added, "If it had just been him, I would've followed your advice. He was more interested in sucking up to Haynes than dealing with an ex-partner. He didn't like me there, that was clear."

Taft had had dealings with both Richards and Haynes. Haynes was a thinking man; he didn't rush to judgment. Not so Ricky Richards, who was always trying to capitalize on a situation, looking for his own glory.

Mac added, "I wonder how Sharon Sealy's doing with the news. She seemed to care about her daughter. But Rayne's sister, Elise, was fairly harsh. Apparently, Rayne stole a boyfriend from Elise."

"Do you think that plays in here somewhere to Rayne's disappearance?"

She slowly shook her head. "I don't know. Sharon and Elise were both convinced Rayne had just run off, maybe with a boyfriend. She's done it before, and Elise talked down about her, but if they'd known or even suspected she was dead, I think I would've gotten a different reaction."

Taft asked a few more questions, but that was about all the information she'd gotten from the detective. She was clearly deeply bothered at learning of Rayne's death. He knew the feeling of looking for someone and then suddenly it's over. The person is gone. Like running into a wall.

"I was at the Waystation earlier with Seth and Patti," she said, shaking her head as if getting back to the point at hand. "From there, they went home again."

"The Waystation seems to be the extent of their limited social life these days," he agreed.

Her eye fell on a plastic packet of hamburger buns that Taft had left on the counter.

"Are those buns from Goldie Burgers?" she asked.

The hamburger buns were in the distinctive plastic bag with Goldie Burger's yellow, white, and green burger logo. Goldie Burger was a local Laurelton establishment that was known for its homemade buns. If their burgers were even half as good as the buns, they would be ten times as successful as they were. As it was, the buns were good, the beef patty kind of scrawny.

"Yep," said Taft.

She snorted, which he took as a derogatory comment on their burgers. She was trying to change the subject, he realized. She'd reported, and now wanted to move on for a while. It was exactly how he'd seen cops react when confronted with hard facts. Some used gallows humor. Others dropped a subject like a hot potato, leaving it in the listener's hands.

"You don't sound like a fan," he observed. "Is that because the burgers are terrible, or maybe because you're going vegetarian or vegan."

"Fat chance. Though my sister's heading that way. She's been touting the benefits of veganism ad nauseum, though I think she cheats."

"I didn't know you had a sister."

"A stepsister, but we're close. And how do you know anything about me anyway?"

She'd finished her wine and when he lifted the bottle and brought it close, she slid her glass over for a refill. "Ah, Ms. Laughlin, did you think I wouldn't do some checking on you?"

"What did you learn?"

"Don't panic. Your deep, dark secret is still safe, whatever it is."

That evoked a half smile.

He brought his own glass to his lips. "So, now that Rayne Sealy's been found, you have more time to work for me."

"I want to know what happened to Rayne," she said.

"Maybe a selfie, that's just so hard to accept. I feel I owe it to Bibi, and it makes me feel bad that I was just asking about her with her mother and then they learn her fate. Seems unfair. And unresolved for me, at least." She took another healthy sip. "So I'm going to keep after it for a while. Seth and Patti aren't doing much anyway, well, except Seth's trips to Best Homes. Maybe he's looking for another job."

She then told him about Seth's latest trip to Best Homes and his meeting with Troi Bevins. "Troi with an 'i.' Possibly another of Rayne's exes."

Rayne's exes were starting to become part of his own investigation, Taft realized. "How many exes are there?"

"I don't know."

"Well, stick on Seth and Troi and let's go from there."

"Okay. You think they're both dealing?"

"Possible. Keep them both in your sights."

She inclined her head, but her brows drew together as if she had more questions. If that was the case, she didn't ask them.

What Taft didn't tell her was that Seth and Patti, and someone at Best Homes, possibly this Troi person, had gotten in the way of one of Mitch Mangella's schemes to buy out Andrew Best from his own business. A hostile takeover. Taft hadn't taken any sides in the corporate shenanigans; he didn't really care how much money and power one guy had over the other, so he'd just done the investigating. What he did have an issue with was drug dealers of any kind. His surveillance had therefore morphed into his own need to quash the flow of drugs into his own community alongside his work for Mangella.

"You do Venmo?" he asked her as she finished her wine

and set the glass aside, shaking her head when he asked her if she wanted another.

"Well, yes. I can do Venmo."

"That's how I'll pay you, if that works."

"I'd like to be paid what I was making with the department," she said.

"Done," he answered. "Tell me what it is, and we'll go from there."

She narrowed her eyes at him. "That was too easy."

"You are a suspicious one, Ex-Detective Mac," he said as they exchanged information to make the bank transfers on their cell phones.

"Is there anything else you want?" Mackenzie asked.

He had a lot of one-liners that came to mind, but let them dissolve on his tongue before being spoken.

At that point there was pounding on his door and the scuffle and snorting of the pugs. Mac looked at the door and back at him in question.

"My neighbor," he said. "I'm dog sitting."

He walked to the door and threw it open. Tommy Carnoff was looking dapper in a black shirt and pants, a tan jacket, and his gray wool driver's cap atop his flowing white hair. The pugs ran inside and straight to Mackenzie, snorting and snuffling around her feet.

"I didn't know you had a guest," Tommy lied as he greeted Mackenzie, sweeping off his cap and bowing at the waist before straightening and jauntily adjusting the hat back on his head.

"Who are these guys?" Mackenzie laughed, leaning down to offer the dogs her hand as Taft introduced her to Tommy. The pugs eagerly sniffed and licked her, curly tails wagging.

Taft was taken by the music of her laughter. He'd come

to expect her to be wry and careful and maybe even a bit cynical. Tonight she'd been damn near humorless. "The black one's Charles, and the fawn one's Camilla."

"Seriously?"

Tommy gave Taft a speaking look. "The black one's Blackie. The fawn one's Plaid."

That did her in. Mackenzie nearly fell off her chair, chuckling and rubbing their heads as each vied for her attention.

"You're going to be furred," Taft warned.

"Well, I'm off," said Tommy. "Winging my way to the land of one-armed bandits. Nice to meet you, Ms. Laughlin."

"It's just Mac." She slid off the stool and went over to shake his hand. The pugs followed as if imprinted on her.

"Thomas Carnoff. Right next door. If you should ever need any help with this dubious man"—he pointed to Taft and winked—"I'm there most of the time."

"Unless he has a date," said Taft.

"Tsk, tsk." Tommy waved a finger at him. "See you Monday."

Tommy headed out the door and Taft corralled the pugs as best he could. They escaped and ran through his condo like sailors on leave, their flat faces smashed close to his belongings, checking things out.

He felt Mackenzie's eyes on him and glanced her way. "What?" he asked.

"You have many facets, Taft." She headed toward the door, placing one hand on the knob. "I'll follow Seth and Troi. If you need anything else, let me know."

"That's it? You're going?"

"I'm . . . yes, I'm going."

He'd thought she'd intended to stay awhile and he was

disappointed, very disappointed, that she wasn't. "Would you like me to look further into the Rayne Sealy death?"

She glanced back sharply. "Well . . . no . . . but . . . you would do that?"

"She's connected to both Seth and Troi and neither of them appears to be the soul of propriety. I, too, would like to know if Rayne's death was just an unfortunate accident. I agree with you, Laughlin. It's a question worth pursuing. I'll check with my connections at River Glen PD."

"Your connections?"

"I know a lot of the same people you do and some others as well." He'd heard the skepticism in her voice and added on a drawl, "I do have some credibility left with the police."

She made a sound of disbelief. "Thanks for the wine."

And she was through the door and gone.

The pugs raced toward the door but they were too late to say goodbye. They turned to Taft and stared at him with their twin humanoid faces, whining a bit.

"You guys' hearts are easily won," he pointed out.

And what about you, little brother?

He looked up, expecting to see Helene. But tonight it was just her voice in his head.

Mackenzie phoned Bibi back after she left Taft's. Bibi was clearly miffed that she'd been put off, though she burst into tears when she heard that Rayne was gone.

"I knew it. I knew it. I knew it," she blubbered. "He killed her. He killed her."

"The police are looking into it." She didn't go on that her death could've been the result of taking a selfie outside of the overlook railing. Not enough was known yet, and

Bibi was in no state to hear anything other than what she believed.

"Would you keep looking into it? Please? Everything's just shit and I need someone to . . . help."

"I'll do what I can," Mackenzie promised, though she wasn't exactly sure what that was. "You didn't tell me Rayne's had lots of ex-boyfriends."

"Well, okay, yeah. Haven't we all?"

"Can you give me some names? So I can get a picture of Rayne's social life."

Bibi reeled off several names and the one that resonated was Troi Bevins. She then hung up without a goodbye, shattered. Rayne's death had hit her hard, amplified by her own marital problems, no doubt.

Mackenzie drove back to her mother's house, let herself in, and turned quickly down the hall to her room to avoid talking to anyone. A lot had happened today and she needed some alone time to pick her way through it.

Chapter Eight

Cooper wrapped up his day at the department, sweeping a file off his desk that he wanted to go home and read more closely regarding Rayne Sealy's death. It wasn't that he didn't know the information from cover to cover already, but her death bothered him. He'd tried to ignore the niggling worry that kept sending up warning signals in the back of his brain. He'd tried to remind himself that there was nothing in the report that showed Rayne's death was anything but a terrible accident.

But . . . searchers had never found Rayne's cell phone, which should have been lying somewhere nearby, in the brush on the bank or in the river itself. There wasn't much of a current at the spot she'd been found but even so, there was no cell phone. He'd asked for a diver and been grudgingly allowed one for a few hours, but again, nothing.

Rayne's car had been found at the Rosewood Center strip mall, parked in a spot not far from the trail head. On the other side of the center's parking lot stood Ridge Pointe Independent and Assisted Living. Cooper hadn't wanted to tell Emma that yes, she'd been right, a young woman had died, but Emma was nothing if not insistent. When the news was out about the victim, Emma had repeated in her blank way, "Rayne? She used to work at Ridge Pointe. She was a hot pants."

Jamie had explained that one of the Ridge Pointe residents had made that particular claim, but that she was a known gossip, as were several others whom Emma knew from the assisted living center.

There had been nothing in Rayne's car, nor at her apartment, which had already been re-rented. The new tenant had allowed them a quick search, which in turn had revealed nothing. Rayne had moved out, taking most of her belongings with her. What had been left were two broken cups and a lopsided swivel chair that had lost its ability to turn. The rest had been packed into boxes and stood in her mother's garage. Sharon Sealy said he was free to look through the boxes, but Chief Bennihof had lost interest in the death of a thirty-something woman who posted dozens of selfies on her social media accounts and made the terrible mistake of stepping over the rail and losing her balance.

But . . . why had she been there? Cooper had looked at her accounts. Her selfies were with friends, at a bar scene, on a date, at a restaurant, on a car trip. Rarely were there pictures of her by herself. There were always others in the background. A number of different guys and a few girlfriends. Bibi Engstrom was around. Also several co-workers from the Coffee Club.

He'd thought about calling Mackenzie Laughlin. She'd been at the Sealy home the night they'd discovered Rayne's body and had wanted to know what had happened to her, had been searching for Rayne at Bibi's behest. Did she know anything more? She'd said she wanted to keep in contact. He'd made a comment about that and had seen the cloud develop over her ex-partner's head. Richards didn't like Mackenzie. Scratch that. Richards didn't like anyone whom he considered to be in his way on his climb up the rungs of the department. Somehow Mackenzie had run afoul of him, probably over that Prudence Mangella thing. The man had been an unwitting cohort to Prudence. He'd truly believed she'd been interested in him as a person. Richards had enough of an inflated opinion of himself not to see what had been so patently evident to everyone else. At the time Laughlin had made the mistake of pointing out the truth, and he'd tried to kill the messenger. Cooper, himself, had attempted to explain that the woman had used him for her own purposes, but Richards wouldn't hear of it. When Laughlin quit the department a short time later, Richards had used her departure as some kind of proof that he'd been right and she was the one who'd messed up, which had made no sense then and still didn't. Maybe it was easier for Richards to have someone to blame other than himself.

Cooper hesitated, glancing at his desk phone, thinking of calling Laughlin. Verbena was just cleaning up her desk as well and looked over at him, eyebrows raised.

He shrugged and turned away. He had his cell phone. He could call Mackenzie any time. Might as well put work out of his head and go pick up Jamie for a dinner out. Harley was eating with Emma tonight at Ridge Pointe.

He put a call in to Jamie as he hit the remote on his Explorer.

"You ready for dinner?" he asked. "I'm just leaving."

"Yes . . ." she said slowly.

"What?"

"Well, we have the house to ourselves. . . ."

His attention sharpened. "And . . . ?" A smile crept across his lips.

"I'm wearing an apron . . . and nothing else. And if you don't get here soon I'm going to turn into a giant goose bump. It's a little breezy in the back."

"Stay just the way you are. I'm on my way."

Too bad he didn't have a siren on the Explorer.

Harley drove Emma and Duchess home in the green Outback that had once belonged to Harley's grandmother, though it was now Harley's. Harley had turned sixteen a few months earlier and it made Emma anxious to see the girl's fingers tight on the wheel. She tried hard to remember Jamie's words about how it was best not to distract Harley when she was driving, but it was all Emma could do. Duchess, picking up on her mistress's anxiety, started a pitiful whining that caused Harley to glance back at the dog in the back seat.

"Could you stop that?" Harley muttered.

"Duchess," Emma said sharply.

The dog exhaled one long doggy sigh but managed to stop the whining.

Emma could almost remember driving herself, but the steps kind of got messed up in her brain whenever she tried to put them in a line. "Processing is difficult for Emma," one doctor had told Mom when she was still alive. Emma had been sitting right there, but no one had paid attention to her.

Mom had nodded, looking kind of mad. "Not mad," Mom had assured her later, when they were out of the doctor's office and on the way home. "Grim. You know what that is."

"Grim," Emma had repeated. She knew the word but sometimes the letters seemed to separate and float away in front of her eyes.

"It's how I feel when I get hard news," was Mom's explanation.

She knew she couldn't drive, but she sorely wished that Jamie had been the one to take her home. Or Cooper.

Harley made the last turn and Emma released a breath she hadn't realized she was holding.

At that moment the skies opened up and rain poured down on them, peppering the roof of Harley's car and making Duchess bark at the noise. Emma waited to open her door and by the time the rain had passed, Harley said, "So long, nice weather. We gotta make a run for it."

They dashed into Ridge Pointe together with Duchess on their heels. After walking the dog back to Emma's room they headed into the main dining area.

"That looks good," Harley said, eyeing the ice cream cart set up in a corner of the room near the kitchen.

"Every Friday. Sometimes they have pink peppermint."

"Is that your favorite?" asked Harley.

"No."

Harley choked on a laugh. Sometimes Aunt Emma just cracked her up.

A woman bent over a walker thumped her way into the room. She spied Harley and Emma seating themselves at a table and worked her way to one next to them.

"Old Darla's deaf," said Emma.

"She doesn't sit at your table?"

"No, she waits for Mrs. Throckmorton." She picked up

the menu that one of the young women who worked there had dropped at their table. "Mrs. Throckmorton has bad breath."

Harley took her at her word. "Point her out so I can avoid her."

"She's not here. She's having some trouble. Jewell says she's a gossip."

"Ah, Jewell." Harley's gaze flicked to Jewell Caldwell. She'd met a lot of the Ridge Pointe residents since Emma had moved in. Some were adorable and some . . . not so much.

"Jewell gossips, too," said Emma.

"No shit."

"Don't swear."

"Sorry," Harley said automatically.

That was the rule in the Whelan-Woodward household. No swearing, but Harley had never been known to follow the rules very well. She tried, sort of, but well, sometimes nothing but a good swear word would suffice.

They ordered dinner, Emma choosing spaghetti, which was always on the menu, with Harley going for the taco salad with chicken. She was trying to be a vegetarian, but it was really hard. Fast-food outlets called to her.

Emma pointed out different residents, some of whom Harley knew already. Like the gossipy Jewell, who had a penchant for blaming others for faults she possessed herself. And deaf Old Darla, along with the halitosis-afflicted Mrs. Throckmorton, who had entered late and seated herself at Old Darla's table. Old Darla didn't seem to mind the other lady's breath, so it appeared all was well.

"Who are they?" Harley asked, pointing her fork at a rectangular table filled with women who looked to be their mid-to-late seventies, chatting away like BFFs. One woman with thick, short silver hair and sculpted cheekbones was staring blankly while the conversation flowed around her.

"That's Jewell's table. Those are her friends."

Harley belatedly saw Jewell. She had a long gray bob and sharp eyes that roved the room. "Who is the pretty woman staring off into space?"

"She doesn't talk."

"Ever?"

"She's a listener."

Harley wasn't sure Emma was right on that. It didn't appear that she was living in the same galaxy as the rest of them.

Emma said, "Sometimes one of them invites a guy to come and eat with them. He's a nice guy. He's nice to me, but I'm not interested in a relationship."

Harley shot Emma a sharp look. Sometimes she wondered if her aunt was putting her on, but Emma was, as ever, completely sincere. She didn't know how to do sarcasm or irony or any kind of snarkiness. She just told it like it was, always.

When they were finished with their meal the waitress appeared to take their plates, and Harley followed Emma as she eagerly led the way to the ice cream cart. Mrs. Throckmorton was in front of them, as was Old Darla.

Old Darla was saying, "—my grandson visits me more than yours."

Mrs. Throckmorton responded, "You don't have a grandson," to which Old Darla reared back and looked like she was going to spit in Mrs. Throckmorton's eye.

The guy from the kitchen came out with a tub of more pink peppermint and plunked it down into one of the circular slots in the stainless-steel counter, his attention on Old Darla and Mrs. Throckmorton. "Whoa, ladies. You gonna throw down right here?" he asked as he settled the carton into one of the slots behind the cart. He looked up and saw Harley, and his expression brightened. He sketched a quick bow. "Greetings, young person. What'll it be?"

Harley smiled a little. He looked like a slacker, but she kinda liked that look. She was with . . . well, *had been*, with Greer, but he'd gone off to college and their close rapport wasn't so close anymore. Harley still really liked him, but things were different now. Her mom had sensed things had changed and had said she was there if Harley wanted to talk about it. Harley had blown her off. She would never let anyone know how deeply she was hurt by the whole thing.

"Pink peppermint," said Emma.

"I thought you didn't like it," Harley reminded her.

She shrugged. "It's not my favorite but I like it."

"And you?" the guy asked Harley, holding up his ice cream scoop.

"Um, chocolate."

"Comin' right up."

A scream and clatter sounded from behind them. Both Harley and Emma turned around and saw that Old Darla had spaghetti in her white hair. Mrs. Throckmorton's plate was on the industrial carpet beside her. At the surprised and fearful look on Old Darla's face, Mrs. Throckmorton burst into tears.

"Whoa," said Harley.

The guy behind the ice cream cart had set down his scoop and was already on his way to help, but an efficient-looking woman with streaked blond hair said, "I've got it,

Ian," and went to Old Darla and guided her away from the table, while one of the younger women squatted down beside Mrs. Throckmorton's chair, offering a tissue.

"Mrs. Throckmorton threw her spaghetti at Old Darla and then dropped her plate," said Emma in her flat monotone.

"Emotional trauma at Ridge Pointe Assisted Living," observed Harley.

Emma said sagely, "That's been coming for weeks."

A middle-aged man with horn-rimmed glasses and an expanding waistline hurried into the room wearing an "all's well" fake smile and tried to talk to Mrs. Throckmorton, but she covered her face with her hands and shook her head.

"That's Bob," said Emma as Ian quickly made her a cone of pink peppermint and one of chocolate for Harley. They walked out of the restaurant to an alcove along one of the hallway wings with two chairs and a table. Old Darla had resisted being pulled away, apparently, and had made her way back to the table. Mrs. Throckmorton put her hands over her ears to the blond woman and Bob, who walked out of the dining room together, having a pretty intense confab as they headed toward the Ridge Pointe offices.

"Somebody's in trouble," said Harley.

"Who?" asked Emma, her tongue circling the ball of ice cream she was molding into a perfect sphere.

"I don't know. It just doesn't look good for these ladies."

One of the girls helping out overheard Harley and shook her head and smiled. "They have the same old arguments about their grandsons, all the time, but they get over it." She moved back toward the kitchen.

"They do this a lot?" asked Harley.

Emma said, "They just get mixed up about their grand-sons. It's very confusing, like your mom and the tattoos."

"What?"

"Jamie likes your baby skin. She doesn't want you to have tattoos on it."

"She told you that?"

Emma nodded. "Mrs. Throckmorton saw her grandson kissing Rayne under the portico and she didn't like it. Old Darla says it's her grandson, but *he* wasn't kissing Rayne. I don't know Old Darla's grandson. I think they're sharing one."

"I'm not sure it works that way." Harley's mind had snagged on the name: Rayne. She knew that was the name of the girl they'd found on the banks of the East Glen River.

Now Emma said, as if she'd followed Harley's train of thought with her own, "Cooper will tell Jamie about that dead body someday." She then girded her sphere of ice cream with the tip of her tongue.

Everyone was trying to shield that information from Emma, as Rayne had been working at Ridge Pointe when Emma first moved in. Harley wasn't so sure that was the answer. Emma could handle more than people believed.

Harley said, "I'd kind of like to work for the police. A detective, like Cooper. I wouldn't want to be a traffic cop or anything. I don't want to hassle people or give them tickets, but I'd like to catch some serious criminals and put 'em away. That would be cool."

"Maybe you could help Cooper."

Harley doubted Cooper would think that was a good

idea. "I need a job to make some money, but I don't think the police department would hire me."

"You could work here," said Emma. "There's a lot going on here."

Harley looked over at the black cat with the white toes who sat at the edge of the room, tail twitching.

"She knows not to come into the dining room," said Emma, following Harley's gaze.

"Smart cat."

"She lets us know when someone's about to check out."

"Check out?" Harley repeated.

"Ian smells like skunk but he said the cat knows when someone's about to check out. That's when it sneaks in their room and gets in bed with them. Then they're dead."

Harley felt gooseflesh rise on her arms. "You serious?"

"Duchess won't let it in my room."

"Jesus . . . I know, no swearing." Harley's stomach clenched, though Emma kept on eating her ice cream. "What's its name, the cat?"

The look on Emma's face was indescribable, somewhere between pain, disgust, and horror. "It doesn't have a name."

"Maybe you should name it?" Harley suggested.

"Twinkletoes," she burst out.

"That's good. Because of its white feet? Makes sense."

"Stupid name," said Emma with feeling.

Harley wasn't quite following which way Emma was landing on this, but that's the way it was with her aunt sometimes. "It really knows when someone's going to die?"

"It sleeps with them."

Through the window to the dining room Harley saw Mrs. Throckmorton rise from the table, looking a bit wild. Her hair was standing on end in places and her eyes rolled around in her head. She lurched away from the table, heading for the dining room doorway.

"Sara!" a woman's voice called to her.

Mrs. Throckmorton looked back, but she kept moving out of the room, walking unevenly as if she couldn't quite move her feet right. She stepped outside the dining room and into the hallway where Harley and Emma sat. The cat moved away from the door, watching her.

Emma said, "Hi, Mrs. Throckmorton."

The woman whipped around and stared at Emma. Harley looked from her to Emma, then back again.

"My granddaughter's dead," she said.

"What?" Emma's mouth dropped open.

"They killed her."

"Who?" Harley asked before Emma could. She gazed at Mrs. Throckmorton with trepidation.

"I thought you had a grandson," said Emma.

"She was lying on a bed of rice," said Mrs. Throckmorton.

"Rice?" Harley questioned.

"You have a daughter named Lorena," Emma reminded. "And a grandson."

"Lorena . . ." the woman whispered.

"I don't think Old Darla has a grandson. You guys get it wrong all the time." Emma went on in her monotone way. She licked off the rest of her ice cream from the cone as Mrs. Throckmorton stared at her.

Harley happened to glance over to the menu, which was displayed on an easel and printed in bright colors, with tonight's special: chicken and gravy on a bed of rice.

As Mrs. Throckmorton moved off, Emma said in a stage whisper, "She isn't reliable."

"Maybe she had a bad dream . . . or she didn't like the menu." Harley motioned her head toward the easel.

Emma's eyes moved to the easel and she read the menu. "You could be a detective, Harley!" For once her voice lifted out of its deadpan delivery.

"Thanks." The idea made her feel good.

Emma leaned into her and whispered, "Old Darla likes Mrs. Throckmorton's grandson more than Mrs. Throckmorton does."

"That's . . . too bad."

"It's a secret, but Old Darla knows how Mrs. Throckmorton feels. I think she wants to have Mrs. Throckmorton's grandson. Unless she has a grandson, too." She frowned then and looked down at her feet. "It's very confusing."

"Why doesn't Mrs. Throckmorton like her grandson?"

Emma shrugged, biting into the bottom of her cone. Harley's chocolate was starting to drip over her fingers, so she got up and went back inside the dining room to throw the rest of her cone away. She grabbed a napkin and wiped her hands, then returned to Emma.

"Why doesn't she like him?" she tried again.

"His name is Thaddeus. Mrs. Throckmorton's daughter is Lorena and Thaddeus is her son."

"You don't like him, either." Emma's unusually cold tone was a giveaway.

"I only met him once."

"But you don't like him," she pressed. She was still basking a little in the thought that maybe she could be a detective. Maybe she *could* work with the police, for Cooper. Why not? She was capable. There must be something she could do there.

"If you can't say anything nice about somebody, don't say anything at all."

"And you can't say anything nice about him."

Emma thought that one over. "No," she finally admitted, biting into the bottom of her ice cream cone.

Thaddeus Charles Jenkins sat in his car, actually his grandmother's sun-damaged blue Cadillac Seville. The old cow hadn't driven it in years. Thad had preferred BMWs in his youth, the Ultimate Driving Machine, if you could ever believe advertising bullshit, cars he really couldn't afford at the time. But life had changed and his needs had changed. And well, the old cow's Caddy filled the bill.

He was parked outside Goldie Burger. He'd spent a lot of time here as a kid. He hadn't been on his regimen at that time. Just ate fries and burgers and milkshakes and pizza and all that kid stuff. Now he was heavy into exercise and a balanced diet with supplements. He was as fit as he'd ever been.

But today's trip to the burger spot was because he was on a mission. He'd killed Rayne in a fit of anger. Sick of her. Sick of the mean girl she'd once been, and the needy, grasping woman she'd become. He'd grabbed up the cup that had flown out of her hand, luckily it hadn't gone over the side of the cliff, an error in his plan that could have had disastrous consequences since his prints were on that cup. Then he'd stuffed all the paraphernalia from their lovers' meeting into her woven purse and left the "crime scene" in a kind of mad euphoria.

Now he had to kill her friend.

Things have to be in the right order.

Through the windshield he watched Bibi Engstrom head to her car, white bag in hand, shoulders hunched, despondent and miserable. He almost felt sorry for her. He had no beef with Bibi. She was like millions of people who led unimportant lives. Unhappy. Going nowhere. Looking for love in all the wrong places . . .

He snorted, thinking of the loser husband who'd left her. She was better off without him. Too bad her life, such as it was, was about to be shortened. He was going to have to take her out because he couldn't trust that Rayne hadn't told her about "Chas," his alter ego, the persona that lived in the alternate reality that was Thad's life outside of his safe room.

He sighed. He'd enjoyed throwing Rayne over the railing, been filled with energy and excitement at watching her bounce down the cliffside. It was unexpected. He'd never done anything like it before and it had been fucking fantastic. He'd run the tape of that scene in his mind over and over again. It never got old. He'd sort of known he was going to have to get rid of her, somehow, but he hadn't really thought of killing her. When the reality happened, he'd been shocked at how good it felt.

The memory even now made his cock stir.

But he had to stay in the moment. He watched Bibi pull out of the lot of Mexicali Rose and turn in the direction of her rental, and pulled out behind her. He knew she was late on the rent and if she paid it, she wouldn't have much left. Her husband had taken half their cash when he'd moved in with his new girlfriend. Nice of him to leave her something, Thad supposed, but neither of them had enough money to last but a few months. He'd been able to hack into their accounts and peek.

He smiled, thinking about his own wealth. He was good with technology. Really good. Especially computers and the Internet and hacking code and the like. He wasn't a braggart by nature, but hey, when you had the goods, you had the goods. His smile tensed. Bitcoin was a capricious bitch. But he'd make it back . . . and then there was the old cow's assets . . .

Bibi drove directly home. She punched the button on her remote for the garage door and drove inside. Not that long ago she'd parked in the driveway, but someone had cleared out the garage—probably her husband—and now Bibi had started pulling inside. The change had given Thad an idea.

He parked across the street in front of what he knew was an empty house and ran lightly up her drive and straight into her garage as she was still getting out of her car, white bag in hand. She blinked at him in surprise. "What? Who are you?"

"Chas."

Bibi's lips parted and her eyes widened. "Chas?" He saw that she knew the name. Rayne had told. It infuriated him and he looked into her frightened face and suddenly wanted her. Scraggly red-dyed hair and all. He went right up to her and punched her in the nose, hard. Blood gushed and she cried out, staggered, and went down hard. He leaned into the car and hit the remote again, bringing the garage door down again. Someone could have seen, he supposed, but he was too amped to care right now.

She was moaning on the ground, writhing a little. He'd really clocked her.

He thought of dragging her into the house, tearing off her clothes, shoving into her. She was like Rayne, waiting for it. He wished he could have wooed her, made her beg for him, but there was no time. And he'd been so furious with Rayne, and her, that he'd just hit her.

She was trying to get up, and he jumped on her prone

body, his hands ripping at her blouse as he cooed, "It's all right, sweetheart."

She reached up and dug her nails in his face, driving a gouge through the skin by his ear.

What—wha—what?

Shit!

He punched her again. And again. Blinded by rage. He didn't know how many times he hit her but his hand hurt and he worried he'd broken a small bone in his fist, the one most likely to snap from a bare-knuckle fight. His skin was split from the force, his blood mixed with hers.

Out of breath, he rolled off her and stared at the ceiling of the garage. One of those fake owls stared down at him from the rafters. It gave him a bad feeling inside.

He turned to look at Bibi's bloodied face. This wasn't how it was supposed to go.

"I'm sorry," he told her.

She gurgled out a response. He thought she said, "It's okay." Then he realized it was her last breath. He'd actually killed her? Beaten her to death? No!

He stared at her for a while, waiting for her to breathe . . . but she didn't. He got to his feet. The door to the car was still open and repeatedly dinging. He hadn't noticed till now. He reached in and grabbed her purse, still on the passenger seat, then shut the door. His hand ached and was covered in Bibi's blood. There was blood sprayed on his shirt as well. The Styrofoam container that held the burger and maybe some fries had fallen out of its bag to the footwell. *No worrying about recyclable containers for Goldie Burger,* the thought as he grabbed up the container and put it back in the bag. His blood smeared on the bag. He snagged her purse and backed out of the car.

His blood everywhere. He could feel the drip from the side of his face.

Fuck.

Using one of Goldie Burger's napkins, he turned the knob on the man-door that led to the side yard. Useless effort. His DNA was everywhere.

He stood for a moment, heart pounding, head feeling like it was squeezed in a vise. He was screened from the front road by an overgrown arborvitae hedge. After a moment he moved along the side of the garage and peered out toward the road. The night was quiet. No one lived in the house across the street and there were no lights on there. They had some motion lights but Thad had figured out how to stay out of their range in his earlier forays down Bibi's street. There was a yard on one side of the house and an empty lot on the other, which was the corner to the main street.

He wasn't supposed to kill her . . . he wasn't supposed to in this way. That had been foolish, and he'd learned not to do anything foolish . . . except when his blood was up, like tonight. He'd wanted to find a way to take her out that could be construed as an accident, like Rayne's death. He'd just gotten too amped.

He ground his teeth. He couldn't leave her to be found. His DNA was under her fingernails, his blood at the scene.

He went back inside the garage, thought a moment. He swiped at the drip of blood beside his ear. Damn her. *Damn her!*

Wrapping his arms around her he pulled her from the garage floor and back into the car, stuffing her into the driver's seat. The keys were on the garage floor. He snatched them up, switched on the engine, and let it run. Carbon monoxide was odorless and colorless and lighter than air and could be explosively ignited.

He stripped off his jacket and shirt, mixed with her blood and his, and went into the house, straight into the kitchen. A roll of paper towels sat on the counter and he ripped off a sheet, using it to open drawer after drawer, slamming them shut again until he found the junk drawer. Right inside was a Bic lighter. Exactly what he was looking for. He pulled it out, then glanced wildly around the room. His gaze fell on a six-inch-wide decorative candle with three wicks on the kitchen table. He grabbed it up and slipped back into the garage, holding his breath. Setting the candle by the main door, he swept up his jacket and shirt and backed out of the garage through the main door. He would have more than enough time to get out before the CO filled the room and ignited, burning all the evidence.

He closed the door almost all the way, then leaned in with the lighter, snapped it on and touched the flame to the three wicks, then pulled the door shut and scurried behind the arborvitae. He calculated that he had enough time, maybe a lot of time, before the place blew, if it blew, he *hoped* it blew, but he didn't want to chance it. He threw on his jacket and wadded up his bloody shirt and made himself move from his shelter and across the front lawn, across the road, to his vehicle. Starting the engine, he drove farther down the street, forced to turn around at the dead end. He was counting down in his head as he turned back, darting a look at the garage as he drove away.

How many people had cameras? How many would be able to recognize the Caddy? He'd removed his front license plate and obscured the back one with mud. That plate was stolen, so if seen, it wouldn't register back to the old lady. Didn't matter. After this he would have to retire the vehicle. It was too memorable.

He drove toward downtown River Glen, half expecting a big *kaboom*, but nothing happened. He knew he should head home, hide the Caddy, but he wanted to *know* when it happened.

He pulled into the lot of a longtime diner that had shuttered for a while but had reopened under new ownership. It had a healthy clientele and he tucked in between a Tahoe and a Toyota minivan, both vehicles looking as well used as the Caddy.

He was about five blocks from the fire department, which was located on the far end of town, away from the central treelined square that marked River Glen's center.

He sat for a good forty minutes before he heard a distant *whump* and then a minute or two later the sirens, growing loud as the fire engines burst onto the road. He'd sunk down behind the wheel and could see the flashing white and red reflection between the buildings as the vehicles raced by.

He was shaking and grinning. More than anything he wanted to cruise by the fire. More than anything he wanted to see the glorious destruction with his own eyes.

More than anything he knew he had to go home.

He battled with himself, but reason won. Swearing all the way, he drove out of town to his home, his lair, his safe house.

He hoped any DNA . . . any sign that he'd even been there . . . was destroyed by the fire. If he was lucky, the husband would be blamed. Or maybe suicide. Why not?

She was terribly depressed. A lot of people chose carbon monoxide as a way.

Not so many fire, though.

That thought made him grimace. He'd been experiencing a pleasant hard-on. Killing someone was better than sex, far better. He'd felt it after Rayne and he felt it now. A hot thrill that burned through him. He would have liked to think the police could choose suicide, but homicide by her husband was fine. He just couldn't have his own DNA trip him up and send him to prison.

Thaddeus Charles Jenkins's face froze into a rictus smile. That was never going to happen. Never.

CHAPTER NINE

Taft was on the phone with Mangella when he got beeped in by Mackenzie. He'd been wrapping up anyway. Basically the call was a fishing expedition on Mangella's part. Something really wrong was going on with the man. Something he was afraid Taft was going to learn. The separation of their working relationship was imminent, it was clear. Mitch was into something he didn't want Taft to know about. He was keeping secrets for unknown reasons. Taft had been walking a tightrope with the man already and that tightrope was growing shakier and shakier and Mangella was thrumming it.

"I'll talk to you tomorrow," he said to Mangella on Mac's second beep.

He grunted a response and Taft clicked over.

"Taft," he answered.

She didn't waste words. "Bibi Engstrom's garage went up in flames tonight. Detective Haynes called me. They found her body inside."

"Whoa." He checked his phone. Almost ten p.m. "What time?"

"Um . . . earlier. Dinnertime, I think. There was an

explosion and the fire department doused the flames . . . they found Bibi's body still in her car."

He heard the stress in her voice. "I'm sorry," he said.

"Thank you . . . it's okay."

Denial. She sounded stressed. "Haynes called you pretty fast."

"I told you I talked to him about Bibi asking me to look into Rayne's death. It makes sense I would be a first call. I'd do the same if the situation were reversed. I'm headed to the station now to talk to them."

"Not without a lawyer."

"Taft, I don't need a lawyer! I just want to know what happened. This isn't coincidence. Something's rotten in River Glen and I mean to find out what it is."

"Wait till tomorrow. You know how they are. They'll put you in the hot seat, make you feel guilty for something you had nothing to do with."

"You're projecting. That's not how I feel."

"Laughlin, listen—"

"I called you because we're working together. But I can take care of myself and there's a case now. Something's going on with first Rayne, now Bibi. They're connected, I just don't know how. One of Rayne's exes, maybe? I don't know. But I'm sure as hell going to find out."

"Tomorrow," he insisted, his voice firm. "It can wait till tomorrow."

"Thanks, Taft. I'm doing it my way."

And she hung up.

Shit.

He glanced down. Plaid was looking at him a bit worriedly, but then that was the fawn pug's perpetual appearance. Tommy had decided to extend his trip to Vegas and had asked if Taft would be able to keep the dogs awhile.

Taft had agreed and his older neighbor had gone dark. It had been almost a week since he'd left, however, and Taft was starting to feel like the forgotten sitter.

"You know the Dr. Seuss book *Horton Hatches the Egg*?" he asked the pugs as Blackie joined his brother and they both looked expectantly at Taft. "Horton is left sitting on the egg while Mayzie, the lazy bird, heads to Palm Beach." They cocked their heads in unison at his voice, which made him smile.

"I'm going out," he told them. "Don't do anything I wouldn't do."

Completely misinterpreting, they both jumped up on the couch and circled around for a good, long nap.

"I didn't say *do* what I—" He cut himself off as he shrugged into his jacket. If Laughlin was facing the police, he was going to be with her. He let the pugs be, aware that he was losing the battle against their never-ending shedding on the furniture.

The River Glen PD hadn't asked Mac to come in. She'd told them she was coming down as soon as Detective Haynes alerted her to the fire and Bibi Engstrom's death. She wanted to be front and center on this. Full transparency. Because the investigation was in its infancy when Detective Haynes had called her, the police had barely had time to deliver the news of Bibi's death to her husband, Hank Engstrom. She appreciated the heads-up, but knew it was also for their investigative benefit, as they were aware of her connection with Bibi.

Mac wasn't worried about what the department would think of her involvement. She knew these guys. Knew them well. She'd insisted on coming down tonight because she needed information. She was boggled, upset, out of kilter. Bibi was dead? How? Why? It didn't seem possible. Taft wanted her to stay away, but he was only looking at things from his own perspective and that didn't apply to her.

Haynes had been at the site, but had told her he was returning to the station, so she drove straight there. It took her about twenty minutes from her mother's house until she hurried through the front door of the department and saw the night receptionist behind the thick plastic screen. The River Glen PD had limited administrative staff throughout the night, and Mac could count on one hand the few times that an evening actually exploded with people, miscreants and victims of crimes and their families, filling up the waiting room and/or jail cells.

As she entered, all was quiet. Haynes would be in the squad room. He might be off his shift, but she knew from experience that he paid only cursory attention to the clock when he was on a case. Bennihof had squawked about it, but since Haynes wasn't one to suck up all the overtime allotment even if he was working, not a lot further was said.

"Hi, Colleen. Detective Haynes is expecting me."

Colleen Dennison smiled at her through the plexiglass. "Good to see you, Officer Mac. This about the deadly garage fire?"

"You got it. Good to see you, too."

"Go on in." She pressed the buzzer and Mac grabbed the door handle and swung it outward, passing into the inner sanctum. She took two steps, then stopped and looked back at Colleen, now only separated by a short counter.

"The Battle-axe here tonight?" asked Mac.

Colleen jerked her head to the closed door on her right and directly opposite Mac. "Right in there."

"Can you tell her I'd like to talk to her before I leave?"

"I'll pass it along."

Officer Mac . . . No longer, but habits died hard.

Mackenzie hadn't been within the secured doors of the department since she'd left and it felt a bit strange heading inside, almost as if she were returning to work. She found Cooper Haynes standing beside his desk . . . and Ricky Richards was right there with him.

"Hi, Mackenzie," greeted Cooper. He was rumpled and haggard and smelled of dank smoke. It had been a long night already.

"Thanks for calling me."

"You're all over the place, aren't you?" Ricky said. A streak of grime ran down the side of his face.

"Call it what you will," she said.

Cooper started right in, ignoring the sniping. He told her how they'd gotten in to look around the garage in the dripping aftermath of the fire department's hoses. The body had been taken away by the medical examiner, and Bibi's husband was at Glen Gen's morgue, which was situated in the hospital's basement. "The crime techs are going over the scene," Cooper wound up. "We've checked with some of the neighbors. So far nothing, but there are some security cameras."

"We should be interviewing him here right now," snapped Ricky.

Interviewing, or interrogating? It didn't take a crystal ball to see where Richards stood on what kind of scene they'd just witnessed. His aggressive tone said it all. The mystery was how he'd hooked up with Haynes again. Her heart stuttered when she considered maybe he was being considered for detective.

"Do you have a problem with me?" Mac confronted him. She was tired of her ex-partner's needling.

He spread his hands and shrugged. Haynes shot him a look, then said to Mac again, "We could talk in the morning."

"We could do that," she agreed tightly. "But I'm here now." She shook her head. "I was just talking to Bibi about Rayne Sealy. Two deaths so close together . . . Any chance this was an accident?"

Ricky snorted and Haynes said, "We've got a long road ahead before we have any answers."

"Foul play," said Mac.

"I'm remembering that you quit the department," said Ricky.

She spread her hands. "Bibi Engstrom asked me to look into Rayne's disappearance and subsequent death, and now Bibi's gone, too."

"We don't have any evidence of homicide," said Haynes. She heard the "yet" that he didn't utter. "Forensics'll let us know what they find."

"Why do you think it's homicide?" Ricky demanded.

"I didn't say it was. It's just the timing. I know her marriage was unhappy. She wasn't shy about talking about it. But it's only been a few weeks . . . days, really, since Rayne's accident, if that's what it was. I'd like more answers."

Ricky started to say something, but Haynes cut in, "Tell me again what kind of investigation you were working on for Bibi."

Ricky heaved a huge sigh, in that "here we go again" way he had when he was bored with a subject. Mac ignored him and reiterated how she'd met Bibi at Portland State and then run into her again at the Coffee Club. How Bibi had requested she search for Rayne, ignoring Mac's assertion that she was no longer part of the police force. How she'd reluctantly taken on the job, and how Bibi believed that Rayne's ex, Seth Keppler, was somehow involved, and how Mac's subsequent tailing of Seth and his current partner, Patti Warner, hadn't turned up anything suspicious. She purposely left out running into Taft and his own interest in Seth. She finished with, "I didn't talk to Bibi about much of anything else. Like I said, she mentioned the shape of her marriage some, but most of our conversation was about Rayne."

"Nothing else?" Ricky demanded.

"Not that I can think of."

"Shadowing Keppler was the extent of your job for Bibi?" Haynes asked.

Mac hesitated, wondering if there was a condemnation in there somewhere, but she decided to take him at his word and admitted that yes, so far, but that she'd learned Rayne had other ex-boyfriends and she was planning on looking into the list, just hadn't started yet.

"You're acting like a private . . . dick," accused Richards.

"I have an obligation to a friend. Bibi didn't believe Rayne died from taking a selfie."

At that moment Haynes's cell buzzed and he looked at it before answering, "Haynes." Listening, he shot Mackenzie a look she couldn't interpret, then said, "Send him back."

"Who?" Richards asked as Haynes clicked off.

"Jesse Taft."

"Jesus!" Ricky declared. To Mac, he accused, "You did this!"

"I didn't ask him to come."

"But you called him," he insisted.

She could hardly deny it. "Yes," she admitted.

"All right," Haynes interrupted. "We'll hear what he has to say."

Mackenzie glowered at Richards. She was half amazed, half glad that Taft was showing up.

They all fell silent and a few minutes later Taft pushed through the door into the squad room. He looked around himself and said conversationally, "Never been back here."

Richards snorted his disdain.

Taft regarded him with a neutral look that could have meant anything. Detective Haynes wasn't waiting to find out and stepped in before more could be said. "You know about the fire and Bibi Engstrom's death."

"Yes. Where's her husband?" Taft asked.

"The morgue," said Haynes. "Mackenzie was just telling us how Bibi had asked her to investigate Rayne Sealy's death."

"Were you on that case?" Ricky demanded of Taft.

"No. But I knew Laughlin was."

"Yeah?" Ricky looked from Taft to Mackenzie and back again. Mac could practically see the wheels turning in his mind.

"I told her I'd help her, if she needed it. Looks like she might need it. So I came."

"Bibi first came to me because she thought I was still a cop," Mac reminded them all. She was feeling raw and wanted answers, maybe answers no one had, but she needed to be in the forefront.

"Did you ever tell her you quit?" That was from Ricky, ever belligerent where Mac was concerned.

"Immediately, when she asked me to find Rayne."

"You said you were friends, and it had never come up before?" Ricky glanced toward Haynes with a look of disbelief on his face.

Mac said carefully, "I thought I made it clear that we weren't that close."

"Trying to distance yourself from her now?" Ricky tried to intimidate her by staring her down.

"Wait a minute. Let me get this straight. Officer Mac's now under suspicion?" Taft drawled.

"No," Haynes said succinctly to him.

Taft added, "Maybe she should have a lawyer."

"Laughlin is not under investigation. Everybody take a step back," said Haynes. To Taft, he added, "Mackenzie told you about Bibi Engstrom's death tonight?"

Taft nodded. "Was the garage fire purposely set?"

"We don't know yet," Ricky was quick to answer.

"Carbon monoxide? Car running? Source of ignition?" Taft looked from one to the other of them.

"We don't know yet," Ricky repeated with an edge.

The adrenaline that had been fueling Mackenzie's energy was dropping off. She wanted to collapse, maybe even cry. She'd experienced the same sag on the job during especially stressful moments and had learned ways to cope with it, but this felt different. Though she and Bibi hadn't been close friends, they had been friends, of a sort. And now she was gone. She remembered the hollow look on Haynes's face after delivering news of Rayne's death to her mother and sister. Hard duties. Emotions could be contained but they existed. She fought for a neutral expression.

Taft asked Haynes, "Got any suspicions?"

"No," Ricky snapped. "Like I said—"

Haynes interrupted, "Bibi's body was in the car. Everything was burned and wet. An errant spark could have set off the carbon monoxide. Could be a suicide. Could have been deliberately set to look like suicide. Could be a homicide. If it was an accident, I'll be surprised." Ricky looked at Haynes in stupefaction as Haynes added, "Thanks, Richards. It was above and beyond to join me at the scene. I can handle things from here."

Ricky's face flooded red. Mackenzie had seen that before, when her partner thought he had everything under control and then was suddenly blindsided. He said, "I don't mind," each word bitten off.

Taft was looking from Haynes to Ricky and back again. Like Mackenzie, he was watching the power play with interest.

"We're about done here." Haynes was pleasant but firm.

Ricky had no choice but to straighten up and move toward the door. He hesitated before pushing through and his gaze fell hard on Taft, as if he were the problem.

Never one to shirk from a challenge, Taft asked, "Got something you want to say to me?"

"You've been fired twice. I think that says it all." With that he strong-armed his way through the door and out of the squad room.

Taft said, "Factually incorrect, as I assume he means my two stints working in law enforcement. I have been fired by clients in investigative services, however, so maybe that's what he meant."

"Let's call it a night," said Haynes. "We'll know more when forensics gets back to us."

"Why do you think it's not an accident?" Mackenzie asked him.

"Seemed staged, I guess. Just a feeling more than anything." He gave Taft a long look. "My advice to you: Don't get in the way. There are a lot of people who share Richards's view. You work for some shady clients. But if you learn anything, come to me first." He swept his gaze to include Mackenzie. "You got that?"

"Yes," said Mac.

Taft gave Haynes a curt nod.

Ten minutes later Mackenzie and Taft were outside the station and heading to their cars, each at opposite ends of the parking lot. Mac was walking to her SUV, then stopped in her tracks. She turned back and started to head inside the station once more, but saw that Taft had slowed his steps and was watching her.

She walked toward him. "I have something I need to do."

"You're going to talk to Haynes some more?"

"No. I have to go back in and talk to somebody else. Nothing to do with this. Thanks for . . . coming, but I really didn't need you."

"Didn't you?" In the darkness, with his face half turned away, she couldn't see if he was joking or not. "Who are you talking to?"

"Not your business."

"True. But who are you talking to?"

"Good night, Taft." Mackenzie headed for the door just as Cooper Haynes's Explorer pulled around from the back of the department where the city rides and the staff's personal vehicles were parked. He held up a hand in goodbye to them as he left.

"Good night, Officer Laughlin . . ." said Taft.

She found herself gritting her teeth as she headed back into the department. Colleen was just going off duty and another woman was taking her place.

"The Battle-axe?" Mackenzie asked Colleen and the other woman, whose nametag read: JANA.

Jana glanced at Mackenzie with alarm and looked to Colleen for direction. Colleen nodded and said she would remind her that Mackenzie wanted to talk to her. As she walked through the door to dispatch, the new woman gave Mac a curt nod. Mac was pretty sure if she tried to explain that political correctness wasn't the issue she would be coolly ignored.

Barbara Erdlich, the Battle-axe, followed Colleen back into reception with brows lifted, headset in place. Mac said, "I wanted to talk to you about Katy?"

"Katy Keegan?"

Mac nodded. "You took her place."

There was something in the Battle-axe's eyes that said she'd registered the point of Mac's questions. Mac hurriedly gave her her phone number and said to call her anytime. The Battle-axe could decide whether she wanted to wade into the he said/she said between her boss and some of the women who'd worked in his department.

By the time Mac was back outside she expected to see that Taft had gone, but no, he was leaning against the back of his Rubicon, one foot on the bumper, waiting for her.

"I don't need a keeper," she told him.

"You going after Bennihof?"

"You're starting to piss me off."

"You are."

"Stop." She turned toward her RAV4, but Taft was hard to put off.

"I can get you in touch with Katy."

"I don't need you, Taft," she rounded on him, all the frustration of the night rising up in a wave of emotion. "Let's get something straight. I have my own life. I have my own choices. I'm working for you. That's it. Leave me alone."

"Mackenzie . . ."

The fact that he said her first name stopped her cold. He'd straightened from his lounging position.

"What?" she managed.

"I'm calling off the surveillance on Keppler."

"What?" she repeated blankly. "Why?"

"He's in a holding pattern. I've got another angle I'm working."

"What angle?"

"I'll call you."

"So, I'm not working?"

"Not right now."

She watched him climb in the Rubicon, back out, and drive away. Had she just been fired? She'd just been fired!

Mac threw herself into her own SUV, then found she was shivering as she sat behind the wheel. Damn the man. He'd pushed her and she'd pushed back because she couldn't push at whatever or whoever had killed Bibi. She wanted answers. And *action*. A plan forward.

To hell with Jesse James Taft.

She switched on the ignition and drove back to her mother's house. The thought of dealing with Dan the Man was so depressing, she almost turned around and headed for a motel. Instead she pulled out her phone and looked up the numbers of nearby apartments complexes she knew in River Glen and Laurelton. Too late to do anything tonight, but she determined she would make the change tomorrow. No more living in limbo. She was taking charge of her own life. She had enough cash for first month's rent . . . maybe last month's, too . . . maybe . . .

*Maybe you should try another police department.
Laurelton?*

Setting her jaw, she pulled into the driveway, thoughts
awhirl. What she was going to do was follow up on Bibi
Engstrom's death, and Rayne Sealy's, and see if there was
any connection. She was off the Keppler case for Taft.
Fine. Didn't mean she couldn't still keep after him. Maybe
she should make contact. Something.

As if the universe was in tune to her needs, her phone
started ringing. At nearly midnight. To her alarm, she saw
it was Stephanie's number.

"Stephanie?" she answered in a careful tone. Her stepsister who mainly texted, rarely called.

"Sorry, Mac. Didn't mean to scare you," she whispered,
responding to Mackenzie's tone. "Nothing bad. Just
wanted you to know . . . Nolan doesn't want me to tell, it's
so early . . . I'm *pregnant!* Don't mention it to Mom. It's
kind of a surprise, but oh, my God! I'm just in disbelief.
And thrilled! Yes! Isn't it crazy! I can't believe it. And
you . . . you're going to be an auntie!"

CHAPTER TEN

T had sat in front of the computer screens in his safe room. His eyes were unnaturally still on the images that spread over the three screens. He didn't see them. He was envisioning the events of the last few weeks, savoring each one, and his heart was beating hard and fast, his blood hot.

He'd been reliving his two kills and his mind had now drifted to the woman he'd met at the Waystation the week earlier. He had a photographic memory and he was recalling the way the pockets of her jeans curved over her butt, the hint of breast beneath the shirt, the hollow of her throat, the "come fuck me" message in her eyes. Thinking about her along with his "kills" had kept him amped most of the day.

With an effort, he came out of his fog. He blinked twice, then felt the cowboy hat still on his head. Carefully he removed the hat and placed it on the metal shelf against the back concrete wall. His safe room was a basement space that ran along the back of the house, a lair that his mother called the dungeon. It had a secret door and steps down to a bomb shelter that his father—God rest his fucked-up soul—had installed in preparation for the end of the world.

He looked over at the wall, at the whiteboard he'd installed. There was one word written on it—*Rayne*—in bright red Sharpie ink. He shivered. He'd gone on the dark web and ordered "knockout drops," probably Rohypnol, they hadn't specified, and he'd brought those drops with him the day he'd killed her, but hadn't had to use them. He'd just had them for backup in case she blabbed. He couldn't have her blabbing . . . gossiping about him . . . telling the world about his flaws . . .

Thad felt the end of the world was near. Life was hard for a lot of people and he couldn't see it getting any better. For a time he'd even tried surviving the coming apocalypse, squirreling himself in the safe room, drinking bottled water and K rations that his father had filled the place with before he'd slipped a rope through the metal ring screwed into the safe room's ceiling and hung himself.

Thad looked up at that ring. "Rest in peace, asshole," he growled, then walked to the end of the long, narrow room where two other rings were also screwed into the concrete ceiling, much the same way. He jumped up and grabbed a ring with each hand, then went through his routine of pulling himself up and extending his legs in front of him in an L-shape, just like the Olympics. He did a number of reps that had him sweating like a pig. He then used the toilet in his safe room and stripped naked before heading up the stairs to the laundry room–cum bathroom–cum mechanical room at the top of the stairs. He threw his clothes in the washer, then stepped into the adjoining shower, turning the water on cold first until he was practically frozen, then steaming hot until he could no longer bear it. Only then did he step out, dry off, throw the towel into the washer, put in some soap, flip the machine on.

Lorena would be back soon. Thad made a face. He didn't like his mother and she didn't like him, but they shared a common outlook: The world fucking sucked. Thad had used his monumental hacking skills to get back at the world. He could extort money from miserable, fledgling businesses who didn't know the first thing about a firewall and he could infect them with malware and hold them for ransom. He'd amassed enough money to make himself rich, but an investment in Bitcoin had gone sour, tumbling in price, causing him to lose damn near all of it. He'd been working his way back, but cautiously, now. Government and private cybersecurity was getting to be more and more of a risk, so he had to proceed with caution and it was pissing him off. If the old lady would just up and die and leave the house to him—he'd sneaked a peek at her will and learned that Lorena had been bypassed—then he could sit back a little and concern himself with other issues of greater interest, but no . . . she just lived *on and on*. It made him slightly crazy. She was past being anything but a drain on society. She should just go. In his loveliest dreams he thought of how he could sneak into that old people's assisted living commune and choke the life from her, but so far it hadn't been feasible. He'd even tried, sort of haphazardly, visiting her from time to time, hoping to hasten her along, but he hadn't had an opening.

So, while she lived on, he'd passed the time counting out the long days, waiting for something to happen. He felt the familiar low-level rage rise up inside him. A taste of bile in his mouth. He, Thaddeus Charles Jenkins, smarter than everyone else, was pissing his life away waiting for his grandmother to die. What a massive waste. If that Bitcoin debacle hadn't happened, if he could have gotten out sooner . . .

He shook his head, pulling himself back from the rim of an abyss he sensed just outside his consciousness. If he should ever fall inside . . . He wasn't sure what would happen but he knew it would be apocalyptic. He couldn't risk it.

He'd turned his attention to Rayne Sealy to combat his lava-like inner fury. He'd first seen Rayne at Ridge Pointe. She'd worked there for a short time. She hadn't been aware of him because he'd made a point of skulking through the place, almost holding his breath. He hated old people. Hated the way they looked and smelled. Hated the way they talked about nothing except the good old days. What good old days? Thad had never experienced any of them to date and wouldn't until his grandmother fucking died.

And then he'd caught sight of Rayne making out with that long-haired asshole outside the front doors as he was driving away one day. He'd wanted to jump out and club the guy to death, he'd felt so possessive, but he'd kept going. He couldn't afford to make a scene at Ridge Pointe. They knew him there.

But then Rayne had been let go and gone to work at Good Livin' where she'd taken up with Seth Keppler. *Fucker*. Thad was disgusted with Rayne. She was indiscriminate and loose. Low morals. It wasn't the way women were supposed to be.

But he couldn't get her out of his head. So disgusting . . . and yet, he wanted her. Once upon a time she'd been above him and treated him like an insect or worse . . . but things had definitely changed, hadn't they? Who was the cockroach now, Rayne? He'd wanted to squash her. Wrap his hands around her neck and squeeze. Cover her mouth to keep her from talking, uttering all those careless junior high, mean girl invectives, words that spewed from between her filthy, sewer lips.

Rayne then lost her job at Good Livin' because of Keppler. Thad hadn't known exactly what happened until she'd told him about it later. Patti, who worked at the front desk, apparently had enough clout at the health club to get her fired. Patti had had her eye on Seth and Rayne, true to form, had jumped into Seth's bed before Patti could make her move. At least that's the way Rayne told it. The result was Rayne got her ass kicked out of Good Livin' and had ended up slinging lattes for the masses at the Coffee Club. Ha! Oh, how far she'd come down from those long ago days in elementary school when she'd held sway over the whole class. He lived to see her on the bottom. Good old Rayne. One of the girls who'd made his life a living hell so long ago. She and her group of friends had tortured him. Not the good kind of torture. Not the kind that made you want to moan with ecstasy. The bad kind. The humiliating kind.

It had taken him years to win back his self-respect. Years and years, and lots of women, and stealing money and planning . . .

His mind shifted again to the girl he'd seen recently at the Waystation. She was the kind of woman who was his reward for the years spent reinventing himself. He'd had her kind before and when they were screaming for him, dying for him, he would walk away from them. Shoot them down. Make them grovel. There were a string of them across the greater Portland area that he'd kicked to the curb. The kind of woman who would do anything he asked, no matter how depraved, and beg for more. He'd seen it in her eyes. Okay, she'd turned him down this time, but there was no question that she wanted him.

But Rayne . . .

He'd expected to do the same with her. Have her and then kick her in the teeth. Let her know how worthless she was. Dirt beneath the heel of his boot. Except she knew him, and though it had been real sweet, fucking revenge to screw her hard and listen to her scream, pant, and gasp, whether with desire or pain, it didn't matter, he'd had to up his timetable. Though he'd intended to keep her until he was sick and tired of her, she'd told her friend Bibi about him. He'd warned her, and she'd told Bibi about him anyway. Whatever came to her as result, it was her fault. She'd asked for it. Even though Rayne had sworn she would keep their relationship secret, she just couldn't help herself. That's how she was made.

In the back of his mind, he'd known that's what would eventually happen, but he hadn't really decided what he would do when she blurted out their secret. Maybe he'd whip her. That idea had intrigued him so much, he'd actually purchased a whip and taken it to the lair. He had images of her hanging from the iron rings while he whipped her and it had filled him with intense sexual desire. He'd toyed with the idea of bringing her to his safe room and keeping her there indefinitely, his sexual toy.

Before that could happen, though, she'd pulled out that camera at the overlook and then . . . the moment had just spun out. He'd seen his opportunity and moved on it, barely thinking. He'd watched in a haze of wonder as she bounced down that hillside. He was giggling as she flew like a limp rag doll and had been hard-pressed to hold back roars of laughter.

The thought of getting caught had been the proverbial bucket of cold water. He'd hurriedly picked up around himself. Made sure he had the cup, the wine bottle and her phone.

Later, recalling that moment when Rayne had flown forward, head down, he'd pleasured himself over and over again. Even now that image sent his blood racing. Better than sex with Rayne. Much better.

And then Bibi . . . if only he'd had more time with her. The fire had been an explosion, a wonderful conflagration that had erased his DNA.

His lips curled, thinking of it all again. He reached down to stroke himself and review every little detail of her death once more, when he heard a car rumble into the garage.

Lorena.

Immediately, he headed back to the lair.

"Tha—" he heard, just as he slid shut the metal door behind him and threw the lock. He didn't want to talk to her. He had better things to do.

Clambering down the stairs, he strode directly to the metal shelves and grabbed up a large coffee table book of Oregon scenery. He opened the hardbound volume and pulled out the grouping of pictures he'd blown up from his eighth grade year, the last full year he'd shared with Rayne and the other bitches from Laurelton Grade and High Schools, the ones who'd sneered at him so much, especially in those early years before he'd learned how to stay off their radar. They were monsters who fed off the misery of life's misfits. Misfits like himself, back then. Thad had

had only one good friend in those grade school days, and that friend had moved away at the start of junior high, leaving Thad to fend for himself through the halls of a school where he always felt like a hated outsider.

Before he'd learned to stay out of those girls' way, skirt the edge of their grade school realm, he'd been in their line of sight. Young, ignorant enough to believe they could be his friends, Thad had left himself open to their mean ridicule. He hadn't known what they were capable of until that red-letter day in the fifth grade when he'd brought a frog to school to impress the science teacher as they were studying amphibians.

He showed the girls his frog, almost blushing with pride. They all recoiled in feigned horror, gasping and giggling and generally freaking out. From that point forward they sniggered whenever they saw him, stage-whispering "Mr. Toad" each time they caught sight of him in the halls. Thad was mortified. He tried to hide it, but he just couldn't. It was a stupid grade school name. Nothing to feel ashamed about, but he did feel ashamed.

In junior high he told himself that name and its association was long over. He convinced himself it was long over. He secretly lusted after Rayne and her two best friends, the most popular girls in the class, the prettiest ones. Luckily, freshman year, before he could further embarrass himself—he'd suffered ridiculous thoughts of buying them roses and writing poems—his family moved to Portland where he finished school away from the triumvirate . . . but he never forgot them. Over time his desire morphed into resentment. He wanted to teach them a lesson. He reinvented himself, no longer the dorky, insignificant dog poop on the bottom of Rayne's shoe, but sometimes he wondered if it was really true. Over the years he fantasized about proving to them that he was better than they were.

Then one day the opportunity arose. There she was, ripe for the picking . . . overweight and now working at the Coffee Club. She didn't recognize him, which boosted his ego. He really had changed. He asked her out on a lark. It was a game. Wondering whether she would find him out. Wondering whether she would call him Mr. Toad again, or whether she would keep her mouth open, eyes glazed with desire whenever he took her.

Three weeks. That's how long it had lasted before she'd opened her mouth for a different reason—and blabbed. He'd wanted it to go longer, much longer. He'd enjoyed how many rungs down she'd fallen, while he was climbing ever skyward, soaring. She was pathetic, really. Desperate. He'd reveled in her debasement. He'd wanted to stretch out the time with her, even though he also relished the thought of the ending. The putdown. He had a mental picture of the look on her face when she learned she'd been toyed with, played for a sucker. The shock. The betrayal. The fear . . . It kept a smile on his face whenever he was with her.

Then she found out who he was.

He'd made a grave error, he could admit it now: He brought her to his place when he had it to himself. Not the safe room, just the house, nosy little twit that she was, she looked through some of the old lady's books and, lo and behold, there was one of his yearbooks, one his mother had kept, one Rayne recognized. And inside was a loose fifth-grade class picture with all the students. He hadn't known it was there, hadn't known it still existed, though it was right there in the bookshelf in the dining room. Thad

had been blind to it for years. He didn't notice Lorena's or the old lady's tchotchkes and other belongings. But Rayne saw it and plucked it from the bookcase and the picture fell out. There was Rayne's picture and his own. Rayne might be dumb as a stump but her avid little eyes realized what she was looking at before he could yank the class picture from her grasp. Putting two and two together, she screamed, "Thaddeus!"

The blood drained from his face. He waited for the condemnation. The whooping "Mr. Toad!" he knew was coming. He could practically hear the scorn in her voice.

But it never came. She was delighted, in fact. She didn't even seem to remember how she'd treated him. She was perfectly happy to just keep going on as before even though she knew who he was. It had boggled him. He'd hardly known how to react . . . at least Rayne hadn't seen the blown-up picture of her that he had in his lair, or the other copied photos pressed between the pages of another hardbound book, pictures of others in her tribe of bitches. Still, having her know his true identity wasn't what he wanted. She might be delighted, but he wasn't. Mr. Toad was going to have his revenge. Her brushing aside the past and complete acceptance of him just showed how truly shallow she was. No conviction. No soul. She was happy to be with the undesirable misfit from grade school now that he had money.

Money . . . *had* money . . . past tense . . . He'd bragged to Rayne about his hacking skills, a rookie move, even while he'd been desperately trying to recoup his losses. He'd used her as a salve, always planning for the big day when he cut her loose, putting it off awhile longer than he'd intended because it felt so good to screw her brains out at that stinky apartment she'd called home. Every time he went there he wore a disguise, just in case someone had a camera, which every paranoid fool seemed to possess these days.

Rayne had teased him about the hooded, bespectacled, masked lover who came to her door. He'd told her it was because he was famous in extremely wealthy circles, but she acted like it was role-playing. That had thrown him, and given him an insight into her other relationships. Jealousy had reared its head. Shocked, he'd tamped that down hard. He'd known he had to get out of the relationship and soon. Otherwise he would be in her evil thrall.

But he hadn't been able to do it. One week turned to two, two weeks to three . . .

She'd made the decision for him when she'd told Bibi she was seeing him. Little bitch. He should've probably thanked her, but he was infuriated. And the camera? She'd been trying to sneak a picture the whole time they were together even though she swore she wasn't. At the overlook he'd barely been able to hide his rage. He'd wanted to strangle her right then and there, crush her hyoid bone and watch her face turn blue, but he'd known he couldn't kill her like that. Somehow he would get caught. There would be some infinitesimal trace of DNA that would point the finger at him.

And anyway, he planned to dump her fat ass. He wasn't going to kill her. He had the knockout drops just in case. . . .

Just in case of what? he'd asked himself, looking at her, knowing she knew he was Thad, not Chas.

Mr. Toad.

He'd thrown down her phone and then . . . *poof.* One moment she was there, the next he'd tossed her over the edge. One moment he was playing with her, the next he was watching her fly. Well, almost. Her foot had gotten tangled up and required one more push on his part. But then she was bouncing down the hill, eyes stretched wide with terror, a diver into an abyss. She'd smacked her head on the way down and her pain reverberated within him, a thrill greater than he'd ever felt before. He'd forced himself to stroll away, a little afraid he could have been seen, even though no one was about.

He was filled with a new kind of awe in his own power. He wished he had a lock of her hair, something personal.

Well, there was one thing. The Hobo bag that he'd shoved everything inside.

Now he dumped out the wine bottle, opener, cups, and assorted trash onto his table, holding on to the bag. Next he plucked the enlarged picture of Rayne from his stash of photos. She'd been slimmer then, and there was definitely a self-confidence in the picture that she'd lost over the years, a come-hither look that had really turned him on. He tacked the picture on the wall and then stared at it while he masturbated with fury and speed into her bag, throwing back his head and howling as he came.

He slowly surfaced to renewed pounding on the upper door. Glowering, Thad cleaned himself up. He doubted Lorena could have heard him but didn't care if she had. He put the picture of Rayne back in with the other photos, ignoring the pounding. His mother always wanted him to *do* something for her.

He let his mind wander to Bibi. He felt that niggling fear about cameras and DNA but he shoved it aside. Not as satisfying as seeing Rayne head down over the rail. A necessary kill, pleasurable in its own way, but he hadn't had enough time.

He went back to remembering Rayne. That first day at the Coffee Club he'd held his breath when he'd stood right in front of her. She'd looked at him expectantly, ready to take his order. He'd stumbled out something, half sure she would suddenly level a finger at him and shriek, "Mr. Toad!" in front of God and everybody, but she barely noticed him. She didn't remember him? Sure, he'd changed a lot. And it was good that she didn't recognize him. But it made him hate her more.

He had a chance to walk away, but he didn't. He wanted her. He warned himself not to do it. Not to engage. Keep his cool. Stay aloof. He even managed to, for a while. But he couldn't sustain. He learned her schedule at the Coffee Club and kept stopping in, acting like she was nothing to him, just another barista. She was friendly, particularly to the male customers. Flirty. Especially if they looked like money.

Eventually he couldn't stand it. What was he waiting for? He turned on the charm and went after her full tilt. She melted like wax. No challenge. Disappointingly easy to win. Her circumstances had diminished over the years and she was ready to do anything for him. All he had to do was ask.

Truthfully, he'd liked having sex with her. He always dominated and she let him. She was so eager for a relationship with "Chas" it was almost embarrassing. She thought the disguises he used were fun. She didn't care that he couldn't make himself kiss that avid little mouth that was only good for blow jobs. She didn't care that he never waited for her climax, though, unless she was faking, she managed to sure meet him there often enough.

All she cared about was whispering that she loved him and wanting him to say it back. "You know I do," was all he could manage, a lie, but she took him at his word. And so the three weeks went.

He hadn't had many relationships beyond what he paid for one- or two-night stands, so it was a novel experience to have someone available, to have *Rayne Sealy* available. He didn't want to give it up, though he knew he had to. The struggle was solely within himself. He liked having her at his beck and call. Loved it when she begged him, and she begged him all the time.

Now he threw open the book to her picture again, staring at her vapid smile. He could almost see the maliciousness, the evil, that hid there. Her hollow heart. There was nothing to her but a shell. She and her friends were all that way.

"THAD!" Lorena's tinny voice carried down to him. She must be shouting her head off.

He jumped up the stairs but stayed on his side of the door. "What?" he demanded loudly.

"Thad?"

"YES."

"Open the fucking door. I need to talk to you."

Lorena, for all her faults, rarely swore so pungently. He had no intention of letting her into his lair, but he sensed she was keen to inspect it, and knowing Lorena, she might find a way in if he wasn't careful.

"Just tell me what you want."

"Open. The. Door."

"Or what?"

"Or I'll find a way to get Mom to cut you out of the inheritance. I can do it. Don't think I can't," she warned.

Is that what she'd really said? The door was thick. Hard to hear through even when someone was shouting. She didn't know that she'd been the one who was cut out of the inheritance. He didn't even want to discuss it with her.

"Thaddeus?"

He chewed on his lower lip. As soon as he realized he'd fallen back on an anxiety giveaway from his youth, he stopped himself and clenched his teeth. "Okay. Fuck it. I'll be there in a minute."

"NOW!"

Fuck you, he silently mouthed, as he ran quickly down the stairs, half tripping on the bottom step and nearly smashing into the metal shelving that held his books. His hand caught the edge of a sharp flange and sliced into his palm. He let out a string of invectives as blood welled. With his uninjured hand he picked up the Hobo purse and stuffed it inside an empty backpack. Then he swept the detritus from that last meeting at the overlook in a trash can. Just in case she somehow forced her way downstairs. Looking at the empty wine bottle, he saw a vision of Rayne's adoring eyes.

He realized, deep in the back of his lizard brain, that he might miss her a little.

Heading back up the stairs, he carefully slid back the door to see Lorena standing there, hands on her hips, glaring at him in that entitled way.

"One of these days I'm going down there, you know." She pointed to his lair as he closed the door behind him, turning the key to thrust the deadlock in place.

"What's the problem?" He wanted to chew his lip. So

wanted to chew his lip. But he kept himself from doing it by staring at her with his meanest glare.

"It's Mother. She's getting batty as hell, and they want to move her to Memory Care. Well, that's just not going to happen. It's already an arm and a leg at that place. You know."

"Yeah, I know." Memory Care. He had a mental image of hundred-dollar bills sprouting wings and flying away.

"I'm going over there to talk to them. They can't move her without my consent. We've already lost enough money on her. I don't know why she doesn't just die."

"Hey, that's my grandma you're talking about."

She gave him a withering look. "Like you give a shit. You're just waiting for your part of the inheritance."

He thought, *My* hundred percent *part of the inheritance.* He'd spent long hours at Ridge Pointe with Gram, even brought the lawyer in to sign. The last time he'd visited Gram had been when the amendment to her will was signed, cutting Lorena out and putting Thaddeus in.

Lorena went on, "She's doing fine in assisted living. They can't make us put her in Memory Care."

"She is fine," he agreed. He didn't want anyone at Ridge Pointe or anywhere else questioning her mental acuity in the last few years.

"So, what are we going to do?"

"You want me to do something?" he asked.

"No, Thad. I want to do it all myself. Just stay in your hole and do nothing."

"It was just a question," Thad snapped. "I wasn't being an asshole."

"Yeah? You sounded like one."

"I love Gram. I can help."

Lorena threw back her head and laughed. "Sure. We both love her. Maybe you don't care if she runs through all her money, but I do."

"I care."

"Fine." She flipped her wrist at him, a dismissive gesture that made him burn inside. "There's just not that much money left," she added, making his heart clutch. "We're going to have to do something, and I'm just not sure yet what that is." She slid him a beady, birdlike sideways look. "How's your computer 'job' going?"

He'd bragged to her about his dealings on the Internet, his appropriation of others' funds. He was sorry about that now. Especially that she knew he'd made money, and lost it. Her attitude, which had been pleasant and coy when he'd been flush, was hostile and belittling now that he was having to start over.

And Gram is running out of money?

"It's going," he said shortly.

"Maybe you could get it going a little faster, before we have to sell this place," she suggested. She turned to the hall tree where she'd hung her coat. Snatching it up, she headed toward the front door where, from his angle, he could just see through the sidelight out to the drive that led to the house. Rain was falling, puddling on a dip in the concrete. The budding irises and daffodils had disappeared, their stalks lying like dead soldiers across the walkway.

After she was gone he stalked through the house and into the kitchen. He had a microwave in the lair and a hot plate, but if he knew he was alone in the house he preferred to eat upstairs. *Memory Care* for the old lady? His mind was in turmoil over the loss of money. He hated that his mother was currently in charge of the finances. An error on Gram's part. She'd corrected the will, but putting his mother in charge of her day-to-day finances? Bad idea. Very bad idea.

Maybe he should go to Ridge Pointe and talk to her again. He hadn't been there since she'd signed. He didn't think she was completely batshit crazy yet. Maybe she would listen to him, turn that duty over to him, not Lorena.

Or maybe it was too late.

"Shit."

He needed to make sure Gram didn't go to Memory Care.

He suddenly longed for Rayne. To be inside her. Pumping away. Furiously making love, or hate, or whatever you wanted to call it, to her. On the heels of that desire came the memory of her flying head down, hurtling over the cliff.

And then Bibi . . . climbing atop her . . . smashing in her face with his fist. He'd wanted to squeeze her head and pop it like a pimple.

Would the police put the two deaths together? He didn't think so. He hadn't worried about it all. Had been on too much of a high, but now . . .

What if they link you to both kills? What if there's no money left? What if you lose THIS HOUSE!

He heard whimpering. Sounds issuing from his own throat. He inhaled and exhaled several times and brought himself under control. He knew that Rayne's death was being treated like an accident, but Bibi . . . did they know it was a homicide? Maybe. But there wasn't any way to trace it back to him, was there? He'd never even met Bibi till the night he killed her. And Rayne, though she'd blabbed about their relationship to her, hadn't given up his name, except to Bibi . . .

What if Bibi knew everything and had *told* someone else before he killed her?

Thad chewed on his lower lip until it bled. He let out an oath upon the realization of what he'd done. Was his freedom in jeopardy? Was the end of the world as he knew it upon him?

What if you only have a few weeks left?

He lurched in a panic back to the foyer, the floor a circle of dun-colored marble except for the carved pinkish rose mosaic in its center. Sheer walls rose dramatically skyward. A curved stairway ran up to the third level, the mahogany rail spiraling dizzily upward, its beauty only marred by the blight of the old lady's attached stairlift, something he planned to remove as soon as the house was his.

But what if that day never came? What if it was never his? What if he was arrested, thrown in prison, locked away forever?

He started shaking all over. He could imagine the wagging tongues, the recriminations, the humiliation he would suffer. What about those other bitches? He could see them. Little girls tittering . . . laughing behind their hands . . . whispering in each other's ears while they rolled their eyes his way.

Loser!

Ugly nerd!

Mr. Toad . . . Mr. Toad . . . MR. TOAD!

Shrill laughter filled his ears. Shrieking laughter. Little girls pointing fingers at him. He tried to bring himself back to reality. That was all a long time ago. A LONG

TIME AGO. He was different now. He was Chas. Women wanted him. Couldn't get enough of him. *Loved* him.

Rayne's face swam before him. She was smiling. *Very soon you'll be getting what you deserve, Mr. Toad. Very soon . . .*

He came to find himself in a fetal ball atop the rose in the center of the marble circle. Luckily, Lorena was still gone, unable to see his fear and weakness.

He climbed to his feet, swaying a bit, still tortured by the vision of his possible future, a future Rayne and the bitches wanted him to endure.

He could see them gossiping about him, laughing at him, infecting others to laugh at him as well.

Rayne was just one of them. He'd had a half-formed plan to get down on his knee in front of her and pretend he was asking her to marry him. That was supposed to be her ending. Where he purposely shattered her dreams by telling her it was over and that she was a stupid cow he'd only used for sex. But instead he'd flipped her into the air and she spun down the hillside. He'd gone from breaking up with her to killing her. Better than the humiliation he'd planned. Much better.

But the other bitches were just as guilty. Just as shallow.

And he knew where they lived today. If he played his cards right, he might be able to replicate the romantic steps he'd taken with Rayne. He could have sex with them— even pretend to pop the question this time!—but in the end he knew he would have to kill them.

Things have to be in the right order, he reminded himself.

He would have to be careful, but it could be done. Nothing like killing Bibi. Not a hurried, clean-up murder. No. They would be more like Rayne's sad ending . . . an elegant romance that would ultimately culminate in a sweet, savage death.

His fear slowly came under control again and he concentrated on what he would do to those other mean girls. His cock rose in response.

One of them lived in Portland. The first one he would stalk and woo.

And the other?

She was right here in River Glen.

CHAPTER ELEVEN

Three days after Bibi's death Mackenzie, who'd packed up her emotions into a mental box, determining to deal with them later, strolled into the reception area of Good Livin'. Patti Warner was seated behind the desk as was a much younger woman who looked like she was still a teen. Her name tag read: GISELLE.

"Hi, Giselle," Mac said, a smile in her voice. "I was wondering about joining the club."

Giselle smiled right back, then looked over at Patti, who was embroiled in something on her phone that had her brows drawn together. "Well, hi. So glad you're here. You won't be sorry. The club's got everything! Umm . . . Patti will help you, just as soon as she's free. You can take a seat over there." She swept a hand to include the row of navy upholstered chairs grouped around a square, rough-hewn table that sported a dull, metallic vase bursting with an eye-popping bouquet of yellow daffodils and cobalt hyacinths. Patti glanced up at her as she clicked off and Mac held her breath. She'd purposely borrowed a pair of Stephanie's aviator glasses, the prescription mild enough that she could navigate without too much effort. She was going to have to get a pair of plain glass ones for herself if she kept this up.

Patti didn't react to her except for a practiced, welcoming smile. "I can sure help you."

There wasn't a lot of enthusiasm in her greeting, but neither was there any recognition and since Mac had no intention of actually joining Good Livin', she counted it as a win.

"I'll be there in a minute," she said, throwing a look at the same row of chairs before turning to the monitor on her desk.

"Okay."

Mac dutifully took one of the navy chairs and positioned herself behind the flowers in a way that allowed her to still see a section of the counter where Patti was seated. She hadn't spoken with Taft since he'd fired her. He'd paid her for her work, but there was a big silence between them. *Fired her* might be too harsh a term, but that's what it felt like. She'd thought about telling him that fine, she didn't need him, she was striking out on her own, following her own path of investigation, showing herself to Patti and Seth, but he would have undoubtedly told her to back off and she didn't feel like hearing it.

In the meantime she'd called Detective Haynes at the station, asking for more information on Bibi's death, and if Rayne's fall had definitely been ruled an accident. She'd half expected to be told it was police business and to butt out. That's what Ricky would have said. But Haynes told her both investigations were ongoing, and that Bibi's husband, Hank Engstrom, was still considered a person of interest in his wife's death.

"So, that one is a homicide?" Mac had pressed, her antennae raised.

"Laughlin, I'll let you know as soon as I can," he'd answered.

"I'll hold you to that."

"Fair enough."

At least Haynes hadn't just blown her off. They'd gotten along well when she'd been a part of the department, even though their paths had crossed infrequently. She'd dealt with the minor miscreants like Doobie Gillis, while he'd worked the investigations. She'd added Hank Engstrom to her list of people she wanted to interview.

Mac had half moved her belongings to Stephanie and Nolan's as Stephanie had insisted when she'd learned Mac was moving out by hook or by crook. The baby wasn't due for seven more months and she wanted Mac to take the spare room and be with her, especially since Nolan was working long hours based on the varying stages of development of the Laidlaw homes that were under construction, homes that dotted the triangular region of River Glen, Laurelton, and Portland. Mac had packed her bag of clothes and ensconced herself in the baby's room, which housed a twin bed and a chest of drawers and was still a shade of pink from when Stephanie and Nolan had moved in. They weren't changing it till they knew the sex of the baby. Stephanie and Nolan hadn't ordered a crib yet, but when they did, Mac figured she'd move to the couch in the den, though Stephanie insisted the twin bed was staying. In truth, Mac didn't know how long this arrangement would last but it was fine for now.

To say her stepsister was glowing was inadequate. Stephanie radiated joy as if she'd swallowed sunlight. She didn't want anyone other than Mac to know yet, but Mac couldn't see how she would keep the news from Dan the Man. One look at her and you just knew something wonderful had happened to her. Mom had been sad to see Mac leave, but she had encouraged her. She'd seen first-hand how difficult it was for her daughter and husband to get along. She hugged Mac before Mac left in her loaded car, telling her she was continually delighted that she and Stephanie had become such good friends. Dan's reaction was a little different. He didn't seem to know how to feel. He had a tendency to look like he'd smelled something noxious on a good day, to Mac's mind, and when he heard she was moving in with his daughter and her husband, he questioned whether they really had room for a vagabond.

"Steph's got a husband," he'd reminded Mac.

"Oh, right. What's his name again?"

He opened his mouth to answer her, but then he caught himself, offering instead a tight-lipped smile. "You know."

Maybe it was small-minded on her part, the urge to needle Dan, but she wasn't going to dwell on it. She was imperfect. And sometimes she reveled in it.

"Hi," Patti said as she swept over. She wore a long skirt and a white blouse with bell sleeves that looked like they were made for getting in the way, natural dust rags. "So, you're interested in joining," she greeted her with a faint lift of enthusiasm in her voice.

Mac had worked out what she planned to say before-hand. "A friend of mine mentioned Good Livin'. Rayne Sealy? I don't know if you know the terrible tragedy that befell her, but . . ." Mac trailed off as Patti's face tightened into a hard mask. "Are you okay? Oh, that's right. She worked here briefly. You knew her?"

Patti breathed heavily and then pulled herself together. "Yes. I knew her. A tragedy. Like you said."

"I'm sorry. I should have been more sensitive," Mac said, watching her. No love lost here. "I was thinking about

Rayne and I've been meaning to get into shape. I think she'd like that."

Patti eyed her sharply. "Rayne?" She sounded incredulous.

"Well, she was employed here, at a fitness place . . ."

"Not for a while. How well did you know her?" she asked sharply.

"Did I say something wrong?"

Patti snapped back into her professionalism, as best as she could and it was clearly an effort. "Rayne wasn't very serious about her commitment to health. I don't mean to speak ill of the dead, but she was a . . . was a . . . was a . . . she wasn't a good employee."

Mac thought she might be seeing the true Patti now. She nudged her a little further. "I don't mean to speak ill of the dead, either, but Rayne and I had our difficulties. I liked her a lot . . . until she, well until I caught her with my boyfriend. Maybe that's TMI."

"Oh, God." Patti shook her head in disgust, holding Mac's gaze. "She went after my boyfriend with everything she had!" Her voice had started to rise and now she glanced over her shoulder. "I really don't like gossip, but I've got to say, I'm surprised you're even trying to be nice about her. I can't. I'm sorry. She's just . . ." She sighed. "Taking a selfie and falling over a cliff? That sounds just like her. But I am sorry she's dead. I wouldn't wish that on anyone." She lifted her hands as if Mac had accused her of feeling otherwise. "I'll get you the paperwork. There's a onetime initiation fee and then we charge monthly to a credit or debit card."

Mac strolled back toward the counter as Patti slipped around the side and into a back room. She returned a few moments later with a sheaf of papers, which she handed to Mac. "You can fill it out here, or turn it in later . . .?"

"I'll come back." She hesitated, glancing at Giselle, who was looking through some papers, but had one eye on the front door. Maybe waiting for someone? To Patti, she added, "Hope it worked out for you and your boyfriend. It didn't for me."

"Oh, it did for me." She was loudly positive about that. She shot Giselle a look that the other woman didn't see, and Mac wondered if maybe Seth wasn't as tied into the relationship as Patti would like. Remembering how angry Seth and Patti had been at the Waystation that first time she'd seen them there, and the second, too, it seemed like there might be trouble in paradise.

"Well, that's good," Mac said with a smile. She'd just started to turn on her heel when she saw Seth approaching outside the glass entrance doors, taking the front steps two at a time. He was in sweats and apparently coming to work.

"There he is now," Patti declared.

Mac tried to duck her head and sneak out with a faint smile of greeting and nothing more as she didn't want to brace him in front of the two women at the desk. Seth, however, did a double take on her. In fact, his eyes did such a thorough inventory Mac had insight into what was feeding Patti's insecurity. It worried her that maybe he remembered her, but he moved right on by and up to Patti. Mac glanced back as she passed through the glass doors and Seth was now chatting up Giselle while Patti's lips were frozen into a hard smile.

Mac was almost to her SUV when Seth suddenly came back outside.

"Hey," he called.

Mackenzie looked up and around, as if expecting him

to be hailing someone else. Her pulse sped up. Maybe this interview was going to happen sooner than she expected. She'd wanted to talk to him, yes, but Seth Keppler was an unknown quantity. She regarded him politely as he moved her way across the parking lot. She hadn't really paid that much attention to his physique, more to his hipster look, but now she saw the muscles stretching the fabric of his body-hugging jacket.

"You were talking about Rayne," he stated flatly.

"Um, yeah. She told me how great Good Livin' was."

"You had a falling-out with her. What's your name? I don't remember you."

"Well, I don't know you, either. Rayne and I were more acquaintances than friends."

"You look familiar."

Mackenzie nodded. "I've heard that before. I remind people of their sister or someone on TV. Happens all the time."

"No . . . I'll think of it," he said, narrowing his eyes.

She almost dropped the act right then and there. She wanted to know if he was Rayne's latest boyfriend. She could believe he was cheating on Patti, although she seemed to have a pretty tight leash on him. But Seth was the kind of guy who would look for a way to slip that leash.

She smiled and climbed into her RAV. He was now going to know her vehicle, have her license number, if he cared to memorize it. Could he look her up from that? She suspected an enterprising crook could learn a lot with a minimum amount of trouble.

She watched Seth return to Good Livin' before she pulled out of the lot.

I'll think of it.

It put her nerves on edge.

* * *

Taft wasn't the most domestic male when it came to housework, but he was vacuuming the furniture for all it was worth. Tommy had returned from his latest sojourn to Vegas and had picked up the pugs. After wondering if his neighbor was ever coming back and if he was, by default, now the owner of two dogs, Taft was feeling bereft that the pugs were gone. Carnoff had suffered an ankle injury on the vacation and extended his trip by a week to recover. He'd thought he'd left a message on Taft's phone and had only learned it hadn't gone through when he showed up at Taft's door, wearing slippers and using a cane. His girlfriend had flown back solo.

"Sorry, Jesse," Tommy had said, thrown from his usual panache.

"No problem. How are you doing?"

He'd lifted his cane to prove that he could stand without its help. "Damn nuisance, but it's getting better. Thank you."

"I like having them around," Taft had told Tommy sincerely.

Carnoff's eyes had twinkled. "Be careful what you wish for."

Now Taft finished his task, put the vacuum away, then headed into the kitchen and the refrigerator. His mind was full of problems. He'd learned a few things recently about Mangella that had chilled his blood and he was still working out what to do about them. There was a thread that tied Mangella to Seth Keppler and it was that thread that had made him pull Mackenzie Laughlin off surveillance. He knew she felt like he'd abandoned her, but he didn't want her anywhere near Keppler until he fully understood the link between the two men.

She's an ex-cop. She knows the risks.

"Yeah, well . . . maybe . . ." He reached into the refrigerator and took out a beer. He wanted to work with her and wanted to protect her at the same time.

Things were winding up at the thrift shop when the bike donation came in. Emma watched the man wheel in the child's bike as Theo was in the back room. "It's just the right size," she told him.

"Yeah? My daughter outgrew it. Can I get a receipt?"

Emma very carefully pulled out the pad of receipts. This was the tricky part. She had no idea what it was worth. Calculating amounts fell into the blank spot of her brain. Harley had told her it was her superpower that she couldn't use numbers very well.

"It's not a numbers game for you," Harley had told her. "That's brilliant."

Emma was still trying to figure out what she'd meant.

Theo came out of the back room with Dummy trotting at her heels. Seeing him made Emma worry about Duchess. She'd left Ian, the skunky-smelling guy who had liked Harley, in charge because she didn't have anyone else. But when she thought about it, it made her feel itchy all over.

Theo quickly scribbled out a receipt and handed it to the man, who folded it into his pocket and left, doffing his baseball cap to them on the way out. "'Doffing' is a good word," Emma told Theo.

"He did doff his hat, didn't he?" Theo smiled. Dummy started barking and standing on his hind legs. This is what he did whenever he got jealous of Theo's attention being elsewhere.

"Stop it, Bartholomew," Theo said, tsk-tsking the little dog in a teasing way. This only made Dummy bark and jump more.

"Should we tag the bike for Paige and Brianne?" asked Emma.

"Yeah, let's. They've maybe come up with a different plan, but I'll call Kendra and we'll keep it for them just in case."

Emma taped a RESERVED sign on the bike. She thought Paige and Brianne might be brats but their mom was frazzled and it would be good for them to have a bike. The bike that Emma had wanted had been purchased and was long gone. That was the way things went at Theo's Thrift Shop.

Emma stayed till closing and Theo drove her to the bus stop as it had started to rain pretty hard. Emma rode the bus and thought about different things, her mind getting hung up on what Jewell had told her.

"Rayne's friend is dead. It looks like her husband did it."

Emma's thoughts had immediately flown back to her own attack. It was always blurry but she knew what had happened. Her heart started thumping and she squeezed her eyes shut, even though she could still see inside her head. "I see his eyes!"

"Oh, shhh. Shhh!" Jewell had started flapping her hands and looking around. "I forgot, Emma. Stop it. You're making a scene! Stop, stop!"

Emma had forced herself to come back from that dark place. She panted hard, sat down on a chair, and put her head between her knees like she'd been told to do whenever she got upset. Get the air moving through. A lot of the fear had passed since Jamie and Harley had moved back to River Glen and she had a family. She knew how to get herself under control before she was out of control. It was a lot better now.

"I'm sorry," said Jewell. "I shouldn't have told you. I just wanted you to be prepared."

Emma's eyes had had little tears in them, but she'd swiped them away. "You just wanted to be first to tell me."

"Well, that's not . . . that's kind of . . . I'm not that way."

Jewell *was* kind of that way.

The bus left Emma off and she walked back to Ridge Pointe. Bob, one of the administrators, smiled at her and asked her how her day was. Emma told him it was good. That's all he really wanted to hear. Then she walked down to her room and got Duchess on a leash, and the two of them went for a long walk around the building three times before dinner.

As Emma stopped at the edge of the dining room, surveying the area for a table—her favorite table was already taken—she saw that "tall drink of water," as Jewell called the man, work his way into the dining room with a cane and wearing slippers. The ladies Jewell often ate with liked him a lot and they were seated at a table near the window tonight. The man pointed the cane at their table and they all smiled and tittered as he winked at them. He liked Emma, too. More than once he'd tried to sit at a table with her, but Jewell had steered him back to the ladies' table, so Emma had never said anything to him.

His name was Tommy and he knew one of Jewell's friends, Maureen, best. Maureen had been at Ridge Pointe Independent and Assisted Living about as long as Emma had. They said she'd had a stroke. One of her arms didn't work too well. She'd been Tommy's "main squeeze" before her unfortunate stroke. Now she was happy to see him, but she was kind of a drifter, too. The rumor was that if there was room in Memory Care soon, she would probably go. Mrs. Throckmorton might be going there, too. They cared for your brain there, which was good because Maureen and Mrs. Throckmorton did not seem to be able to care for their brains on their own. Emma had to keep telling them her name.

The cat rubbed against Emma's ankles, but her attention was on the dining room. It looked like she wanted to cross the threshold and join the diners, so Emma lifted a finger to the cat and warned, "No . . ." The cat stepped back and curled herself near the wall on the invisible line to the hallway.

The older man had the ladies laughing, but then he tipped his hat to Maureen and started to head out. He saw Emma as she claimed a small table just inside the door. He smiled at her, but Emma did not smile back because Jewell and the other ladies who liked him didn't want her to talk to him.

"It's just not seemly," Jewell had told her.

"Seemly?" Emma had repeated.

"It wouldn't be right for a man his age to talk to a girl your age."

Emma had related this conversation to Jamie and Harley over dinner one night and Harley had choked on her glass of lemonade and said, "Aren't you like, forty?"

Jamie said, "I think what she's saying is that Emma is a lot younger than they are."

"Well, she's not a girl," Harley sniffed.

"I think they're jealous of me," Emma had revealed, which had made both Jamie and Harley look at her.

"I think you're right," said Jamie.

So now Emma didn't talk to the man, Tommy, unless he spoke to her first. When she did answer him, Jewell and her friends would look at her as if she'd done something wrong. It reminded Emma of some bad things from long ago, so she wished the man wouldn't talk to her, but today he did.

"You're looking well, Emma."

"You doffed your hat," she responded.

"I did, didn't I?" he agreed, his face wrinkling into a big smile. "How've you been today?"

Emma glanced over and saw everyone at Jewell's table was watching her. Everyone except Maureen, who was picking at her banana cream pie. "Are you Maureen's boyfriend?" she asked.

"I was, mostly, until Maureen had a . . . an unfortunate health crisis."

"She had a stroke."

"Yes. She doesn't really remember me anymore now. We used to go on trips together. Halfway around the world. A couple of Mediterranean cruises. Made it to Australia once."

"That's an ocean away."

"It sure is. Have you ever been to Las Vegas, Emma?"

"No."

"A lot of people call it Lost Wages and there's a reason for that. You can lose your shirt." He chuckled and then the smile slowly disappeared. "I can't take Maureen with me anymore. I still go, but I go with other friends." He glanced back at the table and Emma saw he was gazing sadly at Maureen.

"You don't have to give me your life story," she said soberly.

"I'm sorry if I bored you."

"I'm not bored," said Emma. She, too, looked again at the ladies at Jewell's table. "They don't like me talking to you."

Tommy nodded. "Don't let it stop you. I only talk to them because Maureen is with them. I've seen you with your dog. She's a beauty."

Emma frowned. "She's a mutt."

"I have two pugs. Maybe they can meet your dog sometime? Walk around the outside of the building here? Go to a dog park?"

Emma thought that over. "Duchess has a friend named . . . Dummy."

"Dummy?" Tommy's brows lifted.

"He has a dumb name."

"Duchess is your dog?"

"She might be friends with yours. She's friends with Dummy."

"I'll check back with you and maybe we can introduce them to each other sometime."

"Okay."

He turned and nodded to the ladies at Jewell's table one more time before heading out. The cat batted at his foot as he went by but missed him. Emma looked at the cat, who was now gazing steadfastly into the room.

"You stay there," Emma said to her as Jewell suddenly plopped down in the chair opposite hers.

"What did Tommy say to you?" she demanded.

Emma thought it was kind of rude of Jewell, who was always big on telling someone the rules but not so good at obeying them herself. "He said he had two pugs. Pugs are dogs."

"I know what pugs are. Those are Maureen's pugs. She

helped him get them." Jewell's nostrils flared. "Did he ask you on a date?"

Emma immediately felt uncomfortable. She didn't want to lie to Jewell, but she didn't want to tell her that Tommy had said they would get their dogs together. "He doffed his hat," she finally said, relieved she had some kind of answer.

"He's a very attractive man and, I'm not saying who, but some of the women here would really like to go on a date with him. You and I both know it would be inappropriate for you to go with him, so maybe you could tell him as much. I'm not one to gossip, but he has a bit of a reputation. I don't want you to be taken advantage of, or hurt in any way."

Emma felt her chest tighten and forced herself not to think about being hurt. Though she couldn't feel it anymore, she knew she had a big, jagged scar on her back from a knife wound. "I don't want to be hurt," she agreed.

"Well, it's just best if you keep out of Tom Carnoff's way. He's a regular Casanova with pretty women."

Emma went back to her room a few minutes later. The cat followed her down the hallway and at her door, Emma held up her finger to it once more. "You stay away," she ordered.

She didn't want the cat sleeping with her, that was for sure. The cat cocked its head as Emma opened her door. One sharp bark from Duchess and the feline trotted away.

CHAPTER TWELVE

"So, what do you do all day? I mean, what's a typical day like?" Harley asked, stabbing lettuce and tomato bits on the tines of her fork, sticking them in her mouth and chewing the salad.

Cooper gave Jamie's daughter a look. She'd been dogging him when he was at the house, asking questions. Jamie had noticed it, too. Now, at tonight's dinner, she apparently was finally coming out with it.

"What do you want to know?" Jamie asked Harley now.

"Marissa and I were talking about jobs, and I just thought I'd ask what it's like to be a police detective. Like, do you have a routine, or is it just whatever happens, happens."

Cooper had also heard some of this from his stepdaughter. Marissa was Harley's best friend and clearly they'd had some kind of discussion between the two of them. "A combination of both, I'd say. I check in, see what's waiting for me, maybe write up a report, add to it. Research. Keep following an investigation. Try to answer questions that still remain unless something comes up that takes me away from the department."

"Why are you asking?" Jamie regarded Harley intently.

Harley opened her mouth to say something and Cooper

read her like he had so many others during his time as a detective. He knew she was about to lie. But she glanced at his face and he saw her course-correct.

"I think I'd be a good detective. I want a job," she said.

Jamie made a sound of disbelief. "You're kidding."

"I knew you'd say that," Harley groaned.

Cooper intervened before things got heated. "You have good instincts. Both you and your mom read people really well. So, work toward it."

"I mean I need a job now," Harley said, dropping all pretense. "I want to earn some money. I thought I could maybe help you somehow."

"The department has a budget and it's pretty tight right now. Overtime's been cut back and . . ." He didn't finish. The disappointment on her face said she'd gotten the message.

"Emma said you talked about working at Ridge Pointe," Jamie reminded. She'd stopped eating her own plate of chicken and rice and salad to gaze at her daughter, but now picked up her fork again.

"Well . . ." Harley pushed her plate aside. Cooper noticed the way she'd moved the chicken around without eating it and only nibbled at the rice. Jamie had said she was flirting with vegetarianism but after a few days she would dig into burgers, chicken, pork, whatever. That was Harley through and through these days. Trying to figure out the person she wanted to be. Marissa was the same way.

Cooper thought about Bibi Engstrom's death. The Crime Lab hadn't fully ruled it a homicide, but it wasn't an accident, and suicide, not by carbon monoxide poisoning but by smoke and *fire* from the candle—taken from inside the house, according to Hank Engstrom—was outside the norm, to say the least. And though Bibi's husband had explained about the candle and was an emotional mess, Cooper wasn't completely convinced it was real grief. Verbena had discovered another woman, and Engstrom had immediately lied about her, claiming she was just a friend, which was incriminating. Maybe she was a friend, and maybe she wasn't. The investigation continued.

Detective Elena Verbena, his partner, of sorts, as she'd never been fully named as such, was now heading up the case. Cooper had ceded control, mainly to get Ricky Richards out of the scene. Verbena understood, and they'd basically closed ranks to protect the investigation. Richards was all over the place and Cooper had thought of alerting the chief, but Bennihof wasn't known for backing up his detectives. As chief of police, he was better at schmoozing with the mayor of River Glen and other local government notables. He was a political choice who had mostly been hands off, metaphorically speaking, with his department. However, there were recent rumors that he was "hands on" in other ways. Cooper had yet to verify those rumors. Bennihof hadn't come on to Verbena, but then Verbena was secure in her position. She was a tough, forty-something Latina who took no prisoners. When she got the bit in her teeth she ran until she dropped. If Verbena took on the chief, Cooper was betting on her.

One bit of detail they'd learned was that a blue car had been seen driving out of the cul-de-sac road about forty-five minutes before the explosion that the witness, who lived on the street, didn't recognize. "A Cadillac, I think," he'd told them. It wasn't any of the neighbors', and it had just caught his eye because it reminded him of one his parents had once owned. Maybe it was nothing, but currently it was about all they had.

And then Mackenzie Laughlin was still investigating Rayne Sealy's death. The ex-cop seemed to think it might be linked in some way to Bibi Engstrom's. The department had closed the books on that one, but had she really climbed over that railing to take a picture? It wasn't as if she would be getting a better shot of the chasm and river below, and nothing about her other online pictures read "daredevil." She wasn't into the great outdoors. She was into people and partying.

What had she been doing at the overlook? Had she planned to meet someone? It didn't seem like the kind of place she'd go alone. Cooper had spent a difficult hour with Rayne's mother and sister, breaking the news of her death, and even though they'd been in shock, the sister had burst out that Rayne was selfish and mean-spirited and probably got what she deserved. Then she'd broken into a flood of tears and remorse and said she loved her anyway. The mother had just shaken her head and held her hand to her mouth while tears flowed. Alerting families to tragedy was one of the hardest parts of Cooper's job.

Harley took her plate to the sink and said, "Those old people are crazy at Ridge Pointe," bringing Cooper out of his reverie.

Jamie said dryly, "Not the best attitude if you want a job there."

"I think you said I wanted a job there."

"Because that's what *you* said."

Harley snorted and headed out of the kitchen. Jamie watched her go, then looked at Cooper. "Let it be said, I do not want her to become a cop. I have enough angst dealing with your job."

"Angst," Cooper said, smiling faintly.

"Yes, angst. On late nights, I worry."

He started to reassure her, but she shook her head. She didn't want promises he had no way of keeping. "Noted, about Harley," he said instead.

Taft trudged up the three stone stairs to Mitch Mangella's house with heavy footsteps. He'd worked for the man, one of River Glen's local heroes, in a sense, for a number of years and the demise of their relationship was both sad and a relief.

But something wasn't right in Mudville. Taft had learned from a sometime confidential informant that Seth Keppler was moving fentanyl. How, he wasn't sure yet. The CI didn't know either, but even worse was learning that there was a connection to Mangella. Taft had pulled Laughlin off the Keppler surveillance because of what he'd learned, and the fact that Mangella had started asking about her. Even now, the thought sent a cold bolt of fear to Taft's heart.

Seth Keppler had moved from small-time dealer to the big leagues, and Mangella might be right there with him.

The door opened and Prudence Mangella stood there, treating him to her slightly crooked and knowing smile. "Hello, Jesse. Have you finally come to take me away from all this?" She leaned her cheek in for a kiss and he managed to do the deed without giving away his dark thoughts.

"That's why I'm here," he said.

She chuckled and moved away. She was wearing a belted robe as if she were getting ready for bed though it was barely eight o'clock. Mangella himself came downstairs at that moment, striding down the blood-red carpet runner, having heard Taft arrive.

"Brandy?" he asked, heading into the walnut bookshelf– lined den. The books were classics, displayed for the gold titles on their spines. Mangella read financial reports only.

"Thanks, no." Taft tried to inject just the right note of regret in his words.

"Oh, come on, man. Loosen up. We're celebrating." Mangella slid the doors closed, then poured two snifters and handed one to him, touching the glasses together. The sound was a soft *clink*, but it reverberated in Taft's head.

"What are we celebrating?"

"A job well done."

"I haven't done any jobs for you recently."

"Haven't you?"

Taft stared into Mangella's dark eyes. "What are you trying to tell me?" he asked. Might as well face the music, whatever it was. Let the chips fall where they may.

Prudence slid open the doors at that moment and stuck her face in. "Why am I not invited?"

"Because you're a problem." Mangella moved swiftly to gently push her out and re-closed the doors. She rattled them but knew when her man wasn't kidding around.

"You went to the police the other night. Your friend, Mackenzie? She was there."

The coldness in Taft's heart spread throughout his chest. How did Mangella know? Bennihof? They ran in the same social circle even though Mangella had a dicey relation- ship with law enforcement. The man tiptoed along the edge of the law and everyone knew it.

Richards? He was still trying to romance Pru. And get ahead in the department. It was a problem for another time.

"That's right," Taft answered.

"What were you doing there?"

The question was casual even though he knew his answer would be examined carefully. Taft thought about it carefully. There was a hard line Taft would never cross, but Mangella didn't share the same sense of right and wrong.

"Ms. Laughlin believes Bibi Engstrom was killed. By her husband, maybe. Or, it might be linked to someone else, something else. Not an accident and she doesn't think it was suicide."

"Ms. Laughlin was once a detective with River Glen's finest."

Taft nodded. His answer had Mangella looking pensive.

"She was following Seth Keppler," said Mangella.

"You know Keppler?" Taft asked. A question he would normally never pose.

"You put her onto him."

The conversation was fraught with danger. Taft needed to shut it down. "Bibi Engstrom hired Laughlin to find out what happened to Rayne Sealy, the woman who died taking a selfie at the overlook. Rayne was missing and Bibi wanted to find her. She told Laughlin that Rayne's last boyfriend was Seth Keppler."

"What do you know about Keppler?"

What do you?

"I've heard he's a low-level drug dealer and I don't like drug dealers."

"Oh, I know." Mangella's eyes thinned. "Your sister, and all that."

Taft's blood started to boil. This was an area Mangella had never trespassed into in the years Taft had worked for him.

"I don't like drug dealers, either, you know," he said. "I think Seth Keppler's a problem. I've been interested in a partnership with Andrew Best, and Keppler is friends with Best but his side hustle is in the way. This partnership's been a little secretive and I . . . didn't expect to run into you during negotiations."

This was Mangella feeling him out. It sounded like an apology, but it was anything but. The truth was Taft had first learned of Seth Keppler's extracurricular activities through one of his other clients. A man whose daughter had gotten mixed up with drugs and wanted someone like Taft to dig up the details because he didn't trust the police. There had been rumors for years that drugs had infiltrated River Glen High School and the community at large, but it wasn't until the daughter went to college that her habit was uncovered . . . and a friend of hers overdosed and died.

Taft had taken the job and begun following Seth. The guy was a playboy of sorts, playing one woman off another, taking up with Rayne and then ending up with Patti, who seemed to be clamped onto him in a way other women hadn't managed. Or, maybe she was just Keppler's way to prove his legitimacy. Mangella was acting like Keppler was a stranger to him, but Taft had information that said otherwise.

"Better drink some of that. It's too expensive to waste." Mangella smiled.

Taft took a swallow. He needed the man to think he was able to turn a blind eye. "Laughlin isn't interested in Seth Keppler any longer."

"Good. I wouldn't want her to get in the way."

"In the way of what?" asked Taft lightly.

"Anything." He smiled. "She seems like a nice girl."

Was that a threat? Mangella wasn't being totally honest, but then when had he ever? Taft set the half-filled glass down carefully on a side table. If Mangella was into the drug business, he was going to personally take him down.

Mangella relaxed a bit. "I've always liked that you're a straight shooter, Taft. We work well together."

"We have," he agreed.

"Laughlin is off base with whatever she thinks Keppler's done. Maybe you can tell her. He wouldn't harm this Engstrom woman . . . or the selfie taker."

"Rayne Sealy."

He grunted an assent. "Just get the ex-cop to move on."

"She has," said Taft. *But I haven't.* If Seth Keppler was distributing a powerful opiod like fentanyl, Taft was going to take him down. And Mangella, too, if it came to that.

Mangella tried to fill his glass with more brandy and Taft spent a few minutes dancing around the issue before he could take his leave. Once he was finally free of Mangella and back in his Rubicon, he breathed easier. His face set. Part of him felt like he'd lost a friend, but another part knew he'd never really had one. Mangella had been a source of income, nothing more.

And now he'd crossed that hard line.

He pulled into his parking spot under the carport and walked through a misting rain to his front door, unlocked his condo, and stepped inside. Swiping the rain from his hair he saw Helene standing near the kitchen bar.

You can't blame everyone for what happened to me.

"I only blame the ones that matter," Taft said aloud.

It was my fault, too.

"I don't care," Taft said, angry, knowing he was talking

to himself, aware in a way that this was his Great White Whale, unwilling to let it go.

Don't make it a crusade, the vision warned.

"Too late," he whispered.

Mac's stepsister leaned her head against her husband's chest, closed her eyes, and said, "Mmmm," as she chewed a bite of one of River Glen Grill's classic appetizers, grilled artichokes with their own take on hollandaise. Nolan laughed and set down his fork as he was unable to lift the utensil to his lips.

"You know, food tastes really good," Stephanie said. Her brown hair was swept up into a bun and tiny diamond studs winked at her ears. She seemed to have a smile on her face at all times.

"All food?" Mac asked.

"All food," she agreed. "I'm going to be a blimp if I don't watch it."

Mac looked at her stepsister's still-svelte figure. "Yeah, sure," she said dryly and Nolan laughed.

The three of them were on an impromptu dinner date. Mac had gotten back to their house to find Stephanie and Nolan in a flurry to meet their reservation time and they insisted she go with them, though she'd tried to demur. Now she was glad she'd come. It was nice to see how happy they were. All three of them had rushed out, so Mac was still in her blue shirt and jeans. She'd spent the day trying to get more information on Bibi's death, which was still not declared whether it was a homicide or suicide. The evidence collected at the site precluded an accident. Mac didn't for one second believe it was suicide, but she wasn't about to throw out her theories when she was trying to wheedle information from the police department.

Stephanie and Nolan were a little more dressed up. Nolan had changed into pressed chinos and a white shirt and Stephanie was in a loosely fitting blue jersey dress, which, though she wasn't showing, was one she'd specifically pulled from the back of her closet to have front and center.

They'd been bustled in to their table as they were ten minutes late, and had ordered in a hurry. Now they were relaxing a bit and Mac was sipping on vodka, cranberry juice, and seltzer.

She hadn't heard from Taft since that last conversation. It had been kind of disconcerting, the way he'd acted like the job was over and he was done working with her. Had her meeting with Patti and Seth bothered him more than he let on? Maybe he'd been against it. He'd shut down on Seth as if he didn't even want to talk about him anymore.

And what did you accomplish anyway?

She was beating herself up over her ruse at Good Livin'. She was no detective. She wasn't even a cop any longer.

"I'm going to hit the restroom," she said, scooting back her chair. Nolan and Stephanie were teasing each other and generally looking lovingly into each other's eyes. Nice as it was, it was getting on Mac's nerves.

She cruised by the bar on her way to the ladies' room and saw a woman seated with her back to her. Something about her was familiar, so she slowed her steps, seeking to get a look. She could almost see past her to her companion, and when she finally got a clear look at his face, she received a distinct shock. Troi with an *i* Bevins. His long hair was combed and slicked back from his head. There was a diamond stud in his ear. His head was slightly turned and she could make out a tattoo behind his ear, maybe. But the man was definitely Troi. And the woman . . . ?

Mackenzie was trying not to stare and gain Troi's attention. Then the woman laughed, a bit sarcastically. She'd heard that voice somewhere recently. With the long dark hair and skin-tight jeans that left a spare tire of flesh at the waist beneath a carmine tunic . . . She turned at that moment and Mac got a profile shot. The streak of bleached blond hair curving in at her chin . . . Elise! Rayne's sister. With Troi Bevins.

Well, that was interesting. Mac continued to the bathroom, but hurried through her ablutions so she could see them again on her way out. They were still seated in place, but now Elise had scooched to the edge of her seat and Troi's hand was on the small of her back, definitely edging lower.

She debated approaching Elise. It could be an opportunity to meet Troi, who was suspected of being one of Rayne's boyfriends. Was Troi, then, the boyfriend that Sharon Sealy said Rayne had supposedly stolen from Elise? Elise had denigrated Troi in their conversation the night Mac interviewed her and her mother, but maybe that was why.

As she was dithering what to do, Troi suddenly gave Elise's rear a little love pat and got to his feet. He whispered something in her ear as he headed Mac's way. She realized he was coming to the restroom area and she whipped out her phone and pretended to be lost in it.

"You'll get little frown lines if you're not careful," he said to her as he breezed by. Mackenzie looked up to see him smiling back at her a bit drunkenly. His head was cocked and she could clearly see the tattoo image was of a key.

"I'll remember that," she said, purposely clearing her brow.

He winked at her and kept going. She would have said he was strutting if he hadn't stumbled a bit. Rayne clearly went for a type, or maybe they went for her.

Mackenzie took the opportunity to cruise by Elise, who was once again wearing an abundance of makeup but her face was lit up, radiant even. Mac pretended to look over at an empty bar seat and then focused on Elise. She lifted her brows as if she'd just recognized her. "Hi . . . Elise, isn't it? Rayne's sister?"

"Oh! God . . . yes . . ." Elise blinked a few times. "You're the one who was asking about Rayne, Bibi's friend." Hearing her own sour tone, her eyes widened and she added, aghast, "Isn't it terrible how they both died? You knew that, right. You must have heard. It's terrible!"

The anguish in her voice sounded real enough, so Mac went with it. "Terrible," she agreed.

"I know. Well, and I guess you know, I was so mad at Rayne. But now she's gone . . . and then Bibi." She shuddered. "Her husband must've done it. They were fighting so much and she was so dramatic and I just thought . . . I don't know. He probably did it."

"Or, it was suicide," Mac tried out on her.

"Well, I don't know about that. Are you still investigating for her? No? Right . . . ? Now that they're both gone?"

"I guess not."

Mac saw Troi returning. He seemed to be looking around the room, as if checking out the scene. There were a number of young women in groups and his eye caressed one blond woman who was just meeting a group, bending over to air-kiss her friends, her rounded bottom almost close enough for Troi to touch. For a minute Mac thought he was actually going to do it, reach out and touch her, and she braced herself for the affront and confrontation. But it didn't happen. Troi kept his hand to himself and headed Elise's way. Seeing Mac there he looked slightly alarmed. "Well, hey," he said.

"Hi. Oh, you're together?" Mac asked, feigning surprise.

"You know Troi," said Elise.

"Well, no—" Mac started, but Troi interrupted.

"We just saw each other over there." He waved in the direction of the restrooms.

"I'm Mackenzie," Mac said, taking control.

"Hey," he greeted her again, lifting his chin. "Troi. So, you and Elise know each other?"

"She's the one I told you about who was looking into Rayne's disappearance," put in Elise. "That's when we didn't know what had happened to her."

"Oh." Troi gave Mackenzie a worried look.

"It was a tragedy," said Mackenzie.

"Yeah . . . Rayne . . . yeah . . ."

Elise swallowed and it looked like she wanted to say something but was forcing herself not to.

Mac pressed, "Elise said you dated Rayne."

"Oh, well . . . yeah . . . a little . . . she worked at that nursing home . . ."

"Ridge Pointe," Elise bit out, as if she couldn't help herself. "Before Good Livin' and before the Coffee Club. Rayne changed boyfriends and jobs at the same rate . . . fast."

So much for grief over her sister's death.

"Yeah . . ." Troi shot Elise an uncertain look.

"And now you two are together?" Mac asked lightly, pointing back and forth between them.

"We dated in the past." Elise's voice was brittle.

"Oh." Mac looked to Troi.

"And we're dating again," he said a big goofily. It was a move made to jolly Elise out of her mood, one Mac suspected he used quite a bit. Troi just seemed like that kind of guy.

Elise was looking away, glaring into the middle distance. Maybe she was recalling how it felt when her sister had stolen her boyfriend.

"Well, it was nice meeting you," Mac said to Troi, who answered, "Same," as Mac headed back to her table.

"We almost sent the search squad out for you," Stephanie said when Mac returned.

"Just ran into some people I know."

"That's River Glen for you. You can't go anywhere without bumping into someone you know," said Nolan.

"You're not even from here," said Stephanie to her tall, dark-haired husband, giving him an elbow poke.

"No, but you are."

Mackenzie had finished most of her meal before she'd gone to the restroom and now left the rest on her plate. Stephanie got a doggy bag for herself and Nolan, and they headed back to their house.

Once they were home, Mackenzie waited for a chance to talk to Nolan alone. "You worked for Best Homes before Laidlaw."

"That's right."

"Did you know a guy called Troi Bevins?"

Nolan slowly shook his head. "I don't think so. Why?"

"He's someone I've run across in the course of some investigative work I'm doing. What about Seth Keppler?"

"Well . . . yeah. Seth worked off and on for Best." He spread his hands. "Andrew put up with him. God knew why."

"Andrew Best?"

Nolan nodded. "Andrew went hunting with Seth a few times together, so maybe that was it, but Seth was a slacker at work. They had a couple falling-outs. Seth left to work at a health club."

"Good Livin'. The one near the hospital."

"Sounds right. I don't know if they're still friends. I took the job with Laidlaw and haven't kept in contact with Andrew since then. Andrew can be difficult. He hired Granger Nye and became even more difficult. That's when I left. Nye has my position with the company now. Andrew's right-hand man. Better for all of us." Nolan gave Mackenzie a studied look. "What's your interest?"

"I'm still trying to figure out who Rayne Sealy was seeing."

"I'd be careful around those guys. They play hard."

Mackenzie tried again. "But you never heard of Troi Bevins? Troi with an 'i'?"

He shrugged. "If he's working for Best Homes, he must've come on after I left."

"Okay. Thanks."

She could tell he wanted to ask her more questions, but she wasn't ready to talk about what she was doing. Stephanie had already said she was tired and headed to her bedroom and now Mac did the same. Once alone, in the pink and white room, she sat on the bed and did some serious thinking. Time to figure out some things.

She swept up her cell phone from where she'd tossed it on the bed beside her and weighed the idea of calling Taft. He wouldn't appreciate any of the choices she'd made; she knew that. Still . . . Her fingers hovered over the keypad. In the end she clicked the phone off. Maybe Taft would call her for a new assignment. No reason to change his mind before that happened.

* * *

The cat washed one white-mittened paw with her tongue, rubbing the paw over her black face, cleaning off the white, fluffy cream that the man who smelled like skunk had squirted at her. When he'd first done that she'd run away. She didn't like the way it felt. But the cream was good, so now she stayed nearby whenever he was around, hoping he would put it in a bowl for her, which sometimes he did.

Today he'd lifted up a leg and shot it at her from under his knee. "Pew, pew, pew," he'd said as the cream hit her. "Gotcha!" he declared.

"Ian!" One of the people in the room with all the good smells looked up from where she was stirring a big, steaming pot. The swinging door to the room closed, but not before the cat saw the woman point a big wooden spoon at the man.

"Sorry," he said to the cat. "Duty calls." He pushed through the door and the cat continued cleaning herself. She caught that scent again. Stronger and let her cool gaze travel around the occupants in the dining room.

Finished cleaning, she strolled down one of the hallways, tail high.

Chapter Thirteen

Mac slowed as she drove by the charred remains of Bibi and Hank Engstrom's nearly destroyed home. Half of it was dankly smelling wet timbers and ash. The other half stood dispirited and dilapidated. Hank Engstrom, Bibi's husband, was considered a person of interest and maybe he was the arsonist and murderer. She would have liked to interview him herself, but knew better than to get in the way of the department's investigation at this point. The crime tech team hadn't made a definitive announcement as yet, but in Mac's mind Bibi's death was a homicide. And if that were true and the perpetrator wasn't Bibi's estranged husband . . . then who was it, and what was the motive?

She wished she knew more about Bibi herself, but their relationship hadn't been that deep. Bibi had been in an unhappy marriage and was facing divorce. She'd been clear about that. And she'd been worried first, about Rayne's disappearance and second, that her death wasn't an accident. Bibi had been convinced that Rayne's demise was linked to her mysterious new boyfriend. Maybe Seth Keppler, maybe Troi Bevins . . . or maybe someone else.

Though Rayne's death had been ruled accidental, a foolish and dangerous attempt at a selfie, Mackenzie didn't completely go along with that, either. Bibi's subsequent murder was so fast on the heels of Rayne's death that it seemed like it couldn't be a coincidence.

Maybe she was on a wild goose chase, but Mac was planning on connecting with Troi Bevins later today and asking about his relationships with both Rayne and Elise Sealy to see how, and if, they might play into Rayne's death. She wanted to talk to Seth Keppler as well, but she was still trying to work that one out. He already felt he recognized her and he had a menacing attitude that may or may not be all bravado. She was betting on the former, and well, she didn't want to get in Taft's way, either.

For now she had a few hours to kill. She'd told herself to put her mind to finding an apartment—as much as Stephanie had suggested she stay with her till the baby arrived, she couldn't help feeling like an intruder—but she had no energy for that just yet. It was the kind of task that just zapped strength.

As she drove on she realized she was aiming toward the direction of the trail that led to Percy Peak and the overlook where Rayne had died. She hadn't really planned on following Rayne's footsteps today, but it suddenly sounded like a good idea.

The weather didn't agree, however. As Mac parked at the side of the strip mall, rain suddenly pounded down on the roof of her RAV, bouncing in silver streaks on her hood. She waited inside the vehicle and let a sheet of water wash over her windshield, obscuring everything for a time. March was almost over. If this was a prelude to April showers, next month was going to be a doozy.

She waited, but it didn't let up, and Mac realized how

hungry she was. She switched on the ignition and pulled away from the trailhead, retracing her route to Miller's Market, whose deli she knew served up pastrami sandwiches that were pretty damn good.

She walked in and ordered her sandwich, watching the rain pour down through a window to the street, asking herself if it was really worth climbing up to the overlook in this weather. Once her sandwich was bagged, she moved to the counter where a girl with a sharp face eyed her hard. Her name tag read: CINDA.

"It's a sandwich," Mac heard herself say. The way she was being regarded, it felt like she was trying to buy alcohol underage. She'd tried that once and failed. She'd always looked too young.

"You're that cop?" the girl said, keeping eye contact as she slowly reached for Mac's sandwich, chips, and bottled water. Paul Miller, owner of Miller's Market, was one of the people around town who knew Mac well and had always appreciated having the police looking out for him and his store.

"I was," said Mac. "I'm no longer with the department."

The girl's shoulders slumped and she made a sour face. "Can you get them a message?"

"The police?"

She nodded.

"Yes . . ." Mac lifted her brows in a silent question.

"Will they listen to you?"

"Yes. I think so. What's the message?"

Mac was about to add that Cinda could call the department herself, when she jumped in with, "I saw that girl that killed herself, you know. *That day.* I'm pretty sure I helped her on *that day.* She came in here, to the market."

She stared at Mackenzie, chin out, daring her to argue with her.

Mac took a moment, then asked, "You mean Rayne Sealy?"

"Rain, rain, that's right. Like what we've got going right now." She hooked a thumb toward the windows where the rain had finally lessened a bit but was still a strong and steady drizzle. "She bought a bottle of wine."

"She bought a bottle of wine," Mac repeated.

"Yep." She spread her hands. "She wasn't going to drink it all by herself up there, was she? She was meeting someone. Probably at Percy's Peak. I know she stopped at the overlook to take a picture and she just was stupid, I guess. But she was meeting someone. So, where is he now, huh? Why didn't he come forward after she died? I suppose she could have been a *her*. But I'd bet it's a guy."

Mac thought that over. "What day was that?"

"THE SAME DAY. Are you listening? She went up there *the same day* she was here, buying that bottle of wine. A pinot. I had to card her. I remember she was practically running over the lady in front of her she was so revved. And she was wearing this red blouse, a nice one. I'm thinking maybe I was, like, the last person to see her alive. Freaky, right?"

She was working herself up. Mac saw that she'd had weeks to think about what happened to Rayne and was eager to be a part of the story.

"You'll tell them, right? You'll let them know that somebody was waiting for her. She wasn't going to drink that bottle alone. She was meeting someone. You can just tell."

Mac thought about pointing out that Rayne could just as easily have taken the bottle home with her, but sensed it wouldn't be received well. Cinda had made up her mind and that was that.

"I'll tell Detective Haynes," Mac told her, almost as a means to calm her down as she paid for her items.

She drove through the rain back to the trailhead. Mackenzie ate her sandwich and chips and drank from her bottle of water. She thought over what Cinda had told her. It jibed with her own thinking that maybe there was foul play involved, but she didn't really want to bring an alternative theory to the police. Rayne's case was closed and they would resent someone trying to reopen it. Haynes was fairly open-minded, and Elena Verbena could listen sometimes, but Bennihof liked things tied up and done with.

Could Rayne have been meeting someone, taking a bottle of wine with her? Rayne was known to be a very social person. She could have been meeting someone. Cinda had a point.

Huh.

Mac finished her sandwich and stared through the rain. Was it slowing? It looked like it was slowing. She glanced down at her apartment-hunting notes. There was a service that landlords paid into and posted their apartments for lease, which Mac could join as a would-be renter for a small fee. She'd resisted so far, but maybe it was time to invest in her future.

She eyed the rain again.

Are you believing Cinda because her idea fits with Bibi's certainty that Rayne's death was related to her new boyfriend?

The rain *was* slowing.

Mac made her decision, slapping on her Mariner's cap, stepping out into the precipitation. Bending her head to the wind, she aimed toward the trailhead. She held her jacket close to her neck and trudged up the strong incline.

She was huffing and puffing as she finally reached the overlook. Stopping, she glanced up the trail toward Percy's Peak, which was about a mile farther on. She took a moment to look around, then walked to the overlook rail and gazed downward to the cliff side and river far below. Had Rayne really hauled herself over the rail to stand where? On the teeny, crumbly ledge of land above the river? Maybe. People do crazy, dangerous things for the perfect selfie.

But the bottle of wine . . .

She searched around, kicking wet leaves and debris that had collected against the brush and the bole of a nearby tree. The crime techs had undoubtedly examined the area, but hadn't found anything to change their opinion that it was an accident, apparently.

Mac moved from the overlook and headed farther up the trail about twenty yards. She glanced back, her gaze scouring the area, which was all damp foliage, the trail covered by small sticks, stones, and debris above underlying mud. Hiking farther up the trail, she rounded a corner and stopped, eyeing the upward-winding track. Maybe Rayne had gone farther. Hiked with a friend to the peak before turning back to the overlook. But she'd been wearing a nice blouse. Was that really hiking gear?

Mackenzie worked her way back down, past the overlook, scouring the wet ground. She was about dead even with the closest of the three houses that backed up to the trail when her eye caught on something silvery poking out of a pile of wet debris.

She walked over to it and bent down. With the edge of her coat, she pulled a strip of foil from the dirt, leaves, and small sticks. It was red on one side, silver on the other, a ripped-off piece of the same kind of pliability that wound around the neck of wine bottles.

In her mind's eye she saw Rayne, in her nice, red blouse, pulling a cork from a bottle of wine, ripping off a piece of foil that had covered the cork in the process, smiling up at her companion.

Mac rewound her vision. She looked down the trail and could almost see Rayne hurrying up the path, eager to meet her latest lover, carrying the wine, bottle opener, and . . . glasses? In her . . . purse? Or a bag?

No purse or bag had been found. No cell phone.

Lost in the river . . . or . . .

Her mental vision shifted to the faceless lover. She saw the two of them sharing the wine. Pouring wine into glasses, or possibly both sipping from the bottle?

Mac stuffed the piece of foil into her coat pocket and hurried back down the trail, clutching her hood close, losing her grip on it and running bareheaded down the last part of the trail through the rain and gusts of wind.

She switched on the RAV's engine, backed out of her spot, and aimed the SUV toward Miller's Market again. This time she didn't bother with the hood as she hurried across the parking lot and into the store, glancing around for Cinda. Her heart clutched when she didn't see her at any of the checker stands. She walked past them, thinking hard. Then she saw her standing in front of the deli counter, apparently on break, jawing with one of the young women behind the counter.

Mac hurried her way. As she approached, Cinda glanced over at her. Recognizing Mac, she looked her up and down. "Wow. You really got wet."

The young woman at the deli leaned forward and comically grimaced. "You sure did!"

"Yep. It's wet out there," Mac said with a smile.

"Were you walking in the rain?" asked Cinda.

"As a matter of fact, I was. Can I talk to you for a minute?"

"Well, okay . . . but my break's almost over," said Cinda.

They stepped away from the girl at the deli counter and as soon as they were out of earshot Mac asked, "The day that Rayne came through your station. Do you happen to remember what kind of pinot she bought?"

With the amount of customers that had to have run through Cinda's station since Rayne's death, it was a long shot. But Cinda didn't hesitate.

"'Course I do. I buy it myself. Red Bridge. It's popular around here."

Mac felt a fizz of electricity run through her. She knew the local vineyard, which produced pinot noirs. The Willows. "You're sure about that?"

"Absolutely. Did you talk to the police?"

"Not yet."

"You're going to, right?" she asked, frowning.

She must've heard something in Mac's purposely neutral tone that suggested Mac might not, so Mac assured her she fully intended to speak with the River Glen PD. She just wanted to think about her theory for a little bit more first. "I plan to."

She thanked Cinda, then left her back at her station and walked to the wine section. She found Red Bridge tucked in beside other reds. Mac picked up a bottle and turned it over in her hands.

The foil was red on the outside. The same shade as the piece in her pocket. She picked at the foil with her thumbnail and folded back a tiny section. It was silver on the reverse side, just like the piece she had.

She took the bottle of wine to Cinda and purchased it before walking back into the rain, throwing up her hood belatedly over her wet hair.

Thad drove his pickup down Hawthorne Boulevard on the east side of the Willamette River, opposite Portland's city center, his wipers rhythmically slapping against the rain.

He'd determined he would go after Brenda Heilman, the easier of the two bitches first. *Things need to be in the right order.*

He knew the apartment complex where Brenda lived. She was a dental hygienist and worked at an office only a few blocks from where she rented. Her job almost made her sound decent, but in reality she was a dirty girl, like Rayne. Always out at bars trying to pick up guys. And Brenda didn't seem to have even Rayne's desire for a relationship. She just picked 'em up, brought 'em home, screwed 'em, and let 'em go. Thad had found her on Facebook and had hardly needed to hack into her information to learn all about her. She was giving up information like it was her life's ambition. He knew where she worked, where she lived, who her friends were, what her habits were. She was just the type to meet "Chas" and take him home.

Thad had drifted by her place a number of times, but she'd been gone. No one around. On vacation or something that had taken her away for a while. It was just so like her to make him wait. Fucking bitch.

He'd used the time in between to slowly drive by Bibi Engstrom's house once or twice, needing to relive the thrill of the kill. He'd taken Rayne's Hobo purse with him on those trips. He couldn't wait till he got back in the lair before pleasuring himself. What he really wanted to do was go to the overlook and relive pushing Rayne over, but he knew he couldn't do that. Too risky. He'd heard on the news that they'd ruled her death an accident, but Bibi's demise so soon afterward could be adding some questions. If he hung around both of his killing sites too much, it would put a big, red target on his back. Still, he hadn't been able to help himself. He'd gone up on the trail a time or two, walking past the overlook and heading to Percy's Peak, a regular hiker. But on the way back down he would always slow by the overlook, remembering Rayne's clumsy foot catching the railing before he pushed her through, her flight toward the ground, her body bouncing off the side of the cliff, scattering dirt and small stones that followed her down, down, down to the water far below.

His cock jumped at the memory, and he almost missed the turnoff to Brenda's apartment and had to yank the wheel at the last moment, nearly scraping the bumper of a parked sedan. He earned a sharp beep from a passing motorist at his abrupt move.

Fuck you, buddy. He flipped the asshole off, half smiling behind his aviator sunglasses. He had dear old Dad's cowboy hat on his head. His camouflage.

Killing . . . man, it made him hard.

He cruised by Brenda's apartment complex again. He'd determined her car was the blue Kia Soul, and it was still in the same parking place. Left there while she was gallivanting around, likely on some trip somewhere, screwing day and night. It pissed him off. She needed to be home. She needed "Chas" to make her acquaintance. He wanted to take her down. Bad. Briefly he thought about moving to the third mean girl bitch on his list, but getting to her was more problematic and *things need to be in the right order.* He had to keep remembering. The chance of discovery increased when he deviated.

He gritted his teeth. He couldn't get caught. And the truth was when he wasn't reliving Bibi's death he was in a cold sweat about the way it had gone down. Too many variables. Too many chances to be caught. But so far, it appeared he was safe. So far . . .

Besides, he wanted Brenda. He'd worked up a real appetite for her. He needed to lure her in, have at least one night together, maybe several. Chas could do it. Draw her to him, start a relationship of sorts? At least a string of nights together, about all Brenda was good for. And then a lovely death. Maybe at his place? Again, too risky. The one time he'd brought Rayne over—what the fuck had he been thinking!—she'd found him out. He hadn't shown her the lair because anyone who went there would not be coming out, and he hadn't been ready to be done with Rayne at that time. She'd wanted him and he'd liked it, and he hadn't wanted it to end, even though he'd since learned the ending was better than anything else.

Could he do that with Brenda? Smuggle her into the house and down to the lair . . . ? Love her . . . to death . . . ?

His cock was practically bursting at the thought.

But then what would he do with her? Her rotting body would stink up the place and Lorena might smell it.

Lorena.

Thad growled low in his throat. His mother had been in a mood ever since her meeting with the staff at Ridge Pointe over Gram. Lorena had told them in no uncertain terms that Gram was NOT going to Memory Care. She'd insisted they keep her in Independent Living. She'd half expected them to default to Assisted Living, which neither she nor Thad was willing to pay for, either, but they kept stating that Gram needed Memory Care. Lorena had somehow gotten them to back off. She'd been proud about it, but it was clearly only a reprieve. If they didn't put Gram in Memory Care soon, she was going to be coming home. Thad blamed Lorena for not being strong enough, but when he'd said as much, she'd blasted him again for not helping her.

He was going to have to go meet with the Ridge Pointe pencil-necks himself.

Shit.

He dragged his mind back to the problem at hand: his need to develop a better killing plan. He couldn't have another Bibi Engstrom.

A cold thrill shot through him at the thought, shrinking his hard-on, tightening his chest. If he hadn't been able to burn the place up, they would've found something; he was sure of it. Lucky she'd had the candle. Lucky there was gas. Lucky, lucky, lucky.

That kind of luck doesn't strike twice. No. He had to *think*. Plan. More like what had happened with Rayne, although that had been unexpected, too.

And Brenda, the bitch, wasn't making it easy!

In a fury, he yanked the wheel and got back on the arterial that led southwest to River Glen, his thoughts dark. He wanted, needed, someone. His mind snagged on the girl he'd met outside the Waystation. The one who'd turned him down . . .

But hadn't it really been a maybe? She'd wanted him. He could tell.

Maybe she'd be there again this afternoon.

Stick with the plan.

His own conscience infuriated him. How long was the plan going to take, huh? How long would he be forced to wait?

He argued with himself for a while. He knew better. He *knew* better than to go off on a side adventure. Lady Luck was capricious and might not let him have the girl in the bar and get away with it. He needed to be smart.

But . . . ?

Maybe he would stop by and just see if she was there.

Taft followed Seth Keppler's white F-150 as he left Good Livin' and headed south out of town. This was a break from routine and it sharpened Taft's attention. Maybe this was the break he'd been waiting for. All morning he'd been trying to reach his confidential informant, hoping he could pay him for some surveillance, but the CI was not answering his texts. Maybe he'd given up his burner phone and replaced it with a new one. The man was paranoid at the best of times, and since he'd told Taft about the relationship between Mangella and Keppler he'd been impossible to reach.

He kept traffic in between himself and Keppler's truck. For weeks the man had been barely traveling from home to work, but now he was heading out of River Glen in the direction of the I-5 freeway. Taft had been planning to rent a car for surveillance purposes and had put it off too long. Now he was kicking himself.

He tried to reach his CI again but this time the phone cut off. He'd ditched the burner. Possibly destroyed it.

Hmmm.

Taft checked the time. Three p.m.

Where was Keppler going?

Taft stayed far behind the truck, letting traffic pull between them.

While waiting for Seth to get off work, Taft had taken out his cell phone and pulled up the notes he'd written to himself on Rayne Sealy. He'd promised Mackenzie he would check into the matter. He knew she was disappointed that he'd taken her off the Keppler case, and maybe he had overreacted . . . if Helene were here she would tell him, "Yes, definitely, little brother, you overreacted" . . . but he'd made the choice. He'd spent some time digging into Rayne's story, trying not to double up too much on her own queries. To that end he'd casually asked at the Coffee Club what had happened to her, getting a chorus of voices telling him she'd accidentally fallen to her death by taking a selfie. He hadn't learned anything deeper, so he'd moved on to Good Livin' and a trial membership, which had put him close to Patti and Seth, a decision he'd made in furthering his own investigation as well as Mackenzie's. Mentally, he'd held his breath, half expecting one or the other of them to recognize him, but neither of them seemed to know anything about him, which had made it easier. He'd spent an afternoon working out and had casually asked around about a dark-haired woman who used to work there a half dozen months back or so and had been told he should talk to Patti or Seth. Everyone seemed to know Rayne and the story of the "love triangle" that had gotten her fired. Taft had forgone the one-on-one with either Patti or Seth. A girl named Giselle had set him up with the membership and he'd decided to check back with them later, if maybe at all. He didn't want to travel the same ground as Mackenzie and raise suspicions. But one of the guys who'd been working out on a stationary bike and sweating like a racehorse had wiped his brow and said, "She was at that old people's place before here. Can't think of the name of it, but I heard her talk about it once." He snorted. "She didn't like it there much." Taft knew that Rayne had worked at Ridge Pointe Independent and Assisted Living and had called on the retirement community with limited success. He needed to come up with a good story to spin before they were willing to give out any information on their residents or staff.

Keppler's white Ford entered the freeway heading south and Taft slowed down, allowing several more cars to get in between them. Damn, he wished he had another car. Or another driver to help follow. He thought about calling Mackenzie, but it was too late for today. He was in it now and driving the Rubicon. He just hoped Keppler hadn't seen earlier surveillance and started to wonder about his vehicle.

Keppler was just south of Wilsonville when he took an off-ramp. There was only one car between them as Taft followed. Keppler was stopped at the light and in the lane that turned left onto the side street or straight back onto the freeway. As soon as the light changed, Taft prepared for him to turn left when he darted straight across and back down to the freeway south.

Shit.

Only one reason for that, as far as Taft could tell. He was checking to see if he was being followed. That meant he was watching the cars come up behind him, of which Taft was one.

Taft yanked his wheel to the left and crossed the overpass, glancing down at Keppler's white truck as it entered the freeway once more and kept heading south.

He turned back around as soon as he could and took the on-ramp back onto I-5, hitting the gas as he merged with the other traffic, but Keppler was long gone. Whatever the hell Keppler was up to, he didn't want anyone to know where he was going.

Taft swore a blue streak in his mind, speeding along with the traffic, afraid to go too fast in case Keppler had slowed down up ahead, checking to see if any vehicle was hurrying to catch him.

Was it all a game, or was he really heading somewhere important?

Hard to tell.

Fifteen minutes later Taft gave up the chase. He couldn't catch up to Keppler. The man hadn't laid a trap for him, as far as he could see, but Taft wasn't about to blow his cover. He could go back to surveillance with a different vehicle. The break in routine said something was up, something that could break the case open wide.

CHAPTER FOURTEEN

Three fifteen. Mac pulled into the parking lot of Best Homes, waiting for Troi to appear. She was energized by her belief that Rayne had gone to the overlook intending to meet someone, very possibly her secret lover, and Troi was high on that list. She still hadn't completely ruled out Seth, but she needed to talk with Taft before she braced him again and she didn't feel like talking to Taft. She was hurt. She shouldn't be, really, but she was. She would discuss things with him when she felt better about their dissolution, and that was going to take a while.

Dissolution? You barely worked with him. Get over yourself.

Mac's thoughts drifted to Bibi and her dispirited and charred house. She felt a weight settle on her heart. She'd specifically pushed thoughts of Bibi aside, trusting her ex-colleagues at River Glen PD to get to the bottom of that horrific tragedy. It was easier to think about Rayne. Some of her dogged search for the truth surrounding her death was to fulfill her promise to Bibi, and Bibi had thought there was more to the story.

Troi's silver Audi was parked by a skeletal maple tree

that was just beginning to show bits of pale green budding. She figured he was still at work, but suspected he would be off around three as it was about that time when she'd first seen him meeting up with Seth Keppler. There were a number of Best Homes white cube trucks cruising in and out of a fenced area on the side of the building, a parking area apparently used by the team. Mac had done some research on the company and unlike many independent contractors, Best Homes employed a lot of workers and only seemed to sub out specific areas of homebuilding expertise, like plumbing and electrical.

She sighed. No sign of Troi yet. She'd been waiting for this moment all day. After leaving Miller's Market, she'd gone home, cleaned up, then forced herself to make some appointments to view apartments over the next few days. That done, she'd examined her mental task list and, before she could talk herself out of it, had picked up the phone and called Katy Keegan. Taft had given her the number and it seemed to be embedded in her brain, so she'd placed the call, determined to move items off her task list.

"Hi, this is Katy," she'd answered, causing Mac to lose focus for a moment. She'd been certain she would get her voice mail.

"Uh, hi, Katy. This is Mackenzie Laughlin. We worked together at the River Glen—"

"I remember you," she interrupted. "You quit after I did."

"That's right. Not long after you did. That's . . . what I'm calling you about."

"Oh? What do you mean?" Katy sounded suddenly suspicious.

At that point Mac backed out a bit, explaining that Jesse James Taft had given her Katy's number. When Katy didn't respond, Mac waded in with, "This is about the chief . . . Chief Bennihof."

"Okay," she said carefully.

"I had some trouble with him and heard that you did, too."

"From Mr. Taft?"

Mac couldn't quite read her. She sounded like a hostile witness. Maybe she just didn't want to think about it. "He came onto me in his office. He didn't completely chase me around a desk, but close enough. After that, I couldn't do anything right at work, at least that's the way he made it seem."

There was a long pause, but then she said, "He didn't completely chase me around a desk, either." Her voice was low and bitter, but at least Mac felt they were getting somewhere.

"How do we fight back against a guy like that?" Mac questioned her.

"You're asking me?"

"That's pretty much why I called."

"Look, the man has a roving eye and it's probably bad for the department. I get that. He's the reason I left, too. But there are extenuating circumstances, and I can't help you."

"Probably bad?" Mac keyed in on the equivocation. "It is bad for the department. And it affects morale. I don't know if I'm asking for your help. I'm just trying to get a handle on how pervasive the problem might be. He doesn't have the right to harass any of us."

"He didn't harass me."

"Okay."

"I can take care of myself."

"Yes, but this is about him. He can't just—"

"I chased him around the desk, okay? Not the other way around. You understand?"

Mac stopped midsentence. "You . . . ?"

"I. Went. After. Him." She was succinct and slightly bitter. "I wanted to be his girlfriend. I wanted to have him. Have you looked at the man? I mean really looked at him? He's *sexy*. I like older men and he can be funny. He's good company. Don't make this something it isn't."

Mac thought of Hugh Bennihof. He kept himself in shape and looked good in clothes. His hair was silver and he had penetrating eyes. The last time she'd seen him, he'd even tamed his bushy gray eyebrows and she could admit, grudgingly, that he was attractive.

He was also married.

"I'm sorry if that disappoints you," she was rattling on. "I had an affair with my boss. It's not a crime, even if you want to believe it is. I wasn't a victim. That's all. But thanks to you, it all ended."

"Thanks to me?"

"Yes, Mackenzie, thanks to you!"

Mac almost laughed. She was torn between disbelief and outrage.

"He started looking at someone else, and that someone was you."

"Oh, come on."

"So, I can't help you, Mackenzie. In fact, I don't want to. If I had my way, he and I would still be together, so if you've got a problem with the chief, you figure it out." And with that she hung up.

Well.

She could sense the heat in her cheeks. She felt foolish and was also annoyed at Taft for putting her in this situation with Katy. Damn the man.

You put yourself in it.

She shook her head, needing to displace the whole thing. She knew Bennihof and so did Katy Keegan. Maybe Katy had gone after the chief, like she said. Or, maybe it was a lie to make herself feel better. Mac knew a few victims of sexual harassment who'd twisted the story to take back their power. She'd even felt that herself, wanting to go back to that after-hours scene in his office and replay it with a confrontation rather than her ignominious escape.

Either way, Katy wasn't going to go against the chief. Taft had misunderstood what she was feeling. He wasn't aware of what had gone down between Katy and the chief, and Mac doubted the Battle-axe was, either. But she was glad she knew now. Better than being blindsided. She'd had thoughts that maybe she could air Bennihof's sexual harassment with the female staff and be heard. Now she knew that was an impossibility. She needed more before she took on that fight. A lot more.

Another cube truck drove into the Best Homes parking lot and rumbled toward the fence that housed the company vehicles. Mac straightened in her seat, seeing someone waiting at the gate. She could make out the longish blond hair sticking from beneath the baseball cap that was pulled down over the man's head. As the gate slowly slid backward, he turned his head to look toward the main building. Troi.

Okay, then. Mac settled back down, just letting her eyes peek over the dashboard. She, too, wore her baseball cap. She wasn't sure quite how she was going to approach Troi, what she was going to ask beyond was he, maybe, Rayne's super-secret last boyfriend? Had Rayne hooked up with him again after her affair with Seth? And if that were true, how and when had Troi reconnected with Elise? Before, during, or after his affair with Rayne? Was Troi that last guy who'd met Rayne at the overlook?

A few minutes later her quarry came out of the building and strode toward his Audi. Mackenzie waited while he revved his engine, then backed out of the parking spot and headed toward the main road.

Mackenzie eased the RAV out of the Best Homes lot and followed.

Thad sat outside the Waystation, his truck idling. Need had won out over his rule book and here he was, though he couldn't seem to control his dick. He was jonesing for Bibi and Rayne, and Brenda, and currently the woman who'd driven away in the RAV4 that day. Dark hair, green eyes, sharp wit. He wanted to be inside her so badly he was wondering if there was something wrong with him. The last few weeks . . . since Rayne's death, his self-control had eroded badly. It was like he was fifteen again, when he'd wanted to fuck everything. His mind was full of Rayne. There was a part of him that ached for her, wanted her back . . . except then he remembered her body flying and tumbling and then he wanted *that* again. Strangling Bibi had brought it all back. What he'd really like to do is strangle a woman while he was pounding into her. Brenda. Definitely Brenda . . . but this woman had gotten her hooks in him as well. He should've followed her home that day. Why hadn't he?

Because things need to be in the right order!

Fuck that.

He scanned the parking lot. Her RAV wasn't here. *She* wasn't here. Well, that would have been too easy, wouldn't it? But the guy she'd been with at the bar was here. Thad had watched him enter the Waystation, hitching up his pants. The guy who acted like he was a cowboy. Thad knew about looking the part; he did the same. But this "cowboy" was a fool and a loser. Nevertheless, he'd been talking to the raven-haired girl that Thad was already starting to think of as his.

Brenda's next, he reminded himself.

Well, yes, she was next. He felt angry with the restrictions he'd put on himself. He'd gotten away with Rayne and Bibi, hadn't he? What harm was there in following up on this woman while he waited for Brenda to return from wherever she'd gone? He set his teeth. Brenda was going to pay for making him wait.

He headed inside, taking a quick look around. It was the afternoon and the place was mostly empty. Seeing the "cowboy" at the bar, he sauntered over.

The man gave him a hard look. "I'm waiting for someone," he warned, making it clear he didn't want Thad to sit down.

"I'm not tryin' to take your seat, man," Thad drawled. The voice was an affectation, a distraction.

"Sure looked like it."

"You waitin' for that woman in here a few weeks ago?" asked Thad.

He frowned. "You been here before?"

"She looked like your woman. Pretty."

He'd thrown the "your woman" thing in to make the man feel more comfortable, though it had been clear to Thad that she'd been keeping her distance.

The guy relaxed a bit. "Yeah, well. She busted me a few times, but she's hot, y'know? Whad're ya gonna do."

Busted me? A cold snake of fear coiled in his stomach. She was a cop? He had a moment of panic, though there was no reason for it. The woman didn't even know his name. All he'd done was hit on her, nicely. Still, he hadn't expected her to be part of law enforcement. "She a cop?"

"Ex."

"River Glen PD?"

"Yep." He gave Thad a sharp look. "You're not trying to poach, are ya?"

"Just admiring."

Thad moved a few stools away and got the bartender's attention, ordering a beer. He hated beer, but when playing the part of a shitkicker you needed shitkicker booze.

Could he push it further? An *ex-cop*. He would be wise to steer clear of her. But his dick said differently. Even now it was responding to the challenge. He took a place on the opposite end of the bar from the cowboy and sipped on his beer until he'd cooled off. Seemed like he couldn't think about any of his women without getting hot. He moved his thoughts to Brenda, but imagining what he would do to her gave him a twitch as well. He just had to keep his cool.

Clearly the cowboy did not have anyone coming to take the seat beside him as nothing happened over the next hour. Thad nursed his beer, figured the man had just been hopeful. The cowboy was drinking vodka and he wasn't drinking responsibly. He was starting to get louder and the female bartender was doing her best to ignore him. She was older, but not half bad-looking, so maybe the cowboy was working his moves.

Thad got up and wandered back over his way. The man was going to need a ride home if things continued this way and it sure looked like they were. He debated on his next move. He should just up and go, but he wanted more information. In the end, he decided to leave the bar and wait outside for the man to stagger out.

Thad mentally kicked himself for not memorizing the woman's license plate number. It would have been so easy. He'd just been blinded by thoughts of being inside her and she'd driven away while he'd fantasized. It hadn't seemed so important at the time.

It took another hour for the cowboy to leave the bar. Thad had been about to give up. He'd seesawed back and forth, arguing with himself about all the many and good reasons to give up on the ex-cop. He'd just about convinced himself it was too dangerous, when the guy lurched outside, looking at his phone and damn near tripping down the one step outside the door in the process. Maybe he was calling for a ride.

"Hey," Thad called, climbing from his truck. "I was just comin' back. You leavin'?"

"Yeah . . ."

"You're not drivin', are ya?"

"No . . . no more do-ees. But at least she won't pull me over no more." He held up a finger and pointed it at Thad, swaying a bit.

"That ex-cop?"

"Yeah. Her."

"You live near here? Could give ya a ride, maybe. If it's not too far . . ." He let reluctance color his voice.

"Not that far."

Thad was testing him. The man was wasted, but if Thad seemed too eager, maybe the guy would remember being hustled. You never knew with drunks.

But a Good Samaritan who was rethinking his offer was a safe bet.

"How far?" Thad frowned. He pretended to try to circumvent the man and go into the bar.

"Just . . . just over there." He waved toward the west.

"River Glen or . . . ?"

"Yeah . . . yeah, well, Laurelton, but just across the line, you know?"

"That might be too far for me."

"Oh . . . shit, okay . . ."

"What's your name?" asked Thad.

"Gillis." He was working his phone again, pitching a bit, catching himself each time before he toppled over. "Don Gillis."

"You sure it's just across the line?"

"Fuckin' phone. Fuckin' Uber . . . fuckin' List . . . Lyft . . ."

"I'll take you."

Gillis looked up. "Hey, man, really?"

"I was comin' back for another drink, but I'd better not," said Thad, throwing a longing look toward the bar. "The wife doesn't like me circlin' back, ya'know?"

Gillis said something Thad couldn't quite make out, but when Thad encouraged him to climb into his truck, he complied, practically falling into the passenger seat. "Thanks, man," he said on a burp as he struggled with the seat belt.

Thad hoped he wouldn't puke in his cab. It would be a lot to put up with just for some information.

"Give me some directions," Thad told Gillis, who'd closed his eyes for a second.

"Bitch of a day," he said.

"You got an address?"

Gillis coughed up the street name and Thad headed toward Laurelton, saying, "Point out where to turn as we get closer."

"Sure thing, man. Thanks."

From that point on it was a fairly quiet ride except for Gillis's heavy breathing, which bordered on snoring even though the man was awake. Thad began to feel repelled. At one point he jostled Gillis's shoulder a bit and said, "You there?"

He lifted his head and seemed to try to rouse himself from his stupor. "Yeah . . . sure . . ."

"Your woman didn't show up tonight?"

"Woman? Who?"

"The ex-cop . . . ?"

"Oh. Laughlin. Sure."

Laughlin. Thad smiled. Good. He had a name.

But then Gillis slid him an assessing look from beneath the brim of his hat, making Thad wonder if he wasn't as drunk as he appeared. "She's not my woman yet, but I'm working on it. Okay, pal?"

"Message received."

"What'd you say your name was?"

"Chas." As soon as he said it, he was sorry. If ever Gillis should mention his alias . . . he should have come up with something completely different.

They crossed into Laurelton and Gillis directed him to a narrow street far away from the nicer parts of the city to a tired-looking house down a weed-choked lane. By Thad's reckoning they might actually be outside the city limits of Laurelton as well, maybe in a patch of area owned by the county. There was something scruffy and untended about the roads that made him think so.

"Thanks, Chas," Gillis said as he climbed out.

That chilled him as he watched the man work hard to walk steadily to his front door. He didn't like him repeating his name.

Gillis entered and turned on a light and Thad slowly wheeled his truck around, easing away, watching through his rearview.

Would Gillis remember him? Would it matter? Only if he got near to Laughlin, the ex-cop, and only if she . . . disappeared . . . and Gillis remembered . . .

But he would remember and make a stink. It would all come out.

Leave her alone. You have Rayne and you'll have the others. You don't need her.

"There are other fish in the sea." One of dear old dead Dad's trite lines. The man who would screw anything that moved, according to Lorena. Thad himself was a helluva lot more selective. But he wanted what he wanted. And he wanted *her.*

"Laughlin. Officer Laughlin, previously of the River Glen PD."

He thought of her in his lair. Chained to the wall. Naked. That dark hair lying against white skin. He could have her any time he wanted.

He shuddered with anticipation. He was going to have to do some research on her. He knew he couldn't bring her to the lair. Too dangerous. Too, too dangerous. Lorena was topside, and maybe Gram, too. There was no way he could bring a woman home and keep her a secret from them.

Unless . . . they were gone. Then no one would ever bother him. He could get the money back he'd lost and his inheritance. He could live there forever.

He drove home, hurried down to his lair, and looked

around. He stripped down to his pants and worked out on the rings until he was soaked in sweat. His eyes were trained on the whiteboard where beside Rayne's name he'd written Bibi's in green Sharpie and Brenda's in yellow, which might be premature but she was next on his list.

He walked up to the board, breathing hard. Picked up the blue Sharpie. He didn't know the ex-cop's first name yet. For now he just wrote in her last one: Laughlin.

Mackenzie followed Troi Bevins into the city limits of Laurelton. When he pulled into the parking lot of Nona Sofia's, an Italian restaurant that had been a part of the Laurelton landscape since the nineties, she followed him in but parked her vehicle on the opposite corner from his, tucked behind a Suburban.

Troi didn't notice her as he headed inside.

Mac debated. Maybe this was where she could talk to him. Maybe he was hitting a happy hour.

Mac had eaten at Nona Sofia's twice before, both times with her ex, Pete Fetzler. Both times had been memorable for different reasons. The first time had been her birthday; he was in a good mood and they'd had a nice evening. The second time all they'd done was fight. It was their last date before their breakup. Mac had called off the relationship. Pete had fooled her into thinking he was a different person when they'd first started dating, but she'd learned he was a guy who needed constant ego stroking. She'd been suckered by him, she could admit now. She'd fallen for his good looks.

As she'd realized his true character she'd stopped feeding his need for affirmation and that had not gone well. He'd tried to bully her, and prove he was right about whatever issue came up, even when he was dead wrong, especially when he was dead wrong. His good behavior deteriorated and disappeared entirely. He'd been white-faced and shocked when she'd broken up with him, then he'd harassed her mercilessly, phoning at all hours, name-calling, even following her. She'd just gotten her job with the RGPD and she let him know if he didn't back off, she would get a restraining order and find a way to have him arrested. She was serious as a heart attack and he'd believed her. He'd backed off but told everyone they knew that he'd been the one to "kick her to the curb." She'd tried to be above it, but it had royally pissed her off. Still, making a stink was exactly what he was looking for. A reason to keep fighting, to keep her engaged. She'd swallowed back her anger and shut him out of her life. Most people who knew them also knew the truth.

Mac had just decided to follow Troi inside, strike up a conversation again, pretend they were just two people who seemed destined to run into each other, when he came back out carrying a white take-out bag. Mac stayed in her car and waited as he backed out of the lot. She eased out after him but he was only on the road about four blocks before he turned into a strip mall. She slowly pulled into the lot, worrying that he would notice her, but Troi had already parked and was aiming toward Inky-Dink, a tattoo parlor wedged between a coffee shop and an independent appliance repair store. Inky-Dink's walls and front windows were adorned with an elaborate griffin-like creature that spread toward the other businesses. As Troi entered the shop, Mac saw that there was a smaller version of the griffin on the OPEN sign swinging from the inside of the door.

Mac didn't know this particular establishment, but when she was a cop she'd become acquainted with three brothers who ran a tattoo shop in River Glen. Two of the brothers believed the middle brother was trying to rip them off. A fight had ensued amongst them that had resulted in broken furniture and equipment, and damage to the shop's walls. The middle brother ended up in the hospital with a broken jaw, pointing the finger at his other two brothers. He got even by turning over company records full of flagrant tax evasion tactics. All of them ended up in court and faced huge fines.

It's amazing what you can get killed for if you try to carve out your own niche within the family hierarchy. Taft's words. Maybe he had something there.

She stayed in her car, wondering again if this was a good locale for a stop-and-chat, when Troi came back out, this time accompanied by a young woman whose tattoos ran down her arms beneath her short-sleeved shirt. As Mac watched, they climbed in Troi's Audi and shared what looked like a calzone that Troi had picked up at Nona Sofia's. When they were finished, they leaned into each other and kissed. Then they both got out of the car and were saying goodbye when the girl threw herself into Troi's arms and they hugged and kissed some more, bodies pressed together, grinding a little against each other in a way that most people would find embarrassing in public. After a few minutes of this, the girl skipped back inside the parlor and Troi, once again, climbed into his Audi.

Mac was beginning to think Troi would never land somewhere, when he turned into a shitkicker bar called

Cal's nearer to Portland. It appeared to be on par with the Waystation. Mac left her baseball cap on as this time she got out of the RAV and followed Troi inside.

Cal's was a few rungs up from the Waystation. The walls were paneled in V-groove fir that looked recently stained and the wooden barstools shone as if they'd been oiled. The bottles behind the bar didn't actually gleam, but neither did they look as if the dust had settled for too long like at the Waystation.

Troi strode straight to the dartboard. He swept off his cap, ran his hands through his blondish locks, then stuffed the cap back on and picked up the darts. Mackenzie seated herself at the end of the bar where she could keep an eye on him. He hadn't seen her yet, which was just fine.

He played a couple of games by himself. Did a pretty good job. Then he left the last darts in the board and moseyed over to the bar. Only then did he recognize Mackenzie and give a start. "Hey," he said, frowning.

"Hey, yourself." There was an expanse of bar between them, so Mac moved to a stool closer to him. "Looked like you didn't do too badly." She inclined her head toward the dartboard.

"What are you doing here?"

"I followed you here," she admitted.

Something flared in his eyes. Fear? He then blinked a couple of times. "You're kidding, right?"

She shook her head from side to side.

"Well, then . . . why?" Her words seemed to finally reach the back of his brain. She could almost see the moment when he realized she might have seen him with the girl with the sleeve tattoos. "From when?"

"Since work."

"*Why* are you following me?" he demanded, more aggressively.

"I wanted to ask you about Rayne."

"Rayne!" He gave her a hard look. "I told you what I know about Rayne. Elise and I are back together, so don't be talking anymore about Rayne."

"I was just interested in the timing. I'm following up on what happened to Rayne. After her death you went back to Elise, right?"

He recoiled as if she'd struck him. "No. Elise and me were together *before* Rayne selfied-out."

"Yeah, but Rayne said you two hooked up once more after you went back to Elise," Mac lied.

"Well, that . . . that's not true! Don't you be telling Elise that! That's a fucking lie!"

"You never got back with Rayne?"

"NO. I don't want to speak ill of the dead, but if she told you that, she was lying! Rayne was a liar! She made things up all the time. I made a mistake with her. If you say something to Elise . . ." There was something vaguely threatening in his tone that might have worried her, except he looked like he was about to cry.

"I'm not going to say anything to Elise."

"What the fuck are you doing?" He tried to pull himself together.

Mac believed he was telling the truth about the timing, even if he was cheating on Elise with the girl from Inky-Dink. "I'll be honest with you. I've got a bad feeling about what happened to Rayne. I don't know if it's true. I'm just trying to figure it out."

"Huh." Troi ordered a beer from the bartender and he sucked it down pretty fast. Mac asked for vodka on the rocks, which she could tell impressed him. It was interesting how much cred she got from ordering hard liquor even if she only sipped her drink.

"Tell me about Rayne," she encouraged.

"Nothing to tell," he said, taking the stool next to her. His barriers were coming down a bit, as if her drinking had somehow warmed up their relationship, such as it was. She wasn't a cop any longer, and she wanted him to talk to her like a compatriot. People talked more if they saw you as an equal.

"Rayne and I were just . . . it was a mistake. I told you that before. It wasn't serious."

"You met her through Elise."

"Yeah . . ."

"How did you meet Elise?" asked Mac.

He picked up his glass and kind of jiggled the half inch of beer in the bottom. "I used to go to this bar at this restaurant, Mexicali Rose."

"I know it."

"Elise was working there and we met and hooked up. That's when I was still with Laidlaw Construction." Mac felt herself respond to the name of Nolan's company, but Troi didn't seem to notice. "We were really just kinda casually dating. One time I saw Rayne. She was with Elise, well, not really, they were fighting. Rayne had dropped Elise off and there was something about her being late . . . I don't know. But that's how I met Rayne."

He cut himself off abruptly, then finished his beer. Mac waited till he'd given the high sign to the bartender for another before asking, "So when did you get with Rayne?"

"It was even more casual than me and Elise. We were just . . . look, she's crazy, and I mean, crazy. Well, she *was* crazy," he corrected himself. "She'd do about anything. Elise has . . . some sense. But Rayne . . ." He smiled and shook his head, looking down at his empty glass, remembering. After a moment, he swept back his hair to reveal a tattoo in the shape of a key. "Talked me into this tat and that's where I met Leah . . . you saw her, right?" He shot Mac a sheepish look.

"At Inky-Dink?"

He nodded, grimacing. "Leah gave me this key and Rayne got a lock and it was kinda dumb, but . . ." He cleared his throat. "Leah's just a friend. Elise knows I know her. It's nothing."

"I'm not going to rat you out to Elise."

"It's nothing. It's really nothing."

"So you and Rayne got tattoos together," Mac encouraged.

"It was a wild ride with her. She was working at that old people's place. We had a make-out session outside the building and one of those old ladies about fell off her walker, trying to tap at us against the window. Rayne dared me to pull out my dick and wave it at her, but I didn't."

"Ridge Pointe," said Mac.

He shrugged. "Rayne didn't work there long. Moved on to Good Livin'."

"That's where she met Seth."

"Wow. You know about Seth, too." Troi looked surprised.

"So, what happened between you and Rayne? You got the tattoos and then . . . what?"

"It was fast and furious and Elise was screaming at me. She was really pissed, of course, and well, I don't know. Rayne's fun for a while, you know? I don't want to say nothing bad about her. She was fun. But she wasn't girlfriend material, you know?"

Mac could feel her expression harden. "She was too easy," she said neutrally, though she was starting to really resent the double standards surrounding Rayne.

"Yep." He had no idea the effect of his words on her.

"So you broke it off."

"Yeah . . . we just started not seeing each other. I told Seth about her and he kinda liked her. He's with Patti now, but they weren't really together at that point, so Seth hooked up with Rayne. He did like her. Took her out to his dad's farm and showed her how to shoot."

"And then he broke up with her for Patti."

"I don't know all the particulars, but that's what happened."

"So, after Seth, Rayne was a free agent."

"Yeah. I guess."

"Was she with anybody after Seth?"

"It wasn't me," he reiterated. "I wasn't with her after I got back with Elise, if that's what you're getting at."

"I'm just asking."

"Truth is, after it was over? I tried to not know too much about her. Easier for me with Elise, you know? Elise is kind of the jealous type, anyway, so I'd appreciate it if you didn't say too much about Leah. And Rayne. I swear, I never saw her after Elise and me got back together."

"Okay."

"You're not going to tell her all this?"

"I don't know Elise that well, Troi. It's unlikely the issue would come up."

"Yeah?" He regarded her suspiciously.

"Yeah."

He'd gotten his beer and now he took a long drink.

Wiping his mouth and setting down his glass, he said, "You think something bad happened to Rayne." There was worry on his face. Troi didn't seem to be a terrible guy. He was filled with more heart than Seth Keppler, that was clear. He didn't seem like he would purposely hurt Rayne, even if she wasn't "girlfriend material."

"Something bad did happen to Rayne," Mac pointed out.

"Well, sure. But I mean like . . . it wasn't an accident?"

He regarded her anxiously, as if her answer really mattered.

"That's what I'm trying to find out."

"You should talk to Seth."

She nodded. All signs pointed to him, and he was the boyfriend of Rayne's that Bibi had named. She was just trying to stay out of Taft's investigation, and she also sensed Seth Keppler would be a difficult interview.

"I saw you with Seth outside Best Homes," Mac said, watching him. "In the parking lot. Seth was waiting for you."

Troi looked stunned. "What?"

"You and Seth shared Rayne."

"NO. Well, I mean, Rayne and I were just a good time and Seth was interested, I just. It wasn't like that."

"But you and Seth are friends," she said, though Elise had told her they were sworn enemies.

"No . . . no . . ." He was starting to sweat.

Mackenzie narrowed her gaze at Troi. He was strangely innocent, in his way. Knowing Seth, she came up with a likely answer. "He's your dealer."

"Shhh . . . God! No. I mean, just weed. Nothing illegal. Nothing!"

"He supplied Rayne, too."

"It's not illegal and no, Rayne was a wine drinker."

"Pinot noir?"

"Whatever was around."

"Red Bridge."

He looked at her blankly.

"That was a pinot she liked."

"If you say so. But don't be saying stuff like that about me and Seth. I'm just into weed, that's all. Nothing else."

Mackenzie wasn't so sure, but she wasn't going to push it. At least she had a kind of verification that Seth was a dealer.

"Don't say anything to Seth." Troi was upset.

"I won't. I don't know Seth."

"But you're asking a lot of questions. I think I'm done talking." He half turned away from her on his stool. The interview was over.

Mackenzie paid for her unfinished drink and headed outside, checking the time. A little after five thirty.

She drove straight to Nolan and Stephanie's and after a quick hello, headed to the pink room. She needed to talk to Nolan, who'd said he didn't know Troi. It looked like Troi and Nolan had switched places, Troi from Laidlaw Construction to Best Homes and Nolan from Best to Laidlaw.

But Troi was moving to the back burner for Mac. She didn't see him as Rayne's secret lover. *Secret* was not a word she could really ascribe to the man in any context.

She dropped her bag on the bed and the notepad she sometimes jotted down things she wanted to remember fell out. She could see the top note to herself: One of the outrageously expensive apartments above the River Glen Grill had come available. Yeah, like that was going to happen.

She needed something about one fifth the price or less. Ah, well. She called Mom and checked in on her to learn that she and Dan the Man were heading to the River Glen Grill for dinner. It was all Mackenzie could do to keep from blurting out, "Hang on to your wallet," but she managed to extricate herself from the conversation before that happened.

CHAPTER FIFTEEN

Cooper closed the file on his desk, leaned back, and stared up at the ceiling. Verbena, her desk catty-corner to his, asked, "What?"

He dropped his gaze to meet hers, knowing he was about to tell her, once again, what she didn't want to hear. "Engstrom didn't do it."

She shook her head. "He did it," she argued. She always argued. Detective Elena Verbena blamed the husband first, or the boyfriend, or whatever man was in the victim's life. She rarely leaned toward a woman doer. Cooper found it extremely sexist, but more often than not she was right, so he just listened to her.

And in this case whoever had killed Bibi Engstrom was male. The crime techs had recovered two tiny drops of blood from the kitchen, a part of the flooring that had miraculously survived the explosion that took out the garage. But the blood and the DNA recovered from it wasn't Hank Engstrom's.

"I'm waiting for the full report," Verbena said again, like she had many times before. Bibi Engstrom's body had been burned beyond recognition and was still being processed.

"Whose blood was it?" Cooper asked again. They'd had this conversation numerous times.

Verbena clamped her lips together. She knew she was being recalcitrant.

"It was a homicide. Someone, a man, killed her. Someone whose DNA does not match Hank Engstrom. You've talked to him. I've talked to him. His story doesn't change. He was having an affair, leaving his wife. He's a cheater, but not a killer. His alibi is damn near watertight."

"He could've gone back to the house in that hour that his girlfriend was gone."

Cooper smiled at her. She knew. And though her stubborn ways were annoying, they also created good dialogue that forced creative thinking. Hank Engstrom's alibi was his new girlfriend whom he'd been sharing an apartment with. She'd left him at the apartment when she'd gone to the liquor store before it closed. When she returned he was in the shower. He said he'd been working out while she was gone and the crime techs had found a shirt and gym shorts that attested to that fact. There was no blood on his clothes, nor any trace of Bibi on Hank himself or left over in the shower. The girlfriend said they'd had sex just before she'd made the liquor run, which hadn't been part of Hank's initial report. And then it came out that the girlfriend just threw that in to make it appear that Hank was with her longer than he was, or something . . . it was hard to tell because the lie hadn't been well thought out. The upshot of it was that Hank had looked guilty and that his new girlfriend was lying for him.

But . . . there was the blood. Someone's blood.

For good measure, Cooper added, "Hank's phone was at the apartment the whole time. So, for him to sneak out, accost Bibi in the car or garage, render her unconscious or kill her, fill the garage up with carbon monoxide, set up the candle, and light up the place in the hour the girlfriend was gone . . . maybe less than an hour? . . . and get back to the apartment and in the shower before she returned . . . Can't be done."

Verbena ran her hands through her dark curls. He knew that tell. She was coming around. "Who, then?" she asked.

Cooper shook his head.

"Some other man in her life?" she questioned. The same questions they'd run past each other for days.

"No evidence of that."

"We both agree it's homicide. So who wanted to kill her other than her cheating husband?"

"Don't know the motive yet."

"Take a stab at it," she said.

Cooper grimaced. A preliminary look at the Engstroms' finances hadn't turned up anything particularly suspicious. Bibi and Hank had been renters who were getting by on Hank's salary as a home furnishings deliveryman. They didn't own a lot of things, but they also didn't owe much money, either. Everyone knew about the girlfriend, which was why Bibi had once thrown all Hank's clothes onto the front lawn and locked him out of the house.

Mackenzie Laughlin had dealt with the warring Engstroms, he believed. He thought it was time he talked to her about them.

He glanced over at the chief's windowed office on the far side of the room. The curtains were open and he could see Bennihof at his desk. The old chief had retired several years earlier and Bennihof had been appointed by the mayor. The man had silver hair and a trim physique that came from regular trips to the gym. Cooper had never had serious problems with him as he allowed the detectives to run their cases as they saw fit. There were rumors that he cheated on his wife, but that she stayed with him because of his social connections throughout River Glen. They had two children and Bennihof talked a lot about his son who was on the baseball team at his high school. This seemed to be his only conversation other than when they brought a case to him, when he invariably spread his hands and said something like, "You know what to do." They had no serious guidance from him and that's how the problems with Howie Eversgard's case had developed. Bennihof hadn't defended Howie. He'd pretty much done what he always did, washed his hands of the whole affair. Howie had been cleared of any and all wrongdoing in the shooting that had ended a man's life as it was clearly self-defense, but it was no thanks to Bennihof. The chief didn't have your back. Everybody knew it and Howie had been left to defend himself. The police union had been there for him, but Howie's psychological trauma had sent him out of the department.

Cooper had felt Bennihof hadn't done nearly enough and his opinion of the man had soured. Plus there were rumors that Bennihof was handsy with women. He'd been seen with Katy Keegan from dispatch, his palm on her derriere. Verbena had marched straight to Bennihof and asked for an explanation. He'd assured her Katy had not complained and that she, Verbena, had misinterpreted him. Since Verbena was quick to blame men, no one had gotten all that excited about the whole thing. But then Katy had quit the force, and Barbara Erdlich, who preferred to be called the Battle-axe, had taken over.

And then Mackenzie Laughlin, the talented and decidedly pretty recruit, had left and Cooper really didn't know what had happened there. Maybe something with Bennihof. Likely something with Bennihof because she'd been considered a rising star and then suddenly Bennihof had started finding fault with her. Verbena had once again had a talk with the chief, defending Laughlin, but to no avail.

"Something's off," Verbena had told Cooper quietly. "And I know you think I'm a man hater, which I'm not, by the way, but the chief's become hypercritical of Laughlin all of a sudden."

Cooper had listened to Verbena, who added that Bennihof had told her Laughlin was difficult and couldn't get along with her partner. There was talk of reassignment, splitting Richards and Laughlin up, but then Laughlin had abruptly quit. Cooper had seen for himself that there was no love lost between Richards and Laughlin, but it sure seemed like it was coming more from Richards. He was jealous of his partner's likeability.

Verbena had taken a phone call and now Cooper regarded her dispassionately. She was an attractive woman, too, but she was hard as iron. He sensed that Bennihof didn't really know what to do with her. He'd seemed almost relieved when Howie quit the force, so he could team Cooper with Verbena. Before that, she'd floated between them as no one was seriously partnered at the department. Even now Cooper and Verbena worked together but a lot of time handled cases on their own.

"I'm heading out," he told her. He and Jamie were having dinner at the house of her friends Camryn and Nate

Farland, who owned one of the most well-known estates in River Glen, the Stillwell property, which they'd recently renovated.

"I'm right behind you," she said, wrapping up her call.

Cooper exited through the back door that led to the lot. He aimed for his own vehicle instead of his usual department vehicle, a navy Ford Escape. Since he was going off duty, he hit the remote for his black Explorer.

As he was switching on the ignition Verbena came out the back and waved urgently to him. He lowered the window and she called, "We've got a body."

A body. Turning off the engine, Cooper climbed back out of his SUV. He'd been looking forward to dinner, but now it appeared that was not to be.

Taft wheeled into his carport about the same time Tommy Carnoff pulled into his spot with his black Mustang convertible. Today its top was up as rain had been threatening all day, though it had held off and currently the roads were dry.

"Hello, Jesse," Tommy said as he climbed out, pocketing his aviator glasses.

"Hi, Tommy."

"I haven't seen that pretty lady around for a while."

"You were gone," Taft reminded him.

"So, she has been around?"

There was no use lying to the man. "Nope."

"You're not working together anymore?"

"I'm trying to find out some things for her." He was a little abrupt. Tommy's questions felt like a tongue probing a sore tooth.

"What sort of things, may I ask?"

Taft wasn't in the best of moods. After losing Keppler he'd gone back to Good Livin' to check on Patti, who would usually be waiting for Seth to pick her up before they drove home together. But not today. This evening she'd taken an Uber.

"Come over and have a drink," Tommy invited, apparently picking up on Taft's mood. He started to decline, then decided why not? He had no dinner plans and he was at loose ends. He prided himself on his ability to be on top of a situation, but today he'd blown it.

He said hello to the pugs, who were all about greeting him and demanding his attention. Tommy took off his cap and hung it on a peg by the door, then went into his kitchen, his unit a reverse design of Taft's. A few minutes later he served Taft a gin and tonic without asking what he wanted, and he accepted it and sat down on the couch, letting the dogs curl on each side of him. He gave Tommy a quick encapsulation of Mac's interest in Rayne Sealy, and Tommy cocked his head and looked interested.

"The one who accidentally killed herself," he said gravely.

"Yes."

"Terrible story. Did your lady friend know her?"

"No." He decided not to go into Bibi Engstrom's death. He'd said more than he intended to as it was.

"I knew her," Tommy said.

It was Taft's turn to pay closer attention. "Rayne Sealy?"

He nodded.

"From the Coffee Club?"

"From Ridge Pointe. She worked there for a while. Friendly girl. I'm heading over to dinner there now."

"At Ridge Pointe?"

He nodded. "A good friend of mine lives there now. Do you remember Maureen?"

"Oh. Yes." Taft recalled the lady who'd seemed to corral Tommy's interest the longest.

"She had a stroke," Tommy explained, answering Taft's unspoken questions. "She's been at Ridge Pointe about a year and a half. I still go see her. I have a standing invitation from some of the women who share a table with her." He eyed Taft closely. "You want to go? They all knew Rayne, too."

"Thank you, but . . ."

"Join me," Tommy invited. "I remember Rayne. She was too young for the place, and I don't mean you can't be young and work there, but you gotta be respectful. You gotta care. She was friendly to me, but maybe not so much to the women. Talk to them. They'll give you a different perspective."

"I'll come and talk to them, but I don't need dinner. I'll take my own car."

It was something of a revelation to Taft that Tommy still saw Maureen. He'd thought she was just one of many of Tommy's companions, but she appeared to hold a special place in his heart. Taft followed Tommy to Ridge Pointe and walked in with Tommy toward a grouping of elderly women around a rectangular table.

The ladies immediately urged him to sit down and order dinner, but Taft demurred. Tommy, however, sat down across from Maureen and ordered the same thing she did: a chicken sandwich. Taft held off their insistence on dinner. He wasn't sure who paid and how and didn't want to burden anyone. He managed to get by with a light beer, but was peppered with questions by all the women. He admitted he was asking into Rayne Sealy's death and wondered what they could tell him about her. To a one they looked at each other and dolefully shook their heads. They knew of Rayne, but they were relatively new residents and had never met her. Their friend Jewell could tell him all about her, but Jewell was with family.

"You could ask Emma," one of them said somewhat reluctantly. Collectively they looked over at a young woman who was seated alone at a table. She looked to be in her thirties and wore her long, light brown hair in a single braid. Her eyes were blue and she possessed a frank gaze that nevertheless seemed slightly off-center.

"Emma's not all there," one of the women whispered, for which Tommy chided her. She looked slightly abashed and glanced toward Maureen, who didn't seem to be following the conversation closely.

Taft finished his beer, and since the women were clearly enamored of Tommy, he scooted back his chair and walked to Emma's table. Emma had just finished eating and was just getting up. She watched him out of the side of her eye as he approached and she paused, perched on the edge of her chair.

"Hi, Emma, I'm a friend of Tommy's. My name's Jesse. I was talking to the other ladies about Rayne Sealy and they said that you knew her."

"She took a selfie and she died," Emma said in flat voice.

He could see he was going to need to be specific in his questions. "You knew her when she worked here?" Taft tried.

""Sort of. I was mostly with Jamie, Harley, and Cooper.

Jewell knew her, but Jewell's not here. She left early for Easter."

"Okay. So Jewell talked to you about Rayne?"

"Yes."

Taft gestured to the empty chair opposite her. "Do you mind if I sit down?"

"It's a free world."

Taft eased into the chair and looked at his interviewee. He didn't know what, if anything, had happened to her. Maybe it was autism. Something on the spectrum. Maybe something else entirely. But he thought she was definitely "all there." She just didn't have a ton of accepted social graces.

"I'm trying to determine if Rayne's death was truly an accident." He almost added, "for a friend," but decided not to muddy the waters. "And that means doing some background on her. Find out what she was like. I'd like to talk to Jewell. Maybe next week, when she's back?"

Emma cocked her head, as if in deep thought. "I can tell you what Jewell said about her."

"Great. I'd like to hear it."

"Jewell said she was a hot pants but Jewell gossips. Mrs. Throckmorton saw Rayne kissing the guy with long hair on the front porch. Jewell said Rayne was with Mrs. Throckmorton's grandson, but he doesn't have long hair. Old Darla says that he's her grandson but Mrs. Throckmorton thinks he's hers. Old Darla gets things wrong, but so does Mrs. Throckmorton."

Taft was having trouble following. "Do you know the name of the guy with the long hair?"

She frowned. "I don't think he was Thad."

"Who's Thad?"

"Mrs. Throckmorton's grandson."

"Was Thad a friend of Rayne's?"

She looked at the remains of her half-eaten plate of pasta, her frown deepening. "It's very confusing."

"Sounds like it. How long have you been here?"

"Since we got my mom's money. Jamie had to fight for it. That's how those legal things go."

Taft nodded. "I'm trying to determine how long ago Rayne was here."

"Ask Bob. He thought she was too friendly for here and she quit."

"Bob is . . . ?"

"Supercilious. That's what Harley says. She has a big vocabulary. It means snotty."

Taft fought back a laugh. "Bob is one of the residents here?"

"Bob Atkinson is the administrator. He wants to get rid of the cat, too. He and Jewell are two peas in a pod."

"Who's Harley?"

"My niece. Jamie's my sister and Cooper's her boyfriend. He has a stepdaughter named Marissa. We're a blended family."

Taft realized belatedly that Cooper might be Detective Cooper Haynes, who had a stepdaughter. "Detective Cooper Haynes?" he asked.

Emma's eyebrows shot up. "You know him."

"I know *of* him," said Taft, repeating her words.

"You don't like him?"

"No. I don't have any problem with him." He could practically see the wheels turning in her mind.

"You think he should be finding out what happened to Rayne."

"That's not it. I'm—"

"You think something bad happened to Rayne."

Taft held up his hands, unable to stop her.

"And you think Cooper should do something. So do I. I'll tell him," she said determinedly.

"Her death was very likely an accident," Taft assured her. "I'm just following up."

But Emma was no longer listening to him. He'd given her something to think about and she was gone from the conversation.

"I have to leave," she said, and she moved from the table and headed out the door. A black-and-white cat strolled a few steps after her and Taft assumed this was the cat Bob and Jewell wanted to get rid of.

As if it had heard him, the cat whipped its head around and gave him a cool stare.

CHAPTER SIXTEEN

It was just getting dark as Cooper drove Verbena to sprawling Staffordshire Estates where the body had been found. The development was into its Phase III and homes were in varying stages of production. They passed the illuminated, smiling billboard of Andrew Best, owner of Best Homes, as they entered. Best had erected more homes in Staffordshire Estates than any other builder. Laidlaw Construction was another major contender, but their advertising, a smaller black-and-white sign with the company logo, was far less overt.

There were several trucks, headlights piercing the graying evening, parked along a side road. Cooper nudged in behind them and he and Verbena stepped into the red and blue swirl of the light bar from one of River Glen PD's patrol cars.

Cooper was a little relieved to see the cop at the scene wasn't Ricky Richards but one with years of service under his belt, Bill Tillis. Bill had called in the discovery of the body, and he was with his partner, Owen Lomax, who was younger than Bill but not by much. The two men were standing outside a construction site where the house's framing rose to a second story, which was currently just a flat roof with a few studs pointing to the sky like accusing fingers.

"What have we got?" Verbena asked. She'd tucked her riot of dark curls into a cap. The early April night was growing cold.

"Looks like he fell off," Lomax said in a tone that suggested he didn't believe it. His flashlight was trained on a jean-clad body sprawled alongside the building amidst the dirt, rubble, and puddles left over from an earlier spate of rain, the victim's arms and legs splayed in abandonment.

"His ID reads Granger Nye," Tillis said. "Best Homes foreman. Somebody called in from one of the houses." He pointed to a finished home with a Mercedes SUV in its drive. "Heard something but didn't want to get out and look. About the same time the vic's girlfriend called dispatch and said she couldn't raise him on his cell. Said she tried to call Best, but he didn't answer. We came and found him."

Cooper switched on his own flashlight. "He fell from the second story?"

They all looked upward. "Looks like it," Tillis said.

"Think he was pushed?" asked Verbena.

"Lady with the Mercedes said she heard yelling," Tillis answered, leaving them to their own thoughts on that score.

Lomax played his flashlight beam over the wall and then down to the concrete on the first floor, which was remarkably clean and swept. Verbena shone her light on the victim's face. Nye's eyes were half open and a trickle of blood from the corner of his mouth ran black against his skin. "He's the foreman?" she repeated.

"That's what the girlfriend said," Tillis responded.

"What time did the neighbor hear the shouting?" Cooper asked.

"About an hour ago?" Tillis looked at Lomax.

"About that," Lomax agreed. "The techs are on their way."

"We need to reach Andrew Best," said Cooper. "What's the girlfriend's name?"

"We'll get it from dispatch," Lomax responded.

Cooper and Verbena waited around until the crime scene techs and coroner's van arrived. They moved over to the house with the Mercedes and knocked on the door. The woman who answered didn't want to open her door past the chain. She said she'd said all she was going to say. Verbena asked if she could discern how many voices were yelling and if they were male or female, and she said she didn't know. In fact, she wasn't sure the yelling had even come from that direction and well, if there had really been any yelling at all.

"Doesn't want to be involved," Verbena said as they left, stating the obvious.

"We can come back at her later."

"Explain a few things to her," she agreed.

They tried calling Best but again there was no answer. After a short consultation, Lomax and Tillis took on the task of alerting Nye's girlfriend and any family members to the man's death, and Cooper and Verbena headed to Andrew Best's personal residence. More correctly, Best's *River Glen* personal residence. He owned a number across the greater Portland area and his company had branched out through other parts of Oregon and Washington as well.

Best's home was fairly unprepossessing, a meandering ranch shrouded by overgrown foliage. For all his cheery pictures on the billboards touting his business he was a fairly private man. Cooper knew next to nothing about him other than he built a lot of pricey houses, though he apparently didn't want to flout his wealth on his own home.

Cooper and Verbena walked between high hedges and through a wrought-iron gate on their way to the front door. Cooper pressed the doorbell, momentarily thinking of the Stillwell house, where he was supposed to be having dinner tonight. That home, although larger and more stately since it had been pulled back from the brink of ruin by the Farlands, was also surrounded by thick hedges and a wrought-iron gate, although access was blocked at the end of the drive.

There was a security intercom beside the door and Cooper punched the talk button. It took a full minute before a female voice finally answered in a thick Hispanic accent, "Hello?"

Cooper identified himself and Detective Elena Verbena and said they wanted to speak to Mr. Best.

"He is not here."

"Is there a way we can get in touch?" Cooper tried.

"Nooo . . ." the woman answered uncertainly.

Verbena put her hand on Cooper's shoulder and gave him a small push. He ceded to her and she leaned into the speaker and spoke in rapid Spanish that Cooper, though he knew a few words, couldn't follow. The result was that the woman on the other end said, "Okay," and clicked off.

"What did you say?" Cooper asked his partner.

"I just made it clear her boss would want to know that there was a dead body at one of his home sites."

"You didn't threaten her."

"Cooper . . ." She gazed at him aghast.

He inwardly snorted, though it was true Verbena saved

most of her vitriol for men. Someday he was going to learn what lay in her past that fueled her male-specific misanthropy.

"She says Best isn't here, and that may be, but I want to see her face-to-face."

The woman who eventually opened the door proved to be a middle-aged, worried housekeeper of sorts who spoke in English for Cooper's benefit, but carried on most of her conversation in Spanish with Verbena. She had a lot to say while wringing her hands and while he waited to learn what that was, Cooper's attention wandered. He moved away from the two women, looking around the house, which clearly had been renovated to the cool, mid-century modern style that it had likely been at one time. Best Homes was putting up expensive houses but they were all two-story mini-mansions to maximize square footage. This house was a nice surprise of keeping with its original architecture. Cooper wouldn't have expected that of Best, based on his advertising. More to the man than he thought.

"Meester . . . ?"

Cooper had walked into the living room and was gazing across an expansive backyard with a western view that was currently lit by mushroom-shaped path lighting. It was full dark by now, but he could imagine the beauty of a setting sun blazing in coral and pink across the horizon. He turned around at the woman's voice.

"It's Detective Haynes," Verbena told her.

The woman clearly was anxious about him moving into the living room, so Cooper returned to the walnut planks of the entry where she and Verbena were standing.

Verbena said, "This is Norma Peña, she's the housekeeper for the Best family. She says they're all on vacation. Wife and kids are in California and Mr. Best is unavailable.

She knows why we need to get hold of him, but she's very reluctant."

Cooper regarded her. Lines of distress marked her forehead and her eyes were wide. She was scared to disturb the boss. "He will want to know this," Cooper said to her. They'd agreed not to relate that the dead person was Mr. Nye until they talked to Best himself. "Call him," Cooper urged gently, holding the woman's frightened gaze. "I can get the number if I have to, but it would be better if you call him."

"*Madre de Dios* . . ."

She shook her head, but she pulled out her own cell phone and plugged in the number. When the call went to voice mail, she said in a quavering voice, "Meester Best, thee detectives es here. Police. Someone es dead at your beeldings . . ."

Cooper held his hand out for the phone with a question on his face and she eagerly passed it to him. He said, "Hello, Mr. Best. This is Detective Haynes with the River Glen Police Department. Please call back at this number." He left his cell number, clicked off, and handed Norma back her phone. She made the sign of the cross over her chest before she took it.

In the SUV again, Verbena asked, "How long before he listens to that message?"

"Depends on what he's doing."

"You didn't believe the vacation line?"

He shrugged.

"You could have demanded the number from her," she pointed out.

"We can get it other ways. I don't want to get her in trouble."

Verbena snorted. "If she's in trouble for helping the police over the death of his foreman, he's an asshole."

"There you go again. Making assumptions."

"You think I'm wrong?" she challenged.

"If I did, I wouldn't tell you."

"You wouldn't?" Now she half turned in the seat.

"I prefer to live."

She threw herself back down and muttered something in Spanish.

"I don't know what you said, but it sounded like swearing."

"It was. Serious, serious swearing." The edges of her mouth turned faintly upward. "You think I'm a man hater, but I'm not."

She was right on the first part. He wasn't sure about the second.

"I just want fairness," she said. "And you have to fight for it, when you're a woman."

"What about Bennihof?" he asked. The question just popped out, almost surprising him.

She jerked a little but she didn't pretend to misunderstand what Cooper meant. "He's never tried anything with me."

"But he has with others? Who? Mackenzie Laughlin."

She frowned. "I was thinking of Katy Keegan. Why? Do you think he messed with Laughlin?"

"Not sure. What kind of messing are we talking about?" Cooper was running a little blind. He wasn't in the habit of addressing rumors around the station. Half the time they weren't true and only created more drama.

Elena muttered something beneath her breath, which he thought sounded like "Grab ass." It wasn't like her to keep things to herself and he said as much, but she made a face and said, "I'm not a fan of Bennihof's," and the subject was tabled.

Back at the department, Verbena offered to write up the

report. Cooper said he would help her, but she waved him off. "I'll take care of it this time. Let me know when Best calls."

Cooper had put his phone on silent and now turned it back on to check the time. He saw there was a message from Emma.

"Rayne Sealy's death is suspicious. You should do something," Emma's monotone voice told him and then she hung up.

Emma had been focused on Rayne's death ever since Cooper had had to leave the Whelan house the night Rayne's body was discovered. He didn't know what had precipitated this particular message, but Emma wasn't letting it go.

He put in a call to Jamie, whom he'd pressed to go on to the dinner at their friends' house without him. She had, though she'd made it clear she wanted him to join her at Camryn and Nate's no matter how late it became. Now she let him know they'd all finished dinner but were still drinking wine and talking, and she urged him to come. Sounded good to him so he said, "On my way," as he slid into his Explorer and headed in her direction. He was just cresting Stillwell Hill when the call came in from Best.

"Detective Haynes?" His voice was perplexed. There was dead quiet on his end of the line. Wherever he was, whatever he was doing, he wasn't going to give it away. "You found a *dead body* on one of my properties?"

"It appears to be Granger Nye, per his identification. I understand he's your foreman."

Best inhaled sharply. "Nye?"

Cooper explained about finding the man's body and Best queried him about who'd actually found Nye and what the circumstances were. He sounded strained and worried and finally came out with, "I don't know what I'm going to do without Granger. We're short-staffed as it is."

Cooper let that one pass, then told Best that Nye's body had likely already been transferred to the morgue in the basement of River Glen General Hospital.

"I've gotta . . . I've got . . . I'm not available right now. I need to call, *you* need to call Granger's brother, Terence Nye. He's the next of kin." He gave Cooper the information. "Thank you," he said as an afterthought, and hung up.

Cooper shook his head. Nothing warm and fuzzy about that man. He drove through the opened gates of the Still-well Estate, maybe the Farwell Estate now, and parked in the expansive area in the front. Jamie's Camry was already there. A faithful, if nearly failing, decades-old vehicle that she swore she was going to trade in. Harley was driving Jamie and Emma's mother's car now, which was maybe the newer of the two vehicles but not by much.

He placed a call to Terence Nye as he stepped out of the car into a brisk and surprisingly icy wind that was rattling the hedges and sneaking under the shutters covering the leaded glass second-story windows, making them clatter. Nye answered the phone with a brusque, "Yes?"

Cooper explained who he was and told him about his brother. Unlike Best, he sounded shell-shocked and said he was going straight to the Glen Gen morgue from his Portland home. Cooper then walked up to the front door of the house and rang the bell, which tolled a surprisingly merry tone for such an imposing structure.

Moments later Jamie threw open the door, still smiling from something that had happened as he could hear Camryn and Nate's laughter pealing from down the long hallway.

"Hey there," she said, and he wordlessly gathered her into his arms and held her close.

"A bad one?" she whispered, kissing him. "We were just laughing about their new puppy, who's adorable. And no, I don't want a dog. We've got Duchess to share with Emma sometimes, but that puppy's just a kick."

Cooper didn't respond. He was just glad to have her in his arms and drink in the smell and feel of her. The best antidote to the finality of death.

Chapter Seventeen

Mackenzie's cell rang as she was helping Stephanie clear the dishes from a dinner of chickpea khichdi, a vegan Indian dish that had been flavored with cumin, turmeric, and ginger, and had been really good. Stephanie had been leaning vegan before her pregnancy and now was all in. Nolan was working late and had missed this particular rendition, and Mackenzie wondered if he was sneaking in a T-bone steak or pulled pork sandwich or Kentucky Fried Chicken on the sly.

Her hands were wet and she quickly dried them on a paper towel before picking up her phone, which she'd set on the kitchen counter.

Taft.

Immediately her pulse raced and she had to school her features. "I'm going to take this in my room," she said, sweeping up the phone.

"Who is it?" Stephanie asked.

"It's . . . work . . ."

"You're working? What are you doing?"

"Same thing as before," Mac called over her shoulder.

"What is that?"

Mackenzie entered the pink bedroom and closed the door behind her. She made a point of not sharing the details of her work with her stepsister from her days with the police and had generally kept to that. She knew squirreling into the bedroom without saying who was on the phone would raise her stepsister's antennae, but she didn't want to talk about Taft. Especially since she didn't know what this was about.

Another reason to get that apartment.

"Laughlin," she answered, registering the cool tone of her voice.

Taft didn't waste time. "The foreman of Best Homes, Granger Nye, was killed in an apparent accident at the work site. He fell from the second story of a house under construction."

"What?"

"Maybe it's an accident," he said, his own tone suggesting he didn't think so.

Mackenzie's head whirled. "What? When?"

"Earlier today. I heard from some contacts. It'll be on the news. I wanted to reach you before you heard from someone else."

"Why? You think this has something to do with . . . Seth Keppler?" Seth was the only intersection of their two investigations.

"This investigation's growing. I stopped your surveillance because I didn't want you to get caught in the crossfire."

"So you're making decisions for me. I was a cop, Taft," she reminded him. "I can take care of myself."

"There are people involved . . ."

He was struggling to say what he felt, which was strange for Taft. She squinted in thought. "Mangella?" He didn't immediately answer and she quoted, "'It's amazing what *you* can get killed for if you try to carve out your own niche within the family.'"

He barked out a laugh. "Something like that."

"Which family are we talking about? Seth and Patti . . . and this Granger Nye? What did he do that got him killed?"

"I don't know if he was killed. I just know this thing has gotten hot. I want you to stay out of it, and—"

"Hold it right there. I learned today there's a very good chance Rayne met somebody on the overlook, so I met with Troi Bevins today and asked some questions. I want to talk to Seth, too, and I was going to tell you—"

"Leave Keppler alone."

"—that I was going to interview him. See, I knew that's what you'd say. You want to tell me why? Give me all the connections? I can make decisions for myself."

"I know."

He was weakening some. She marveled at how well she'd gotten to know him in such a short period of time.

"I need some help," he admitted.

Mackenzie almost laughed. "That hurt, didn't it?"

"Here's the truth. I don't want you anywhere near Mitch Mangella or his wife and that's why I pulled you off Seth, but I need someone, like I said before, because I can't be in two places at once."

"What's with Mangella? You gotta tell me, Taft. Eyes wide open."

"I'd like to talk in person," he said slowly.

"I could meet you . . . now?"

"Come to my place."

That was a bad idea. She could feel it in her bones. Something about the intimacy. But she wanted to go. "I'll be there in half an hour."

She was actually there in twenty minutes. She brushed her teeth and her hair and ran out the door. Stephanie chased after her.

"Where are you going?" she called as Mackenzie headed toward her SUV. "Was that the guy you're working for?"

"Working with," she threw back over her shoulder. "An ex-cop."

"Be careful!" was her worried warning as Mackenzie backed out of the drive.

Taft opened the door and led her into the kitchen as soon as she arrived. Once again she perched on a barstool as he stood behind the counter. She hadn't gone to all the trouble over her looks this time. She wasn't going to let herself fall into that trap again. This was business.

Taft didn't waste time. "Before we get started I wanted to tell you that I've been following up on Rayne. Haven't learned much beyond what you already know. I ended up at Ridge Pointe Independent and Assisted Living and asked a few questions. Rayne may have been seeing one of the resident's grandsons while she was there. Another to add to the boyfriend list. You might want to follow up."

"Okay . . ." She was a little bowled over that he'd followed through on his promise. "What about your investigation?"

"Keppler fell out of routine and I followed him today and lost him." He was clearly chagrined. "I think he's making a move and I could use another set of eyes on him *with* me. Not alone."

"Tag-team him?"

"Yes."

"Okay."

"Mangella has Seth on his radar. He's going into a

partnership with Andrew Best and he wants Seth out of the picture. I don't know if he knows of Keppler's involvement with drugs or . . ."

"If he's part of the deal?" Mackenzie suggested.

"If he is, that's it."

She'd never heard him sound so coldly certain.

"Then tonight I heard about Nye."

"You think Nye is connected to Seth . . . ?"

"I don't know the connections. Maybe Nye overheard something he shouldn't have . . . caught Seth at something. Maybe he was with them."

"Them meaning Andrew Best and Mitch Mangella."

"Let me tell you about what happened with Seth . . . Want a glass of wine or . . ."

"No, thanks. Just go ahead."

He then launched into how he'd been following Seth down I-5 toward Wilsonville and how he'd chosen to bail rather than have Keppler tag his SUV at the overpass. He reiterated that Seth appeared deeper in the drug trade than he'd originally thought and reminded, "You were the one who saw Seth waiting for Troi Bevins outside of Best Homes, so the stink of drug dealing, drug trafficking, possibly hangs over that business. I don't know how far up the ladder it goes, but Nye's death takes everything to a new level."

"You don't know he was murdered."

He half smiled. "I don't. But I'm operating on the assumption he was. I've met Granger Nye before. Kind of a formal, stiff guy. Not the kind to catch a beer with after work. He's fairly new to the job and he just doesn't seem to fit in with Seth and Troi."

"Nye took over the job my stepbrother-in-law had," Mackenzie reminded.

"I don't know how well he was fitting in. Andrew Best liked Seth Keppler, even though he kept hiring and firing him."

"Maybe because of the drugs?"

"Maybe."

"Best liked to go hunting with him."

Taft nodded. They'd covered this ground before and he wanted her to go over it again. Mackenzie appreciated that Taft had gone out of his way to learn what he could about Rayne, but he clearly wasn't all that interested in what she was doing. He hadn't given her a chance to explain about the piece of foil from the Red Bridge wine bottle she'd found at the overlook and she wasn't sure he would deem it as important as she did anyway. His focus was on Seth Keppler.

She said, "I told you I met with Troi today. I followed him," and then went on to explain about Troi's romantic entanglements with Elise and Rayne and Leah. "Troi's more . . . I don't know, *doofus*-like . . . an innocent rather than a criminal mastermind. I asked him about his meeting with Seth outside Best Homes and he was stunned that I'd been following him. I'd heard that they were rivals, from Elise Sealy, but Troi said Seth just sells him weed. Acted like Seth was small-time, like you said."

"I don't think he's small-time anymore."

She nodded once, silently agreeing.

"I wouldn't give Troi Bevins an out-and-out pass," Taft added. "You don't know who he's involved with."

She lifted her brows. "Like Mangella. One of the clients you're a fixer for?"

He wanted to argue that point, but didn't. They both knew Mangella was fluid with the law. And who knew how many other unsavory clients Taft had. She'd heard the rumors.

"So Mangella is in partnership with Best and now Best's foreman is dead."

Taft nodded. "Your stepbrother-in-law was the foreman for Best before Nye."

Mackenzie said, "Yes, but Nolan is no part of this." When Taft didn't answer right away, she doubled down, "I guarantee it. He left Best Homes and went to work for Laidlaw because Best was difficult to work with."

"Okay."

"Okay?" she challenged. "You don't know Nolan. He's a good guy. A *really* good guy."

"I'm not disagreeing."

"I just don't like the way you said that."

"Laughlin, I don't know your brother-in-law. I didn't say he was part of it. Maybe he saw something while he was there. You don't have to defend him."

"It sure sounds like it. You should talk to him."

"Well, I'd like to talk to him."

They looked at each other. Then Mackenzie pulled out her phone and quickly dialed her stepsister. "Is Nolan back?" she asked Stephanie.

"He's just walking in now."

"Tell him I'm with Jesse Taft, and I want to bring him by. He has some questions about Best Homes for Nolan."

She wondered if she should go into Granger Nye's death or if Stephanie had already heard, but Stephanie changed her mind by asking, "Is this the ex-cop you're working with?"

"Well, yes."

"Sure. Bring him by. I'd like to meet him. I'll tell Nolan."

Mackenzie clicked off. Stephanie had sounded way too

eager and Mackenzie wondered if she thought something romantic was afoot between her and Taft. Irked, she said, "Let's go," then got up so fast she nearly knocked over the stool. She straightened it and headed for the door with Taft switching off lights and following behind her.

The Redfield home was a modest ranch with warm light emanating through the picture window, illuminating the neat front lawn. Taft parked behind Mac's SUV and then met her in the driveway, and they walked to the front door together.

She hesitated on the stoop.

"You're rethinking this, aren't you?" he said.

"No."

"Yes." He almost smiled. "You're not sure how to explain me."

"I'm working with you. That's the explanation and it's the truth."

"Why are you so nervous?"

"Damn it, Taft. Just . . ." She didn't finish. Just shook her head and threaded her key into the lock.

Taft didn't really think Nolan Redfield was part of the stream of drugs that might be flowing through Best Homes via Seth Keppler and likely others, but he wanted to talk to the man.

And you want to be with Mackenzie.

He glanced behind himself, but there was no Helene. She was, as ever, just in his head.

Nolan Redfield was over six feet and had a slightly distracted smile on his face as he was introduced to Taft and shook his hand. The smile dropped off almost immediately as he asked both of them, "You heard about Granger Nye?"

Mackenzie assured them they had. "That's kind of why we're here," she added as they seated themselves in the living room. Redfield's wife, Stephanie, joined them by perching on the arm of her husband's easy chair. Mackenzie sat on the edge of the small sofa that Taft sat down in. He could feel Stephanie's gaze assessing him closely.

"What do you want to know?" Redfield asked into the lull after the introductions.

"Anything you can tell me about Andrew Best and Best Homes operations," said Taft.

"Are you trying to investigate Nye's death on your own?" Redfield slid a glance toward Mackenzie.

"Taft . . . Jesse . . . has been working on a case for a while."

"And you're on this, too?"

"Yes," Taft answered for her.

"Well, I'm sorry about Nye. I didn't know him. He took the job I had there."

"That's what Mackenzie said," Taft agreed. "What did you think of the Best Homes operation? Was it efficient? Did everyone get along?"

Nolan snorted and Stephanie gave Taft a wry look. She said, "Nolan was miserable there. It was hell."

"That's not really true," he tried to say.

"*Hell*," she repeated. "He wasn't the only one who was glad when he quit."

Nolan explained, "I took the job with Laidlaw Construction. I'm one of several foremen there and it's better."

"Less money in the beginning, but no Andrew Best to deal with," said Stephanie.

"I've heard Best's difficult," encouraged Taft.

"You heard right." Stephanie tossed her hands in the air and then dropped them down to her thighs. "That smile in his picture? You never see that. That man is intense. All the time. If Nolan made one mistake . . . It might not even be a mistake, but if Andrew thought he made one, he was furious and he didn't get over it."

"You said he hired and fired Seth Keppler," Mackenzie reminded Nolan.

"That's true," Nolan said reluctantly. He looked Taft in the eye and asked, "What do you think happened with Nye? They're saying it's an accident."

"It could be," said Taft.

"But you don't think so."

Mackenzie's gaze drilled into Taft and he knew she was wondering how far he was going to go into his investigation. He decided to push a little further. "Did you ever feel there was something else going on?"

Nolan frowned and said nothing. His wife twisted around to squint at him. "Honey?" she asked, when the silence pooled.

Nolan said, "You brought up Keppler. I guess I know why."

"Why?" Stephanie asked.

"Drugs. He was Andrew's connection . . . at first . . ."

"At first?" Mackenzie pushed when he trailed off.

"What happened later?" asked Taft.

"You never told me there were drugs," Stephanie said. She put a hand to her stomach and made a face. "I'm going to throw up." And she got to her feet and hurried down the hall.

Mackenzie sat up straight. "Should I help her?"

"Maybe . . ." Nolan said with a frown and Mackenzie followed after her, clearly torn between leaving Taft alone with Nolan and helping her stepsister.

As soon as she was out of earshot, Nolan said, "I didn't want her to know. I didn't do anything about it, and maybe

I should've. I just wanted out. You think Nye was involved and he got killed over it."

"I don't know," Taft said truthfully. "The police will investigate."

Redfield said, "You don't think they're going to come to the right conclusion."

"Oh, I'm sure they will."

"You're holding something back."

The man was too astute by far. What Taft wasn't saying, what he hadn't said to Mackenzie, either, was that there was political pressure being brought to bear on the pathologists to render causes of death that might be not as truthful as they should be. Mitch Mangella had a lot of sway. Likely Andrew Best did, too. Taft didn't trust Chief Bennihof to always make the tough choice when it came to River Glen's heavy hitters.

"I agree with you that Keppler's drug distribution was small-time once," said Taft. "It may be getting bigger now."

"Keppler is someone to watch out for. Mackenzie asked me about Troi Bevins, but we were two ships that pass in the night. Never at the same place at the same time."

Mackenzie came back out of the bathroom. "She's okay. She's pregnant," she explained, though she'd already told Taft.

They heard retching coming from down the hall and Nolan got to his feet. "That doesn't sound okay."

Taft said, "We'll let you be. Thanks. If you think of anything that might help, give me or Mackenzie a call."

"I will." He walked quickly down the hall.

Taft led the way out the door with Mackenzie bringing up the rear this time. They stood in a fine, misting rain outside for a few moments.

"Nolan's not any part of whatever's going on with Keppler," she said, hugging herself against the damp April night.

Taft nodded.

"I want to hear you say it."

He laughed. "Look, I'm going after the truth. That's all."

"That's good. So am I. The truth."

"Okay."

"I just want to get something straight," she began as a brisk gust of wind threw a slap of water against Taft and he turned toward Mackenzie, who'd pushed herself his way at the same time. He bumped her and she staggered and he grabbed her, holding her steady.

His nose was inches from hers. "What do you want to get straight?" he asked.

"That we're . . . working together. Not against each other."

Her voice trailed off to be caught by the wind.

For a wild moment he thought about kissing her. Every cell in his body told him to.

Very carefully he dropped his hands from her arms and took a step back.

"I'm not out to get your brother-in-law. Are you worried about him?"

"Of course not." She drew herself up straight.

He took a step away. "Yeah, well . . ."

"Everyone's warned me about you. Don't trust him, they said. He plays fast and loose. For the record, I think they're wrong. At least I hope they're wrong. And I want to work, and I want a job, so I'm trusting you, Taft."

"No, you're not." He almost laughed again. "Good night, Laughlin."

She said firmly, "I'm just not sure I like you."

"Oh, you like me," he threw over his shoulder.

And you like her way too much.

Arrogant son of a bitch.

Mackenzie let herself back into the house, asking herself what the hell happened there. Somehow that had gotten away from her.

Stephanie was right inside, pale but smiling.

"He's cute," she said.

"Didn't you warn me to be careful working with him?"

"Yeah, but he's cute."

So many words came to mind. Curse words. Serious turn-the-air-blue curse words. She fought them back and chose instead: "So are llamas, but they'll spit at you."

Stephanie nearly keeled over laughing. "Man, this morning sickness has started to be all day, but Mac . . . this is going to be so much fun!"

Mackenzie wasn't sure she appreciated the humor. She snorted and stalked down to the pink and white bedroom.

But the wry curve of Taft's lips bare inches from her own felt burned on her retina.

She grabbed up a pillow and held it over her face. When that didn't block the image she threw the pillow down and sank onto the edge of the bed. She was aware there was also a smile on her lips and that was the worst of all.

"You know better . . . you know better . . . Jesus, Mac . . ."

She heard Stephanie talking to Nolan. Not the words, the cadence, and then a trill of amusement from her and a deeper chuckle from him.

Get that apartment tomorrow.

Chapter Eighteen

Friday afternoon Thad sat in front of his computers, chewing on his lower lip. Last night's death at Staffordshire Estates had caught his eye on the local news feed. He didn't know the man who'd died, but he had a new interest in the River Glen Police Department since he'd learned the woman from the Waystation was an ex-cop. As he read the article he memorized the names of the officers and detectives who'd been at the scene of the accident. The reporter had tried to catch an interview with any member of law enforcement and had failed, though he did have a quote from Andrew Best, owner of Best Homes, the development company the victim worked for.

Best said, "It's a tragedy that Granger Nye fell to his death. We at Best Homes are saddened to lose such a fine man and loyal employee."

Thad smirked. They always said something like that. Total company bullshit. Nobody probably gave a flying fuck about the guy. And what about this Nye? How did a company foreman accidentally fall off a building?

His thoughts moved away from the story, and his gaze fell on Rayne's Hobo purse. He had to close his eyes and force himself free of the desire to relieve himself inside its folds. This hold Rayne seemed to have on him irked and somewhat alarmed him. He couldn't wait much longer for his next fix.

He glanced at his whiteboard, but his gaze turned inward.

Laughlin . . . ex-cop . . .

Dangerous. Very dangerous. But what was life without danger?

His mind then tripped to Gillis. Had the man sobered up this morning and thought about the Good Samaritan who'd given him a ride home? Had he started overthinking it, wondering why "Chas" had asked him about the ex-cop?

Had the police found any evidence that would tie him to Bibi Engstrom's death?

Cold fear pooled in his lower back and his body went into overdrive, his senses heightened. He jumped from his chair, yanked down his pants, grabbed the purse and folded it around his dick.

Bang, bang, bang!

"Thad! THAD!" Lorena's tinny voice filtered down to him.

"Fuck."

He threw down the purse, yanked up his pants and stalked up the stairs, his boner slowly dissipating as he had to deal with his goddamn mother.

"What?" he shouted through the sliding metal door.

"It's Mom. I've got to go get her. They're freaking out over at that place. She's gotta come home."

"Keep putting them off."

"I can't. You've got to come with me, Thad!"

Oh, Jesus.

"You can handle it," he snapped.

"I need your help so get THE FUCK OUT HERE!"

He covered his ears with his fists and jumped back down the stairs two at a time to the lair. "Leave me the hell alone," he snarled to himself.

BANG!

She'd kicked the door. Hard. He almost ran right back up. He'd like to snap her neck.

But then everything went quiet. He hesitated, listening, but Lorena was gone. Good. He tasted blood and realized he'd chewed into his lip. He made a sound of annoyance. Damn. He couldn't have Gram back. Couldn't. If that place was so desperate to move her, she must be loonier than he remembered.

He stared longingly at the purse. No . . . no . . . he didn't have time for that. Damn Lorena. DAMN HER AND GRAM. He couldn't kill Lorena. He still needed her. But she was a problem.

Was it even true about Gram? Maybe Ridge Pointe was just fine with where she was and this whole thing was one of Lorena's lies just to get Gram *under her control!*

Thad pressed his palms to his temples. He howled out a primal scream that reverberated through the lair. He waited half a minute, then did it again.

The relief he'd hoped for didn't come.

He went back to his computers and realized blood was dripping down his chin.

He'd bitten that deeply into his lip.

Shit!

He headed to the sink and cleaned his face off, staring at his reflection in the tiny mirror above it. His lip was swollen and still oozing blood. He had to keep licking it off. He turned sideways and saw the scab that ran down by his ear to his temple, courtesy of that bitch, Bibi Engstrom.

He needed a way to bring himself back under control. When had he lost control? When had that happened? He'd been so cool, so careful for so long, but he felt shaky now.

Rayne. It had happened with Rayne.

His fury knew no bounds. He wished he could kill her again. Those other mean girls. He needed to get those other mean, mean girls!

Stop being distracted, he warned his reflection.

With that thought in mind he grabbed his father's hat, jammed it on his head, and ran up the stairs. He would check on Brenda again. The dirty whore had to come home sometime. If she wasn't there, he'd go to the Waystation, see if the cop was there.

But if Gillis was perched on a stool he might have to do something about him. Or that shithead he'd played pool with. The guy had accused him of cheating and Thad had been immediately incensed. He was many things, but he was not a cheat.

He glanced over at Rayne's name, scrawled on the whiteboard, and the colorful list of names. Rayne's and Bibi's and Brenda's and the cop's . . .

He ran lightly up the stairs, wondering if he should bring a rope, something to tie Brenda up with if she tried anything. The idea excited him. Something new. He pictured them making love on her dirty bed with him slipping the rope around her neck. . . .

Lorena was right outside the door. "You're going with me," she ordered. "We need to bring her back and you're good with her. She'll listen to you. I don't know what you do down there all the time, and I don't care, but you need to help me. Then I'll leave you alone. After we get Mom."

Thad felt a growing rage. She had no right to order him around. He could picture the rope around his mother's neck. He could picture himself tightening it, hanging her body from the chandelier . . .

She was staring at him.

He nodded.

Not yet. He would go with her to pick up Gram.

But sooner or later he would have to find a way to get rid of Lorena.

Emma straightened the stack of washcloths she had on her bathroom shelf, aligning the corners. She'd just gotten back from a walk with Duchess around the building. Duchess had done her business and then sniffed at the ground, tugging at her leash. Emma had allowed her to lead them toward the hiker's trail. They had gone partway up that trail together a couple of times. Duchess wanted to run like crazy, but Emma had to hold her back. She couldn't let the dog off leash unless they were at a dog park.

"That would be bad," she said aloud. Duchess could scare someone.

She came out of the bathroom and Duchess was sitting on the kitchen floor, her eyebrows moving up and down as she looked at her bowl. The dog started whining.

"Too many treats make you fat," Emma said to her. Again.

Duchess gave a sharp bark.

Emma sighed. Duchess wasn't a good listener.

Knock, knock.

"Emma? Are you in there?" Jewell called anxiously through the panels.

Duchess barked and barked. "Shhh," Emma told the dog, giving her a stern look, as she went to the door.

Jewell burst into the room and Emma took a few steps backward. "Have you heard? Have you heard?" Her voice was shaking.

"Uh—"

"Twinkletoes slept in Sara's bed! The cat was *in her room!* Sara's really frightened. They need to get rid of that cat! It's not right!"

"The cat slept in Mrs. Throckmorton's bed?"

"It shot out of her room this morning!" She shuddered and looked over her shoulder at the door, as if the cat was coming for her.

Emma wasn't sure what she felt about the cat. She really didn't like the name they all called it. But the cat belonged at Ridge Pointe, so she said, "The cat lives here, and you can't take away someone's home."

"Emma . . ." Jewell pressed her hand to her chest. "The cat is a stray and there's something wrong with it."

"Is Mrs. Throckmorton dead?"

"Emma!"

Emma blinked at her.

"No! Goodness, no. She's alive. Her daughter and grandson are here now, talking with Bob and Faye." Jewell sniffed. Jewell did not like Faye who also worked in the office. She liked supercilious Bob Atkinson, the facility director, who made more rules.

"So, the cat was wrong," said Emma.

"They don't die the day Twinkletoes shows up. You know that, Emma. It's afterwards. Sara's daughter is taking her home. Maybe she'll be safe there, but I don't know. It's like a . . . hex, that cat!"

"Mrs. Throckmorton is going home?"

"That's what I heard."

"You were eavesdropping?"

Jewell glared at Emma, her brows in a dark line. "They're in a meeting room and they're loud. Sara is rightly upset. Old Darla's making things worse. She can't keep anything straight and she's in the way. They've trapped the cat."

"What?" Emma's heart flipped over painfully.

Jewell held up her hands. "I just wanted to keep you informed."

"You wanted to gossip."

"Honestly, Emma, I know you have problems, but I really don't need to be chastised all the time." With that Jewell twisted the doorknob, yanked the door open, and slammed it behind her.

Emma grabbed up the keys to her room and headed out, turning to Duchess who, as ever, wanted to follow her. "We'll go later. I need to save the cat."

Duchess barked twice and her gaze switched from Emma to her bowl again, her tail sweeping the floor. Emma pretended the dog agreed with her, but Duchess just wanted a treat. That's how dogs were.

When she reached the Ridge Pointe lobby she walked around the center fireplace and looked through the glass wall to the meeting room, the special room with the circular table. Mrs. Throckmorton was seated there, her head down. Bob and Faye were there, too, along with Mrs. Throckmorton's daughter . . . Emma couldn't remember her name . . . and Thad.

Bad feelings settled over Emma. She didn't like the way Thad looked at her, and she was suspicious of the way he treated Mrs. Throckmorton. Emma had overheard him whispering to his grandmother about how much he cared about her, how he was the one she could depend on. Emma was pretty sure he was lying. He seemed like a liar.

She could see Mrs. Throckmorton was crying, and Emma walked to the door and pushed it open.

"Emma, this is a private meeting," said Bob in a harsh voice, rising from his chair.

"Mrs. Throckmorton is crying."

Faye had jumped up, too, and now she came to the door. "You can talk to her later," she said in a soothing voice.

Emma felt Thad's eyes on her. They seemed to burn right into her. She couldn't make herself look at him directly, but said, "Thad was kissing Rayne."

Faye gently touched Emma's arm. "This is a family meeting, Emma."

Emma pulled away. "You've trapped the cat?"

"Who told you that?" Bob sounded angry, but like he was trying to hold it back.

Faye said, "No, the cat was put outside."

"Twinkletoes!" Mrs. Throckmorton said, tears in her voice.

Faye held the door open, waiting for Emma to exit. Emma backed out of the room and Faye closed the door.

Emma stood there a moment as Faye walked back to her chair. She shot a look at Thad. He was staring at her. She hunched her shoulders and headed for the outside door to the front portico. She needed to find the cat and save it before they got rid of it.

Jesus . . . Christ . . . Thad felt his heart thundering in his chest. That . . . woman . . . that *retard* . . . *God!* They'd all turned to look at him when she'd said he was kissing

Rayne. When had she seen him? Never! They couldn't associate him with Rayne. They couldn't!

He could feel the blood drain from his face. There was a buzzing in his ears. They were still talking about Gram and Gram was crying, moaning that she didn't want to leave, just like she'd moaned that she didn't want to leave her home when they'd first brought her here. She didn't know what she wanted. She was as loony as they were saying, as loony as that *retard!*

He wanted to kill her. She'd caused him irreparable harm. He had to say something, do something.

"I don't know what she's talking about," said Thad, glad his voice sounded normal.

"Whatever, Thad," said Lorena, turning back to Bob Atkinson, who was being a pure asshole about the money and Gram's care.

They were taking Gram out today. Of course he didn't want her to come home, but now with the retard's words hanging over him like an arrow, pointing down on his head, a marker that he'd *killed Rayne*, Thad's mind was changed. He needed to get away from this place and never see these people again. Never come back here.

"We'll take my mother tonight and Thad'll figure out how to move out her things and furniture. That should make you happy."

"It's not about that, Mrs. Jenkins. It's the level of care," Bob tried to say, but Lorena was in pure bitch mode and just waved her arm at him and glared at the other woman, Faye, who clearly felt he and Lorena were not up for the job.

Too bad.

Twenty minutes later they were helping Gram out to Lorena's car. Lorena had wanted to take the Caddy, but

Thad had told her it wasn't running right—he couldn't afford it to be on the road—so they were in her Honda compact with Gram in the passenger seat and Thad folded into the back. Gram was still sniffling and it was driving both Thad and Lorena crazy.

"We didn't want this, either, Mom," Lorena snapped.

Thad asked, "How are we going to get her upstairs?"

"The stair lift, *Thad*."

"I don't think she can do it, *Lorena*."

Lorena glanced at Gram, then in the rearview to Thad. "We'll do it. You'll do it."

Unable to help himself, he stated firmly, "I don't know what that weird woman was talking about. I wasn't kissing anyone."

"Oh, give it up. I saw the way you looked at her, too."

"Who?" Thad asked, unable to help himself.

"That Rayne girl. When she was there. The one that killed herself."

Lorena threw it out like it was no big deal. Like she knew it and everyone knew it and there was nothing anyone could do about it.

Thad found himself chewing his lip, breaking open his cut again. He licked the blood and forced himself to stop gnawing.

"And what happened to your face?" Lorena asked, looking at him in the mirror again.

"What do you mean?" Thad went cold all over.

"That scrape by your ear. Somebody claw you?"

"Rayne did it," sobbed Gram.

Lorena glanced at her and Thad stared in horror at the back of her graying head.

"Rayne's dead, Mom," Lorena said tiredly to Gram. "She killed herself."

Gram didn't respond, just sniffled.

Thad forced himself not to cover the scab on his hand protectively, the remains of the wound from Bibi's fingernails. His blood was pounding in his ears. His mother and grandmother were dangerous to him. He felt like he was going to explode.

As soon as they were home and Thad had managed to belt his grandmother into the stair lift and then walk up the stairs beside her and get her into the room closest to the master bedroom—*Lorena's* bedroom, not the one at the end of the hall he sometimes used when he wasn't in the lair, which was unfair and he was going to take over the master as soon as they were both dead—Thad headed to his F-150. He needed air. He needed away from *them*.

He looked around the garage. He'd thrown a drop cloth over the Caddy, hiding it. Lorena hadn't mentioned it. Didn't care. Thad's Ford truck was in the carport alongside the garage. When Lorena was gone, he would sell her car and move his truck inside.

He moved forward to the workbench and the cabinets his grandfather had ordered when the house was built. His grandfather had died less than a year after he and Gram had moved in, but he'd stocked the garage with tools and miscellaneous landscaping gear. Determinedly, Thad started sorting through Grandpa's cobwebby lawn and outdoor items. Part of them were dear old Dad's, too. After Grandpa died, his parents and Thad had moved in with Gram, but his father had taken his life soon after. Thad snorted as he sorted through the spades and clippers and rusting cans of Raid, getting ready to load up his truck. Lorena could make a man want to kill himself, for sure.

He gathered up a first load to put in the truck bed. He already had the knockout drops in his glove box.

CHAPTER NINETEEN

Mac checked her online source of apartments on her phone and saw there was a new one open at a small complex that she knew in Laurelton, close to Highway 26. It wasn't far from the Barn Door, which served up seventy-two-ounce steaks free to anyone who could eat one and all the fixings on the plate that came with it. The restaurant had been popular for a long time, but its clientele was diminishing in the age of a rapidly expanding vegetarian and vegan culture. Mac had been at the Barn Door once when a huge, bearded dude with a shaved head had managed to put down one of the enormous steaks. He'd gotten his meal free, but he'd looked a little glassy-eyed, as if he was having trouble keeping it down, as he'd staggered for the door and out of the restaurant.

The price of the apartment was right so she clicked on the manager's number and waited for them to pick up.

She'd tried to put Taft out of her mind, but he'd been the first thing she thought of every time she woke during the course of a very restless night. She'd finally given up and had switched on her bedside lamp at four-thirty, jotted down some notes about things she needed to talk over with him, before lying back down and staring at the ceiling. She hadn't felt this way in a long time about a man and it was troublesome. She tried to remember how she'd felt about Pete, but her ex-boyfriend was way too far in her rearview to educe any romantic response.

Taft, on the other hand, seemed to have her nerve endings in thrall. Her autonomic system was on high alert from the most minor message from her brain, sending electric tingles from neuron to neuron, shooting through her whole system if she thought too hard about that man's lips.

She'd pushed thoughts of him aside with an almost physical effort with varying degrees of effect over the course of the morning. She'd checked on several apartment complexes and spent some of the morning with Stephanie, mindlessly shopping, glad her stepsister had switched her conversation to baby talk rather than anything more to do with Taft. She'd driven by Good Livin' twice on her apartment search and had noted Keppler's car both times. She hoped Taft would call and put her on the job in some way and didn't want to approach Keppler again till she'd gotten his okay. She wasn't sure Seth was Rayne's last lover . . . she kind of thought he wasn't . . . so she was willing to be patient and stay out of Taft's way, especially since Seth appeared to be into illegal drug trafficking of some kind.

She'd also checked the news cycle, hanging on anything to do with Granger Nyc's death, but there was precious little. No one was saying it was anything but an accident. Detectives Haynes and Verbena were in charge and Haynes had given a non-answer to the media, which meant the police weren't labeling it an accident yet.

Her mind flipped back to Jesse James Taft's lips.

"Damn . . ." she whispered. At the same moment the manager answered and they worked out an appointment time of four p.m. She immediately started feeling anxious about losing out. The one-bedroom unit was on the second floor, about the center of the complex, and she suddenly wanted it so badly she could hardly stand it. She told herself that there would be something else if she didn't get it, but the tactic didn't work. She wanted this one.

With that in mind, she drove over early. Three o'clock. If he wouldn't show her the unit yet, she would just wait.

The manager's unit was on the bottom floor with an OFFICE sign tacked onto the outside. The complex itself was L-shaped, two stories with a center outdoor stairway and one on each end. It was gray shingled and had a gated, designated parking area underground, and also an above-ground blacktopped area at the backside for visitors and residents with more than one or two cars. In front of the building there were about three spots marked with time limits, several fifteen-minute-ers, and one for one hour max. Mac pulled into the one hour max limit. She had a good view into the manager's office.

Her cell buzzed and she saw it was Taft. Immediately her nerves buzzed in anticipation and her pulse increased. She gritted her teeth and wanted to smack her palm to her forehead. She felt like a teenager and she had not enjoyed her teenage years. She answered with, "I hope this means you have work for me. I'm seriously trying to get an apartment and I need an income stream."

"Where's the apartment?"

"Near the Barn Door. You know it?"

"A Laurelton landmark," he said dryly. "Leaving River Glen, huh?"

"I grew up in Laurelton."

"Welcome home," he said, a smile in his voice.

Did he know? Had he seen her reaction? There had been

a moment of awareness between them; she was sure of that. They'd both played it off like it was nothing, but *did he know?*

"Do you have work for me?" she asked, her eyes on the SUV that had pulled up. A young couple had gotten out and were now walking into the office, holding hands. Were they going to look at her apartment? She was starting to feel very competitive.

"I've had someone keeping tabs on Keppler for me," he said, "but he's been off the grid for a few days."

She felt a pang of rejection that he'd turned to someone else. "So you do have someone on surveillance."

"In a sense."

"What does that mean?"

"One of my CI's is a watchdog. He's been gathering information. I'm waiting to hear from him."

"Information on Seth?" If she'd thought about it, she would have known he had confidential informants at his disposal. Any good investigator did.

"I have something else in mind for you. I want to take my measure of Andrew Best, and I'm thinking about how to go about it. He knows me by reputation through Mangella. I've never met him, and I'd like to keep it that way."

"You want to get up close and personal without him recognizing you."

"I want to see where Nye died. The possible crime scene."

"You think someone killed him."

"I think there are a lot of connections to Keppler and your friend Bevins and Andrew Best, maybe Mangella, that could circle back to Nye."

"Troi Bevins is not my friend," she protested. "Okay, so what do you want me to do?"

"We could go look at a Best home together."

"What's the play?"

The couple had come back out with the manager and were climbing the middle stairway to the second floor. Mackenzie gritted her teeth. She was set on this apartment but it looked like the gods were against her.

"I think you and I are in the market for one of the homes near where Granger Nye fell. We'll go to Best Homes offices and will undoubtedly be fobbed off to someone else rather than Best, but it's likely Best will be around because of Nye's death. We'll get as close to that particular house as they let us. I think we should show up as a married couple."

"Really?" The thought boggled her, but she recovered enough to say, "A ruse. Not exactly how we do it in the department."

"Good thing you're not a cop anymore."

Bantering with him only made things worse. She said crisply, "I can play that out."

"Okay, I've made an appointment for five thirty this afternoon. Mr. and Mrs. John Adams."

"Well, gee, I don't think I can make it that fast. Can you wait?" She checked the clock on her dash. "I've got things to do. I need this apartment."

"I want to get there just before closing."

"Do you have ID for us?"

"Won't need it yet. We've put money down on a Laidlaw house and only have until tomorrow to back out of it and buy a Best home. They're going to talk to us fast and deal with details later."

"Okay," she said.

"Good. Come to my place and then we'll go over there together. See you soon." And he clicked off.

Did she have enough time? Not if these people didn't get moving. She had all kinds of thoughts on how to stop them from renting the apartment. Taft's less than honest tactics ran through her mind. Ruses. Ploys. Lies. She was veering away from the rules she'd abided by in the department in a big way. She wasn't sure if that was bad or good.

She waited while the couple and manager came out of the unit and back down the stairs to the office. They were inside for a good twenty minutes, and Mackenzie's heart sank. This was not going well. When the young man and woman finally came out and headed toward their vehicle, Mac stepped from her RAV. "Hi," she greeted them. "Are you looking at the unit up there?" She pointed to the apartment.

"We just signed for it," the woman answered her.

Mac's heart sank. Well, great.

She watched them leave, then walked into the office half an hour early. The manager looked up at her expectantly. Mac didn't waste words. "Hi, I have a four o'clock appointment to look at the apartment on the second floor that you and that couple just came out of."

He straightened up as if she'd goosed him. "Ah . . . yes . . . I was just going to call you and tell you it was rented."

"Well, thank you," she said coldly.

"Okay . . . Yeah." He was about Mac's same age with a patchy beard and a few leftover adolescent pimples, and she guessed by his uncomfortable behavior that he hadn't had much experience at the job.

"Do you have anything else coming up?" She was so bugged she could hardly think straight.

He smiled at her, relieved she wasn't going to go into a full-blown hissy fit. "Possibly . . ."

"Possibly. What does that mean?"

"Well, we have a situation that is . . . well, um, one of our units should be available soon? Maybe. It's an end unit, which is a little more money?"

"Which floor?" Mac asked tersely. She tried to hold his gaze but his eyes were darting all over the place.

"Second."

"I would like to put money down on it."

"I don't know for sure—"

"I would like to put money down on it," she repeated. "In case it comes up."

"I won't know for a week or so, so . . ."

"I'll write you a check for first and last month's rent, right now."

"And a security deposit," he said, looking around as if he was searching for someone to help him. Then his gaze finally fixed fully on Mac. She'd tried harder with her appearance this morning than she usually did. Her hair was brushed back and clipped into a low ponytail, and she'd actually added earrings and light makeup.

He seemed to like what he saw. "Sure, why not?" he said with a shrug, and Mackenzie pulled out her checkbook from her purse before he could change his mind.

Half an hour later she was driving back to Stephanie and Nolan's house, grinning. She got it. The apartment. She had a place to live of her own and a plan! The first serious step she'd taken toward the rest of her life since her decision to leave the department. She almost felt jubilant.

Inside the pink and white room, she searched through her clothes for an outfit to become Mrs. John Adams. She decided Mrs. Adams's first name was Brooke and that

she leaned toward jewel tones. Mackenzie shook out a
royal blue skirt and the silk blouse that matched it. Yesterday's rain was a memory, but there was a cold, kicky
breeze outside and she needed another layer. The dull gold
cardigan sweater she teemed with the blue made her look
a little like a cheerleader. Hmm. She switched out the skirt
for a pair of jeans and was more satisfied. This time she
fixed her hair to hang loosely, brushing it until it crackled.
She eyed herself critically, carefully adding some extra
mascara and dark pink, almost red lipstick.

Stepping back, she examined herself critically.

"You look . . ."

She couldn't quite finish the comment to the colorful
vision in the mirror.

Stephanie's mouth opened in shock a few minutes later
as Mackenzie tried to sneak out of the house. "Where are
you going?" she asked.

"I have a date with destiny."

"I don't know what that means." Stephanie couldn't
take her eyes off her.

"I dress up occasionally," Mac said a bit defensively.

"No, you don't."

"Is it too much?"

"The shoes are wrong . . . for whatever you're doing.
You need heels. Those flats are—"

"I'm in jeans. I'm not wearing heels," Mac interrupted.

"Heels look good with jeans." She held a hand to her
stomach.

"Sick?" Mackenzie asked with concern.

"Same old, same old. Everything was going fine—
perfect!—and now I can't even look at food without my
stomach churning."

"You still glow."

Stephanie snorted.

"I'm not kidding. Pregnancy looks good on you."

"Are you meeting Jesse?" she asked hopefully.

Mackenzie didn't know how to answer that. She didn't want to foster Stephanie's new-found interest in her possible love life. "I'm on a job."

"For Jesse?"

"For Taft, yes."

"Does it have something to do with that foreman who died, Granger Nye?"

Mackenzie detected a hint of worry in her voice and said, "As far as I know, his death was just a terrible accident."

"If you knew differently, you'd tell me, right?"

"I don't know anything. I'm not a cop anymore, Stephanie."

"Yeah . . . but you're something." She looked Mackenzie up and down.

"I'll check with you later," Mackenzie said, and swept past her and out the door.

Half an hour later she was at Taft's place and was rethinking her costuming. She'd gone overboard, as if she was back in drama class.

Then Taft came out in pressed jeans, a black shirt, and a dark jacket. He looked hip and cool where she looked . . . she didn't even know. Theatrical?

He smiled as she got out of her SUV and his gaze swept over her. "You look great," he said.

"Thank you," she answered cautiously. "I was going for a character. Brooke Adams."

"Brooke? Okay."

"There are a couple of things I want to get clear. Last night, and today, a lot of names were tossed about that possibly had something to do with Seth's extracurricular activities outside Good Livin'. One of them was Mitch Mangella, who you work for."

"I do *some* work for Mangella," he clarified.

"And you think Mangella might be involved in Seth Keppler's drug deal."

"I hope to God he isn't."

"That would be a deal breaker."

"Of course," he answered coldly.

"That's why we're going to see Andrew Best. You're worried that he's a part of it, maybe a big part of it, because he's connected to both Seth Keppler and Mangella and now his foreman's dead."

"And Troi Bevins."

Mac wasn't going to argue with him about Troi again. She'd come to her own conclusions about the man, but there was a chance she was being played by him. It was unlikely, but she couldn't rule it out entirely.

"When we're done with this, I have a couple of things I want to talk over."

Taft had driven them all the way to Best Homes, and they were pulling into the parking lot and he was checking the time on his dash. "What?"

"I don't have time now."

"Give me a sample." He stopped the car, cut the ignition, and gave her a look.

"Taft," she said, exasperated. Annoyed, she kept the information about Rayne and the wine bottle to herself and said instead, "Katy Keegan says she went after Chief Bennihof, not the other way around."

Taft gave a derisive laugh and climbed out of the car. Mackenzie scrambled out the other side.

"What's that supposed to mean?" she asked.

"That's a story she's telling you. I saw her after he caught her alone in his office. She was making excuses for him, but she was trying to make it right in her mind. It wasn't good."

"She flat-out told me she chased him down."

They were walking toward the company offices, and he stopped before taking the two steps that led to Best Homes's wraparound stamped concrete deck and massive entry doors. "So she lied to me, or she lied to you," he said. "Which do you think it is?"

Mac had already considered that Katy might have decided to go after Bennihof after his first harassment as a means to take back her power. "Victims sometimes blame themselves and try to normalize a sexual predator's attack."

"Straight out of cop psych class. And the truth." He went up the stairs and held the door open for her. "We're a bit late, Brooke. You ready?"

"Yes . . . John."

CHAPTER TWENTY

Old Darla sat at Emma's table, her face contorted with fear. "They took her away. She was tagged to die, so they took her away."

Emma looked from Old Darla to Jewell, who was sharing dinner at a separate table with her friends. They were all looking over at Emma and Old Darla as well. Emma wished she were still working at the thrift shop, but they'd closed for the day and she'd just gotten back, walked Duchess, and was now at dinner. There was too much drama going on now. "The cat didn't sleep with Mrs. Throckmorton."

Emma had searched for the cat for a long while, worried they'd lied to her and it was trapped somewhere. But then it had strolled up to the door, meowed, and been let in by one of the old men, who was generally cranky but liked the cat. Emma had been relieved but was still worried for the cat's fate. Maybe it should've stayed away.

She said to Old Darla a bit louder, "Bob said the cat did *not* sleep in Mrs. Throckmorton's bed. Jewell gave the cat a bad reputation, but it's not true. Mrs. Throckmorton is alive and well and with her family. That's what Faye said."

Bob didn't like the cat, but he liked telling people they were wrong. And he'd been telling Jewell she was wrong, which had not gone over well with Jewell. He'd also told Jewell, and Jewell had told Emma, that one of the residents had seen Mrs. Throckmorton urging the cat to come inside her room with her. Bob said Mrs. Throckmorton had then forgotten why the cat was there and had gotten scared.

Old Darla didn't seem to hear her loud voice. Old Darla didn't hear much of anything. Now she looked toward the entrance door and squeaked. Emma followed her gaze. There was the cat, sitting in the doorway. Ian wasn't here tonight. It was Friday and he had the night off. He was the one who usually gave the cat treats.

Emma tried not to worry for the cat.

Old Darla suddenly said, "They said Sara's daughter picked her up, but she's my daughter."

Emma frowned at Old Darla. That was not true. Mrs. Throckmorton's daughter was Lorena—she'd remembered the name—and her grandson was Thaddeus. Emma had never heard that Old Darla had any grandchildren. Harley had told her that Old Darla had a "loose connection" and Emma thought she was right. Old Darla kept mixing everything up.

Raising her voice once again, Emma said firmly, "*Mrs. Throckmorton's* daughter is Lorena, and she came to Ridge Pointe yesterday and picked her up to take her home." She purposely left out that Thad was her grandson because Old Darla was too confused about him.

Old Darla's eyes fixed on Emma. "That house has too many stairs. All those houses do. I remember when they built them. They won't take her there."

Emma was glad they weren't talking about grandsons

again, but she had seen with her own eyes Lorena helping Mrs. Throckmorton to her waiting car, so they'd gone somewhere. "Lorena buckled her into the car," she told Old Darla.

"All those houses have too many stairs," Old Darla declared, pointing her finger at Emma three times. "It won't be safe there. That's why they put her in Ridge Pointe in the first place. *She couldn't do the stairs!*"

"Maybe Mrs. Throckmorton is going somewhere else," said Emma. She didn't like Old Darla pointing at her.

"I tried to fight them but they built them anyway." She waved her arms around, growing upset, pointing past Emma. "Too close to the trail. They're monstrosities. The city should have never allowed them!"

"Monstrosities," repeated Emma.

"I fought them . . . I fought them . . ." Old Darla's face collapsed into tears.

"But now Mrs. Throckmorton lives there . . . ?"

"She has my daughter and grandson!" She started wailing and Emma worried she was going to spill the chicken soup in her bowl. She'd hardly eaten any of it.

"Be careful," said Emma. She wondered if the administrators had gotten it wrong and it was Old Darla who should go to Memory Care, not Mrs. Throckmorton.

Scott, a weekend administrator, looked into the room. His gaze zeroed in on Old Darla, and he came over to their table and laid a hand atop one of Old Darla's that was lying on the table. Old Darla snatched her hand back and wouldn't look at him. "Darla, are you finished?" he asked, smiling but not really smiling. He was being patient, but Emma knew it was fake.

Old Darla wasn't answering, so Emma explained, "Her friend Mrs. Throckmorton is gone."

"Yes, she's gone home." He flicked Emma a look. Across the room Jewell and some of her friends were looking over, too.

"My grandson is coming for me," Old Darla whispered.

"I'm sure you'll see him soon," he said and it was a lie. They did lots of lying around here.

"Old Darla doesn't have a grandson," said Emma.

"Yes, I do!" she flashed. "Yes, I do!"

Scott soothed, "I'm sure he'll come see you soon. Let's get you back to your room."

"But it's not the truth," said Emma.

"I think I know what Darla needs." He turned back to Old Darla, who was peeking up at him. Her head was down because she was embarrassed. "Looks like your soup's gone cold. I'll get you a warm bowl and have it brought to your room."

Emma could tell he was kinda mad. She just wasn't sure if he was mad at Old Darla or her.

She watched as he helped Old Darla from the chair, to her walker, and down the hallway. They passed the cat, who took a playful swipe at Scott's ankle.

"Be careful, cat," she muttered.

She thought about Mrs. Throckmorton's house. She knew those houses that Old Darla didn't like. Three of them above the trail. Maybe she would pay a visit to Mrs. Throckmorton sometime. Her house wasn't that far from Ridge Pointe and she might like the company.

"If we see Andrew Best, he'll focus on you," Taft said into her ear as they entered the Best Homes offices. "Like

Bennihof, he warms to attractive females. I know you can act, so just do what you do."

"What do you mean?" Mac pulled away a bit from the warmth of his breath on her ear.

"Before you became a cop, you were in theater arts."

"How do you know that?"

"I did my research on you. You have an associate's degree in—"

"How long have you been researching me?"

"Laughlin. Your curriculum vitae isn't hard to find."

"That was a lifetime ago. I changed course to have a career."

"Okay."

She narrowed her eyes at him. Now who was playacting? She wanted to be outraged. She felt used, somehow. No, that was bullshit. He was right, goddammit. She wanted to play this part.

"Just want you to know, I'm not sure Brooke even wants a Best Home," she said. "They're a little on the traditional side and I prefer mid-century modern."

Taft rubbed his right hand across his jaw to cover a grin and reached with his left for hers. They walked up to the front desk holding hands and were greeted by a young woman with perfectly coiffed blond hair who told them their appointment was with Racquel, who was ready to show them around.

"Is Mr. Best here?" Mackenzie asked with a little shrug of her shoulders. "I'd love to meet the owner."

"I'm sorry, he's busy today."

"Oh. Oh, that's right." There was a horrified gasp hiding in Mac's tone. "You had that accident last night! I saw it on TV. Awful." She flicked a look at Taft whose eyes were sparkling with repressed amusement at her performance. "Maybe we should have come another day?"

"We have that deposit . . ." he said.

"Right." Mackenzie nodded and frowned. "We put money down on a home in Staffordshire Estates by that other builder . . . Laidlaw Construction? I do like that one," she said to Taft.

The woman at the desk was looking kind of tense. She glanced down a long hallway and said with relief, "Here's Racquel."

Racquel was tall even in black flats, and she was dressed in black pants, a white blouse, and a gold jacket. An iridescent green Best Homes pin with her name on it was tacked to her lapel. She asked, "Are you only interested in Staffordshire Estates, because we have many wonderful properties elsewhere as well."

"Oh, no. It has to be in Staffordshire Estates," said Mac.

"Well, I can show you some we have available, but we've had an unfortunate accident at one of the sites and so it will be limited, I'm afraid."

"Oh, I know. I'm so sorry. We're just kind of under a time crunch."

"We have money down on another property," Taft admitted, showing off his dimples with a faintly regretful smile. He'd shaved his beard close to a five o'clock shadow. With his jeans and black shirt he almost looked like a model, and Racquel and the woman at the desk both noticed.

"I'll show you what I can," said Racquel. "Should we go in my car? I'm sure you know that Staffordshire isn't that far from here. We have two models that we can walk through."

"That would be great," said Mac.

They followed Racquel outside to a white Mercedes sedan. It was decided Mac would sit in the front beside Racquel and Taft would sit in the back. Racquel chatted of the wonders of buying a Best Home on the short trip, and Taft, reining in his usual bombastic style, asked Racquel a lot of seemingly small-talk questions about Best Homes that she eagerly answered in glowing terms.

"We're number one in the area. I know you said you've offered on a Laidlaw property, but we really are the best in the business!" she chortled.

That line could get pretty old, pretty fast, Mac thought.

Taft said, "I've heard that, but are you really?"

They'd fallen easily into their roles without rehearsing. Mr. Adams was the skeptical male who was the hard-ass on the purchase, the man who needed his hand over the end of the bat to win, whereas Mrs. Adams was motivated by prestige and social climbing.

"I know it sounds like a joke," Racquel said, shooting Taft a smile through the rearview mirror, "but it's the truth. You want a Best home. You really do."

"You'll have to convince me," Taft said, an answering smile in his voice.

"Challenge accepted," said Racquel, her shoulders squinching in as if she wanted to hug herself with delight.

Mac tried very hard not to mind.

When they arrived at Staffordshire Estates, Racquel drove them to the oldest part of the development, a ring of houses around a central park with a center gazebo and a play structure surrounded by laurel hedges. The houses themselves were sixties-style ranches, some with added second stories, some with basements.

"I just wanted to show you these. They're called the Villages. Victor's Villages, after the original developer, but shortened to the Villages. They have their own homeowners' association and the dues are a little more economical."

"They seem very nice, but they're not quite what I'm looking for," Mac said regretfully.

"I understand, Mrs. Adams. I just wanted to give you an overall look of Staffordshire."

"It's Brooke. Please."

Taft said, "We're really more interested in your newer plans."

"Well . . ." Racquel drove them out of the Villages and farther down a wide, winding drive to a second section of homes, which were mostly finished. The third section was right beside it, and though most of those homes were under varying stages of construction, there didn't appear to be any work being done.

"We've shut down work today on Phase Three," said Racquel, "but the houses in this section are of the same design as Phase Two. The models are open."

The periphery of the lot of one of the houses under construction that abutted Phase II was staked out with crime scene tape, and a number of vehicles surrounded it. Seeing Mac's gaze, Racquel added, "There are houses toward the back of Phase Three that are further along, but we'll have to stay off-site, I'm afraid."

"That's where it happened, isn't it?" Mac said, expelling her breath.

"We hadn't had an accident in over a year."

"It was your foreman?" Taft inquired.

"Yes."

"Looks like the police are investigating," he added.

Racquel determinedly drove them down another street

and parked in front of a white, two-story home with gray shutters. "This is our most popular model."

As they got out of the car, Mac asked, "Is this model the same as the one where the accident happened?"

"No, that's the second floor plan."

"Could we see that one?" asked Mac.

Racquel's lips tightened. "Well, since we're here. Let's see this one."

She walked them through and spent all her time talking to Taft. After they'd toured the second floor and returned to the kitchen, Mac said, "I don't mean to be rude, but this house plan is too . . . *meh* for me." She looked at Taft. "What do you think?"

Racquel had bristled at Mac's remark but now she turned to Taft. "The other floor plan may be more to your liking . . ." she said doubtfully.

"Let's take a look," said Taft.

By the time they were through the second model home, which was a lot like the first although the roof was flatter and offered more room upstairs, it had been full dark for over an hour. The neighborhood lights had switched on illuminating the front yards of all the houses in diffused white circles. Several garage doors were open where family members had returned home.

"It's a nice neighborhood," Racquel said, sliding Taft a sidelong look from beneath her lashes.

"I'd like to drive through the new section. Phase Three," Taft told Racquel.

"Like I said—"

"Quick drive," he interrupted, spreading his hands.

"I'm not sure . . ."

But she was waffling and in the end Taft got his way.

They drove into Phase III, past the house where Granger Nye's life had ended and through the snaking streets bounded on both sides by structures in varying stages of construction. Here the lighting was bright bulbs on poles that spread cold white light over the area.

And as they circumvented the house with the yellow crime tape Mac recognized Cooper Hayne climbing out of his city ride and striding toward a man in a hard hat who could only be Andrew Best.

Taft drawled, "Looks like Mr. Best is meeting with the River Glen PD."

Racquel said, "What?" whipping her head around to gawk as they passed by.

Mac's attention was so split that she barely registered Racquel had asked her a question as they circled back and once again passed Andrew Best and Cooper standing outside the house where Nye's body had fallen from the second story.

"Brooke?" Racquel asked, as she aimed the nose of the Mercedes out of the development and back toward the Best Homes offices.

"I'm sorry," Mackenzie said. "What was it you said?"

"I was asking which section of the development you—"

"Hon, I know you probably like Phase Three best, but I'm leaning toward the Villages," Taft interrupted.

Mackenzie half turned to look at him. It was dim inside the car but she thought he was hiding a grin. "Well, babe, I'd have to disagree." She turned back around and said to Racquel, "Why are the police here? It's rather frightening."

"Well, they have to investigate the poor man's death, and we're cooperating to the fullest, of course."

She was getting kind of snippy, so Mac pushed, "It

seems like they think it's more than an accident. I don't know how that's going to play out, for your development, I mean. When someone dies suspiciously in a house, it's hard to sell afterward, or so I've heard."

"It was an accident." She glanced back at Taft and said, "The Villages are hard to get into, I'm afraid."

"But what if it was murder?" Mac pressed. "What about the neighbors? I'd be scared to go out of my house, I can tell you."

Racquel touched her toe to the accelerator and said firmly, "Well, let's go back and talk about what appeals to you."

She was all business after that, directing everything to Taft and nothing to Mackenzie. She hustled them into an anteroom at Best Homes, one eye on the clock as it was getting into the evening. Mackenzie started to sit down and then said, "The restroom?"

"It's down the hall." She inclined her head in the direction of the hallway from where she'd first appeared.

Mackenzie left Taft with her. She didn't really need to use the facilities but she wanted to get away from Racquel. Seeing Detective Haynes on-site was a good indication that there were questions regarding Granger Nye's death, no matter what Racquel said. She couldn't wait to talk to Taft about it.

The rest of the Best Homes staff appeared to have left, and the place was quiet as she made her way to the ladies' room. Coming out of the facilities she heard a male voice emanating from one of the offices around the last corner. The door to the room was shut but his voice was loud and Mackenzie recognized it. Seth Keppler.

What was Seth doing at Best Homes?

She hesitated. If he came out and caught her, she had no excuse. Still . . . She moved closer.

". . . following me. I don't give a shit. I'm going there tomorrow and he won't be in the way. He leaves me alone. Fuck, man, I'm doing everything I can. I wouldn't have come here if it wasn't important." A pause. "Soon as he's gone, come here. I'm in your office."

Mackenzie tiptoed away, hearing the call was winding up. Was he talking to Andrew Best? Whoever it was, she didn't want to be caught eavesdropping and was worried that if Keppler decided to leave the office he would see her before she could get Taft and vamoose.

Racquel was showing Taft a packet of information when she slipped back inside the door. The room had a window to the inside entry and compared to the dimness of the rest of the building was lit up like a film scene.

Mac grabbed her stomach. "Babe, I think I ate something wrong."

Taft gave her a hard look, alert. "You want to go?"

"Yeah, I think so."

Racquel said, "I'm so sorry you don't feel well, Brooke. I could get you some sparkling water from the kitchen if you—"

"No, thanks, I really just need to go."

Taft got up from the chair and moved toward her, putting a solicitous arm around her. "The baby?" he couldn't help himself from saying. She could read him and knew he was getting a little kick out of the whole thing.

"Don't forget your packet." Racquel practically thrust it into Taft's free hand. "I don't have your cell number. Do you have a card?"

"I'll call you tomorrow," Taft said, guiding Mackenzie out of the room.

Racquel followed them a few steps. "My number's in the packet."

Taft nodded to her and then he and Mackenzie were out in the night air. The rush of cold was almost welcome.

"What?" he asked her as they slammed shut the doors to the Rubicon.

"Seth Keppler's in an office inside, maybe waiting for Best?" She quickly related what she'd overheard in the conversation.

"Damn it. What's Keppler doing here?" Taft muttered as he pulled out of the lot, his expression tense. "I asked my CI to put a tracker on Keppler's truck, which he did."

"An illegal tracker?" She supposed she should've guessed. "Who is this guy?"

"Someone close to this investigation. He went out of his comfort zone to place the tracker."

"Okay. Fine." Clearly he didn't want her to know and she got that. "I didn't see Keppler's truck at Best, did you?"

"No." Taft was clear on that. "Once we're out of the lot I'll pull over and we'll wait and see where he goes next." He looked troubled. "He must be driving something else, or he Uber'd over. A Best Homes cube truck? Shit. You heard Seth say he was 'going there tomorrow'?"

"Yes, and 'he won't be in the way,' whoever he is."

"Not Best, I'd wager." Taft was thinking fast. "Don't know why I haven't heard from my CI. I suppose Seth could ride share back as well. Why doesn't he have the F-150? If he knows about the tracker, he knows he's being watched."

"He did mention something about 'following me.'"

"Damn." Taft looked as angry as Mac had ever seen him.

"Where do you think he's going tomorrow?"

"To the meeting. The exchange. The big finale . . ." Taft's eyes were on the traffic as he took a left onto the street and drove toward the place he could pull off and meld with other vehicles, a gas station. "Wish we had your RAV to catch him both ways. If he turns right . . ." He shook his head.

They sat for a couple of minutes in silence, then he drew a breath and asked, "What do we know about Keppler?"

She sometimes forgot he'd been with two different police departments; his moves were so outside of procedure. But it was the question always asked about the players in an investigation: What do we know about him or her?

"Seth's worked off and on for Best Homes and he's a friend/frenemy to Andrew Best. He's currently employed as a trainer at Good Livin', a workout guy. He's dangerous, likes guns. Hank Engstrom, Bibi's husband, described him as gun crazy." Mackenzie's gaze was trained on the street. "He dated Rayne Sealy, then jilted her . . . for Patti? He moved on to Patti, in any case. He drives a white F-150 Ford truck. He's Troi Bevins's weed dealer and Troi dated Rayne before Seth."

"What else?" he asked, although he sounded sort of far away, like his mind was working a different path.

"I'll have to think. What do you know about him?" she asked him.

"Seth Keppler's from a small-time crime family."

"Oh, right. The vicious kind."

"He's serious about his workouts. He took the job at Good Livin' after Best let him go, but he's still tied in with Best. Maybe Best got nervous about having Seth run his side business out of Best Homes and that's why Seth was hired, fired, hired again, fired again. Best wants him close but not too close."

Mac nodded. "Can't quite let him go."

"And Keppler's moved from small-time to big-time in the drug business. Moved away from whatever his family is into to a new level of crime, which may include both Andrew Best and Mitch Mangella. I don't want it to be with Mangella, but it doesn't look good. At any rate, Seth recently made a jump up."

"How recently?"

"I don't know."

"But when you realized it, that's when you took me off the case," she said.

He didn't deny it.

"I'm still on the case," she told him. "Mine and yours. What's the tie-in that you think is with Mangella?"

She was afraid he might not answer her, but he said, "Mangella wants Seth out of the way while he's working on a partnership with Best, so there's something there. My CI has been doing some digging for me."

"What if we just follow him home? What if he just goes there?"

"Then we'll figure out where he's going tomorrow," he said.

Mac shrugged. Easier said than done. "Maybe south . . . like when you were following him?"

He grunted. "His family's mostly east, near Gresham, but . . ."

Mac suddenly remembered, "Troi said Seth would take Andrew Best to his dad's farm to shoot. Where's that?"

"Dead end. His dad's gone. He was the patriarch and

he and Seth never got along anyway. You're sure Troi said his 'dad'?"

"Yeah."

"Hmm. The Kepplers don't have a farm, to my knowledge."

"Then where did Seth take Best shooting?"

Taft leaned back against the headrest. "He had a stepfather once, years ago . . . but like with his father, he and Seth were at odds. Seth has anger issues. Wouldn't be surprised if he's a roider. Doesn't make for sustaining relationships."

"The information you have on Keppler is pretty in-depth."

"Like I said before, I have friends in high places."

Taft's phone buzzed. He pulled it from his jacket pocket and looked at the number. After a moment, he answered, "Taft."

Mackenzie couldn't make out the words but she thought it was a male voice. Taft listened in silence and then said, "Good," and hung up.

"Your CI?" Mac guessed.

He threw her a smile as he switched on the ignition. "Yep."

"We're leaving?"

"He saw Uber pick up Keppler and followed. It was lucky timing because he wasn't planning on surveilling him with the tracker in place. He followed him to Best and he's in the parking lot. He saw us leave."

"So we pick him up tomorrow outside his town house and see where he goes."

"I'll follow him and let you know—"

"No, I'm in at the start."

"This has gotten bigger than—"

"I'm going with you, Taft," she insisted.

"I have other things I need from you. I want to know the status on Granger Nye's death. You can check with Cooper Haynes, and I'll let you—"

"Hell, no. You can get that information from those *people you know in high places*."

"Let me do the reconnaissance and I'll call you."

"You won't," she charged.

"No, I will. I mean it. I will. Go home now. Get ready."

"I'm going with you," she said again as he drove them back to her vehicle. She was still arguing as he pulled into his slot beneath the carport, but he wasn't listening.

"I'll call you. Promise. Goodbye, Laughlin."

Son of a bitch.

She gave him a tight smile, got out of his SUV, and stalked to her car. He could push her off all he wanted, but she determined right then and there she was going to follow him to wherever he was going and he could just eat it.

CHAPTER TWENTY-ONE

T had left Lorena and Gram at the house and climbed into his truck. They'd picked up Goldie Burgers on the way home and had eaten them in the kitchen together like they were one happy family. What a joke. Thad had wolfed down the meal, still seething about the retard at Ridge Pointe and his mother's *and* grandmother's comments about Rayne. Now Lorena and Gram were upstairs, settling down to watch television in Lorena's room. Lorena didn't like it much and had angled to put Gram in Thad's room, as he had a TV and the spare room didn't, but he'd put his foot down and for once Lorena had just thrown up her hands and snapped, "Fine."

What the fuck was he going to do with them? He couldn't live with them. They both needed to go. He'd had dreams of burning down the house with them in it, but that would destroy his lair. He was going to have to get rid of them a different way . . . and soon.

He was heading toward Brenda's apartment again. He'd loaded up the truck bed with whatever he could find around the house and the garage that might be useful in case things went awry as he romanced her. Twine, two gunnysacks from the original Stillwell Feed and Seed, a box of latex gloves, several gallons of bleach, and a smattering of other tools were loaded under a gray tarp he'd stretched across the bed. He did not have a gun, which bothered him a bit, but he'd never been into firearms.

He was passing by the Waystation on his way home, his head full of plans for Brenda, hoping she'd finally come back from wherever she'd been. His mind snagged on Laughlin, and he yanked the wheel and pulled into the lot. He had a feeling he was going to be disappointed that his quarry still wasn't back, so he might as well learn more about the woman who'd bewitched him at the bar. He thought about her and then got a distinct shock.

She reminded him of a slimmer, prettier Rayne.

"Aaargh!" he howled as he threw the truck into park. Rayne was the one who'd bewitched him. He hated her. *Hated* her.

He dug his hands through his hair and bit his lip. The rip he'd torn broke open and blood ran down his chin. He had to wait till it stopped bleeding and swore in his mind at both Rayne and the raven-haired Laughlin ex-cop.

It took twenty minutes before he got himself in hand and presentable. His anger once again on a leash, he swept up the cowboy hat and jammed it on his head. It looked like Gillis's vehicle was here. He didn't see the ex-cop's vehicle but maybe . . .

He entered the Waystation and saw Gillis at the bar, alone. Of course, he couldn't be that lucky.

"Hey, man," a voice greeted him.

Thad looked over and saw it was the guy who'd called him a cheater standing by the pool table, a smirk on his face. Thad's blood boiled and he had to internally scream at himself to keep from overreacting. It was worrisome that the fabric of his controlled demeanor was fraying, but he managed to hold it together. In a moment of clarity he recognized he'd crossed the Rubicon into a new world. Before Rayne, he'd been satisfied with living his life online, but since having her, killing her, that satisfaction was gone. He needed more. He needed a woman to love and kill.

Thad ignored the asshole. He was just about to turn back and head out when Gillis looked over and saw him. His brows drew together, then cleared.

"You!" he called, waving him over. "C'mere. I owe you a beer!"

Thad almost left anyway. His hope of finding the ex-cop at the bar had been a serious misstep. If he wanted her, he could find her online. Why hadn't he done that? There had to be something about ex-River Glen PD cop Laughlin somewhere. With his skills, it wouldn't be hard. He'd been too distracted, waiting for Brenda to return, worrying about Lorena and Gram . . . and Gillis.

And now the man had recognized him.

He could kick himself for letting his cock drive his decisions. He lifted his chin in recognition and sauntered over to Gillis.

"Did I say thank you?" Gillis asked loudly. Too loudly. It almost hurt Thad's ears. "You took me home. I owe you, man. Hey!" He signaled the bartender.

Thad resisted the desire to pull his cowboy hat lower over his eyes. He wasn't wearing his boots today. Was dressed more like usual in jeans and a close-fitting dark T-shirt that showed off his physique.

"Can't stay, man," Thad said, remembering to drawl. "Gotta get goin'."

"Aw, c'mon. One beer. Or did you like vodka, like Mac, maybe. Can't remember."

"Beer's fine." Actually he hated beer, but he drank it upon occasion just to keep up his persona.

"Give him the same as me," Gillis called to the man. Then, to Thad, "Did you find her?" as he took a long swallow of his own beer.

"Who?" he asked automatically.

"Mackenzie. You were looking for her, right? I remember that part. You asking about her." As Thad's blood chilled, Gillis wagged his finger at him.

Mackenzie Laughlin.

The bartender snorted as he brought over Thad's beer.

"Hey," Gillis said to him, affronted, but the bartender, a young man with a hoop earring, just waved him off as he left.

Thad was getting in deeper and deeper. Not only Gillis but the bartender knew about his interest in Mackenzie. He was going to have to leave her alone. He was going to have to stay away, because if he had her, if he got her to the lair, and then she disappeared, which was kind of his thinking on her, just have her disappear—poof!—and these jokers remembered he'd been asking about her . . .

He could bury her in the lair, maybe. Or outside, between the houses, maybe. The people who lived next door were rarely in residence. Fucking elites lived in Colorado half the time. Maybe he could get away with it. But it was dangerous.

"Told ya she was mine," Gillis warned him, smiling, trying to sound sorta friendly about it, but the thin line of his teeth gave him away.

Thad decided right then and there that he would kill Gillis. Maybe not right away. An accident. Some drunken evening he would run the sucker off the road or something. There were lots of ways to kill people and get away with it. He just had to come up with the right plan. But Gillis deserved to die for getting in the way of his plans for the ex-cop.

Maybe there's a way you can still have her. Gillis and the bartender won't think it's you. Especially if you keep showing up, become one of the regulars. Talk about some other woman you're with. Brenda. Or Rayne. Just don't use their names.

No one will suspect you.

"Chas!" Gillis said suddenly, snapping his fingers. "I remember!"

Thad forced a smile and nodded at the asshole.

Now it was too late. He would have to deal with Gillis at some point.

He drank his beer and tried hard not to give his churning thoughts away. He managed to leave the bar after choking down the beer, touching the edge of his cowboy hat at the pool player who still tried to get him into a game.

His thoughts were black as he drove through the darkening skies toward Brenda's apartment. He had a sensation of doom that he couldn't dispel. Nothing was working out. He could feel himself on the edge of that vortex. One wrong step and he would swirl around and around like a leaf in an eddy, caught for eternity.

Traffic was a bitch. Everybody getting off work for the weekend. Neon bar signs beckoned the crowds as he drove up Hawthorne, already certain and fuming that Brenda wouldn't be there. She'd obviously quit her job as a dental hygienist. Probably a good thing. He liked the profession, but he thought about her dirty hands in someone's mouth. She was a party girl. Liked to go out at night with her

BFFs, a bunch of empty-headed women with too much makeup looking to get laid. Thad knew enough about Brenda to be repelled. He'd purposely steered clear of her, hating her from a distance. But then he'd hooked up with Rayne and things had changed. He'd found Brenda less repulsive. Of course it was sickening the way she ran through men like Rayne had, but if he was the last one, then that was worth something.

He drove past her apartment complex and there was her car . . . in a different spot. She was back! She'd moved the vehicle. She had to be back. . . .

He drove around the block, unable to find a parking spot on the street. Shit. He slowly cruised by her place again, turning into the lot at the last minute, parking in an empty numbered spot, thinking. If the apartment owner came out and found him in their slot he'd be fingered and that was a no-go, but he had to know if Brenda was really home.

As he sat there, hands on the wheel, Brenda herself suddenly appeared, tip-tapping in heels to her Jetta. Thad's heart beat hard and fast at the thought that she might see him. But she was oblivious. She backed out of her parking spot with a chirp of tires and headed up the street.

He was beside himself. She was *here*. Right in front of him as he edged onto the street behind her. Man, that black skirt was short. He caught a glimpse of a shiny, hot-pink blouse beneath her black jacket. Her brown hair was down to her shoulders, thick and bouncing. He wanted to bury himself in its tresses.

But then his mind imagined her on vacation at some resort, on a lounge chair, dripping in coconut-scented oil, basking in the sun, some guy beside her reaching over to rub his hand along her thigh, suddenly slipping his fingers between her legs, digging inside her bikini bottoms, sliding into her wetness. She would be begging for him. Squirming for him to take her. Her fingers raking his back as her body convulsively arched upward.

"Cheating bitch," he whispered.

He shadowed her to a swank club, not too far from her apartment. He parked and then debated on the cowboy hat, but it didn't look like that kind of place, so he left the hat in his truck. Climbing out, he tugged on the lines that held the tarp in place over his equipment and followed Brenda into the club.

The music was loud, but slow and sexy. His first impression was bodies everywhere, gyrating to the music or pressed up against one another. It felt like a disco right out of the seventies with a mirror ball cascading little squares of refracted light over the scene. Brenda had just landed at a small bar table at the far side of the room, which was being saved by a couple of girlfriends. The three of them were laughing and talking, and to place her order Brenda had to grab, literally grab, one of the young male waiters and wink at him and whisper in his ear.

Thad worked his way closer to their table, but not too close. He wanted to observe for a while. He'd never gone hunting quite this way and it was pumping adrenaline through his system. He kept his eyes on Brenda's table, watching as the waiter came back with a clear martini sporting a lemon twist, straight alcohol, he thought with an inner smile. Wouldn't take too many of those before she was loose and ready.

There was a table near them of a bunch of guys who seemed out of place. They were looking around in a dorky way, taking it all in with a kind of awe. Had to be newbies.

Thad uncomfortably remembered that he'd looked much the same way when he first started hitting bars.

One of them, who looked like he was barely old enough to drink, or maybe he wasn't and just had good ID, made the mistake of walking up to Brenda's table. She and her friends regarded him with smirking smiles and kept looking at each other as if to say, "Can you believe this guy? This nerd. This *ass!*" Thad recognized the look and in his head he heard young girls squealing, "Mr. Toad! Mr. Toad!" It was all he could do to keep from staggering from the dizziness. He sat down hard on a barstool just vacated by a woman who'd been asked to the dance floor.

Brenda was the worst of the bunch at her table. She clearly had spent money on some breast enhancement, but apparently hadn't bothered to improve the oversized nose he remembered from grade school. It was still too big for her face, even though he could admit she was the best-looking of all her friends.

He debated if he should approach her. Maybe he should wait for her to leave. He could grab her, tie her up, drag her to his lair . . . except he was parked in a public spot. There was no way he could quietly kidnap her without the whole world seeing.

About twenty minutes in, Thad was feeling better. He didn't have to kidnap her. He just needed her to invite "Chas" home. How hard would that be? He'd ordered himself a Coke and asked the bartender to send her over another of what she'd been drinking. It turned out to be a Grey Goose vodka martini. Thad watched the waiter take it to her and when she shook her head and said she hadn't ordered it, he pointed to Thad.

Brenda smiled in delight and raised the glass to her lips, meeting his gaze. He lifted his chin at her in recognition.

When she didn't immediately invite him over, he took it upon himself to step over to her table.

"Thank you," she said, looking him over. A puzzled frown wrinkled her brow. "I know you."

"I don't think so," he answered in a deeper voice than normal, but his pulse blasted into hyperdrive. "It's Chas."

"Brandy," she said. "This was very nice of you." She lifted the drink in a salute to him before taking another sip.

Brandy, huh? If she thought that made her more attractive, she could think again. She was still a bitch and a whore with a big schnozz no matter what she called herself. She'd taken the drink from him, hadn't she? Those things cost an arm and a leg in this place and he was going to get his money's worth.

"Well, Chas, I would invite you to our table, but it's just girls tonight." Her friends both looked at her and then at each other, stifling giggles. She was lying. One of them said, "That's right. It's BFF night!" and the three of them joined in laughter together.

"But I appreciate it," Brenda said again with a smile she probably thought was just the cutest. Thad nodded to her and returned to his barstool only to find that someone else had snatched it.

A few minutes later he left the bar, infuriated. He checked the ties on his truck bed, still untouched, and climbed inside. It was a shock that she had blown him off. He knew he looked good. His body was in great shape and he'd purposely walked in without a jacket so everyone could see how he looked in a tight shirt.

But Brenda hadn't cared.

Her little smirking smile was etched on his brain.

He waited in the truck. It took two more hours before she stumbled out. She never went for her car. Just waited outside yakking away with her friends and then the other two got in a Lyft car together while Brenda waved at them. She then waited for her own Lyft and as the driver turned back out of the lot, Thad followed.

He parked on the street this time as there was a spot available. Good. On his many trips past her place he'd determined there were no outside cameras; the building was too old or the management didn't care. Of course, some of the apartment dwellers could have those Ring cameras outside their doors, but he knew there was nothing on the stairway and Brenda's place was the first door along the third-floor hallway. With the cowboy hat pulled down across his face he felt fairly safe he wouldn't be recognized.

He watched the Lyft driver pull back onto the road and he lithely ran to the back stairs and up to the third floor. The paint was peeling and he thought the place smelled ever so slightly. If he weren't so enraged he'd almost feel sorry for her. He could make her life better with his ill-gotten gains. He could marry her. Take her away from all this. Maybe if he dangled a nose job in front of her?

What was he thinking? He hated her. She could wallow in her low-class life.

The door was cracked open. The stupid cow hadn't even shut it all the way. She deserved whatever she got.

He pushed the door open with his elbow. He could see a light and hear her in what he assumed was her bedroom. He quickly stepped in and closed the door behind him. It made a small clicking sound and he froze, but he realized she was kind of singing as she apparently got ready for bed. His eye caught sight of the chain lock. With a smile he slid the lock in place, his pulse running light and fast, then turned back around. There were small potted plants on every available surface, like a fucking greenhouse. Maybe that's all she had for companionship.

I'm good at this, he thought. He caught sight of himself in the mirror on the wall by the kitchen and smiled at his reflection.

"What the fuck, man?"

Thad's head whipped around. Brenda stood at the end of the hall, glaring at him. He'd expected her to be sloshed but she seemed surprisingly sober.

"Your door was open," he said.

"You're the guy from the bar! Who are you? I know you. I know I do!"

"I'm Chas." He swept the cowboy hat from his head. He'd almost said "Thad."

"Get the fuck out!" She came toward him hard, actually *charged* him.

"Whoa, whoa!" He held up his hands.

"GET OUT!"

Her hands were out, fingernails heading his way. She was bold, he'd give her that. As she neared he simply hauled off and slammed his right fist in her face and that oversized nose burst out with a spurt of sudden blood.

She opened her mouth to scream and he jumped forward, held his hand roughly over her mouth. They tumbled to the floor together. She was spitting and tried to bite him and he hit her again and she went out cold, turning into a limp rag.

Bitch!

His fist hurt. Really hurt. Same damn hand he'd injured over Bibi. These women . . . these terrible *whores*.

Breathing hard, he got to his feet. Had anyone heard?

He listened hard, but there was no sound anywhere. Good.

Very deliberately, he stripped off her clothes. He listened to her chest. She was alive but her breathing was uneven. Thad ripped down his own pants to his ankles and settled himself on her.

Bzzzz . . .

He froze before he could enter her.

Her limp, outstretched arm slowly twisted a bit and her cell phone fell from her hand, sliding onto the thin carpet and waiting there like a grenade, screen glowing.

He saw the text: Bringing friends. Hope you wanna party!!! A line of emoji party hats followed.

The roommate.

He quickly pulled up his pants, panicked. How much time did he have?

Brenda stirred and said something.

She could identify him. And she might finally remember who he was.

He'd dropped his hat on the kitchen table and now he swept it up, thinking. There were no fingerprints.

He'd touched the chain on the door.

He ran into the kitchen, his gaze frantically searching the counters. Paper towels. He grabbed up the roll from amidst a half dozen pots of African violets. He hurried around the wall to the living room.

She was gone.

What?

Slam!

He jumped at the sound. The door to one of the bedrooms.

He hurried down the hallway. "Brenda?"

"I know who you are," she said, crying from behind the panels. "You're . . . Thaddeus Jenkins!"

Shit!

He slammed his shoulder against the door. His hat flew off. There was no lock and the jamb splinted and broke under his weight.

Smash!

Pain exploded in his head. He staggered. Saw stars. Vaguely he realized she'd smacked him with one of her vile plants from her windowsill and was reaching for another. Blood ran down his face.

He swung into her, throwing all his weight on her. She dropped the plant and fell to the bed, Thad on top of her. He wrapped his hands around her neck and squeezed and squeezed and squeezed. Her hands came up, struggling to release his fingers, the pressure. She scrabbled madly, her eyes bulging, gasping and cursing.

He slipped into unconsciousness for a minute, an hour, an eternity. One second he was teetering on the precipice of the canyon, the next he was back. He let go of her and stumbled to his feet. She was dead. Her eyes locked open. There was blood everywhere. Hers and his.

The bleach . . . in the truck . . . but the roommate . . .

He staggered back toward the living room and saw the roll of paper towels unspooled on the floor. Snatching up several sheets he used them to open up cupboards and was rewarded with a nearly full bottle of bleach beneath the bathroom sink. He poured the bleach over Brenda and her bed. He saved a few inches of it sloshing in the bottom and lurched back with the bottle toward the living room. Drips and swatches of blood on the carpet. He drenched them with the remaining bleach. Then he swiped at the chain lock as he released it.

His hat.

He hurried back to the bedroom, found it sitting in the hallway. He grabbed it and jammed it on his head, moaning at the pain, then he headed down the stairs to his truck.

He moaned all the way home, a high keening he couldn't seem to stop. He hadn't put on the latex gloves. He'd intended to romance her. He'd intended to *romance her* and she'd *attacked him!*

There was no sound in the house as he hurried toward his lair. He cleaned himself up at his washbasin, shocked that he was really no worse for wear in appearance. His head throbbed like a son of a bitch, but she hadn't got her claws into him. His eyes were dilated. Concussion, maybe.

Nothing had gone as he'd planned. Nothing! And yet . . . as he thought about it, as he remembered the way her bloodied face had turned blue and she'd gasped for air and begged him for mercy as he squeezed . . .

He shuddered from head to foot. He would take a shower in the dead of night, when he was sure Lorena wouldn't get up and check on him. For now, he was going to pleasure himself with the memory of the kill.

CHAPTER TWENTY-TWO

It was still dark as Mackenzie drove through a sheeting rain in Stephanie's car to Seth and Patti's town house. She was a little afraid Taft would get up before she did and be parked somewhere nearby. She saw Keppler's Ford truck sitting in the driveway and thought about the tracker Taft's confidential informant had placed there, and wondered if Seth knew it was there.

A few blocks away she passed a Best Homes cube truck parked on the side of the road and thought, *Oho.* Taft had theorized that Seth was picking up a Best Homes truck and she would bet this was the one he'd taken. Taft's CI undoubtedly had let Taft know the same, so she drove a few more blocks and worked her way into a parking spot that gave her a somewhat limited view of the truck, but might make her invisible. The rain was a hindrance and a help. Visibility was crap, which made it hard to see the Best Homes truck, but it also made it difficult to see inside the vehicles on the street through the fogged windows, so she had some camouflage.

She slunk down in her seat and just let her eyes look

over the steering wheel. She hadn't seen Taft's Rubicon, but maybe he, too, would be driving something else.

She was pissed off at him. He was trying to protect her because he thought things had grown too dangerous. So who made him the one to choose for her?

Time crawled by. She thought about that female astronaut who'd decided to kill the woman who was the rival for her lover's affections. She'd driven across about five states and had worn Depends so she wouldn't have to stop at the bathroom. Homicidally crazy she might have been, but if too many hours elapsed Mackenzie would have to figure that out. She'd forgone breakfast just so she could last for hours.

She peered through the darkness. Was that a man walking through the rain? She shrank down farther and watched as her quarry turned the corner where the Best Homes cube truck was parked. A few minutes later, headlights cut through the faint gray morning light and the Best Homes truck rumbled into view and down the road. Mackenzie hesitated before turning on her engine. Where was Taft? She didn't believe he wasn't around.

She waited an excruciating five minutes. The Best Homes truck was out of view. If she waited much longer she would lose it entirely.

She forced herself to hold tight. Her brain screaming at her to get rolling!

But then a vehicle turned out from the same block where the Best Homes truck had gone. It was a light brown sedan with no lights.

Mackenzie let it also get nearly out of sight before she pulled onto the street behind it. She didn't recognize the car but she just knew it was Taft. The morning was growing faintly lighter, which was a relief because she left her lights off, too.

Cooper slipped out of the bed he shared with Jamie into the dull morning light, stopping a moment to look down at the sweep of her lashes against her cheek as she slept on. He pulled his pants over his boxers and grabbed the sweatshirt he'd tossed across a chair. He'd worked late the night before and Jamie had asked him a lot of questions about the Nye investigation when he'd returned. Cooper hadn't been able to tell her much. Even if he could confide work-related issues with her, he just didn't have a lot of information yet.

Sweeping up his phone, he headed downstairs barefoot, listening to the rain being thrown against the windowpanes. He set the cell on the counter and quickly started a pot of coffee, searching through the cupboards for a mug. He'd stayed at Jamie's house a lot, most nights, in fact, but still hadn't completely familiarized himself with her kitchen. It was Saturday morning and Jamie wasn't working, though she'd been substituting pretty steadily throughout March and now into April. He was glad she could sleep in.

His mind was on Andrew Best. The man had reluctantly, very reluctantly, agreed to meet with him yesterday at the scene of Granger Nye's fall. He was still being cagey about where he'd been at the time of the man's death. Clearly he hadn't been with his family on vacation as he'd first intimated, and Cooper thought maybe he'd been somewhere close by.

Had he been involved with that accident? In person, or as a director of some sort?

His cell, on silent, lit up. He glanced over. Verbena. Picking up the phone, he headed into the living room to answer, the farthest corner of the house from the master bedroom. "Early," Cooper answered.

"You didn't call last night after your meeting," she said.

"Best didn't give me anything."

"So, your feeling is?"

Cooper thought a moment and said, "He's hiding something. I don't know what. Could be just that he was somewhere he wasn't supposed to be. Could be something to do with Nye. Tox screen?"

"Not yet. But we finally got that Ring camera footage from the house at the end of the Engstroms' road."

The owner of the home at the end of the cul-de-sac had been gone and when he'd returned he'd been reluctant to help them. He was one of those guys suspicious of government as a whole and the police in particular, so it had taken them a while to convince him they really needed to see what had happened at the Engstrom home.

Verbena went on, "The Engstrom house is outside of its range."

Cooper nodded even though she couldn't see him. It was as they'd suspected. "Did they get anything?"

"Several cars came down the street within the two hours before the house went up. Checked them out. An older Cadillac Seville, blue, front plate missing, but had muddied plates on the back. Tech's trying to bring the numbers up. The other vehicles have been okayed."

"You think our guy's the Caddy?" The DNA from the blood spot said whoever had left it was male and their theory was that he could have been Bibi's killer.

"It's an anomaly. We're searching other cameras around

the area, seeing if we can pick it up on the street and find where it went."

"Okay."

"What's next on Nye? His brother keeps calling."

Terence Nye was certain his brother, Granger, had been killed and wouldn't let it go. He'd fast become more nuisance than help.

"I'm going to recheck with the neighbors."

"That witness knows something," Verbena said, referring to the woman who'd heard yelling at the site and then swiftly recanted her testimony.

"Let's check with the housekeeper again, um . . . Peña?"

"Norma Peña."

"See if she can remember a little bit more about Best's whereabouts."

"On it," she said. ""I'll push on tox, too."

Cooper acknowledged and they hung up a few minutes later. It was unlikely the results of Nye's screening would be available until after the weekend. He would check with the neighbor who'd recanted everything she'd heard and see if her memory could be jogged.

He poured himself a cup of coffee and sat down at the kitchen table just as Jamie came downstairs in her robe, her hair tousled. "What's going on?" she asked, pouring herself a cup of coffee and seating herself opposite him.

Cooper smiled at her. The best part of his life was his family and he was grateful for all of it. "Want to get married?" he asked her.

"Yes," she answered without hesitation.

She looked at him over the rim of her coffee cup and he picked up his cup and did the same. He watched her eyes crinkle with humor and his own lips formed a grin.

They smiled idiotically at each other a long time.

* * *

Mackenzie followed Taft down I-5 toward Wilsonville. There wasn't a lot of traffic out this early so she had to hang way back. She still didn't have proof it was Taft in the brown sedan but she was banking on it. A rental, most likely. From the moment he'd jettisoned her, he'd made plans and he wasn't taking his Rubicon on this sojourn.

They passed Wilsonville and hit a stretch of I-5 that began to stretch from urban and suburban to more rural. Grassy fields bordered the freeway on both sides. Mackenzie couldn't see the Best Homes truck. It was too far ahead. She was keeping Taft's vehicle in her sight and counting on him doing the same with the cube truck. Or maybe he'd planted a tracker on it? Highly possible.

About a mile farther on Taft exited the freeway, and Mackenzie slowed down even further to take her time doing the same.

The brown sedan turned right and after a few moments she did the same. Taft then got caught at a light and she looked around for another car, any car, hoping it would get in between them. She was relieved when a pickup truck belching a lot of diesel smoke rattled up behind the sedan before Mackenzie had to.

She was just congratulating herself on the screen when Taft's vehicle suddenly pulled into a gas station. Her pulse jumped. Should she drive on past, or turn in, too? He wouldn't know Stephanie's car, but he might be looking to see if someone was following him as well. She glanced ahead. Was the Best Homes truck still on this road? Should she just keep going and hope she caught up with it?

The brown sedan parked in an unmarked area of concrete at the gas station's outer edge. She confirmed Taft was the driver when he stepped into the drizzling rain, a black baseball cap on his head, and stood by his car, his eyes on her.

He'd made her.

Damn.

There was nothing for it but to pull in beside him and roll her window down, earning her a spray of precipitation slapping her face. "How long have you known?" she asked.

"A while."

"Why aren't you following the truck anymore?"

"Because I know where it's going."

"Oh, really. How? You've been holding out on me?"

"Actually, you sent me in the right direction. His step-father, Larry Perkins, has a farm."

"Maybe they like each other better than you know. You have the address?"

He nodded.

"I'm coming with you."

"Your part of this whole thing was Rayne," he reminded her. "This drug operation is—"

"I don't give a shit, Taft. I'm coming with you. I'm still on Rayne. I still want to know what happened to her, and I might learn something by getting Seth to talk. But I want a part of this, too. Don't just shut me out because I'm a woman."

"That's not why—"

"Yes, it is. Overprotection. Stop it."

He lifted up his hands in surrender, thought a moment, then shook his head and made a sweeping gesture to indicate she should get into the passenger side of his car. "Hope you're wearing hiking boots."

She wasn't, but she didn't care. She quickly grabbed her anorak from the back seat, parked and locked the car, then jumped out and dashed through the rain to the passenger side of the sedan. Inside she was hurrying as well. She sensed he could change his mind in an instant.

"Do you have a gun?" he asked as he backed out and turned around.

"Well, no. Not anymore. You?"

He nodded. "If things go sideways, stay out of the line of fire."

She nodded back at him and tugged the hood of her anorak over her head. It seemed the best way to respond to his grim tone.

About a half mile farther they turned onto a two-lane road with fields on either side and farmhouses punctuating the end of long lanes. The road wound on for some time before angling west where a ridge of trees ran in a semicircle around a distant property where Mackenzie could make out a few grayed roofs.

Taft said, "Larry Perkins's farm. I'm going to find a place to park on the road and then we're going to hike to those trees." He drove a bit farther until there was a wider pull out on the side of the road. He slid into it and yanked on the e-brake. Mackenzie could tell by the sticker on the windshield that she'd guessed right: The car was a rental.

He glanced down at her sneakers as they both got out. Mackenzie waited for some comment, but he just opened a rear door and reached for a small backpack that had been wedged beneath the driver's seat. From the pack he pulled out a Glock, which he then tucked into his hip holster. He slid the backpack over his shoulders and started out. He'd come prepared and she hadn't. She'd given up her gear when she'd given up her career in law enforcement. Not so Taft, apparently.

"I checked out an aerial view," he said as they headed

toward the ridge. "We're lucky in that we have cover to recon the area, but it's likely the reason Keppler chose his stepfather's place. Protected from view by the trees."

"You think the stepfather is who Seth meant when he said, 'He won't be in the way'?"

"Unless there's someone else." Taft shot her a look as rain drizzled down his cheek and jawline. "Just one more reason to be careful."

Mackenzie shivered a little and concentrated on keeping up with Taft as they worked their way closer. By the time they reached the ridge and were in place, looking through Taft's binoculars on the white farmhouse and several out-buildings, it was after nine. A Best Homes cube truck was parked in front of a graying shed, the most dilapidated of the buildings. There was no one in sight.

"I want to see Keppler with my own eyes," Taft muttered and they settled in to wait. Mackenzie didn't have to worry about an unwanted bathroom trip. She felt dry inside and out, as if there was no liquid left inside her body's cells. Her mouth was a desert. She would have liked to call it anticipation, but in her heart what she felt was fear.

But it was too late to let Taft know he might have been right about how much she would help on this foray, and she doubted she could make herself admit she was wrong anyway.

The scream from down the hall sent a jolt through Emma as she headed into her room with Duchess, who was following at her heels after their walk. They'd gotten caught in the rain, which had come down in a wild, cold rush. She'd fed Duchess before they left and now she tried to hustle the dog inside. Duchess shook herself mightily before trotting through the open door, the one that was always supposed to be closed.

Duchess began urgently barking at the scream.

"Stop," Emma told her, practically having to push her head back inside the room in order to keep her from bounding down the hall. After Duchess was inside and Emma had the door shut and locked, she hurried down the hall to find out what happened.

Jewell was standing at the edge of the dining room, by the kitchen. She threw a wild-eyed look at Emma and grabbed her by the arm, squeezing hard. Emma immediately tried to pull back but Jewell's grip was intense.

"The cat slept with Old Darla last night and is still in her bed and Old Darla won't wake up," Jewell exclaimed.

Emma's heart clutched. "Is she dead?"

"She's unconscious."

"Excuse me . . ." Supercilious Bob practically pushed them both back into the dining room. "Stay out of the hallway. The ambulance is coming."

"Where's the cat?" asked Emma.

"Honestly, Emma!" Jewell glared at her. "What about our friend? What about Old Darla? All you can think about is that cat?"

Emma thought about reminding Jewell that she didn't really like Old Darla and would never sit with her.

"Old Darla was fine last night," Jewell went on. "Just fine. And then that . . . *devil cat* . . . got in there and killed her!"

Bob overheard her and whipped around. "I don't think the fact that Darla needs medical attention can be blamed on Twinkletoes."

Faye came out of Old Darla's room carrying the cat, who was squirming to get free, its eyes wide.

"The cat doesn't like to be touched," said Emma.

"Too bad for the cat," said Jewell.

Emma heard the *woo-woo-woo* of a siren and soon an ambulance pulled up. The cat shot out of Faye's arms and out the door as soon as one of the ambulance drivers opened it. The drivers brought a cot that had been raised to normal bed height. Emma couldn't remember what those things were called, but she knew they would put Darla on it and take her to the hospital.

Old Darla's face looked kind of gray and her lips were parted, eyes closed. She looked kind of dead but Emma did see she was breathing.

Faye said quietly to Bob, "I couldn't reach her daughter, but I told her grandson."

Emma frowned and looked at Faye. "Old Darla has a grandson?"

Faye said patiently, "Why don't you both go into the dining room or back to your rooms?"

"I'm not leaving till I find out what happened," warned Jewell. "There's something really wrong around here. First Sara, now Darla . . . There's something really, really wrong."

Bob had walked to the front doors with the ambulance drivers, supervising them from inside the building as the ambulance men put Old Darla into the back and slammed shut the doors. He heard what Jewell said and strode back over to them. His mouth was twitching. He was 'totally pissed' as Harley would say.

"Jewell, I'm sure you know that Darla wasn't in good health."

"Did she have a heart attack? A stroke?" Jewell demanded.

"She's being checked out by medical professionals."

"I think it was a stroke," said Jewell.

Emma saw someone approaching the front glass double doors that the ambulance guys had just gone through. The ambulance took off with its lights flashing but there was no siren this time.

The person who pushed into the building was Harley. She had a bunch of papers in her hand, and she waved at Emma and held up the papers as she turned toward the girl at the office counter. Emma knew she was applying for a job.

"Come on, ladies," Bob said, holding out his arms and heading toward Jewell and Emma. He wanted to push them back into the dining room. Emma ducked under his arm and race-walked over to Harley.

"Leave the cat alone, Emma!" Bob called, certain he knew where Emma was headed.

"Where's the cat?" asked Harley, looking around.

"Outside. Faye had it in her arms, but it got away and ran out." She pointed to the area beneath the portico.

Bob came steaming over. He stopped near Harley and put on a smile. "Have you signed in?" he asked.

"Sure did," said Harley with an answering smile.

Emma knew Harley didn't mean it, but maybe Bob knew it, too, because his smile faded and he looked like he wanted to say something more but couldn't find the words.

Emma told Harley, "Old Darla went to the hospital in the ambulance. She had a stroke or a heart attack."

"Uh-oh," said Harley.

"We don't know what happened," Bob contradicted, swooping into the conversation. "Emma, I think we should all get something to eat before the breakfast room closes.

It's after ten, and you know the kitchen needs at least a half hour to prepare for lunch."

"Harley, can you have breakfast with me?"

"Already eaten, Emma. But I could go for an orange juice."

Jewell was hovering inside the door. Today she wasn't going to sit with her friends because they were long gone. Instead, she chose a chair at Emma and Harley's table. Emma debated on telling her she didn't want her there, but it seemed kind of rude.

Harley said, "It's Jewell, right?"

"Yes, hello. You're Hayley."

Harley opened her mouth to point out the mistake, but Jewell ran right over her. "Twinkletoes is a menace," she said. "We need to send a clear message that we don't want that cat anywhere around."

"Twinkletoes is a menace?" Harley tried, but couldn't hold back a laugh. "Sorry. Kind of an oxymoron."

"A what?" Jewell narrowed her eyes. Emma could tell she didn't know what an oxymoron was and maybe thought it was an insult. Emma didn't really know what it was, either, but knew Harley wouldn't be that mean.

"Opposites. Like Iron Butterfly. A cat named Twinkletoes doesn't really sound like a menace," said Harley. She was scanning the menu. "Maybe I will have a biscuit. Yum."

"All I know is that that cat causes problems. It wouldn't hurt my feelings if it never came back."

Emma didn't like hearing that. She knew that she should change the subject. That's what Jamie had told her to do when she was in an uncomfortable conversation, so she gave it a try. "Who is Old Darla's grandson?" she asked Jewell.

Harley had caught one of the waiter girls' attention and asked her for the orange juice. The girl then looked at Emma and Emma ordered a bowl of oatmeal. Jewell just sniffed and said she only wanted a cup of tea. As soon as the girl was gone, Jewell said, "He's the one with the long hair that was kissing Rayne under the portico. I told you."

Emma frowned. "But Mrs. Throckmorton said it was Thad."

"Are those the two that got in a fight?" asked Harley.

"It's confusing," said Emma.

Jewell snipped, "They each have a daughter and a grandson. Sara's daughter is Lorena and her grandson is Thad. I don't know Darla's daughter or grandson. They don't come by too much. I think they're just too busy. But her daughter was called this morning after *that cat* stayed in Darla's room."

"You said the boy with the long hair was kissing Rayne," said Emma. "But Thad does not have long hair."

"That wasn't Thad!" Jewell half rose from her chair. Emma worried she might be having a heart attack or stroke, too.

"Whoa," said Harley.

Emma reminded Jewell, "You said Mrs. Throckmorton thought it was her grandson kissing Rayne. Was it Old Darla's?"

"I don't know why you're flogging this dead horse. Poor Darla is in the hospital and Sara's been taken away and it's all that cat's fault!!" Jewell threw back her chair and fled the room just as the waiter girl brought their order. She left the orange juice and Emma's oatmeal and took Jewell's tea away.

Harley lifted her brows at Emma, so Emma explained, "Jewell doesn't like the cat."

"No shit."

Emma held herself back from telling Harley, "No swearing," though it was difficult for her. "And Jewell doesn't like to be wrong."

"Does it matter really whose grandson was kissing that Rayne girl?"

Emma thought that over. "Rayne is getting a bad reputation and it's too bad because she's dead and she can't stop them from gossiping about her. I want to talk to Mrs. Throckmorton and I'm going to go walk to one of the three houses above the trail. That's where she lives."

"Yeah? When?"

Emma looked out the windows and saw the rain, which was now running off the eaves. "Not today."

"I could go with you," said Harley. "I kind of like these crazy old people. If everything goes right, I could be starting work here soon." Harley drank her glass of orange juice, then stopped and said in surprise, "Emma, you're smiling."

"I smile," Emma protested.

"No, you don't. Not usually. Are you glad I'm going to be working here?"

"Very glad." Emma could feel that Harley was right. She was smiling and she *was* very glad that Harley would be at Ridge Pointe. It was like having family moving in with her.

Thad stared at the television where Brenda's dog-faced roommate was sobbing out her fear, anxiety, and horror over finding Brenda dead and bloody in her bedroom. He was stunned when the reporter broke from her to one of the women she'd been with at the bar. She said Brenda hadn't left with anyone but several men had attempted to engage her and one had even bought her a martini.

Thad grabbed his head, digging his own fingers into his scalp. His head still ached and he almost wanted to make it worse, feel the pain. He was lucky Brenda hadn't gotten her fingernails on him or there would have been more of his blood mixed in. The bleach should save him. Women and their fucking *talons*.

Bang! Bang! Bang!

"Thad!" Lorena called down to him.

Thad stared at his whiteboard. He didn't remember putting a yellow line through Brenda's name but he had. Bitch was dead. He picked up the markers corresponding with each name and put a red line through Rayne's and a green one through Bibi's. They were all dead.

"THADDEUS!" Her tinny voice was louder. Man, he wanted to shut her up.

He stalked to the concrete steps and stared upward. He could just see the faintest strip of light around the door's edges seeping into the dimness of the stairway.

"I'm taking Mom out for a drive in the Caddy. What the fuck do you have it covered for?"

Thad's heart lurched. He touched the side of his face where Bibi had raked him with her claws. There'd been blood on his clothes that night, maybe traces of it on the Caddy's seats still.

And there was the possibility the Caddy had been *seen*.

He raced up the stairs and slid open the door. Lorena had already walked away from him toward the kitchen and the garage. He strode after her.

"The Caddy's not running well," he clipped out.

"I don't care. Mom wants to go in the Caddy, fine, we'll go in the Caddy. Anything Her Highness wants."

"Take your car, Lorena."

"I'm not doing this for my health. She wants to go in the Caddy. I'm taking her in the Caddy."

"Fuck, I'll take her," he declared. "She wants to go for a drive, I'll take her in my truck. It's clean and decades newer."

Lorena paused at the door to the garage, her narrow face garnering a feral look. "Why don't you want me to take the Caddy? What are you hiding under that tarp?"

"Jesus Christ. Nothing. Okay, fine. Take the Caddy. Drive it off a cliff, for all I care. But I'm not picking you up when it breaks down. Don't even call me. You and Gram can just sit in the rain till kingdom come!"

He turned back around, his heartbeat thundering in his head, throbbing where that piece of crockery had raised a hard bump. The precipice felt near. Time was running out.

He needed a woman. Needed to have sex with her to relieve himself. He hadn't been able to have Brenda. She'd *attacked him*, the bitch! She'd . . . attacked . . . him! He'd had to kill her before Chas could romance her.

He pressed his palms to his temples. What was he going to do? How was he ever going to feel better?

Mackenzie Laughlin.

NOOOOOO! He raced to the lair, slamming the door closed and locking it tight behind him. Not the ex-cop. Be smart. Move on.

Things need to be in the right order.

Deviate and risk everything. He needed to make a plan. He needed to wipe Mackenzie Laughlin off the whiteboard and make those mean girls pay. He needed to NOT BE DISTRACTED from his mission.

He thought of Rayne and a wave of loneliness washed over him. He shook his head and turned that thought to dirty Brenda. He was glad he'd killed her. She'd come at him with those claws. Bibi had gotten her nails into his flesh and had ripped a strip off. He was furious with her, glad she was dead, too.

He needed to make a plan. A plan . . . a plan . . .

He glanced up and saw his father's cowboy hat where he'd placed it back on the shelf.

Chas needed to make an appearance.

CHAPTER TWENTY-THREE

"There he is," Taft whispered and Mackenzie leaned forward. Without the binoculars she couldn't make out the person's face from this far away, but he walked a lot like Seth Keppler. He was heading from the house to the Best Homes cube truck, carrying a toolbox.

"If he takes off, we'll lose him," she said.

"If he takes off, we'll check the house," said Taft. "I'm a little worried about Larry Perkins."

Mackenzie nodded. If they were caught entering the house, it was at least some plausible deniability about why they'd entered uninvited, and Larry Perkins's fate was truly still a question mark.

But Seth Keppler did not get in the cab of the truck. He walked through the now light drizzle around to the back, which was facing Mac and Taft. He rattled up the back door and dropped the hydraulic tailgate, the hum of its lowering reaching her ears. Keppler then disappeared inside the bowels of the vehicle, too deep for them to see him. A few minutes later he hopped out with several large, rectangular plastic bags filled with white powder, which he hunched over to protect from the rain.

"Bingo," said Taft.

"What is that?"

"Don't know, exactly. The mother lode. He had it in the van. Couldn't have been just loose in there. Too risky. That van is tricked out," he said, staring through the binoculars. "The floor or the walls. It's why he wanted to transport using a Best Homes truck."

"He's taking the stuff to that shed."

They watched in silence as Seth moved a stack of heavy packets to the gray shed.

"He's coming back," Taft said a few minutes later and Mackenzie could see him hurry forward and jump onto the tailgate. They heard the hum of it lifting him up again, and soon he came out hunched over another armful of large packets.

He made a couple more trips, and then he stayed in the truck for quite a while, and Taft surmised he was putting back whatever panel he'd removed to get the stuff out.

"I've been surveilling Keppler awhile. The scope of this operation is fairly new," he said.

"Why did you start watching him in the first place?"

"A client wanted me to keep an eye on him," he admitted.

"Mangella?"

"No." He was clear on that. "That was just an unpleasant side discovery, one I haven't figured out what to do about yet."

"Who, then?"

Taft didn't drop the binoculars from his eyes but she saw the grimace of his lips. She thought he wasn't going to answer, but then he said, "Debra Warner."

"*Patti*'s mother?"

"Not all of my clients are borderline mobsters. Some are just regular people. That information is for your ears only, by the way."

Mackenzie almost smiled. She knew the only reason he'd told her was because he was regarding her as a team member, which was exactly what she wanted. "She was worried about Patti with Seth?"

"She wants to believe he's a straight arrow but she probably knows better. I gave her information on his family when I started watching him, which didn't infuse her with confidence. This dance between Keppler and Best . . . I've been looking to nail down what that's about."

"You think Best knows about Seth's side dealings?"

"I'm still trying to get a handle on Best, but he doesn't strike me as the kind of guy who would be unaware of something like this"—he nodded toward the Best Homes truck—"going on in his company."

"Agreed," said Mackenzie.

"Okay, he's leaving," Taft said as Seth climbed into the truck's cab after closing the tailgate and back door. He switched on the engine, and then turned the truck around and started heading back down the long drive.

They waited till the truck had rumbled onto the access road leading toward the farmhouse's drive, then they waited some more. There had been no movement inside the house, but that didn't mean the place was entirely empty. The rain took a break and after a time they crept down from the ridge through wet grasses. Taft worked his way to the gray shed, which had a large, shiny silver new padlock on it.

"The wood around this lock would splinter if I pushed hard enough," he mused.

"Seriously?" she whispered. "What about the DEA? We ready for them?" Mackenzie had never actually worked with the Drug Enforcement Administration, but she knew they didn't like amateurs messing with their job.

"I'd like a little more proof Keppler's not moving powdered sugar," he said.

"Oh, sure. Good idea. He's just the kind of guy for that."

"I'm going to check for another way in. Keep a lookout."

Taft turned toward the corner of the building and moved out of sight. Mackenzie's nerves were on high alert. She glanced down the drive, but there was no sign of Seth Keppler returning. She thought about how far she'd come from when she'd first agreed to follow Seth to discern if he'd had anything to do with Rayne's disappearance up to today's discovery of a whole lot of something far more powerful than powdered sugar.

The creak of an opening door had her whipping around to stare at the house, heart pounding. She automatically reached for the nonexistent gun at her hip. She wanted to yell to Taft, but took a moment to reconsider.

An older man stutter-stepped outside, then swayed for a moment before collapsing with a thud onto the porch floorboards.

Mac glanced back to where Taft had disappeared, then at the house itself, trying to see inside the rooms. The man on the porch began a raspy moan. If there was one person in the house there could be others. She stepped forward and saw Taft at the end of the shed, examining the corner boards. She signaled him to come over.

He reached into his pocket for his phone and texted her:
What?

Man on the porch. Moaning. Fell over. Older.

Taft looked toward the porch but obviously couldn't see
anything. He gave her a high sign and came to where she
was standing. They carefully crossed the yard together in
silence. Taft had his gun in his hand as he drew close. Mac
was right behind him.

A wheeze and a cough greeted them and Taft took a
quick look, then holstered the gun as he headed up the side
porch stairs. Mackenzie looked past him to the man lying
on the wooden floorboards.

"Mr. Perkins?" Taft asked him.

"Help," he said, coughing some more, reaching a hand
up. Taft carefully handed his gun to Mackenzie, then aided
the man to his feet. Perkins's sleeves fell back and there
were rope burns on his wrists.

"That bastard . . . that bastard . . ." he said, and then
dropped his head to his hands.

"What happened?" Taft queried. Perkins waved for Taft
to help him back inside the house and Taft did so, asking,
"Is there anyone else here?"

"No. No. But he'll be back."

"When?" Taft clipped out as he eased the man into a
chair.

Perkins wore a red plaid flannel shirt, dungarees, and
gray wool socks, no shoes. His gray hair flopped in front
of his eyes and he brushed it back with a shaky hand.

"He was always a little shit. Now he thinks he's a big
shit. Works out and meets people at that club. They got him
into it, but he wanted to go, y'know?"

"You're talking about Seth Keppler, your stepson," said Mackenzie.

Perkins looked up at her beneath bushy white-gray brows. "Ain't no stepson of mine. His mom and I divorced. That ended it." He made a face and moaned again. "Strapped me to a chair this morning when I told him to get out. Took me hours to get the penknife outta my pocket. It's good to have a knife. Got myself free. He's gone, but he'll be back."

"What's in the shed?"

"Ketamine. You know what that is?"

Mackenzie nodded. It went by a number of different names, Special K being one of them. A powerful hallucinogenic that was one of many so-called date rape drugs.

"We know what it is," Taft assured him.

"Seth was always a crafty little prick, but now he's got into this." Tears filled his eyes. "Mister, I'm no part of it."

"Do you need medical help?" Mackenzie asked.

"I just need you to get Seth the fuck off my property!"

"There's a new lock on the gray shed. I can get around it, with your permission," said Taft.

Perkins flapped a hand at Taft. There was blood welling in the rope burns. He looked at the marks and dolefully shook his head.

"Do you have some salve in the house somewhere?" Mac asked.

"Upstairs bathroom, mebbe. I'm okay, honey." To Taft, he said, "Tools in the garage. Crowbar. Pull the whole damn thing down, if you want, but do it quick. I don't know who Seth's in business with, but there's a lot of money riding on this."

Mackenzie remembered a recent drug bust in Thailand

where a shipment of ketamine worth over a billion dollars was confiscated by the authorities.

Perkins added, "Don't know how you got here, but I'm sure glad you're here. Seth's a fool if he thinks they'll let me live."

Taft took back his gun from Mackenzie and headed in the direction of the garage. Mackenzie told Perkins she would find the salve and worked her way up a narrow stairway to the top floor. She found the bathroom easily enough and there was a large jar of salve and some adhesive tape in the medicine cabinet. She'd worried Perkins might be playing them, but then changed her mind. Those wrist burns were real. Even so, as she headed back downstairs to Larry Perkins, she checked a couple of rooms on the way down. Nothing unusual upstairs but at the bottom of the steps she turned toward the kitchen and an anteroom at the back of the house. One look in the anteroom and she felt herself go still. It was lined with guns. Every kind. Handguns, rifles, automatic weapons . . . There was a gun case filled with rifles next to a pegboard dotted with handguns of every size.

Hank Engstrom had said Seth Keppler was crazy with guns. Hank Engstrom was right, which begged the question: How well did Hank know Seth . . . ?

Mackenzie returned to Perkins, who allowed her to roll up his sleeves and apply the salve. They could hear the screech of boards as Taft ripped the shed apart.

"Our car's a ways away," she told him. "Do you have one?"

"Got my truck in the garage."

Mackenzie was beginning to feel the pressure of passing

time. "Can you get to your truck, so you can be gone before Seth returns? Do you need help?"

"Hate leaving my property," he said.

"Only temporary."

He barked out a laugh as he got to his feet. He wasn't all that steady and he leaned on Mac. "You ever dealt with the Feds, missy? Temporary can be a loonnngg time if they feel like having it be."

They'd taken about two steps when they heard a shout. Taft. Yelling.

Before Mac could do more than turn her head, the front door burst open and Seth Keppler practically ran inside. "What the fuck are you doing?" he screamed, then stopped short upon seeing Mac. "You?" he asked incredulously.

Larry Perkins pushed Mackenzie away from him as he teetered in front of his onetime stepson. "Get outta my house!"

Seth reached forward and grabbed him by his collar, practically lifting him off his feet. "How do you know her? What have you been up to? Who've you been talking to? I told you to stay out of it, didn't I? Didn't I warn you to stay out of it? You said you wouldn't be a problem."

Mackenzie was pressed against the wall, her eyes on Seth. She reached a hand out automatically to help Perkins, wanting him to stand down for his own sake.

Seth flicked a look at Mac. "You've been following me . . ." he hissed, hitching a thumb over his shoulder. "I saw your car parked out there on the road. Knew someone had been following me. Decided to come back on foot and here you are. All that bullshit about Rayne Sealy! What the hell is your deal?"

Mackenzie swallowed. "That wasn't bullshit. You killed Rayne," she told him. "You threw her off the overlook."

The look he gave her was incredulous. "You're out of your fucking mind."

"Maybe she saw something, something you couldn't have her know. You killed her."

"You're wrong and you got yourself in a big mess here. What am I going to do with you?"

Perkins suddenly threw himself at Seth, toppling them both over. Mac yelled at him, then turned toward the back of the house. The gun room. She needed a gun. She burst into it and glanced around wildly.

Bang!

She jumped at the shot. Half ran, half dived for the handguns. Grabbed a Glock. Her hand was on it when a bullet zipped past her head and splintered into the bottom of the wood rifle cabinet.

She screeched and ducked, half fell to the ground, gun in hand. Flipped the safety. Knew it could be unloaded, the chamber empty. But Seth was the kind of gun enthusiast who wouldn't be caught dead unawares. At least she hoped.

The back door suddenly slammed inward and Taft burst in, both hands on the gun he held in front of him. "Put it down!" he yelled at Seth.

Mackenzie had the Glock in hand and was twisting to meet Seth Keppler, who had hesitated in the fraught moment when Keppler couldn't seem to decide who to shoot while staring down the barrel of Taft's gun.

He chose Mackenzie, aiming at her. Taft didn't hesitate. Squeezed off two shots *BANG. BANG*, the noise ear-shattering in the small room. As he pulled the trigger he dove for Mackenzie, slamming her against the floor. Her head smacked hard, causing her to see stars at the same moment Seth's gun went off. *BANG!* She felt Taft's body jerk at the impact.

"Taft!" she screamed, shocked.

Her gaze flew to Seth, who stood in stunned disbelief, his mouth hanging open. His left hand was pressed to his chest. He pulled back his hand and stared at the blood, then slowly sank down the wall, his gun still in his right.

Mackenzie's attention slammed back to the body atop her. "Taft," she said again, softer, scared silly.

"I'm okay," Taft muttered. He pulled himself off her with an effort. Mackenzie scrambled toward Seth, grabbed his gun. He didn't resist.

She turned back to Taft. "You're not okay. You can't be. You were hit."

He slowly got to his feet. Mackenzie jumped up, ready to grab him if he toppled over. He steadied himself, feet planted apart, and looked down at Seth Keppler, whose lips were moving. He was trying to say something.

Mac said, "He shot you. I felt it."

"What's he saying?"

"Taft . . . Jesse . . ."

"He's not going to make it," Taft said, and Mackenzie turned to see that Keppler was staring blankly straight ahead, though he was still breathing.

"Where were you hit?" she asked. She put the Glock she'd grabbed and Seth's handgun on the floor, then reached for her cell phone in her back pocket. It wasn't there and she glanced down anxiously, seeing it had skidded a few feet away. She lunged for it. "Where were you hit?" she asked Taft.

"Beneath the shoulder," he admitted.

She had the phone in one hand. She watched him pull back his jacket. The bloom of red against his shirt made her dizzy.

"Nine-one-one. What is the nature of your emergency?" the operator answered.

"A shooting," Mac said crisply, going into cop mode, forcing herself to stop thinking of the spreading blood on Taft's shirt. "Multiple injuries. Hurry . . ."

Chapter Twenty-Four

It all hit the fan.

Larry Perkins, Seth, and Taft were taken by ambulance to local hospitals, though Taft, who was the only one awake and aware, lobbied for Glen Gen and his request was granted. Mackenzie got the keys to Taft's rental and drove like a madwoman to Glen Gen, ignoring all speed limits and wheeling into the lot with a screech of tires, a sound that perfectly fit her mood. Taft's gun had been confiscated by the local police. The officers had then looked at Keppler's arsenal of weaponry with raised brows and had stationed themselves outside that room, waiting for the crime scene team.

Mac arrived right on the heels of the ambulance, but she was turned away when she tried to follow Taft and the EMTs into the emergency cubicles and then on to surgery. Taft tried to assure her he was fine, but he was white-faced with pain and shock and she knew it wasn't true.

Federal agents and local law enforcement were working the crime scene. Mac learned that Taft had already put in a call to DEA as soon as he'd gotten an up close and personal with the drugs in the shed. He'd just placed the call to them when Keppler charged into the house. He then raced to the back door, intending to sneak in through the gun room, unaware Mackenzie had already blasted into the room with Seth on her heels.

Mackenzie had learned that Seth was also in surgery with two shots to the chest from Taft's gun. Larry was in surgery with one shot to the chest from Seth's. Both were touch and go. Mac had been seen herself and was happy to learn she was not concussed, but her head still hurt like hell from where it hit the floor.

Seth's other bullet had gone through Taft below his right shoulder and embedded into the wall beneath the display of handguns.

Mac had spent most of the day at the hospital, fielding calls, pacing, and generally waiting to hear about Taft. It took them a while to get him into surgery as his injuries weren't life-threatening, thank God.

She'd heard from Cooper Haynes, who let her know crime scene techs, local police, and the DEA were all over the house. Cooper Haynes was working the Granger Nye case and had met with DEA members at Best Homes as well, much to Andrew Best's dismay. There was an on-going search of Best Homes cube trucks to see if any others had been modified for drug smuggling. No word on that yet.

"How you doing?" one of the male nurses asked Mac.

"Fine." She lifted a glass of water up. The staff at Glen Gen, though unable to stretch protocol for her, had been nothing but nice.

She glanced at her phone and caught a text from Haynes. DEA was annoyed that Taft and Mackenzie had intercepted the shipment before it had landed into the hands of its final destination, the kingpins who would divide it up and sell to willing customers.

She thought about heading out and getting something to eat other than cafeteria food, but when she looked out the window she saw several news crews that had come and gone all day, attempting to interview her and learn more about Taft. Channel Seven, always the most aggressive news station, had cornered her when she'd gone outside to switch cars back with Stephanie, who'd uber'd to her car at the gas station, switched it with Mac's RAV and brought it to her before catching uber now. Mac's "No comments" had been splayed across the local news and were getting regional play as well because of the size of the confiscated haul of ketamine.

Finally, Taft was out of surgery and doing fine, or so the hospital staff told her, as they still wouldn't let her see him. Mackenzie exhaled and sank into one of the chairs outside the OR. She was exhausted.

Mom called about five thirty and said, "How're you doing?"

"Fine."

"You sure? Even when you were with the police, nothing like this happened."

"This turned out to be bigger than any of us knew."

Mac wondered if Keppler's drug involvement was going to come back on Mitch and Prudence Mangella. Andrew Best was already in the DEA's sights. Taft had said there was something between Best and Mangella. Important heads could roll.

"They say this drug dealer is involved with a lot of others in the community," her mother said, speaking Mac's thoughts aloud.

"Seth Keppler. Yeah, there are some ties . . ."

"Are you going to keep doing this and make me worry?"

"I'm not trying to make you worry, Mom."

"Who is this man you're working with? Jesse Taft? An ex-policeman?"

"I'm sorry, I have to go. I've got a lot going on."

"I'm just so happy you're safe. You just don't know." She exhaled and drew a deep, deep breath. "There is something else I need to talk to you about."

Mac's heart nearly stopped. "The cancer . . ." she whispered.

"No, no. Nothing like that. I'm doing great. It's Dan."

Dan the Man? "What about him?"

"He has . . . I'm . . ." She cleared her throat. "We're splitting up."

"You are?" Mac was totally taken aback. This was what she'd prayed for but now that it was here, she hardly knew how to feel. "Are you okay with it?"

"Yes."

"Mom, you sure? I know you know how I feel about him, but if you're happy, then—"

"I'm not happy. Dan's, well, I don't have to tell you . . . among other things, Dan's too cheap. I've had enough worrying about my life. I have enough money and I don't want to penny-pinch. I'll be thrifty. I can take care of myself. I'm not going to put myself in debt, but I'm tired of this. Always making excuses for him. Always looking over my shoulder, second-guessing me on my finances. He has his own money, and I have mine. We've never truly melded most of our funds, which is good. Now I need to live my life."

Mac felt an easing of her tension. "You're absolutely right."

"Maybe you'll come back and live with me," she said hopefully.

Mac didn't immediately respond. She didn't want to disappoint her mother, but it was time to move on. She talked about a few other things and let her mother go off on Dan awhile, then eased herself off the phone. She digested the news, then put in a call to Stephanie. They'd seen each other during the vehicle exchange, but Mac had been preoccupied, and Stephanie had just said over and over again how glad and utterly thankful she was that Mackenzie was okay. Now Mac asked her, "Have you talked to your father today?"

"Yes, I finally told him about the baby. He was, well, a little underwhelmed. Kind of pissed me off."

"He didn't say anything about my mom and him?"

"Oh. Just that she's dumping him and it's not because he took twenty-five thousand out of the only account that they shared to put down money on one of those super-expensive apartments above the River Glen Grill."

"Oh . . . shit . . ."

"Yeah. That's my dad. He transferred the money to an account of his own and now he's moving into the apartment and keeping the rest of the money to help pay for his lifestyle." She laughed without humor. "I told him he was going to be a grandpa and that's what I got in return. I didn't really want to tell you, with everything that's going on with you. How's your head, by the way?"

"Just a big knot. I'm the lucky one."

"Hang in there. You need anything, just ask."

"Thanks, Stephanie." A lump was developing in her

throat, so she ended the conversation before she could embarrass herself. No matter how little she thought of Dan Gerber, the fact that he'd given her Stephanie as a sister was worth everything.

Thad couldn't believe his eyes. He'd been chewing his lip into a bloody pulp, waiting for more news on Brenda when all of a sudden ex-cop Mackenzie Laughlin popped onto the news. He was on his computer and saw the clip, so he delved further into the story, playing every news article he could find. It was a breaking story. All about a big drug bust. There was a guy in surgery at River Glen General who'd been instrumental in breaking up the ring. Thad took out a pen and wrote down his name: Jesse James Taft. Mackenzie had been involved with him in the bust.

Channel Seven broadcast a picture of Taft in uniform from his days with Portland PD. He'd left or been kicked out of not one but two departments. Thad looked him over carefully and felt a snake of jealousy uncoil inside him. Chas would give Taft a run for his money, he told himself. Chas had power.

But Chas had failed with Brenda. She hadn't fallen for his charms.

She didn't give you a chance!

"Stupid, dirty bitch," he muttered.

And Mackenzie Laughlin had blown him off as well.

But she wanted you. She did.

"Next time," he whispered.

Except for this guy. *This guy*. She was with this guy and he was good-looking enough. Better than Chas, maybe. Tough-looking. An ex-cop, just like she was.

It was time to give up on her. Go back to his original plan. Take care of those mean girls who had turned into such wicked women.

Things need to be in the right order.

He realized he was breathing hard. He was at war with himself and didn't want to follow his own rules. He tried to turn away from the news feeds that had Mackenzie Laughlin and this Jesse James Taft. He didn't want to think about them together. Working together, sharing a smile, rushing to the bedroom or bathroom, maybe in the shower, bodies slick with water, him pounding into her as she moaned in openmouthed ecstasy . . .

He shook his head and went back to work on investing. He'd blown so much cash that he had little to work with. Nearly impossible with such a small investment nut to build it back up. If he could get his hands on Gram's accounts, he could start over.

He closed his eyes and willed himself to relax. Luckily, Lorena had not taken Gram out in the Seville. All that threatening to drive the Caddy and then she'd done just what he'd told her, taken Gram for a ride in her own car. She'd maybe believed him when he'd said the car wasn't working and had just wanted to twist the knife. Lorena understood him, he realized. Way better than he'd ever given her credit for. It was a growing problem. She'd understood his fear somehow, though she hadn't known the why of it, hadn't understood that someone might pick up the car on camera and match it to one outside Bibi Engstrom's home the night of her death.

And the threat was still there.

He needed to keep moving. Like a shark. Not stay in one place and be pinpointed. Thad tried hard to get himself out of this place and concentrate on the third mean girl, but his thoughts traveled back to Jesse James Taft.

He knew where the man lived.

Sunday afternoon Taft was released from the hospital and Mac was back to pick him up. She'd gone home to the pink and white room and spent a dreadful night tossing, turning, and reliving the same nightmares chasing through her unconscious mind. This morning she'd returned Taft's rental car and had Uber'd back to Stephanie's, then had gone straight to the hospital. She'd seen Taft the night before, but when he'd tried to include her in plans to spring him, she'd left before he could convince her and had planted herself facedown on her bed.

Now, as she helped him into her RAV, she tried not to be intrigued by the few more days' beard that had seemed to only add to his rough attractiveness.

He was cranky about his wrapped torso. The bullet had traveled through his chest, just below his right arm, ripping through muscle and sinew. He'd been put back together through surgery, but full mobility was going to take a while. Though he knew he'd gotten off lucky, he was still glowering.

"If I haven't thanked you for saving my life, I'm doing it now. Thank you," she told him as they entered his condo and he sank down in the one recliner in the room, while Mac perched on the couch.

He smiled faintly in acknowledgment, then said, "Seth Keppler isn't going to make it."

She'd heard the same. At least Larry Perkins was holding his own.

"His co-conspirators are lucky he won't be able to talk," Taft added. A lot of the animation in his face that she'd come to expect wasn't visible right now. She suspected he was also feeling the low-grade depression, almost PTSD, that came from taking someone's life, no matter what kind of scumbag he or she might be. Officials from the police and DEA were waiting to question them both more at length.

"I got a call from Keith Silva," Taft said after a moment of introspection.

Mackenzie frowned at him. "You know Silva?"

"He also wanted to thank me for making sure Keppler got what he deserved."

"Silva knew Seth Keppler?"

"I think he wanted him out of the way."

Like Mangella had wanted him out of the way.

Mackenzie thought the words, but she didn't say them. With Keppler unable to talk, others involved in the ketamine distribution ring were claiming innocence and pointing fingers solely at Keppler. Andrew Best was at the head of the line, corroborated by a witness who'd previously said she'd heard two men yelling the night of Granger Nye's death, but hadn't known who they were. Now she absolutely, positively, no further questions need be asked, claimed one of the voices was Seth Keppler's. With her testimony in place, the theory was that Seth had fought with Granger Nye when Nye discovered his underhanded operation and use of Best Homes as a cover and had confronted him. The two men had argued and Seth, either by design or accident, then pushed Nye from the second story to his death. Whether it was true was a question yet to be answered.

"What's Silva's part of this?"

"He warned me once that Mangella had a lot of power. I think he knew I was pulling away from Mitch and wanted to make sure I didn't do anything I would regret."

"Like what?"

He shrugged and his lips tightened as he was reminded of his injury. "I don't know. I don't have anything on Mangella. Around me, he walked the tightrope. I think Silva was preparing for the future."

"So, with Silva Mangella has a new go-to guy?"

His dimples flashed for a second. "Looks like it."

"What's our next move?"

"You done with Rayne?"

"I think so. Seth wouldn't admit to pushing her over the railing, but he's not the kind to admit to anything. He was her last boyfriend, so maybe he was the one. I'll never believe it was an accident."

"What about Troi Bevins?"

She gave him a sharp look. "Well, he was before Seth." She narrowed her eyes at him, wondering if he was trying to say something without saying it. "And I think he's getting a raw deal."

"You don't know that."

"No. I don't. But I'd still like to help him in some way."

So far Andrew Best had bobbed and weaved at everything the authorities had tossed at him, claiming innocence while he threw suspicion on anyone else in his circle of influence. Most notable of that group was his employee Troi Bevins, who'd had a sometime friendship with Seth Keppler, though Troi had insisted Seth was just his weed connection, nothing more. Still, Troi was being held and questioned about the ketamine bust and no one at Best was stepping up to help. They were all covering their own asses.

His girlfriends were the only ones who seemed to care. Elise Sealy had called Mac and begged her to do something, saying it was Mackenzie's fault Troi had been taken into custody, which made no sense at all.

"Is he lawyered up yet?" asked Taft.

"I don't know."

"Laughlin, you've got a soft spot for that kid."

Troi's other "friend," Leah, had also shown up at the jail to protest Troi being held, which had given Elise some serious consternation. She'd called Mac a second time, ordering her to get rid of the tattoo artist, saying, "You need to kick her skinny butt down the road!" Again, Elise had been unable to explain why this should be Mac's problem; apparently, it just was, in her mind. Mac had not responded to the request.

They heard barking outside and a light tapping at the door. Mac answered and found Tommy Carnoff with Plaid and Blackie off leash. The two pugs tore inside as soon as the door was opened wide enough. Tommy held their leashes in hand.

"How ya doing?" he asked Taft, who said that he was fine in a little testier voice than usual. Tommy explained about the dogs, "I'm taking them to the kennel for a few days. Maureen's back in the hospital and I might be spending a lot of time there."

"You can leave them with me," said Taft.

Tommy eyed him critically. "I didn't want to overload you."

"I'll take care of them," said Mac.

"You planning to be around here then?" Tommy brightened.

"Well, I . . ." She glanced at Taft, who gave her a bland

look back that could have meant anything. "Yes," she said. "But only while he recovers."

"I don't need a nursemaid," said Taft.

"It's strictly business," Mac added.

Carnoff coughed into his hand, but it sure sounded like he said, "Poppycock."

Mackenzie helped him bring over the dogs' beds, food, treats, and toy stuffies, whereupon both pugs jumped on a plush hedgehog who looked like he'd seen better days and tussled over it. A few minutes later, Tommy touched the brim of his hat and left. Once he was gone, Mac made sure the pugs were fed and asked Taft, "What would you like to eat? Goldie Burgers? Mexicali Rose? River Glen Grill? Take and Bake pizza? It's a little early but I'm game for anything."

"I can find something to eat here. I keep telling you I don't need a nursemaid."

"This isn't about you, Taft. The dogs need my touch."

He snorted but stopped arguing.

The pugs had bolted their food down, and Mac hid a smile and bent down and cooed to them. Plaid came straight over but Blackie caught sight of the prize hedgehog and zagged right. Realizing her mistake, Plaid immediately turned an about-face and chased Blackie into the kitchen. The battle for the plush toy included plenty of growling and yipping.

Taft leaned back in his chair and grimaced. He glared at the point of his injury. They'd put his arm in a sling to control movement, but now he jerked the sling off.

"Think that's a good idea?" she asked, and the look he sent her could melt steel.

She decided to change the subject. "Troi did not have anything to do with Rayne's death. Seth was the last guy."

"You sound like you're trying to convince yourself."

She had a mental image of Seth's look of incredulity burned on her brain. He'd acted as if she were speaking in tongues, and the memory wouldn't leave her. It bothered her like an itch she couldn't scratch.

Taft admitted, "I could actually go for a Goldie Burger."

She smiled. "I can do that."

"Thanks, Mackenzie."

His seriousness got to her. It was so out of character. "*De nada*. I'm going to stop by Stephanie's and pick up a few things."

"You planning on staying the night?"

She met his gaze and her heart beat a little faster. "High probability," she said as she headed out the door.

CHAPTER TWENTY-FIVE

Thad sat in his F-150 and watched Mackenzie walk to her car, a grin on her face, and felt a burning jealousy so intense he hardly knew what to do with it. He was afraid she'd see him. There were only so many visitors' spots and he kicked himself for racing over here without more thought. Things were getting flaky in his mind. He needed to clamp down on himself, control dangerous urges.

He slid his truck into gear as she got into her RAV and pulled onto the street. He hoped she was going to her current residence because he had no information on where that was yet. He'd discovered her mother lived in town and had been planning to stake out that address until he'd learned today about Jesse James Taft's existence in her life. It hadn't taken him long online searching to come up with his address and as soon as he'd seen the RAV4, he'd known it was her. It matched the one he'd seen her climb into outside the Waystation and her appearance had clinched it. This time he memorized the license plate as he kept a safe distance behind her.

Things need to be in the right—

"Shut the fuck up," he said aloud.

Mackenzie turned away from Laurelton toward River Glen. Maybe she was going to her mother's house.

But then she turned on Wishing Well Street and his skin felt suddenly electrified. *What is she doing here?*

Taft worked himself out of the recliner, annoyed with the dull pain radiating throughout his right side. He knew he should take another pill. Keep ahead of the pain. But he wasn't going to.

The pugs snuffled by the door and Plaid was already whining for Mac. "You too, huh?" he said as he stood to one side of the window so he couldn't be seen as he glanced through the blinds.

You like her, Helene said.

Already established, he silently answered back.

Don't make stupid mistakes this time.

He watched Mac pull out of the lot. He was just turning away when he saw the gray Ford F-150 follow after her, the silhouette of a man in a cowboy hat at the wheel. The license plate was plainly visible and Taft memorized it, then went to the kitchen for a notepad and wrote it down.

He walked back to his chair, thinking about it. It was entirely possible Mackenzie and he were being watched by the authorities. They'd been in the center of a multimillion-dollar drug bust yesterday and were very likely on the Feds' radar.

But . . .

He picked up his phone and placed a call. "I need a license plate number."

* * *

At Stephanie and Nolan's, Mac swiftly packed an overnight stuff bag. One night, maybe two. That's the most Taft would be able to handle no matter how much he needed help. Helplessness was not something he could handle.

Stephanie had heard her come in and now leaned a shoulder against the doorjamb of the pink and white room, one arm wrapped somewhat protectively across her stomach. "Where are you going?" she asked.

"It's just for a night or two."

"Aha, you're staying with *Jesse James* Taft. Sounds like an outlaw. His name was all over the news today. How is he?"

"Okay. I think." She picked up her bag. "He saved my life."

"Then he's at the top of my good list. I just wish you were staying. Nolan's on his way home, but I like having you here."

"I'll be back."

"And then you're moving out for good."

"Not that far away."

She smiled, then said, "I don't want to sound like I'm paranoid, but I just learned something awful."

"What?"

"A girl I used to be friends with was killed on Friday night. Murdered."

Mac frowned as she walked toward the door, Stephanie following behind her. She looked back at her stepsister. "Really? Here?"

"In Portland. It was on the news yesterday, but I didn't think it was her. Someone came in and strangled her. They called her Brandy, first. Her roommate found her. I knew her as Brenda Heilman."

"I've hardly seen the news. Didn't want to watch myself."

"Yeah . . ."

Mac saw the tightness in Stephanie's face. "You want me to look into it?"

"Maybe, yeah . . . I guess. But the weird thing is, you know that girl who accidentally fell from the overlook taking a selfie? Rayne Sealy?"

They were standing together on the porch. Mac was ready to dash to her SUV before the rain could start again. Now she gave Stephanie her full attention. "What about her?"

"She was a friend, too. In fact the three of us were best buddies in grade school for a while. Kind of drifted apart later."

"You knew Rayne?" Mac demanded.

Stephanie blinked. "Did you?"

"Stephanie, that's the case that I've been working on. That's how I ran across Taft, in the first place. He and I were investigating different cases. I was trying to find Rayne. Her friend Bibi asked me to and then Rayne died, and then Bibi . . . was killed . . . and Taft was working on this drug bust that happened."

"Bibi?"

"The garage fire. The police haven't fully said it was homicide. There were indications that she may have tried to kill herself with carbon monoxide, but I don't think it holds up."

Stephanie shivered and looked around quickly, drawing her sweater closer around herself. Mac, too, felt a cold frisson slide down her back. "Your friend Brenda was murdered?" she asked.

A gray truck passed by the front of the house, a man in a cowboy hat at the wheel. They watched the back of it until it turned onto the main road and then Stephanie said, "I'm going inside and locking all the doors."

"Do that," Mac said. "Maybe I should stay till Nolan gets home?"

"No, no. Go on. Rayne's death was an accident and I don't know anything about Brenda. It was probably an ex-boyfriend. Isn't it always? I'm just letting myself get spooked."

"I told Taft I'd go to Goldie Burger, but I'll come right back after I drop it off for him. You want a burger?"

"No, I've got food. Meat doesn't work for me right now anyway. Nolan will be home soon."

"Call me if he gets home before I return, otherwise I'm coming back."

"Okay."

Stephanie closed the door and threw the lock as Mac race-walked toward her RAV. Strange developments. She hadn't told Stephanie that she thought Rayne had been murdered because she didn't want to frighten her more than she already was, and anyway, Seth Keppler was no threat to anyone right now.

But Bibi's death . . .

And now this Brenda's . . .

Were the deaths all tied together through Seth?

Mac was still mulling it over as she approached the drive-through at Goldie Burger. There were two cars in front of her. Did that make sense? Seth Keppler, drug dealer, also a mastermind killing young women?

The two vehicles slowly placed their orders and moved ahead of her and she was finally able to place her own order. She added fries and a couple of Cokes, even though she rarely drank soft drinks. Her mind was frazzled. Her head still ached some.

She would lay it all out to Taft when she got back, see what he thought.

As she turned back toward Laurelton and Taft's condo, she didn't notice the gunmetal gray F-150 that trailed her out of Goldie Burger's drive-through.

Thad followed after her as she headed back in the direction of her lover's place. What had she been doing at Bitch Stephanie's house? How did she know what was in his mind? She was too attuned to him. Eerily so.

Was that why she'd been at the Waystation? Did she know? *Did she know?*

You approached her, not the other way around.

A cosmic connection, then?

He didn't know how to stop her. How to keep her from reaching the condo of her lover, the ex-cop. He had to stop her. He had to.

He needed to take her to the lair.

How? What did he have?

He had a pickup full of supplies. He could use something. What?

He had to stop her!

How?

And then he knew. It was mostly blocks of city between River Glen and Laurelton but there was that one stretch of county property with nothing built on it. They were almost there. She was rounding the corner. He pulled the truck up close to her SUV, hugging her bumper as she made that turn. His beautiful truck would take a hit, and that would hurt, but he had had to do it. Had to.

She's onto you!

He punched the accelerator hard and the F-150 jumped forward.

Wham! He smashed his truck into her bumper. The RAV spun on the wet pavement and Thad hit her again, slamming into the SUV's side and pushing the vehicle off the road and into the swale below.

Mackenzie lost control of the wheel. What? What was it? *Slam!*

The RAV skidded off the road sideways and down a few feet into the grassy area below street level. She banged her head again and it took a moment to gather her wits. This time she really might be concussed. Damn, if she wasn't going to have to have herself looked at and—

Her driver's door suddenly wrenched open. Outside in the rain was a man in a cowboy hat.

"What happened?" she asked dully.

He suddenly grabbed her shoulders and yanked her out of the car. She tried to stop him. She grabbed at his arms but he was strong. She wasn't tracking well.

"Sorry, Mackenzie," he said through his teeth.

"Wha—"

She saw the blur of his fist coming and then nothing.

Taft waited for an hour. She'd said she was going to stop by her stepsister's first, so maybe she'd gotten to talking to her. It was early for dinner anyway. She'd said she was coming back, but she hadn't said when.

He resisted the urge to text her. He hated being weak in front of her. He'd meant it when he said he could get by on his own, but the truth was he wanted her here.

He waited for some word from Helene, but there was none. The drug bust today had gone a long way in helping vanquish some of his ghosts regarding her death from an overdose. It hadn't been his fault, but her dealer had been one of his acquaintances. Ten years older with an unfaithful husband who'd stoked her unhappiness, Helene had spent time partying with her younger brother's crowd. She'd hooked up with one guy in particular and had gone down a drug-fueled rabbit hole with him. They were both gone now. Had been for a long time.

His phone buzzed with a text. The gray F-150 belonged to one Thaddeus Jenkins. He plugged the address into an app of River Glen and his brows drew together as he saw where it was. He was pretty sure that was one of the houses above the trail.

CHAPTER TWENTY-SIX

Mackenzie came to slowly. Everything hurt and she didn't understand it. Her head hurt. Her arms hurt—her *wrists!*—it felt as if they were being flayed and her limbs were being dragged from her body. She visualized being on a rack and slowly pulled apart. Shuddering, she finally opened her eyes and looked at her right hand. It was strung with twine through a ring that was screwed into a concrete ceiling. Both hands, arms . . . were strung up. She was hanging from the ceiling and her body weight was cutting off her circulation, turning her hands white. With an effort, she got her feet underneath her and released the tension. Felt immediate relief. Thank God she could stand.

Why? her dulled brain asked. *How?*

She blinked and felt the cold.

She was naked.

Memory flooded back. She was driving . . . driving to Taft's place and . . . there was food. The burgers! She'd picked up burgers and she'd stopped to get her clothes and . . .

She heard footsteps and a man was suddenly standing

in front of her. He was bare-chested, stripped down to his jeans. He looked familiar but she couldn't place him.

"You're awake," he said, grinning. He was breathing hard and sweating. "Had to sneak you in, pack you down here, but I did it. I did it!"

"Who are you?"

He stared at her, a flash of anger in his eyes. "You know. You've been tracking me, bitch."

She didn't have the strength to argue, just waited, her mind racing. Where was she? How long had she been gone?

Very slowly the man reached for a cowboy hat on a metal shelf and jammed it on his head. She had a glimmer of recognition then. He was the man who'd tried to pick her up outside the Waystation.

"Chas," he said.

"I haven't been tracking you."

"I saw you. I saw you with *her*."

"Her? I don't know you, Chas."

"On Wishing Well Street. I saw you with her!"

"Stephanie?" Her pulse leapt. This was about Stephanie? Had her stepsister been right about the connection to Rayne and Brenda? But this was someone new. Someone else. Who?

"I don't know you," she tried again.

"But you were with her. And she knows who I am, doesn't she? She knows very well."

"You saw me outside her house tonight?" Mac said, thinking of the gray F-150 that had cruised by as they were standing together on the porch.

"Things need to be in the right order, but you got in my way, didn't you?"

Mac willed her sluggish mind to catch up. She needed to play along. To buy time. "Where am I?" she asked.

"You're with me." He spread his arms and turned around. "You like it? It's where we'll make love until you die." He pointed behind her and she carefully turned her head to see a whiteboard with names written in different colors and crossed out with the same: Rayne's in red, Bibi's in green, and Brenda's in yellow. Her own name was written on the board in blue, still viable.

As she watched he walked over with a pink Sharpie and added *Stephanie* to the list.

"You'll be pleased to know you're the first to visit me here. Rayne got close, but I made mistakes with her. She knew too much."

"Rayne didn't fall. You killed her," Mac said, her eyes on the whiteboard.

"I didn't want to," he answered regretfully.

"And Bibi . . . ?"

"I didn't want to kill her, either! But Rayne talked about me to her. I wanted to make love to her, like I did Rayne. And Brenda, *Brandy*," he sneered. "She wanted me. Things just got out of control, so . . ."

Mac wished she knew what time it was. Wondered if Taft was starting to question where she was.

"So, now it's just you and me, and we'll make love all night and all day. Forever." Mac tried to hide her feelings of revulsion, but he must have seen something in her expression because he drew near and whispered coldly, "Don't worry. Nobody's coming to help you. You're mine now. . . ."

Emma clipped the leash on Duchess's collar, and the two of them walked down the hallway and stood outside the dining room where Harley was taking orders from a table of four men who usually sat together. They all seemed to be flirting with Harley. That's what they did with pretty girls.

Harley managed to walk away from them before she rolled her eyes on her way to the kitchen. She nearly ran into Emma on her way.

She looked down at Duchess and said, "Oh, I wish I could pet you, but I'm working."

"How are you doing?" Emma asked.

"Good. It's okay. You taking Duchess for a walk?" she asked.

"We're going to Mrs. Throckmorton's house." Emma had already been there once today. She'd knocked on the doors of all the three houses and of course it was the last one where Mrs. Throckmorton's daughter, Lorena, had finally opened the door.

"Wait a minute. I said I'd go with you. I can't right now and it's getting dark."

"I went earlier but Mrs. Throckmorton was taking a nap. I said I would come back today. I have a flashlight."

"Whoa. If you wait till tomorrow we can go together. I'll come here directly after school."

"I want to look for the cat, too."

"Somebody said they saw Twinkletoes earlier," said Harley.

Emma wasn't so sure, and it could be that Harley was just saying that to get her to stay. Old Darla had died at the hospital today and Jewell and everybody else was blaming the cat. "Supercilious Bob tried to catch her. They want to get rid of her."

"I don't know that that's true." She looked toward the kitchen. "I have to put this order in."

"Okay."

Emma watched her leave, then headed out the door with Duchess. She would have liked Harley to go with her, but she'd told Lorena that she would be coming back today and it was important to keep her word.

Thud, thud, thud.

Mac heard the noise above the pounding inside her own head and realized someone was beating on a wall somewhere above them, maybe a door. Chas's face grew rigid and fury made his eyes bulge. "Bitch!" he screamed.

"Thad?" a woman's distant voice called.

Chas ran across the room and then up a stairway; she could see the bottom concrete step. "Go away!" he screamed. Mac shivered. Just how unhinged was he? It made her heart go cold.

"There was a young woman here today to see Mom. She seems kind of off and she lives at Ridge Pointe."

"You let her in?" Chas demanded, aghast.

"No. But she's coming back."

"Well, don't let her in."

"She said it was confusing which grandson kissed Rayne at that place. She said Mom thought it was you. I don't know what she really wants, but I told her it couldn't be you because you're so damn anal about no public displays of affection, in fact no displays of affection whatsoever."

"JUST DON'T LET HER IN!"

"Stay down there in your fucking den and die," she snarled. "You're as crazy as your bipolar father."

Mac heard a bolt turn, a heavy metal door slide back and slam into the wall with force. There was a sharp, "Thad!" and then a quick, aborted scream. Scuffling and shrieking and Thad roaring in fury. The sounds of the fight grew more distant and Mac quickly examined the twine around her wrists. It was pulled tight, knotted. Could she work her way free? No . . . She needed a tool. Where? How?

There were books on the metal shelving in front of her, across the room a ways. And office supplies of a sort. A box cutter. That was a box cutter!

If she swung herself by her wrists, her feet could reach the shelving. She would have to wrap one foot around the metal corner post of the shelving to stop her momentum, then attempt to grab the box cutter with the toes of her other foot.

Impossible. Her head was throbbing. Her wrists were killing her.

She gritted her teeth and ignored the pain. She swung herself forward, moaning against the burn at her wrists. Her feet came up and she missed hooking her right around the post and swung backward, but she'd dislodged several of the books. One dropped to the floor. The box cutter shifted and she held her breath. If she pushed it back much farther it would be out of reach.

She heard footsteps on the stairs, stomping heavier than when he'd ascended. If she'd thought he was breathing hard before, now his chest was rapidly rising and falling. The cowboy hat had fallen off during the tussle and there was a streak of blood across his torso she didn't want to think about. His eyes were bright, almost feverish.

He came at her and grabbed her face and started kissing her. It took Mac by surprise and she wasn't quite sure how

Nancy Bush

to handle it. She held herself still as his tongue thrust into her mouth. She wanted to bite it off but knew that would serve no purpose other than making things worse for her. She concentrated instead on fighting back the pain in her head and wrists.

"Who was that?" she managed to get out when he finally moved from her mouth to her ear. One of his hands was painfully crushing her breast.

"Oh. Lorena. *Mother.*" He laughed, almost a giggle. "She won't be bothering us anymore."

"Who's the girl from Ridge Pointe?"

He pulled himself away from her, angry. "Stop talking. She's not a girl. She's a woman. And a retard. She's attractive, though. Her name's Emma." He seemed to get hold of himself again and cocked his head, as if listening, maybe thinking. Then he walked away and searched through the Sharpies, producing one in purple. He added *Emma* on to the whiteboard. "Don't worry," he said, coming back to Mac and running his tongue down her cheek. "We'll have enough time together." He touched his fingers to her chin, which was swollen and tender. She realized he'd hit her with an undercut. "Sorry about that. I didn't want to hurt you. I just had to get you in the truck. You're not like those gossips."

"Like . . . Rayne?"

"And Brenda and Stephanie. The mean girls. The trio." He stepped back and said in a falsetto, "Mr. Toad! Mr. Toad!"

Mac wanted to defend Stephanie. There wasn't a mean bone in her stepsister's body. But that line of conversation wasn't going to get her anywhere. "She called you Thad. Lorena."

"Nope. There's only Chas. As of today, Thad is dead."
He sounded as if he'd just decided that.

Mac could feel a swirl of air in the dungeon-like room.
Thad, or Chas, had left the door open at the top of the
steps. She didn't think he would be foolish enough to leave
it open by mistake. She guessed that Lorena might be dead
as well and any hope of help from her was over.

Emma knocked on Mrs. Throckmorton's door. It had a
metal ring she could smack that made a thunking sound.
She'd used it earlier in the day and Mrs. Throckmorton's
daughter, Lorena, had answered right away with a scowl
on her face. Emma had told her she should turn that
frown upside down, to which she had said some very rude
remarks, and when Emma had said she would come back
later in the day, she'd said, "Don't bother," in a snarly tone
Emma hadn't liked. That's why she'd brought Duchess
with her this time. She thought Old Darla might have
been right and they—Lorena and Thaddeus—were keeping Mrs. Throckmorton in the house with too many stairs.
And besides, Emma had promised she would be back.

This time Lorena didn't hurry to answer.

Emma knocked again and waited. She looked through
the skinny windows on either side of the door. Her eyes
widened as she saw that funny chair on the stairs was
coming down the side of the stairway. She watched as it
came to a stop. Lorena was sitting on it. She stared through
the window back at Emma and Emma went cold from
the inside out. "I see his eyes!" she whimpered, causing
Duchess to growl low in her throat.

Lorena lifted an arm to point at Emma. Her face was

covered in red, red blood as she tried to get out of the chair. One foot was out, then the other, and Lorena suddenly pitched forward and down the steps to slide onto the cream-colored marble floor with the big rose in the center.

Chapter Twenty-Seven

Taft called Nolan Redfield and asked if Mackenzie was still at their house. He got Stephanie on the phone, who immediately sounded worried. "No! She was here, but I texted her that she didn't need to come back because Nolan was back. Isn't she with you?"

"Not yet."

"That's been over an hour ago! Longer!"

"Don't worry, I'll find her."

He clicked off. He'd tried to clamp down his worries, telling himself he was being paranoid. But he knew something was wrong. Could feel it in his bones. He'd lost his Glock to the police after the bust today and wouldn't likely get it back for a while. He had another handgun, a .38, in his wall safe. He went to it now, unlocked it, and pulled the gun and some ammo out. He loaded the gun and headed for his Rubicon. His whole side felt like it was on fire.

Stay ahead of the pain.

He was glad he hadn't.

Dong, dong, dong, dong. The metallic clanging must have been from the front door, Mac determined. It made her own head ring. Thad/Chas had been taking his time, and she'd been wondering just how long she could put up with this before she would break, when the clanging started.

Dong, dong, dong, dong. It went on some more until Thad/Chas was infuriated. He threw Mackenzie away from him, nearly setting her swinging, and roared his fury. She stopped herself with her foot as he raced back to the stairs.

Immediately she tried to swing herself forward again. Reach the box cutter. Two tries and she hooked her right foot around one corner. Her wrists felt like they were being cut off. She could hardly see, her head hurt so badly. With the toes on her left foot she edged the box cutter toward her. She squeezed her eyes shut, then opened them again, concentrating on moving it ever so carefully.

"What the fuck!" she heard Thad/Chas exclaim.

There was a high, keening feminine cry.

Mac shivered and the box cutter fell onto the floor with a clatter, sliding toward her.

But not far enough.

Shit.

She stood on her feet, releasing the pulsing pressure on her bound wrists. Her ears were tuned to what was going on upstairs, while her eyes were glued to the box cutter, tantalizingly just out of reach.

Thad ran upstairs and saw Lorena working her way across the floor, almost swimming toward the front door. Through the side light Thad saw the retard. He jumped over Lorena and threw open the door, grabbing Emma by the shoulders.

He didn't see the dog until it leapt up and bit off half his ear.

Thad screamed in shock and fury. He tossed Emma aside and grabbed for his ear. The dog was on him, its jaws snapping onto his arm. He kicked and thrashed and tried to run but the dog held him fast.

And then a man's voice. "Emma, call off the dog."

"Duchess, down," she said in her monotone voice.

The dog released him but kept up a soft, hair-raising growl. Thad glanced back and there was Mackenzie's lover, a gun in his hand, trained on him. He thought of charging him, pushing him aside, and running out the door. He could get away. Race away. Get in the truck and leave.

"Do it," Jesse Taft told him.

Lorena was crying on the floor and the dog's lips were back showing its teeth, snarling and snapping, but it stayed by Emma's side.

Emma asked, "Where is Mrs. Throckmorton?"

"Upstairs," Lorena cried. "Thad will kill her. He will kill her!"

Thad looked from one to the other of them. The precipice yawned. A Grand Canyon waiting to swallow him up. He couldn't go with them. He couldn't.

Bang!

The sudden shot rang through the room.

Bang! Bang!

In his peripheral vision Thad saw Taft throw Emma down to keep her safe. Who was shooting?

The dog was barking its head off. Barking and snarling. Lorena was crying. A cacophony of noise.

Thad realized vaguely that he'd been shot. The shock had covered the pain. He looked down to see he was bleeding from his stomach.

And Lorena was gazing up at him through the rivulets of blood that ran down her face from the series of blows he'd leveled at her head when she'd run to her bedroom and he'd grabbed up the cut-glass vase with its fake red roses on her side table. Her smile was that of a madwoman.

As he met her gaze, the handgun dropped from her hand and she laid her head on the marble floor. "I got you," she said, and went limp.

Mackenzie was still trying to get her toe close enough to the box cutter when a barrage of footsteps clattered down the stairs. She braced herself for what, she didn't know.

And then Taft was there . . . and a woman she didn't recognize—Emma?—and a medium-sized scruffy dog whose eyes darted back and forth and had a bloody mouth.

"Mackenzie," Taft expelled. He held his cell phone to his ear with his left hand. A gun was in his right hand, a .38, held down at his injured side.

"You need some clothes," Emma observed.

"Your coat," Taft said to her, then was on the phone with 911, tersely giving directions.

Emma looked down at her full-length coat and slowly undid the belt.

"Box cutter," Mackenzie said, as soon as Taft had clicked off. She was so glad to see him she could feel emotion swelling in a wave of heat inside her, burning her nose and eyes.

Taft spied the tool and snatched it up. The dog growled as he started to cut her loose, responding to the urgency, but Emma shushed her and kept her by her side.

As Mackenzie fell into Taft's arms, Emma solemnly handed over her coat and Taft reluctantly released Mackenzie long enough to help her on with it.

"Your wound," she said, shivering within the woolen folds. He pulled her close again.

"Need to rub your wrists," he said. "Make sure the blood's flowing."

Mackenzie held her arms out of the sleeves. Taft grabbed first one, then the other, rubbing vigorously.

"I was supposed to be taking care of you," she said, despising the quaver in her voice, unable to stop it.

"We're both okay," he said softly, his breath in her hair.

Mackenzie's eyes were closed but she heard Emma say, "Thad kicked Duchess, but Duchess wouldn't let go."

Taft lifted his head and said, "Duchess is a very good dog."

"Yes, she is," Emma agreed soberly.

"You know him? Thaddeus Jenkins?" he asked her.

A long time passed. Mackenzie opened her eyes to see Emma frowning hard.

"He's Mrs. Throckmorton's grandson. It's very confusing, but he's not the boy who was kissing Rayne. That was Old Darla's grandson, but Mrs. Throckmorton mixed it up. Old Darla died from a stroke and I feel bad. I don't know her grandson's name but somebody said he got arrested today. He has long hair and tattoos and even though Jewell didn't like his long hair, I did. But then Jewell's a gossip and says things she shouldn't. If you can't say anything nice, you shouldn't say anything at all, which is why I'm not going to talk about Thad anymore." She turned her gaze toward the whiteboard and said, "My name is on that list."

Taft and Mackenzie both looked to the damning indictment of Thad's murderous crimes and his plans for the future.

"He can't hurt you now," said Taft.

"He is too deeply injured," Emma said after a moment of thought.

The sirens approaching in the distance were a welcome sound. Taft helped Mackenzie up the stairs and they met the cavalry. Cooper and Verbena and even her old partner, Ricky, who actually looked worried and chastened when he glanced at Mac, giving her an idea of what she must look like. There were others as well, along with an ambulance. One look around and the EMTs called for a second one.

Thaddeus Jenkins aka Chas was dead on the scene and his mother, Lorena, had lapsed into unconsciousness from her head injuries. Cooper looked a bit dumbfounded to find Emma and Duchess on scene, and he put Emma on his cell phone to talk to her sister, Jamie, just as Emma's niece, Harley, arrived at the house, out of breath and white-faced. Relief flooded her expression and she gave Emma a high five, as did Cooper.

Detective Verbena asked Mac some questions, but quickly realized she was in no condition to be interrogated. They urged her toward an ambulance but she left with Taft, who took her to Glen Gen to be checked out. "I never thought I'd be back at the hospital so soon," she muttered as they went inside.

They saw some of the same hospital staff members from yesterday and this morning. One of the ER docs concluded that Mackenzie had a concussion and he also insisted on rechecking Taft as well. By the time they were released Stephanie and Nolan were waiting for them.

"I can't trust either of you," Stephanie said, her eyes noticeably wet. "You've both got to come home with us."

"I've got pugs waiting for me at my place," Taft told her with a faint smile.

"Mackenzie, you definitely need to come back with me," Stephanie said firmly. "You need to rest."

"But there are pugs at Taft's."

"Oh, for God's sake." She tossed up her hands and shook her head. Her husband came up behind her and wrapped his arms around her. "I've been thinking about it, you know," she said. "Thaddeus Jenkins. He was that nerd kid in grade school. He was . . . my God, he turned out to be one of those guys," she exclaimed. "Those sick and twisted terrible predators! Rayne used to make fun of him and Brenda did, too, and I laughed with them." Tears filled her eyes anew. "I laughed with them and I felt bad but not bad enough. Do you think it's my fault?"

"You can't say that," Mackenzie told her.

"There's no predicting," Nolan agreed.

"I should've stuck up for him. I should've never been a part of it."

"Let it go," Taft said gently.

"Steph, I'm going to stay with Taft tonight. Don't worry. Don't blame yourself," urged Mackenzie.

"Was he coming after me, too?" she asked in a small voice.

Taft told her, "Whatever he was or wasn't planning to do, he won't be able to any longer." Then he tucked his good arm around Mackenzie and they walked to his Rubicon.

EPILOGUE

No, she didn't sleep with Taft. She wanted to, she really did, but she was too beat up and he probably was, too. He insisted on giving her his bed while he took the couch. She was both disappointed and relieved. Disappointed because she'd wanted nothing more than to lie in bed with him, be that close to another human being, wrap herself completely within the safety of Jesse James Taft. Relieved because, well, she wanted something more long-term. A working relationship. Something that would last, and a night together after emotional upheaval just wasn't going to cut it. Oh, bullshit. She wanted a helluva lot more than just one night, that was the truth of it, and that was going to take some work.

The next few weeks passed by in a blue of healing and questions from authorities. Mackenzie and Taft were interviewed separately by the police and DEA. There were enough deaths and injuries in the wake of that one weekend's events to put both of them under a microscope. Seth Keppler never regained consciousness and passed away in his sleep about two weeks later. To date Larry Perkins was still alive but barely. He was still in the hospital. Mackenzie hoped for his recovery, but she wasn't sure that was going to happen. Though Thad had died that night at his grandmother's house, his mother was expected to make a full recovery, though she had a long court case ahead of her for killing her son. Her mother, Sara Throckmorton, was discovered asleep upstairs, out cold, actually, as she'd been given a form of Rohypnol by either Thad or Lorena. Mackenzie wanted to blame Thad entirely, but there was evidence at the house that Lorena may have been the one to tamper with her mother's food and drink, so there were more black marks in Lorena's column. Her mother had been moved to Memory Care at Ridge Pointe, a decision made by her lawyers.

Brenda "Brandy" Heilman's death was linked to Thad by DNA as was Bibi Engstrom's. Rayne's demise would be forever listed as an accident, which bothered Mackenzie deeply, and only made her more determined to go after miscreants of every kind and try to get justice for them.

Granger Nye's death was still under investigation. Though Andrew Best was certain Seth Keppler was to blame, the jury was still out on that one. Detective Haynes hadn't specifically said so but Mackenzie felt he wasn't giving up. Troi had been cleared of any wrongdoing, so that was a plus. As Emma had said, Troi was the grandson of one of the recently deceased residents of Ridge Pointe, Darla Mandell. According to Troi, he'd met Rayne through Elise and then had later been seen in a make out session with her outside Ridge Pointe. Mackenzie wondered what had happened since between Troi and Elise and Leah, but at least Elise had stopped calling her and demanding some kind of action.

Tommy Carnoff's onetime girlfriend, Maureen, had been moved to a nursing home and was doing okay, according to Tommy. It had left Blackie and Plaid with split parenting between Tommy and Taft, which suited everyone just fine.

Two days earlier Mackenzie had stopped in to see Emma and Duchess at Ridge Pointe in her rental car as her RAV was still being fixed, and had learned Emma wasn't as satisfied with the Ridge Pointe Independent and Assisted Living as she'd thought she would be. She'd said she missed Old Darla and Mrs. Throckmorton and the cat, which had disappeared around that same weekend.

Emma had related, "I might move home with my sister. She and Cooper Haynes are getting married. But I want Twink to join us and I don't think she will."

"I'll have to congratulate Cooper," Mackenzie told her. "Twink's the cat?"

"It has a dumb name so I shortened it. But it's gone."

"Maybe it will come back."

Emma had looked skeptical. "It didn't like Duchess. They were frenemies."

"Maybe you can tell someone here about it, or your sister, or your niece. . . ?"

She'd shaken her head, said, "You don't have to give them your life story," and had gone in to dinner.

Then today, to Mackenzie's surprise, Chief Hugh Bennihof had come to see her at Stephanie and Nolan's. She'd been stuffing her boxes into the back of her SUV when he pulled into the drive behind her.

"I'd like to offer you your job back," he told her, smiling as if he was bestowing the biggest award on her that anyone could ask for.

She'd answered carefully, "I'd like to be a detective."

That had thrown him. "Well, that takes some years on the job. There are quite a few candidates ahead of you."

"Like Bryan 'Ricky' Richards?"

"I'm not saying it couldn't happen, but it would be a wait."

It would never happen. She'd known it before she'd even asked. She hadn't decided quite what she wanted to do about him, but she'd already determined she wasn't going to put herself in any situation where he was her boss.

"Thanks for the offer," she said coolly.

Her tone had given him his answer and his face took on a pissy look. Mackenzie thought about Katy Keegan and was leaning more and more toward thinking she was trying to take back power rather than really wanting a relationship with the man. And anyway, she wasn't giving up her job with Taft to go back to the department.

Now she looked around the mess of boxes and belongings that she'd piled in her new living room and felt satisfied. She and Taft were going out for those Goldie Burgers they'd missed the night she'd been abducted. It wasn't a date in the usual sense. It was a working meal. Taft was bound and determined to bring down his own frenemy, Mitch Mangella, and he'd asked Mac to help him. No more sidelining. She was part of the team.

The cat switched her black tail back and forth. The people in the house had lured her in with good smells, but they'd never let her go back out. They had a litter box, and a scratching post and squeaky toys the cat found off-putting.

She picked up a paw and licked it, gnawing a bit on her claws and pad, but one ear was cocked, listening for the door. When the man came home today and the woman started complaining about the messy child who stumbled after the cat and made loud sounds and grabbed the cat's tail and squeezed hard, there would be a moment or two when the door was held open.

Today she was going to escape and go back to the place with the white, fluffy cream and the man who smelled like skunk.